LISA JACKSON

LIAR, LIAR

ZEBRA BOOKS are published by

Kensington Publishing Corp.
119 West 40th Street
New York, NY 10018

All Kensington titles, imprints, and distributed lines are available at special quantity discounts for bulk purchases for sales promotion, premiums, fund-raising, educational, or institutional use.

Special book excerpts or customized printings can also be created to fit specific needs. For details, write or phone the office of the Kensington Sales Manager: Attn.: Sales Department. Kensington Publishing Corp., 119 West 40th Street, New York, NY 10018. Phone: 1-800-221-2647.

Zebra and the Z logo Reg. U.S. Pat. & TM Off.

First Kensington Books Hardcover Printing: July 2018
First Zebra Books Mass-Market Paperback Printing: June 2019
ISBN-13: 978-1-4201-3599-2
ISBN-10: 1-4201-3599-6

ISBN-13: 978-1-4201-3602-9 (eBook)
ISBN-10: 1-4201-3602-X (eBook)

10 9 8 7 6 5 4 3 2 1

Printed in the United States of America

Author's Note

For the sake of this story, I did take a few liberties with the locations and police procedures within the pages of *Liar, Liar*.

Books by Lisa Jackson

Stand-Alones
SEE HOW SHE DIES
FINAL SCREAM
RUNNING SCARED
WHISPERS
TWICE KISSED
UNSPOKEN
DEEP FREEZE
FATAL BURN
MOST LIKELY TO DIE
WICKED GAME
WICKED LIES
SOMETHING WICKED
WICKED WAYS
SINISTER
WITHOUT MERCY
YOU DON'T WANT
TO KNOW
CLOSE TO HOME
AFTER SHE'S GONE
REVENGE
YOU WILL PAY
OMINOUS
RUTHLESS
ONE LAST BREATH
LIAR, LIAR

Anthony Paterno/
Cahill Family Novels
IF SHE ONLY KNEW
ALMOST DEAD

Rick Bentz/Reuben
Montoya Novels
HOT BLOODED
COLD BLOODED
SHIVER
ABSOLUTE FEAR
LOST SOULS
MALICE
DEVIOUS
NEVER DIE ALONE

Pierce Reed/
Nikki Gillette Novels
THE NIGHT BEFORE
THE MORNING AFTER
TELL ME

Selena Alvarez/
Regan Pescoli Novels
LEFT TO DIE
CHOSEN TO DIE
BORN TO DIE
AFRAID TO DIE
READY TO DIE
DESERVES TO DIE
EXPECTING TO DIE
WILLING TO DIE

Published by Kensington Publishing Corporation

PROLOGUE

San Francisco
Now

*N*o! No! No!

Forcing her way through a gathering crowd that had been barricaded across the sloped street, Remmi shielded her eyes with one hand and stared upward through the thickening fog to the ledge of the Montmort Tower Hotel. "Oh, God." Squinting through the fog to somewhere near the twentieth floor, she saw a woman balanced precariously on a ledge, her back to an open hotel room window, sheer curtains billowing behind her.

It couldn't be.

It just couldn't!

Not when Remmi was so close . . . so damned close. Please, no!

"Jesus, Mary, and Joseph, she's gonna jump!" a tall man said under his breath. He wore a heavy jacket and stocking cap, and a one-year-old in a hooded snowsuit was strapped to his chest. He quickly sketched the sign of the cross over his chest and the baby. Red-faced from the cold, the child began to whimper, but his father barely seemed to notice.

Sirens wailed as fire trucks and police cruisers collected near the base of the stalwart San Francisco hotel, an Art Deco edifice of concrete and marble that had withstood earthquakes and fires, riots and time, rock stars and politicians. It pulsed with the fierce, eerie lights of emergency vehicles. People were talking and milling around, jamming the roped-off area of the steep San Francisco street.

High on the ledge, a woman with short, platinum hair, the hem of her pink dress dancing around her knees, wobbled on her matching heels, swaying enough to make some of the onlookers gasp, while others screamed.

Don't do it!

Heart in her throat, her pulse a surf in her ears, Remmi pushed her way through the throng held at bay by police officers and yellow tape strung hastily over A-frame barricades. Twilight was descending, the lights of the city winking through the thickening mist, the streets shiny and wet, the bay nearly invisible at the bottom of the steep hillside. Most of the crowd, heads tilted back, stared, gape-mouthed, hands to their chests, up to the thin ledge where the woman balanced so precariously.

"This is horrible. Horrible!" a woman in a stocking cap and padded jacket whispered. She was transfixed, as they all were, but couldn't turn away. Her gloved hand was clamped over that of a boy with ragged brown hair and freckles, a baseball cap crammed onto his head.

"Let me through." Remmi shouldered her way closer to the police line. "Come on."

The gloved woman observed, "She looks like Marilyn Monroe."

"Marilyn who?" her son, all of about twelve, asked,

earbuds visible beneath his baseball cap, acne vying with fuzz on his jaw as he stared upward to where the would-be jumper stood.

"A–a beauty queen . . . actress from the fifties."

"So *really* old."

"No, no . . . she's dead." Gaze aloft, the woman shook her head. "Died a long time ago. Overdose of sleeping pills. Or . . . or something." Her forehead crumpled as she thought.

"Then it's *not* her."

"I know."

"Just someone who looks like her." The kid's eyes were focused on the ledge high overhead. "Is she really going to do it? Will she land in that fountain?"

His mother was shaking her head. "I hope not. I hope she doesn't . . . Dear God." She, too, made a hasty sign of the cross over her chest.

"Impersonator?" a man in a long overcoat who had overheard the exchange asked.

"I–I guess." The woman again.

"There've been a lot of them," the man said with a snort, as if the woman's life was of no importance. Callous jerk.

"The outfit. Pure Marilyn." The woman in the stocking hat was nodding, her head bobbing slowly, graying curls springing from beneath the knit cap. "But one impersonator . . . in particular. Kind of famous. What was her name?" She snapped the fingers of her free hand, the sound muted through her glove. "It was . . . it was, oh, I almost had it . . . But gosh, I can't remember. Doesn't matter."

Didi. Her name is Didi Storm, Remmi thought, her heart frozen in her chest. *And it* does *matter! What's wrong with you people? Acting as if a woman contemplating suicide is just an interesting sideshow!*

Overcoat pulled a face of disbelief. "An impersonator of a dead woman . . . long dead, by the way. She's gonna take a swan dive off the Montmort? Doesn't make sense."

"Does suicide ever make sense?" Knit cap snapped, her lips pursing a little.

"Sorry. I was just sayin'—"

On the ledge above, the slim woman swayed, and the crowd gasped. Firemen were gathered at the base of the hotel, and someone in a uniform—a sergeant, Remmi thought—was addressing the throng: "Stand back. Give us a little room here."

Water beading on his Giants cap, the kid observed, "Man. It looks like she's really going to do it."

"Oh . . . oh, no. Come on, let's go. I can't watch this." The mother hustled her son through the gathering throng of horrified lookie-loos, and the boy, reluctantly, his gaze glued to the would-be leaper, was dragged past nearby observers holding cell phones over their heads in sick efforts to capture the horrible moment. Mother and son disappeared, melting into the ever-growing throng.

Remmi didn't listen to any more speculation. Heart pounding, fear driving her, she pushed her way through the crowd, past a businessman in a raincoat who, like so many others, was filming the macabre scene with his phone, while people around her murmured or gasped. All were transfixed by the horror unfolding right before their eyes. Traffic had been halted, headlights of the stalled cars glowing in the fog, horns honking, emergency workers barking orders. Somewhere a deep voice was humming an old song she'd heard in Sunday school class. What was it? Then the words came to her:

> *This little light of mine,*
> *I'm gonna let it shine.*

Remmi's eyes turned upward, the song fading, her gaze transfixed on the woman teetering high above, the fog wisping around the building. *Don't do it,* Remmi silently begged as she forced her way through a knot of women with umbrellas. Throat tight, she glanced up at the ledge. *Please, Mom, don't jump!*

To Remmi's horrified dismay, as if the would-be leaper could actually hear her, the woman moved suddenly, a high heel slipping over the edge. The crowd gave up a collective gasp, then a scream, as she suddenly plummeted, arms pinwheeling, hair a shimmering, moving cloud in those horrifying seconds as she tumbled in free fall through the thick San Francisco evening.

Let it shine, let it shine, let it shine . . .

PART 1

CHAPTER 1

Las Vegas, Nevada
Twenty Years Earlier

"You can do this," Didi told herself as she drove her vintage, specially equipped Cadillac through the city. Neon lights sparkled and shone as daylight slipped away and Las Vegas became a beacon in the twilight desert.

God, she loved this town, with its hot, dry air, bustle, and excitement, and, most importantly, the glamour and glitz of the tall buildings that spired upward into a vast, star-spangled sky. The city itself was almost surreal in its stark contrast to the quiet, serene, eerie desert at night.

Well, it wasn't quite night yet, and she had no time to think about anything but her mission, one she'd been planning for the better part of a year. A tiny frisson of excitement sizzled through her blood, and the back of her mouth was suddenly dry with anxiety.

"You can pull this off," she said, the words a familiar mantra intended to calm her jangled nerves, push back her fears. She stepped on the gas as she reached the outskirts of town. Her chest was tight, her fingers clammy over the steering wheel, a million doubts creeping through her mind.

She would have preferred to have the top down on the big car, to let the warm Nevada breeze stream across her face and through her hair, but she didn't want to muss her makeup, nor her hair, and, really, with the twins, it was best to keep the convertible's roof snapped into place and just leave the windows cracked enough to let in some air.

In the back, strapped into their car seats, were her two infants. Her heart twisted at the thought of her precious little ones. A boy and a girl, six weeks old and sleeping, cooing softly as she drove, not knowing their fates. "Oh, babies," she whispered, guilt already gnawing through her soul. What she was planning was unthinkable. But she was desperate, and everything would work out for the best. No one would get hurt.

She hoped.

Despite herself, she crossed the fingers of her right hand as she gripped the wheel. Was she making a mistake? Probably. But, then, it certainly wasn't her first—or fiftieth, for that matter.

Swallowing hard, she fought a spate of hot tears and steeled herself. She had to do this, *had* to; it was her one chance, *their* only chance for a better life. Sniffing, she blinked and wouldn't let the tears fall and ruin her mascara. She needed to look good, perfect, to pull this off. Not like a sad sack of a clown with black streaks running down her cheeks.

Involuntarily, seated in the soft white leather, she straightened her shoulders. *You can do this, Didi. You can.* She pressed a high heel a little more firmly on the gas pedal, and the Caddy responded, leaping forward, tires eagerly spinning over the dry, dusty asphalt.

But what if something goes wrong?

"It won't."

It couldn't.

Just to be on the safe side, she sent up a quick prayer, something she hadn't done much of since she'd shaken the Missouri dust off her boots, bought a bus ticket, and headed west when she was still a teenager. She'd left her family, and God Himself, in the huge Greyhound's exhaust.

Tonight, everything would turn around.

Over the roar of the car's big engine, she heard a soft sigh, one of the babies probably dreaming.

Oh God.

Setting her jaw, she flipped her visor down to shield her eyes against the sun's glare and reminded herself that she couldn't back out now—her plan was set, the wheels in motion. As Las Vegas became a strip of glorious lights reflected in her car's oversize rearview mirror, she pushed in the cigarette lighter, then let her fingers scrabble on the seat beside her for her purse. She shook a Virginia Slims from the glittery cigarette case she scrounged out of her clutch. A few hits of nicotine would calm her. She cracked open the side window and, after lighting up, held her cigarette near the window—no second-hand smoke for her babies! *That* was definitely a thing these days, and as long as she was a mother . . . oh, Jesus, how long would that be? . . . she would keep the babies safe.

Really? Who are you kidding?

Condemning eyes reflected back at her in the mirror as she headed steadily west, where the blazing sun was settling over the cliffs of Red Rock Canyon. While the nicotine did its job, she turned on the radio to an oldies station and heard the Beatles singing "Let It Be."

Bam!

Paul McCartney's voice was drowned out as she hit a pothole, and the car shuddered, a loud thud sounding from the rear end of the Caddy.

Oh, puh-leez.

She couldn't break down. Not now. Not when she'd finally screwed up her courage and set her plan in motion. Fearing that one of the car seats was too loose, that the strap securing it might have failed in this old car, she glanced over her shoulder. Nothing seemed out of place. And the car was running well, no popped tire, no bent axle. The babies were still safely bound in their car seats.

For now.

"It was nothing," she said aloud. Maybe something had shifted in the trunk or a prop had gotten away from its bindings in the specialized cargo space she'd had retrofitted into the big car so that she could use it in her act. God, how she loved to pop out of the "empty" white Caddy, in a scanty outfit . . . well, those days were gone, at least temporarily, until she got rid of the remaining fat and sagging skin from her latest pregnancy with the twins. So far, she'd lost a lot of that weight, but things had shifted, and her skin was not as taut as it used to be when she'd been a nubile teenager, and tonight she'd had to wiggle into some damned tight undergarments to even slip into her current outfit—her favorite pink Marilyn Monroe dress.

The jeweled gown's seams were straining, but scarcely being able to breathe was well worth the trouble. Didi knew she looked spectacular.

Cutting the radio, she kept the pedal to the metal, all the while listening for that disturbing noise again. She detected nothing more than the thrum of the engine, the whine of the tires, and the rush of wind through the partially opened window. Since the clunk had stopped, and there didn't appear to be anything mechanically wrong with the car, thank God, she clicked on the radio again, this time to a current pop station. She squashed her cigarette on the tab in the ashtray, adjusted her sunglasses to fight the glare of those last eyeball-searing minutes before the sun sank over the ragged mountaintops, and told herself she was ready.

Tonight, her bad luck was going to change.

Forever.

Remmi hardly dared breathe in the tight cargo space of her mother's ancient Cadillac. She rubbed the back of her head where it had bumped against the inside of the wall when Didi, at the wheel, had hit something and Remmi had bounced enough to slam the back of her head against the metal roof. *Ouch!* She was surprised her mother hadn't heard the thud, stopped the car, and discovered her oldest daughter stowed away in the area where Didi usually hid the props for her stage act, a part of the voluminous trunk sectioned off in this boat of a white Cadillac.

Fortunately, Remmi had bit back a scream despite the radiating pain.

Now, she was sweating. A lot. Drops drizzled down her forehead and off her chin, and covered her back. The space she was wedged into was tight. Claustrophobic. But she didn't want to think about how she could so easily be trapped inside. There was a latch of course, but it could jam. She didn't want to think about it and swiped at the beads of sweat on her chin.

For a split second, as the huge car's speed increased and she felt as if Didi were being intentionally reckless, Remmi considered calling out, letting her mom know she was hiding in the space, but she held back. Didi would kill Remmi if she found out her teenager had stowed away in the car. Well, actually, Remmi hadn't intended to stow away at all. She'd been hiding. From her mom.

And it had backfired.

Big-time.

Cautiously, Remmi peered through a small slit between the cargo area and the back seat, a tiny peephole Didi had installed. The scent of cigarette smoke reached her nostrils, and she heard music from the radio. The twins, her half siblings, were silent for once, not crying, but Remmi couldn't see them. From her vantage point, she saw little more than the back of her mother's head, Didi's blond "Marilyn" wig securely in place.

Why the costume?

Remmi hazarded a quick glance toward the wide rearview mirror and caught a glimpse of her mom's face, sunglasses over the bridge of her nose, lips pouty and colored a glossy pink, even a signature mole drawn near the corner of her mouth.

Oh, Mom, what're you doing?

Remmi wished to high heaven that she hadn't decided at the last possible second to hide in the cargo space. She'd thought Didi was working, and Seneca, the twins' nanny, had retired to her room for the night as the babies had fallen asleep in their shared crib. Remmi, whose room was part of the converted garage on the far end of the house, had thought she was safe, that no one would check on her until her mother returned sometime after her last show, usually after 2:00 AM. She'd planned to sneak out her bedroom window, and with the keys she'd already lifted out of the drawer in the kitchen, she'd intended to drive her mother's crappy old Toyota into the night. The windows of her room were mounted high, slanted panes near the apex of the sloped ceiling, accessible by climbing onto the headboard of her bed and scrambling over, impossible to reach from the outside without a ladder.

But she'd done it.

She'd slid through the narrow opening, hung by her fingers from the sill, then softly dropped to the dusty ground below, the heat of the desert still simmering, the sun beginning to sink in the western sky.

All to meet a boy.

A boy who was probably bad news. Or worse. But there was something about him, something that caught her attention and made the blood pound a little in her ears when his dark eyes found hers. Even now, stuck in the sweltering cargo space, her heart trip-hammered and the back of her throat went dry at the thought of Noah Scott. Older, with a bad-boy reputation, he was definitely *not* Didi-approved. Which made him all the more attractive, she decided. But she couldn't help herself. God, he was sexy. She had dreams about his hands on her body and how kissing him made her tingle all over, even in places she hadn't realized were meant to tingle.

Stop it!

She couldn't think about him—fantasize about him. Not when she was trapped in Didi's Cadillac, going to God-only-knew-where.

Earlier, she'd snagged the keys to the Toyota, just after dinner, waited for Seneca to close her door, gave it another ten minutes, then slid out of the window and dropped lithely to the ground. She'd just settled behind the wheel of the Camry (she'd taught herself to drive on the sly and was fairly adept, even though she was still only fifteen) when she spied her mother's Caddy rounding the corner of the street leading to their driveway in this crummy part of town.

Crap!

She'd sunk down in the Toyota's battered driver's seat, barely peeking over the dash as Didi had driven into the garage. Counting out three minutes in her head, she'd waited for Didi to head into the house. The second her mother was inside, Remmi had slipped into the open garage and thought she could sneak into her room, as it was just a few steps down the short hallway. Once Didi was past the kitchen, Remmi would be able to quietly ease the door open and make her way to the bedroom.

No one, especially her mother, would be the wiser.

She'd thought.

Listening over the thudding of her own heartbeat, Remmi had wrapped her fingers around the doorknob when she'd heard the distinctive click of Didi's heels approaching her direction.

Crap!

Rather than try to make it outside, where, if Didi chose to lock up, Remmi wouldn't be able to get back into the house, she'd slipped away from the garage door and silently opened a back door of the monster of a car. Without thinking, she'd rolled into the back seat of the Caddy and engaged the secret lever Didi had installed. The seat back had flipped down, and Remmi had forced her body into the cramped cargo space. Without really thinking, she'd found the inside latch, and the rolled leather seat had sprung into place once more, clicking into place as Didi emerged from the house with one of the baby carriers.

Remmi, peeking through the specialized peephole, had held her breath and silently prayed, *Don't let her find me, oh, please God, don't let her—*

The Caddy's back door flew open. Muttering to herself as she'd secured the carrier into position, Didi didn't seem to notice anything was amiss. She'd quickly returned to the house. Remmi had reached for the lever but never got the chance to escape. Less than a minute after strapping in the first carrier, Didi had reappeared with the second.

Once both car seats had been locked into place, Remmi had been trapped.

Only then did she notice that Didi was dressed in her favorite Marilyn Monroe costume, all pink and shimmery. She'd climbed behind the wheel and jammed her keys into the ignition. The massive car with its huge engine had roared to life, and Didi had backed out of the garage without a word.

Five seconds later, she'd rammed the Cadillac into drive, hit the gas, and headed to the desert. With her infants strapped into the back seat of this boat of a car, and Remmi hidden in the trunk, Didi drove as if the devil himself were chasing her.

Why?

What was with the full-Marilyn regalia?

And where to?

Remmi bit her lower lip nervously.

Where the hell was she headed?

"Son of a bitch!" Noah kicked a rock hard enough for it to hit against the weathered side of the barn and bang so loudly that the dog sleeping on the porch gave a startled bark. Roscoe, who was a mix of some kind of sheepdog and who knew what else, raised his speckled, shaggy head, yawned, wagged his stub of a tail, then settled back on the old rag rug that was his bed, his nose buried in the faded fabric, eyes bright and focused on Noah.

"It's okay," Noah grumbled, but it wasn't. Not by a long shot. Noah was itching for a fight. He was supposed to meet a girl. Not just any girl, but a girl he'd just met the other day at the lake. She wasn't his usual type, was a little on the nerdy side, and young, too, but she was smart and hadn't been intimidated by him. The daughter of some weird showgirl, a woman impersonator, he thought. Didi Storm. Yeah, that was the mother's name. Like him, the girl, Remmi, had no real dad in the picture, and he could see she would soon become a knockout. Her brown hair was streaked a reddish gold—naturally, he'd guessed, from the blasting Nevada sun. Freckles dusted a long but straight nose, and her eyes, somewhere between green and gold, flashed with intelligence and humor. He'd tested her, and she could give as well as she could take. Built tall and lean, with small breasts and hips that barely flared, she didn't seem to care that she wasn't as curvy as some of the girls she hung out with.

Including that bitch Mandi Preston, who, while they'd all been swimming in the lake, had made a point of pressing her impressive boobs up against him. She was a tease, and as those massive breasts, held in place by a slip of a red bikini bra, had grazed the bare skin of his back, he'd had an immediate reaction, a hard-on forming despite the cool water. He'd tried to hide his boner, but it had been impossible, and Mandi had known just what she'd accomplished. It was a game with her, but he wasn't interested in her. Never had been. All blond tousled hair, bubblegum-pink lipstick, and high-pitched giggling, he'd found her too . . . commercial? Too much like a TV bimbo? No, maybe she was just a fake. He knew she was smarter than she pretended to be; he'd seen flashes of it, and the flirty dumb act bothered him.

Not so Remmi.

She said what was on her mind and didn't seem to care what anyone else thought. She'd seen the display in the lake as she'd lain on a towel and read a book. Over the cover, she'd watched as Mandi had splashed and rubbed up against Noah. Arching a dark eyebrow, she'd caught

Noah's eye, given her head a shake, and closed the paperback. As she'd scooped up her towel, flip-flops, and small cooler, he'd waited for his damned cock to cooperate; then he'd followed her to the parking area.

"What?" she'd asked when she unlocked the door of a beat-up Toyota and slid into the sunbaked interior.

"I don't know you."

"You're right. You don't." She'd jabbed her keys into the ignition.

"You got a license?" he asked. If she was sixteen, he'd be surprised.

"So how is that any of your business?" She'd flashed him a cool smile and started the engine, stomping on the gas and backing up so quickly she'd nearly hit him—he'd jumped back, just in case—then, sliding her sunglasses over that long nose, she'd nearly clipped a signpost that listed the rules of the swim park. He wondered if she'd done it on purpose, as if she were thumbing her nose at authority.

Or maybe he'd just hoped so.

Didn't matter. He was hooked, and he'd caught up with her twice more at the lake, bringing his own ratty towel and stretching out beside her as she pretended to read. Maybe she was really trying. But her gaze kept straying from the pages of the paperback, a battered copy of a Stephen King novel, to the lake, where the water shimmered under the harsh sun. Boats, sometimes pulling skiers, cut through the clear water, engines churning, frothy wakes widening behind them. Swimmers kept closer to the shore, moms with toddlers or teenagers hanging out in packs.

Remmi came alone, most of the time.

He liked that.

In fact, he liked her.

And it surprised him.

She was, after all, jailbait, or so he'd thought. She

couldn't be sixteen, despite the car. She was kind of on her own, helping out with her infant siblings, working at a burger joint, and waiting for school to start. And she liked computers, was kind of a geek when it came to the Net, something that was completely foreign to him.

Yet, he'd felt a kinship with her, as if they were both some kind of misfit. He was out of high school and fast running out of options, his job as the clean-up guy on construction sites a dead end. His life at home the same. He needed to move on. But tonight?

Remmi.

He felt a jolt of anticipation fire his blood and mentally kicked himself when his thoughts took him to imagining her warm lips and soft body. Shit, what was he thinking?

Nothing good.

Then again, not so bad.

Oh, hell, who knew? Maybe he was making a bigger deal of it than it was, but say what you will, hadn't she agreed to meet him tonight? In a park not far from the edge of town. They planned to go dirt biking in the desert. Alone.

Despite the fact that he was supposedly grounded.

By his stepfather. Ike Baxter, a big, burly guy with swarthy skin, a thick salt-and-pepper flattop, and eyes drilled deep into his skull, seemed to think he could tell Noah just exactly what to do. If he ordered, "Jump," Noah was supposed to respond, "How high, *sir?*" Yeah, right. Ike could go jump into the deepest lake around, preferably chained to a cement block. God, he hated that miserable son of a bitch. What his mother saw in him escaped Noah.

But there it was.

And the big jerk-wad had grounded him because his "chores" hadn't been done in a timely fashion, the task in question being setting fence posts in cement-like soil *after* a ten-hour stretch at his job. Well, screw that.

"Shit," he said, and swiped at the sweat running down his face. Mad at the world, Noah eyed the stucco house with its cracked walls and missing roof tiles. Even though he knew it was near-suicide, he considered "borrowing" the crappy Yamaha motorcycle on which Ike was forever tinkering. The dirt bike was a beater, circa 1968, in Noah's opinion, but something the old man treasured and called "classic." Noah snorted his disdain at Ike's lofty notion of the relic. Still, the bike had some kick in it, and he needed to get out. Now. While he could. Cora Sue, his mother, was MIA again, probably down at Slaughter's, sipping vodka, getting wasted, and trying to forget the landscape of her pathetic life. As for his old man? Ike had taken off an hour or so ago, but not before rattling off a list of chores for his stepson, an edict reinforced by a threat that, if he failed to get them done, he'd be grounded "for the rest of the month, maybe more. We'll see." Who knew when the fucker would show up again? As if Noah cared. Ike Baxter was a hard-ass son of a bitch who didn't like his wife's "snot-nosed smart-mouthed jackass" any more than the jackass liked him. Yeah, Stepdaddy was a real dick-wad. Too good for Cora Sue, but she gravitated to losers, one after another, including his biological old man, who'd done a quick vanishing act before he was born. Never had he met the "sperm donor," as Cora Sue had so appropriately named Ronnie Scott, though she'd chased him rigorously and futilely for child support that never appeared. The only help she'd ever gotten from Noah's dad was in the form of Ronnie's widowed mother, a religious nutjob who had taken care of her grandson while Cora Sue waited tables at one of the smaller casinos just off the Strip.

The last Noah had heard, dear old dad was banging

out license plates or doing laundry or some other menial labor while serving time in prison in California. Noah didn't know which lockup housed his father, and he didn't much care.

With that thought, he jogged to the hovel of a house, where his room consisted of an attic space that was hot as hell in the summer, colder than a well digger's butt in winter, and tight enough that he could stand only under the crown of the roof. His bed was a sleeping bag tossed over a mattress lying on a plywood floor, but there was a window, and through that small pane of glass, he could view the stars at night and watch the sun come up each morning.

And neither Ike nor Cora Sue bothered him in the attic; they pretty much left him alone.

Things could be worse.

Then again, they could be a whole lot better.

The sun was hanging low in the sky as he hurried up the dilapidated steps to the porch. Roscoe thumped his stubby tail, and Noah, in a hurry, gave the old shepherd a quick pat on the muzzle before crossing the dusty floorboards and opening the creaking screen door. He stepped into the house and found the single key dangling from a nail pounded into a post near the back door, snagged it, started outside, then hesitated. Knowing he was crossing a line, he walked through the kitchen and down a short, hot hallway, where pictures of Cora and Ike's wedding, at one of the local drive-through chapels, were posted. Ignoring the shots of his younger, happier mother and the man who would become his tyrant of a stepfather, he slipped into the second bedroom, which was now Ike's den. Unerringly, Noah went to the heat vent behind the scarred metal desk, removed the vent's grimy cover, and stuck his arm down the dusty hole to a spot where the vent bent back under the house.

His fingers scraped not one, but two plastic bags, and he withdrew the first to find a wad of cash. The other small sack was either more money, which was unlikely, or Ike's stash of "feel-goodies," as he referred to the weed and ecstasy and whatever else he'd scored and hidden away. This one was enough. From the looks of it, there was nearly a grand hidden inside the first bag.

After pocketing the plastic bag and replacing the vent, he headed for the attic stairs and climbed the steep, ladder-like steps to his "room." Once there, he went to his own hiding spot, a board near the only vent in the ceiling; he slid it out of place and reached beneath the convex arch of a roof tile. He retrieved a sock holding several hundred dollars. Not enough to start a new life, but when added to the money he'd taken from Ike, he should do all right.

Maybe.

He didn't take the time to think it through, just backed down the staircase, and headed outside, the screen door banging behind him, Roscoe giving up a disgruntled "woof." Noah didn't bother with the steps, just took a flying leap off the porch and ran across the parking area to the shed, another one of Ike's private spots.

Inside, the shed was an oven, stifling and breathless.

A wasp buzzed angrily near an umbrella-shaped paper nest tucked in rafters low enough to touch; the building was small and compact, not quite as large as a single-bay garage. Weathered siding smelled of oil and dust, mingled with the lingering scent of stale cigarette smoke from stepdaddy's last Camel Straight. Tools lined the walls, and motorcycle parts were strewn on a bench that ran along one side of the shed, beneath the single window, where cobwebs and grime covered the small panes. The Yamaha was propped against the far wall, and without a second thought, he rolled it out of the dingy building, down the short ramp, and onto the sparse gravel of the parking area between the sagging garage and the back porch.

He kick-started the old bike into life, and the engine caught immediately. Then he was off, the back tire sliding a little as he slipped from the scant gravel to the asphalt of the two-lane. *Take that, Ike,* he thought, grinning smugly. It was time to give a little back to the man who didn't think twice about back-handing him; he was a burly son of a bitch with a cruel streak that he tried and failed to control. There would be hell to pay when Noah returned, but maybe he wouldn't. Maybe he'd just keep riding west; he was old enough at eighteen to do what he wanted, even if it was on a stolen motor bike.

Oh, hell.

His mother, if she knew what he was doing, would have a heart attack. But how much did she care? If his whereabouts weren't engraved on the bottom of a martini glass, she wouldn't have a clue, right? No, Cora Sue left all of her child-rearing and now teen-monitor duties to Ike the Spike or his paternal grandmother, the sperm donor's aging and oh-so-religious mother. As far as Noah knew, his grandmother still regularly wrote to her felon of a son and, no doubt, spouted the same Bible verses and quotes to Ronnie as she did to Noah. She plucked them at random, from the Old Testament as well as the New. They were often butchered and spun for her own purpose, but they continued to ring in his ears.

"Do to others as you would have them do to you" and "Be joyful in hope, patient in affliction, faithful in prayer . . ." and Noah's personal favorite, "For all have sinned and fall short of the glory of God. . . ." *Amen to that, Granny!*

He wouldn't dwell on the consequences of what he was doing. Not now, anyway. With the hot wind in his face, the Yamaha whining high and steady, only to catch, then thrum again as it wound through the gears, and his pocket full of the old man's ill-gotten money, he steered the bike steadily west, where the desert stretched toward the mountains that were on fire, backlit by the setting sun.

His heart surged.

He felt free, and though it was probably a temporary sensation, one he might regret, he didn't care. At least not for the moment.

He flicked his wrist, shifting as the motorcycle screamed down the highway, passing a few cars heading toward the lights of Las Vegas. Sin City. And his home. At least for now. Probably not for long when Ike discovered his stash and bike missing.

But who the fuck cared? Live for the moment, baby, that was his new motto.

Grinning, he wound the bike up, engine revving, tires humming, and eating up the dusty asphalt strip as he cruised by the park.

Remmi wasn't on the bench where she'd said she'd be. Disappointment welled inside him, and he waited, driving the bike in figure eights, then gassing it and popping a wheelie, as the seconds and minutes rolled past.

What do you expect? A girl like that. Emphasis on girl, *and she is way out of your league. A braniac who reads books and doesn't give a crap about what every other girl her age likes isn't going to be into you.* Still he waited and argued with himself, coming up with a dozen legitimate reasons why she hadn't shown up: the car wouldn't start, she'd been found out, she'd fallen asleep, she got called into work, she had to babysit those twin siblings, and on and on.

Still he hung out, feeling the heat rising from the parking lot pavement, watching others come and go, mothers, and babysitters, even a dad or two, or a grandparent; all stayed only long enough for their kids to play in the sand and the fountain while they chatted on their cell phones.

But no Remmi.

He checked his watch and noticed the sun was beginning to set over the ridge of mountains.

Fine. She wasn't going to show.

Angry again, he pressed on the gas and sped out of the parking lot, racing to the part of town Remmi called home. He didn't see her in the lengthening shadows surrounding her house, and even after several passes, he didn't catch sight of her. The house was quiet, almost as if no one was home, just one lamp blazing from a back window, and the nanny's car, a small Honda Civic, parked in the drive. Was Remmi inside? He drove loudly past twice, and neighbors across the street peered through the windows, but no one stirred in the Storm house. Either she didn't hear him, couldn't respond, or just didn't want to see him.

Fine.

He couldn't wait forever, he decided, and hit the gas, speeding along the narrow bit of rapidly declining suburbia and onto the main road, his back tire skidding a bit again before it caught and the bike righted itself.

Adrenaline burning through his blood, he wondered if he'd ever see Remmi again, told himself it didn't matter, though that was a hard and fast lie considering his sense of disappointment.

He pushed the bike ever faster, around a slow-moving pickup loaded with bales of hay, and then farther, the Yamaha whining in his ears, the wind screaming past as he headed unerringly west and into the Mojave, now burnished by the rays of the dying sun as it stretched silently to the mountains.

CHAPTER 2

Didi hankered for another cigarette as she drove, but resisted the urge. She'd already broken some unwritten law by lighting up with her twins in the car, and she'd just have to wait. Instead, she reached across the bench seat and opened the massive glove box, another place she kept props, then with one hand and an eye on the road, she scrounged around until she found an opened tin of Altoids. She popped two, hoping her breath would smell fresh for the upcoming meeting.

Her heart was pounding a million times a minute at that thought. Hands tight on the steering wheel, she gave herself an internal pep talk. "You can do this. You know you can. It's for the best. For you. For the kids. For everyone." But she blinked against an unexpected gush of tears and refused to let them fall from her eyes. Not only did she not want to appear weak to herself or to *him,* she didn't want to ruin her so carefully applied makeup.

She checked the Caddy's dash, noting the time. She couldn't screw this up. Her next set started at ten, and she'd promised she would be there. And she would be.

Nothing could go wrong. It just couldn't. She stretched her fingers over the steering wheel, feeling them tense despite all her best intentions.

She'd been planning this night for months, ever since the midwife had given her the news that she'd be delivering twins. Not one baby, but two. Oh, Lord. She'd wanted to argue with Seneca, but the woman, who had some Jamaican blood in her, was a skilled midwife and nursemaid. Tall, elegant, with sly, watchful eyes, Seneca knew how to keep her mouth shut as well as help with the birthing and caring of babies without the inconvenience of hospitals full of staff and visitors with their watchful eyes and wagging tongues. Doctors, nurses, aides, and whoever else within the walls of even a private hospital would have been hard to buy off—there were just too many people involved—but Seneca, though not cheap, not by a long shot, could keep her mouth closed. Seneca's tight lips, coupled with her skilled hands, made her well worth the trouble and expense, and even if Didi really couldn't afford the midwife/nursemaid right now, she would soon be able to.

Didi might not be much of a celebrity, as she darned well should be, but right now she had to filter the publicity around her and make sure her secrets were secure. Or else her plan would backfire—and she couldn't risk that. She had a future to think of. Not just for herself, but for her children. She hazarded another quick glance at the back seat, where her babies were cooing and gurgling. Little Adam and Ariel. Her throat grew thick, and she turned her eyes back to the road and searched for the spot where she would exit this strip of highway. Within minutes, she found the back road that dissolved into gravel and wound through the cholla and yucca before turning onto the broad expanse of Mojave. Her throat was tight and as dry as the dust that plumed from beneath the white-

walls of her Caddy as she tore past Joshua trees and followed the dirt bike and ATV tracks through the uneven
desert.

One of the babies started to cry, and she let out a sigh.
"Not now," she said softly. "Please not now." To distract
herself, she turned on the radio again but didn't even notice what was playing. It didn't matter.

Her nerves were on edge, but in an hour, maybe less,
this part of her plan would be over. And then . . . And
then . . . ? Phase two.

"God help me," she whispered, and despite her vows
otherwise, she pressed in the lighter again and searched
her bag for one more cigarette.

Just one.

Stomping on the accelerator, Brett Hedges drove as if
he were trying to outrun a damned avalanche. And he was.
The storm of emotions roiling within him, propelling
him, was chasing after him, nipping at his heels, threatening to swallow him with all its vengeful fury.

Just who the hell did Didi think she was?

Baiting him?

Taunting him?

Threatening to expose him and using a *kid* to do it?

A mental image of her beautiful face swam before his
eyes. Sly green eyes, pouty slick lips, high cheekbones,
and a naughty come-hither smile that was part innocence
and part pure sensual guilt. With a sexy, sassy attitude and
a body to match, she'd lured him, teased him, and thrown
out her proverbial bait, and he'd snapped it up, hook, line,
and sinker.

The damned part of it was, he'd probably do it all over
again, even knowing the consequences.

Maybe . . .

As dust spun from beneath the Mustang's tires and the engine roared, he sped across the desert, the sinking sun at his back, the luminescent glow of Las Vegas deep into the horizon, the million stars in the clear, dark sky beginning to show. He drove steadily to the stupid meeting point that she'd insisted upon.

He'd told her he would drive to the city, have the meeting in a hotel room in one of the large casinos, but no. She wanted a face-to-face in the middle of the damned Mojave Desert.

It seemed over the top. Nearly insane.

Then again, Didi was nothing if not a drama queen, so here he was, racing across an uneven track of what couldn't even be called a road, in the middle of the fucking Nevada desert. The back of his neck twinged, that same feeling that was always a warning, telling him he was making a big mistake, maybe a colossal or epic error in judgment, by agreeing to her demands.

For a second, he sneaked a peek at the passenger seat, where his briefcase lay. Inside: blood money. Next to it: his pistol. A Glock G-19. With fifteen rounds in the clip.

Just in case.

His back teeth ground together as bugs spattered his windshield and dust filled his nostrils.

Shit, shit, shit!

Pounding on the steering wheel with one curled fist, he thought of all kinds of scenarios, nasty ones, where he would put her in her place. His guts curled at the thought of paying that lying bitch, who, less than a year ago, was all wet lips and hot pussy, a woman who was, as it turned out, as crazy as she was sexy, as cunning as she was erotic, a woman he never should have touched, let alone slept with. Oh, hell, this was a mess, and he was right at the center of it.

But he wasn't going down without a fight, he thought,

as he heard the first cry of a lonesome coyote over the growl of the Mustang's engine. Inside his somewhat battered briefcase, he had a little surprise for Didi. Some of the bills weren't legit, but near-perfect forgeries, a fact she wouldn't be able to discern until she'd really examined each bundle, all strapped neatly. Professionally. By the time she'd realized her mistake, it would be too late. She wouldn't be able to go to the cops without selling herself down the river for attempting extortion and selling her own infant. He wasn't sure about the laws, but what she was attempting was darned close to human trafficking in a way, even if he was the kid's father.

Right? Maybe.

Did it matter? No.

The upshot was that she would be cornered as well as broke.

He felt a grim satisfaction at that thought. Didi would get what she'd deserved, the con artist becoming the mark. It all had an ironic and gratifying ring to it, he thought, though the sprinkling of legitimate fifties and hundreds within the straps did bother him. A necessary cost of doing business.

He only wished he could be a fly on the wall when she finally discovered that the illicit tables had been effectively turned on her.

As he thought about that, he allowed himself a grin, and for the first time since he'd rented his car in L.A., the warmth of the lowering sun was welcome against his back.

In the back of the Cadillac, Remmi fought nausea. The car was speeding, engine humming, and Didi didn't seem to care as the tires hit rocks and potholes that caused it to bounce. The cargo space was beyond hot, the air stale, and Remmi held onto the grips on either side of the tight space, handholds made especially for Didi when she was hiding within this cramped space as part of her routine. Now the straps helped Remmi from hitting her head again and kept her body, even wedged as it was, from shifting and banging against the sides or ceiling. Her head still throbbed from the first time, and she couldn't chance Didi hearing a suspicious noise, though that scenario seemed far-fetched right now as she was driving like a bat out of hell to a place only she knew. The longer the trip, the more woozy Remmi felt, and the more her fear mounted. Wherever Didi was taking her twins, it wasn't a good spot, of that Remmi was certain.

What if Didi was somehow plotting to get rid of Ariel and Adam? Remmi's heart twisted, and she didn't really believe it because she felt at some level her mother really did love her infants, even if they were fatherless, and once again, Didi Storm, aka Edwina Maria Hutchinson, was thrust into the role of single mother. She'd stuck by Remmi despite the lack of a husband; surely, she would do the same for the twins. Or would she? Hadn't Didi taken extraordinary measures to hide her pregnancy, wearing tight girdles in the first few months, which, combined with her morning, afternoon, and night sickness, had kept her from showing, but then, when the two babies began gaining weight in utero, Didi had stopped working, claimed an illness shrouded in mystery, and quietly had her babies at home, with Seneca as midwife and Remmi as her aide. Remembering the birth, Remmi felt even more queasy. Afterward, when the two infants were breathing on their own, wailing and cleaned, their cords cut, the detritus of afterbirth and blood dispensed with, Remmi's heart had soared at the wonder of birth and the creation of the perfect tiny humans, but during the protracted labor and birth itself, she'd nearly vomited.

Didi had taken to the twins, a boy and girl she'd quickly dubbed Adam and Ariel, but still she'd kept her secret, and Remmi had been advised to do the same. There had been the unspoken threat of some kind of illegality, possibly no official birth record for either child, and Didi had warned her daughter that the babies could be "taken away" and "put into foster care" or "put up for adoption," all of which was probably BS, but Remmi had dutifully held her tongue.

And now this. A secret run through the desert in the Caddy, while dressed in her flashiest costume? It didn't make any sense. Not only that, Remmi knew, somehow it wasn't right, almost seemed sinister. But what was her mother's plan? Remmi didn't doubt that Didi had one, and she almost banged on the panel separating this tiny cranny from the back seat, but didn't. If Didi realized her eldest daughter was stowed away and now a part of whatever plot she'd hatched, Didi would flip out and possibly even slap her again, so Remmi bit her tongue and tried to ignore the headache throbbing to the pulsing beat of some song Didi was listening to, the guitars and drums pounding through speakers mounted in the cargo space.

But as the beat thundered and the smell of cigarette smoke filled her space, the heat intense, Remmi almost gave up and pounded her fist on the panels. She was poised to do it when the music stopped suddenly and the car shifted, turning widely, still bouncing on the uneven terrain, slowing slightly. Whatever Didi was involved in, it was about to go down.

Remmi bit her lip, worried. And Didi was clearly nervous. She never smoked unless she was stressed to the max, at least not around the babies. Whatever this was, it was bad, bad, bad.

Maybe she should reveal herself.

What if something really bad was about to happen?

She'd told herself that Didi wouldn't do anything to put her babies, her specially equipped monster of a car, and her own self at risk, but what did Remmi know? Didi was nothing if not theatrical, and though she seemed very inclined to save her own skin, she'd been acting weird lately, ever since the birth of the twins. And now she was lighting up again, a sure sign that she was anxious. Yeah, Didi smoked, but not one after another, and the set of her jaw, the little worry lines near the corners of her glossy lips, visible in the mirror, were indications of just how serious this all was.

Remmi started hyperventilating and told herself to calm down, that everything was going to be fine, that Didi had been in more than her share of scrapes and had always landed on her feet. Hopefully this time would be the same.

On the ridge overlooking a wide span of the Mojave, the Marksman waited.

Patiently.

Double-checking the holographic sight on his rifle, making certain it was aimed perfectly, he felt the dying sun on his back. The Remington was held in place by a hog saddle on a short tripod and aimed at the desert floor, where trails from motorbikes, ATVs, and SUVs criss-crossed through the sparse vegetation. The evening was still hot, only a whisper of wind sliding over him.

Nearly go time.

A glance at the dead body lying face down, blood staining the sand, confirmed the fact that everything was in motion.

He turned back to his sniper's nest, once more checking for scorpions and Mojave greens, rattlers common to this part of the desert. He scanned the dips and ridges of his hiding spot but found it clean. Settling in, he ignored the little trail of blood that ran down a bit of a slope toward him and didn't listen to the sounds of the coming night, the insects, and the occasional cry of a coyote. He needed to focus, and as he did, a song came into his mind.

As always.

Whenever absolute concentration was necessary, the prayers and rhymes and songs of his youth would seep into his brain, the rhythms and tunes soothing, though some people might think it hypocrisy or heresy or even worse for the religious or patriotic ditties and phrases to be part of his plan of action. He didn't care, though. He needed a clear mind, a focused eye, and a steady hand. He didn't choose the mantra, it chose him, day by day, different as the seasons, constant as the rising sun. Once the Lord's Prayer had sifted through his gray matter:

> *Our Father who art in heaven,*
> *Hallowed be thy name . . .*

Another time a song he barely remembered from vacation Bible school:

> *Jesus loves me*
> *This I know*
> *For the Bible*
> *Tells me so . . .*

But today there was another one, the refrain simple, the earworm incessant, which was just perfect:

> *This little light of mine, I'm gonna let it shine . . .*
> *This little light of mine . . .*

His entire family would have been horrified that these inspirational songs and catchphrases and prayers were what he used as a calming bath for his brain, a steadying force, but did it matter? Sometimes he even invoked prayers in Latin, a dead language he'd been forced to learn at the insistence of his ultrareligious grandmother, who had been raised Roman Catholic before she found her born-again faith. Despite her conversion to a strict evangelical sect, she retained some of the trappings of her Catholic roots, her affinity for Latin being one of them. Granny. May she rest in peace. "*Requiescat in pace*," he said aloud, softly, not for the dead person here, in the desert, but for that pale-lipped, curly-haired woman with skin the color and texture of beef jerky, who had alternately wagged her finger at him and laughed uproariously, from her gut, mouth opened wide, gold caps glinting in the firelight. A miserable, God-fearing, and hilarious old bitch. "*Requiescat in pace*," he repeated, then spat into the dirt, sending a camel spider scurrying to hide under a nearby rock.

It shouldn't be long now.

He closed his eyes for a second.

Listened hard.

It sounded like a car's engine was getting closer. Yes, there it was . . . and another? From the opposite direction? Oh, yes . . .

He couldn't help but smile as he opened his eyes, searching the desert floor for the pinpoints of headlights and the telltale plumes of dust.

There it was. The distinctive rumble of a big car's engine. He slipped his finger onto the trigger.

And then he saw them, the tiny glare of twin headlamps, coming in from the east.

And fast.

Right on time.

CHAPTER 3

"Gotcha." Brett trained his eyes on the headlights blazing, twin beacons glowing like gold eyes in the desert, moving steadily in his direction.

As if the driver of the approaching car heard him, the vehicle slowed, wheels sliding through a clump of cacti, a pastel fender glinting in the last streaks of sunset. Didi for sure, and in that big monster of a car, the white Cadillac convertible she used in her shows.

Of course.

She had to make a flashy entrance.

Always. No matter how serious the situation. But then again, maybe she didn't realize just how serious this was. Again, he glanced to the passenger seat. Could he do it? He wondered. It would be easy enough to threaten her, but to really pull the trigger?

He remembered, just ten damned months ago, first meeting her after one of her shows. It had all started with him sending a message to her dressing room. He'd gone to see her perform at the suggestion of a friend. Though the casino had been older, a seedy throwback to the fifties

that was rumored to have been sold and slated for demo-
lition, there had been a bit of nostalgic charm to the place.
He'd ordered a double martini, then turned his disinter-
ested gaze to the stage when the drink had arrived.

The curtain had gone up, and to his surprise he'd been
instantly captivated. From the moment he'd first spied
her "appearing" magically from the inside of what had
seemed to be an empty, if gleaming, pearlescent white
Cadillac, its finish so glossy as to look wet, he'd been gob-
smacked. Didi, in a sequined gown, fluffy blond wig, and
bubblegum-pink lips had resembled Marilyn Monroe so
closely, he'd had to look twice. And hard. Man, she'd
been a knockout.

Seated in the front row, at a table nearly abutting the
stage, he could have sworn she'd singled him out, that the
glances she'd sent his way had definitely been hot. He'd
interpreted them as come-hither invitations that had caused
all sorts of erotic images to spring to mind. He'd downed
three or four martinis during her set, his gaze drawn to
the sexy performer who changed costumes during the act,
becoming different celebrities while singing and actually
performing a little magic as well.

Brett had been mesmerized. Stupidly, he realized now.
He'd sent the message to her dressing room via a waiter
and then had ended up buying her more than a few drinks
when she'd appeared without all the stage makeup, looking younger, more innocent, and even more beautiful in
tights and a shimmery, belted tunic. She'd been blessed
with a fresh face and was quick with a soft, sexy laugh.
Her large eyes glimmered, or had it been the booze? Who
knew? The upshot was that one thing had led to another,
and they'd spent more than a week together, primarily in
his hotel room with a glorious penthouse view high above
the city. He'd lost his sanity for what had, in reality, been

only a few nights, but it had been long enough to reel him in forever.

In hindsight, the seduction appeared to have been part of a greater plan that had blossomed into her extortion plot. She'd probably set her sights on him from the onset, and he'd been stupid enough to think he'd fooled her with his alias and back story about his identity. All along, it now seemed, she'd known he wasn't who he'd claimed to be, that even the ID he'd carried and left "carelessly" in his wallet had been a lie.

One night that week, in the early morning hours, he'd felt her stir and slide out of the covers to tiptoe to the bureau where he'd tossed his billfold. As he'd watched through slitted eyes, she'd opened the wallet and studied its contents. The room had been dark, for the most part, the only illumination from small digital numbers on the television and digital clock, as well as the ambient glow from outside the window, seeping past the open blinds, the neon lights of Las Vegas giving the room an otherworldly half-light. He'd expected her to take some of the cash or slip one of his credit cards into her purse. He'd been mistaken. She'd just looked at each thin card with its magnetic strip and unknown available balance, not bothering to photograph any of them or pocket a single one. As quietly as a mouse, she'd replaced his belongings exactly as she'd found them, going so far as to pat his wallet, as if for good luck or as a sign of affection before returning to the bed.

He knew better now, but in those wee hours when she'd spooned her supple body up against his, her smooth rump cuddled into his crotch, he'd trusted her, and his erection had stiffened against her skin. She'd snuggled closer, moving against his cock, making soft mewling noises as he'd reached around to cup one of her incredible breasts. Her nipple had tightened, and he'd groaned, then pushed her into the bed and thrust deep into her silky, moist heat. Their coupling had been fierce and raw, and even now, as he drove, knowing full well the depths of her deception, loathing himself, he felt a twinge in his crotch.

After that night, when she'd left his wallet on the bureau, their affair had blazed white hot for four or five more nights, before he'd left the city, promising to call and never bothering. She was, he'd decided, a fling. Nothing more. Part of a wild, erotic week of his life that he would remember from time to time, and he would smile, wondering what had happened to her. He might even search her out, via the Internet or some other means, perhaps try to reconnect, but he hadn't believed it, because deep down, he'd suspected she was trouble, the kind of trouble he wanted no part of.

For the better part of a year, he hadn't heard from her.

Until that fateful call telling him he was a daddy. And, oh, by the way, she knew his true identity and that his family was loaded.

So she'd never bought his story that he was single, a salesman for a high-tech firm who visited this part of Nevada as part of his territory. He'd made it clear that he'd been looking for fun and that was all, and she'd acted as if she'd understood—no strings attached.

And then, after hearing nothing for three quarters of a year, she'd dropped the bomb that he was a father to a newborn son, and she had the DNA test to prove it.

Maybe.

The whole thing smelled of a con job.

He felt to the marrow of his bones that he'd been set up. From the very get-go.

She'd played him, played him good.

But no more.

Tonight was the end of it.

It's now or never.

Didi spied the approaching car, and her throat turned as dry as the dust spraying up from the Caddy's tires. The babies. Her babies. Was she making a huge mistake?

"You can do this," she said, determined. Yes, this was the biggest con of her life, and yes, she was nervous, but it was close to going down. Heart thudding, she told herself she should feel some sense of exhilaration rather than angst, but one of her little ones started to cry, and she had to shut out the sound for fear that her damned milk would let down and gushers of milk would stain her dress despite undergarments that had been guaranteed not to let that happen. Geez, how had her life turned to such a mess, all deception and lies? She'd once been a Missouri farm girl, filled with promise and enthusiasm, but that girl, Edwina Maria Hutchinson, had died a quick death the minute she'd turned eighteen, took the bus out of the small town she'd called home, and, two days later, landed on sweet California soil. At that moment, Edie, as she'd been known in the Midwest—she had even gladly embroidered it onto her tight cheerleading sweater—had died a quick death, and Didi Storm had been born.

Even at eighteen, she'd known she'd been blessed with the face of an angel and the body of a she-devil, and she'd been certain she would take the entertainment industry by her new surname, which was one of the reasons she'd chosen it. Didi Storm. It just had such a great ring to it, y'know? However, like so many others who had believed they were the next big thing, she'd been sadly mistaken and horridly disappointed. No, she'd not become a household name like Meg Ryan or Demi Moore or Jennifer Aniston or Julia Roberts or whoever. There were dozens of women who had, and Didi had been determined to become one of them. She'd start out at the bottom, take bit parts in soap operas or do commercials, anything just to get a toehold on stardom. But it hadn't panned out, not at all, she thought bitterly as her Cadillac hurtled through the desert. Because stupidly . . . stupidly, she'd let herself get pregnant, and all of her dreams had gone up in dust—or, more accurately, in piles of dirty diapers, sinks full of baby bottles, and long, sleepless nights with a baby girl.

If she hadn't been so foolish as to become a teenage mother, she was still certain, she would have made the big time. Instead, she'd spent hours as a waitress in a seedy bar or going to auditions or rocking her colicky infant while staring at the television in the studio apartment she'd rented in Sherman Oaks. The tips had been okay, and at least she hadn't had to stoop to turning tricks or fall into the trap of becoming some kind of porn star with more than one X in her name. No, she'd scraped by, and deep into the nights, though exhausted, she'd watched dozens of old movies and learned to mimic the stars of the silver screen. Marilyn Monroe, with her combination of innocence, sexy charm, and breathy voice, quickly became her favorite, and she'd practiced every nuance of the blond bombshell's on-screen personas. But Didi hadn't stopped with Marilyn, not when she had been able to watch hours of MTV with its endless music videos. She taped her favorites, then replayed them over and over, studying the dance moves and singing styles of the female artists she adored. Cher was the best, but Whitney Houston, Madonna, and Joan Jett all were close seconds. Didi loved the most flamboyant and independent, the pop stars and rockers who dressed to suit themselves, their costumes brilliant and outlandish, their attitudes sassy and outspoken—women she'd emulated while trapped with a sickly infant.

Yeah, pick your poison, boys, she'd thought, Didi does it all. And had for years. All because she'd drunk too much rotgut tequila one night and thrown caution to the wind. She'd ended up with a mother of a hangover that hadn't really ever gone away, considering she'd conceived Remmi that night.

The daughter who had stopped her from getting to the big time.

The pregnancy that had started her downfall.

If she hadn't been knocked up with Remmi, who knew how bright her own star would have shined. As it was, she'd made a name for herself of sorts by bathing in, and reflecting, the luminescence of much bigger celebrities.

"Shit," she muttered under her breath but told herself she'd learned her lesson. Now, she knew how to use a baby to get what she wanted. She just had to hold onto her nerve a little while longer.

She'd started her impersonation act as a way to put food on the table and pay the rent while still dreaming of making it big and hoping her talent would be discovered. It was a stopgap until she was discovered and soared to the heights of celebrity, but now, nearly fifteen years later, with gray hairs beginning to sprout, her boobs starting to sag, her skin not nearly as tight as it had once been, she was still doing her routine at a dive off the Strip in Sin City.

But not for long.

Nuh-uh.

Tonight was the big score.

Her eyes narrowed on the approaching car—a Mustang, from the looks of it—speeding over the dry terrain. Getting closer by the second. Near enough to spy the driver, a dark silhouette of a man who was about to be taken down a peg or two.

"Here we go."

She slowed to a stop only twenty feet from the Mustang, whose headlights appeared to glow an evil yellow as the dust settled between the two idling cars.

"God," she whispered, then turned in her seat and said to the two infants who were beginning to whimper, "It's showtime." Then as the babies started to wail, she got out of the car and opened a back door. "Shh, shh, shh, little one," she whispered as she unbuckled one of the car seats. "Hush now. It's time to meet your daddy."

What?

Your daddy? Is that what Didi had said?

And what did she mean by "showtime"?

Remmi couldn't believe her ears. Had her mother really hauled her twins out here in the middle of the damned desert at twilight to meet their father? Even for over-the-top drama queen Didi Storm, this seemed far-fetched.

And who was this guy?

As the car door slammed shut, doors locking with a resounding click, Remmi wriggled to get a better view through the crack between the back seats, but she couldn't see anything other than headlights burning through the dusty windshield.

Didi had never named the father of her twins, even though Remmi had asked her mother over and over again, just as she had about her own father, but until this moment, Didi's lips had been sealed about the paternity of any of her children. "Some things are better left unsaid," she'd asserted. She'd also been vague when Remmi had wanted to know if her father knew she existed. She'd never heard one whisper from him in her entire life and had assumed he didn't know he had a daughter. Because of Didi, whose personal mantras about men included "Keep them guessing" and "The less they know, the more they'll want to know. Everyone wants to sniff around a secret." In Remmi's opinion, Didi had that one down cold. Didi's life was more of a secret diary, as opposed to an open book, and even that very private journal had had a few dark pages ripped from its binding. "A woman needs an aura of mystery to keep a man interested," Didi had once advised her eldest daughter. "Otherwise he'll go sniffin' around any horny bitch who breezes by. Ya know what I mean?" This piece of advice was followed by a knowing wink. Didi had been in full regalia, her favorite glittery Cher outfit, all netting, sequins, deep plunges, and an over-sized black wig. Seated at her makeup station in her "dressing room," which had been little more than a large closet, Didi had met Remmi's curious gaze in the mirror as she'd applied a shimmery coat of lip gloss. "You get me?"

"Sure." Remmi had nodded appropriately, as any other response would have been met with anger.

"Remember that," Didi said, standing and taking stock of her slim figure in the glass. She swatted a bit of lint from her shoulder, then, satisfied with her appearance, added, "Now, you wait here. I'll be back after the first set and drive you home." Then she was off, leaving Remmi alone in the small room to dabble with her mother's precious makeup and to note that all of Didi's theories about life, love, and especially men didn't really mean much as they certainly hadn't worked out for her, evidenced by the trail of burned-out romances that had flamed oh-so-hot for a while, then inevitably sputtered and died. Mostly because of Didi's mercurial temper, but also because, in Remmi's estimation, her mother always picked losers, never anyone solid. In every case, any man who Didi had pronounced as being "the one" had ended up with the title of "sick, damned bastard" only a few months later. All wrong.

In a flash, she thought of Noah, and with a twist of her heart and more insight than she wanted, she wondered if her attraction to him was genetic, if she'd inherited her mother's fascination and proclivity for men who were obviously all wrong for her.

Don't even go there. She couldn't think of Noah right now, or anything other than the drama unfolding in front of her. Through the slit, she saw her mother's backside, swinging in the beams of the Caddy's headlights. In heels, blond wig, and a tight dress, she sauntered as one of the baby carriers swung from one hand.

What the hell was Didi going to do?

In the sweltering secret compartment, Remmi was sweating, her heart racing a million beats a minute. Even the bit of air sifting in from the back seat didn't cool her off or ease her anxiety. Biting her lip, Remmi wondered if she dared pop out from behind the false wall to get a better view of her mother and whatever she was doing, of the spot where the beams of the facing sets of headlights embraced. Or maybe she should even fling herself out of the Caddy and demand to know what her mother was doing with one of her siblings.

Whatever it was, it was wrong. Remmi felt it.

But if she exposed herself, Didi would be furious. Out of her mind with anger. And whatever she was plotting would be blown to smithereens. No, she had to remain hidden. It was the safest move. For her. And for her little brother and sister. Oh, Lord, she hoped so.

But as Didi walked farther into the distance, Remmi sent up a silent prayer that whatever her mother was doing, it wouldn't be the disaster that seemed so imminent.

> *Hide it under a bushel?*
> *No!*
> *I'm gonna let it shine.*
> *Hide it under a bushel?*
> *No!*
> *I'm gonna let it shine . . .*

Soundlessly, the Marksman mouthed the familiar words, the lilting, deeply ingrained tune sifting through his brain as he stared through the sight of his rifle. Everything was going perfectly, unfolding just as he'd been informed it would happen.

Well, other than the dead guy.

That was a wrinkle he hadn't foreseen.

He didn't bother glancing at the corpse again. Would deal with it later. Right now, he had to concentrate.

Through the sight, he saw that the two cars had stopped, were idling about twenty yards apart and facing each other. His lips twisted as he recognized the woman, all curves and shimmery dress and ridiculously high heels. She was already out of her classic Cadillac, its interior light casting a weak glow.

He zeroed in on her and forced his heartbeat to slow. He had to remain calm. Steady.

He adjusted his sight just a hair. Watching, he saw her bend over the back seat and withdraw a bulky infant carrier, and it appeared heavy, with a kid inside. Then she rounded the big car and opened the opposite door, only to withdraw another carrier. It too looked heavy.

Deftly, she kicked the door closed.

Far in the distance, over the sound of a lonesome coyote's cry, he heard the high-pitched whine of a motorcycle's engine. The driver was winding the bike through its gears. From the corner of his eye, the Marksman thought he saw a trail of dust at the far end of the valley. No way. And yet, the glimmer of a single headlamp boring into the twilight caught his attention.

No.

Not now.

Don't let it get to you. It's just some cycle junkie out on a joyride. It has nothing to do with the job.

But the rider could be a witness.

Just like the dead man.

He stole one last glance at the unwitting stranger he'd had to kill.

Concentrate.

Deal with the situation when it becomes a problem.

Sweat began to bead over his brow, and he let out a slow breath of air.

A low moan rolled on the slight breeze, and the hairs on the back of his neck raised. Again, he glanced over at the dead man. Unmoving. Silent. The guy hadn't been breathing five seconds ago. And he'd been shot through the heart. Or damned close to. He was dead. Had to be.

Still, the Marksman's skin prickled as the sound, low and guttural, whispered over the dry soil again, but the body didn't move.

A ghost?

Someone else hiding in the shadowy landscape?

He swallowed back fear and stared at the cacti and scrub and rocks jutting out of the desert floor, but he saw no movement in the coming night. With renewed effort, he forced his gaze back to the drama unfolding in the valley below.

A bead of sweat slithered down from his hairline and along his jaw, but he ignored it. He couldn't, wouldn't break concentration.

The driver's side door of the Mustang flew open, and the driver, a tall man carrying what looked like a briefcase, sprang from the interior. Leaving the door open, the interior light dim but steady, he strode toward the approaching female.

Here we go.

His finger was ready on the trigger.

Not yet.

Wait.

The exchange has to happen first. Remember. And do not hit the kid.

Steady . . . steady.

Let it shine, let it shine, let it shine . . .

CHAPTER 4

This is such bullshit!

Glock tucked into the back of his pants, Brett hauled his briefcase out of the car and wondered why he'd agreed to meet her like this. The middle of the desert at dusk. God, it was all so *Didi*. He should have just talked to his attorneys and let them handle whatever arrangements were necessary and legal.

But then, he wouldn't have been able to get back at her, would he? No. This sounded like the best solution, a plan to get a little of his own back. He only hoped he could pull it off. And he'd end up with his son. If everything went as planned. He could lie with the best of them, when called to, and this situation certainly warranted evading, or even reinventing, the truth. But he never liked it. Always felt uncomfortable. Not so his father. Nor his brother. God, if Brett only had the balls and swagger of his older sibling, the ability to lie easily and so convincingly through his teeth, maybe he wouldn't have ended up in this mess. Oliver Hedges Jr., who called himself OH2, was ruthless, even cruel when he needed to be. As the old man had been before his accident. The particular quality of sheer will to do whatever it took, and Brett lacked it. Nor had he ever cultivated his brother's cutting-edge, take-charge, and "damn the consequences" persona.

It just wasn't who he was.

Hence, his current untenable situation.

Caught in Didi Storm's seductive trap.

His fingers clenched around the handle of his brief-case.

There might have been a slim chance Didi wouldn't have seen through his fake identity when they'd first met. But no, she'd apparently known who he was, and their whole meeting, which he'd thought had been his idea, was really hers.

But what was done was done.

He just had to fix it.

And he would.

Right now.

He rounded the front end of the car and stepped into the bath of light cast by the Mustang's beams. The night was closing in, the sky dark aside from a line of illumination throwing the jagged mountains into relief, the air dry and still warm, the sound of his footsteps muffled by the layer of dust. And there she was. Didi Storm in all her glory. He stared at the woman he'd so lusted after. Damn, but she was still beautiful. Sauntering toward him, taking her time, wearing outrageous heels and a short, short skirt, she was still sexy as hell, and she knew it. Lips shimmering in a knowing smile, she hauled two baby carriers toward him.

Two?

What was this?

A back-up car seat? Or . . . ?

Holy Christ.

Could there really be two infants?

Twins?

His stomach clenched.

Were they his? Hers?

She'd sent the DNA profile. One. Not two. A son.

But right now, there were definitely two babies; he heard them both crying. Stereo. Good Lord.

What kind of nutcase was she, deep down? Bargaining with her own child . . . or possibly children? He stopped walking in front of his car. Let her come to him.

This could all be a show. Remember who you're dealing with.

"Brandon," she said in that breathy Marilyn Monroe voice that he'd once found sexy. Now it sounded fake. Anxious. Well, good. "Oh, wait. That's not right, is it? You weren't Brandon at all," she said. "That was just your alias, the one you used when you tried to pick up innocent girls."

He set his jaw, felt the Glock pressing into his back, and noticed the tension in the air. The desert at night. Where some people came to find inner peace under a vast star-flung sky.

"You weren't exactly innocent," he reminded her. "You set me up."

"Tit for tat, I guess."

"What is this, Didi?" he asked as she neared. He motioned from one of her hands to the other. "Two kids?"

"Mmm. Yeah. Turned out that way." Her cat-who-swallowed-the-canary smile made him want to strangle her. "Guess I forgot to mention that. Twins. A girl and a boy."

"You're kidding." But he could tell she was dead serious.

Shaking her head, she kept her gaze locked with his. "Two babies, and they're both yours."

"How would I know that?"

"DNA doesn't lie." She was so damned sure of herself. So smug. He wanted to strangle her.

"You could have mentioned it."

"And ruin the surprise?" She chuckled softly, but it was a nervous laugh, and for the first time, he sensed a deeper disturbance in the night. Something more was going on here, he could feel it, smell it in the dust of the desert, hear it in the whispering thump of bats' wings overhead. The warning hairs on the back of his neck stood erect, and it was all he could do not to reach for the pistol pressing into his back.

Didi's gaze slid to the briefcase clutched in his hand.

Of course.

"It's here," he said and stopped short. To prove his good intentions, he slid the locks, and the case opened. Stacks of tens and twenties were strapped into each side. "Two hundred and fifty grand."

She swung the carriers around, to show the faces of the tiny babies. They were red from crying, and the two infants were probably scared. "Which one?" she asked, and despite her determined exterior, she seemed to waver a bit, her eyes actually shimmering with tears.

"What?"

"Which kid do you want?" Her voice actually cracked as she pointed from one carrier to the next. "Adam or Ariel?"

No, no, no!

Whatever Didi was doing out here was wrong, so damned wrong. And she had to be stopped. Remmi was sure of that. *It's up to you. No one else is out here.* Frantically, she stared through the slit in the back seat and the windshield to the space in the desert between the two cars where her mother and some guy were squaring off. The baby carriers were now on the ground between them, an open briefcase near the man's feet.

For the love of God, it looked like an exchange of some kind.

Didi was trading her babies? To their *father?* No, no . . . that couldn't be right, Remmi thought frantically. She wouldn't be . . . *selling* her own children. But what then?

Hadn't Didi said recently that things were going to get better? When pressed, she'd been cryptic and only laughed to say, "We're about to win the lottery, honey," and Remmi had chalked it all up to her mother's fantasies about the damned tickets she'd purchased every week for as long as Remmi could remember.

But this . . .

No, she wouldn't. *Couldn't.*

Then what?

Frantically, she pressed the release to the back seat. Nothing happened. She tried again, her hand slick with sweat. Again a no go. "Come on, come on," she gritted, clawing at the damned release as she realized that without a special key, she couldn't get out. When the doors to the Caddy locked, so did the secret compartment. Fresh panic washed over her. Somehow, she had to stop this . . .

But she was trapped.

"You want me to choose?" Brett said, staring at the twin carriers. The girl, dressed in pink, was sniffling, as Didi had carefully leaned down and placed a pacifier in her tiny mouth, while the boy, in blue, had stopped crying on his own and was watching his mother and blinking. "That's crazy."

"You're paying for one," she said, straightening.

"I thought there was only one."

"Your mistake. If you want the second one, it'll be another two-fifty."

"You greedy bitch. You're certifiable."

"Am I?"

"You can't sell your own kids."

"Sure I can. You're their damned father. You can . . . you can think of me as a surrogate, okay?"

"That's not how I think of you."

"Doesn't matter," she said, though she flinched a little. Then she was all business again. "So, who do you want? Adam?" She pointed to the infant in his blue blankets. "Or Ariel?" Her manicured finger moved to the baby swathed in pink and lavender. "Your choice."

"I'm not making a . . ." He let his voice trail off. She had him over a barrel. They both knew it. A muscle in his jaw worked, and he wondered what would happen if he just took both kids. Would she call the cops? Claim kidnapping? Then what about the money?

"Or I can make the decision if it's too hard for you."

"The boy, then," he cut in, and she nodded as if she'd expected the answer. "You said I had a son."

"And I wasn't lying."

"But you didn't mention the girl."

"We were talking about one child, okay? But if you want Ariel, you . . . you can have her." Didi swallowed hard, as if her words were choking her. "But you'll have to pay another quarter mil." She tilted her head to the side and waited, chin lifted defiantly, platinum hair glistening in the headlights.

"This is insane!"

"Probably. But here we are. And now you have a son. Just like your old man wants."

His head snapped up. She knew that?

Her smile was cold as death. "That's right. I know all

about you, Brett, and your family. You've got what you wanted, and so do I, so let's just call it good."

Damn, he wanted to throttle her, but maybe that could come later. In a split second, he remembered her naked body—so hot, trembling with need, so moist. All a setup?

Didn't matter. Not now. He passed over the briefcase, and she examined it, unbuckling both straps and eyeing the bundles of cash, mentally counting and confirming that each stack was complete.

"It's all there."

Her eyes narrowed, and she warned, "You better not have cheated me."

He snorted, thinking of the scam she'd pulled.

Her lips knotted, and she dropped the opened packs of money back into the case, then cast one longing look at her son before picking up the carrier with the delicate pastel blanket. "Let me know if you want Ariel," she said, though it wasn't with any enthusiasm. "Maybe we'll be able to work things out."

"Yeah, right." Pissed, he grabbed the carrier with his son and turned back to the Mustang as she took his daughter, *his damned daughter,* back to the Caddy. He'll never see the girl, he knows that. Didi won't allow it. But she's greedy and a spendthrift. She'll blow through the cash he gave her and discover most of the bills are forged. Then she'll be back and threatening to expose him, but she won't have a leg to stand on as she will have to cop to selling her own baby.

Maybe they'll be able to work something out.

When pigs fly.

At the open door of the Mustang, the same bad feeling of unseen eyes observing them, that something dark and evil was lurking in the shadows, was even more intense, and the hum of that motorcycle's engine was getting louder. Closer. He saw it then, the bike's headlamp bouncing over the uneven terrain about a quarter of a mile away.

Quickly, he strapped the carrier with his kid into the back seat.

How about that?

He had a son.

And a daughter you may never meet.

Didi's heart twisted as she turned back to the Cadillac. *It's only for a little while. Remember that. You'll have the baby back soon.* Tears stung her eyes, though her back was ramrod straight, and she wouldn't let that son of a bitch know how much she hurt inside, how her heart twisted at the thought that she was giving up one of her infants, if only for a few days.

What if something goes wrong?

"It won't," she whispered as she reached the Caddy and unlocked the door. "It can't." Expertly, she snapped the car seat into place.

But when he realizes he's been duped . . .

Oh, sweet Jesus . . .

"It will be all right," she said and, after tossing the briefcase onto the seat next to hers, slid into the interior, immediately pressing in the button of the cigarette lighter with fingers that shook. She couldn't think of what she'd done, just about the future. Soon her plan would be complete. "Oh, God please," she whispered. This was the best she could do. For herself. For her kids. She knew it. You didn't get more than one shot at the big time, and since she'd failed when she'd landed in Hollywood all those years ago, this, the twins, was it. She started the car, then hit the gas. She didn't want to give Brett the chance to discover he'd been tricked. Cranking on the wheel, she headed back the way she'd come and found the damned motorcycle in her path.

"Idiot!" she ground out, just as he blew past and did some kind of wheelie thingie, riding the bike as it stood on its back wheel.

To think that Brett even considered taking the second kid. Oh, yeah, right. That would *never* fly, and besides, how could she explain it? Unfortunately, she was far from an A-list star, but she did have some kind of following, a few fans, and there had been rumors about her time off, that she might be knocked up. She'd managed to hide the fact that she'd borne twins but hadn't been able to hide her pregnancy. Seneca and Remmi, the only people who knew she had given birth a second time, would both keep their mouths shut, so she was home free.

Almost.

She glanced at the briefcase she'd cast so casually onto the passenger seat. A quarter of a million dollars. Enough to change a girl's life forever. The lighter clicked, and she found a cigarette, lit it, and inhaled deeply. "Oh, baby," she whispered, imagining her life and how it was going to change.

For the better.

But just wait until Brett realized she'd conned him, pulled a switcheroo. The son of a bitch was going to hit the roof when he realized he didn't have a son after all, that she'd dressed the twins in each other's clothing: Adam became Ariel, and her daughter became her son. She'd thought Brett might check but figured he'd been too stunned to discover he'd fathered two kids, not one, to think about it.

"Serves you right," she said, taking another long drag and feeling the nicotine swirl through her bloodstream.

This way, knowing he had a son, the DNA/paternity

report being on a male, Brett would come back to the well. His old man would insist upon it, and then she'd really put the screws to him. No measly two hundred and fifty thousand, no way. This time she'd ask for a cool million. Surely an heir, a *male* heir, was worth that to that greedy chauvinistic old man.

In the rearview, she saw the Mustang begin to move.

Away from her.

"Good."

She sped to the spot where the dirt tracks became gravel and slowed for a curve.

Crack!

A sharp report echoed over the valley.

And again.

Crraack!

What?

Gun shots? A car backfiring? What?

Her gaze flew to the mirror again, and then, after a pause, two more shots blasted in rapid succession and then—

Blam!

The earth shook violently.

With the explosion, the Caddy shimmied, tires bouncing.

Panicked, Didi hit the brakes. The big car fishtailed.

In the rearview, she caught a glimpse of a huge fireball rising into the desert sky.

Oh. *God!*

Night became day.

Brett's Mustang was nowhere to be seen.

Her heart clenched. Her stomach heaved. Her worst fears screamed through her brain. *His car blew up! He and everything in it, including precious Ariel, are destroyed!*

"No! No! No!" She screamed, her hands gripping the

wheel as she stood on the brakes. The white Cadillac shuddered to a stop. Dust rained down on her. This couldn't be happening. She twisted around to stare out the back window. "Please, please . . . oh, God, please, no." Her throat was tight, her grief unbearable. Not her baby. Nothing bad could have happened to her precious Ariel. "No," she whimpered, starting to sob. Horror scratched at her soul, tears ran from her eyes, and for a split second, she thought about turning the car around, driving to the inferno and . . .

And what? What can you do?

The cops will be out here in minutes, and how can you explain what happened out here? Besides, you don't know . . .

"Oh, God. Oh, dear God . . . oh, oh." She was trembling, shivering from the inside out. She had to do something, *anything!* But the raging inferno illuminating that barren part of the desert was burning out of control. No one could have survived.

"Forgive me," she whispered, then hit the gas and tore away, gravel spraying, mascara running into her eyes, a bump sounding in the rear of the vehicle. Oh, no . . . not a flat tire, not a piece of the Caddy falling off. She blinked and tried to see. If a part of her car were left out here . . . And did she hear a moan? No, that was the pitiful sound escaping from her own throat.

She saw no incriminating piece of her car in the darkness behind her, but would she? Of course not. Unless it reflected off that hellish glow from the fire . . . oh, God, she thought she might be sick.

The car is not falling apart. You're just freaking out, imagining it, making things worse by your stupid imagination. Stop it. Get a damned grip!

The front right tire careened into a rock and something—some kind of scrub brush—scraped the side. She heard another thud. Told herself to keep driving, to quit imagining that her sturdy, vintage Caddy was losing pieces, and to try not to think of the child she'd left with Brett.

Oh, Lord. Her baby. Her sweet little baby. "Ariel," she whispered, gasping and sobbing. She couldn't stop the tears nor the shaking. Terror and self-loathing roiled within her as she drove. Why had she done this? Why? For a few lousy bucks? A quarter of a mil? Or to get even with the hustler who'd gotten her pregnant? Why? Her baby . . . *nothing was worth her baby's life!*

Cigarette forgotten, she found a new mantra and started spewing it out loud, as much to drown out the demons in her head as anything. "Don't think about it. It never happened. Don't think about it. It never happened. Don't think about it . . ."

Just go, go, go. Ooh, sweet Jesus, God, no. Don't think about it, don't think about it . . . Oh God, oh God, oh God.

Heart thudding, she thought she heard the first sound of sirens wailing in the distance. Heading this direction? Or to some other catastrophe?

Didi Storm couldn't take the chance.

Despite all of her guilt, she couldn't, wouldn't, let the police and the world know what she'd done.

She pressed her foot harder still on the accelerator, and the power of over two hundred horses responded, racing beneath the hood of her prized car, propelling them forward toward the incandescence of Las Vegas.

CHAPTER 5

S omething was very, very wrong here.

Watching her mother return to the car through the peephole in the back, Remmi bit her lower lip, her mind racing.

Adam? Didi brought Adam back?

But not Ariel?

Didi left the girl dressed in her brother's clothes with her "daddy"?

That's how it appeared. Once the transfer for the brief-case had been made, Didi had sauntered back to the car, tossed the case onto the front passenger seat, strapped the baby carrier into place on the wide back seat, then climbed in and began driving. Fast. Somehow managing to light a cigarette. *What had just happened? And what was in the briefcase?*

Money.

Of course.

With a sinking feeling, Remmi knew.

Her mother had sold her child. The baby had been born with a price on her head.

Remmi thought she might be sick and was only vaguely aware of the sound of a motorcycle's engine revving near-by and her mother muttering a loud "Idiot!"

The exchange of cash for an infant was unthinkable, even for Didi Storm.

Remmi decided she could hide no longer; she had to find out what was going on. No more conjecture. Maybe there was a plausible, even reasonable explanation. She pounded on the back of the seat just as an explosion rocked the car, the Caddy shuddering and groaning as a burst of light was visible in the rearview. With a scream and some unintelligible words, Didi floored the monster of a car, and Remmi was thrown back, her head striking the roof. She moaned, blinked, and thought she might throw up as the big car raced across the uneven canyon floor. One of the car's tires struck a pothole or a rock or something. Remmi was tossed around in the tight space and bumped her shoulder.

Damn!

Reflexively grabbing hold of a bar that held the hidden props in place, she clung for dear life.

Something had gone horribly wrong out here. She knew that much. Now, Didi was fleeing, but what had happened to Ariel?

And what was that blinding flash, that explosion that had spooked Didi?

Not the other car. Please, God, not the other car!

But what else would blow up like that in the middle of the Mojave?

Then she heard her mother's voice, even and toneless, saying over and over again, "Don't think about it. It never happened. Don't think about it, it never . . ."

Remmi's heart turned to stone.

What had her mother done?

Tears blurred her vision, and she bit back sobs as she

thought of her baby sister. Ariel. Sweet, tiny girl. For the first time in years, Remmi began to pray.

Please be with innocent Ariel. Please, God, please . . . Keep her safe.

Blam! Blam!
What the hell?
Gunshots?
No way!

Braking, Noah spun his bike around. Dust kicked up in a cloud that obscured the stars and moon for a second as he got his bearings. Had he really heard shots, or was it a firecracker or a car backfiring?

Heart hammering, he waited. He'd seen the two cars, nose to nose in the desert, and a couple of people getting out to meet in the space between them, a man and a woman. Some kind of drug deal, he figured, as a lot of shit went down at night in the desert, yet there was something surreal about the rendezvous, something a little out of whack. When he'd kicked the bike into gear, roaring closer, the bigger vehicle swung around, turning back toward the lights of Vegas. That's when he'd recognized the boxy car's silhouette as a vintage Caddy, about the same make and model as Remmi's mom's big boat of a car. Was it Didi's ride? Was the woman actually Didi herself?

What the hell was she doing out here?

And the gunshots?

No! Not gunshots.

But . . . Oh, Jesus . . . then what?

Over the pounding of his heart, his bike idling, he squinted through the night as the big car sped away.

What the hell was Didi Storm doing out here, and did it have anything to do with the reason Remmi hadn't shown? He revved the bike just as he saw movement from the corner of his eye. A shadow stealing down the mountainside.

He froze. Focused on the shifting umbra . . . too big for a coyote, too tall for a mountain lion. Had to be a person.

Oh, hell.

Another quick movement and a flash of light.

What the hell?

The guy was definitely *shooting.* At the damned *car.* He swallowed hard. Noah revved his engine. Couldn't let the assailant just fire away. Popped a wheelie and caught the would-be assassin's attention. He leaned forward, and the front wheel hit the hardpan hard, then he punched it. Hitting the gas and zigzagging across the desert, sure to rattle the guy.

What to do?

Draw fire?

That was crazy.

But the thought that Remmi, or at least her nutcase of a mother, was somehow involved spurred him on. He hit the gas and the bike tore forward. Closer to the Mustang. Knowing he was playing with fire and not giving a damn. He figured he could outrun the bastard. "Hey, dick-wad!" he yelled over the roar of his engine. "What the fuck do you think you're doing?" And why the hell wasn't the driver of the sports car speeding away? Was he already hit?

Another round of reports from the rifle, aimed at the car, the sitting duck of a Mustang as the killer approached, walking steadily across the desert floor.

"Drive, you idiot!" Noah yelled.

Flashes from the rifle's muzzle. Another burst of gunfire.

Papapapapa—

"Oh, shit!"

KaBOOM!

A fiery explosion rocked the desert.

"No!"

Blinding light flashed in a ball of fire that soared toward the heavens.

Noah's bike bucked, its front wheel lifting off the shaking ground. Muscles straining, he tried like hell to hold onto the grips.

Crack!

Another shot.

Pain, searing and deep, cut through Noah's shoulder just as he saw the gunman take aim again. "Damn it!" He punched the gas. The bike leapt forward, dusty desert air screaming past him.

Don't let go!

But his left arm was useless.

Blam!

This time, the bike took the hit and bucked, the front wheel spinning wildly. Noah tried to hold on and failed, his body flying through the air.

Thud! His head smacked against the ground, his bones jarring on the hardpan.

"Oooh." Agony wracked his body, and he felt the blood oozing from his shoulder, the burn of scrapes on his face and hands. With all his strength, he tried to move. Failed. Sucked in his breath. Coughed out dry grit that he'd inhaled. The world spun crazily for a second—night stars obliterated by the flames, shadowed red rock seeming to swim and dance before his eyes, darkness plucking at the edges of his consciousness.

Get up! Get up now!

He blinked. Tried to clear his head. Attempted to focus. Spat blood. Oh, God, he was in trouble. As if through watery glass, he saw the fireball, the sports car burning in a garish pyre, flames licking toward a smoky sky.

And in front of the hellish glare?

A lone silhouette.

The figure of the tall, lanky gunman who was steadily approaching, a rifle hanging from one large hand, the bill of a baseball cap visible and maybe a thick moustache above a square jaw. Or maybe not.

And he was coming for him.

Why the hell had he goaded the guy? What had he been thinking? That all of this somehow had to do with Remmi? Sweating, fear propelling him, Noah tried to scuttle backward, to crab-walk away, to force himself to his feet, to run as if the hounds of hell were chasing him, but his muscles refused to respond.

Run, damn it. Run like hell.

He set his jaw. Using all his strength, he pushed away from the advancing figure, then collapsed.

His brain was screaming, *Run!* He tried to scramble away, to scurry backward, to find a hiding spot, to outrun this . . . this assassin, but he couldn't so much as force a finger to move. Terror gripped him, adrenaline poured through his veins, but his damned muscles were frozen. Unable to propel him.

Still the attacker came.

Walking slowly.

Taking his time.

Enjoying the moment.

Humming something familiar.

Panic strangled Noah. He couldn't speak or scream or do anything. Worse yet, the blackness kept tugging at him, shrinking his awareness.

He couldn't let it. He had to fight! His life depended upon it. He was as sure of that as he was that this man intended to kill him.

Move, damn it, Scott! Move your sorry ass. NOW!

With a Herculean effort, he attempted to get his legs under him.

Nothing.

Oh, crap.

Try again!

Still no movement.

Too late!

Noah wretched, spitting up blood.

Slowly, and with deadly determination, the shadowy figure lifted the rifle to his shoulder. For a split second, Noah saw his face in the reflection of the burning pyre that had once been a Ford Mustang. Do I know you? he thought crazily.

And there was something more. That tune, off-key but recognizable. Something he'd heard as a young kid when his grandmother was alive, something she sang along with the hymns from her Catholic youth, something that seemed so out of place.

His stomach convulsed as he faced the killer. The man's lips moved as he glared down at Noah.

. . . Let it shine, let it shine, let it shine . . .

The Marksman took aim.

Click!

Noah heard the sound of the hammer striking just as blackness dragged him under.

CHAPTER 6

P lay it cool.

Rubbing her head and peering again through the slit between the back cushions of the Cadillac, Remmi kept quiet. Confronting Didi now would only cause more trouble. As it was, her mother was a wreck, obviously upset, chain-smoking and crying, her perfect makeup ruined as she sobbed and drove, first onto the pavement from the sparse gravel road in the desert and then steadily into the city, where people were crowding the streets of the Strip and the neon glowed in bright, dizzying colors. As the big car slid onto the side streets and Remmi recognized the neighborhood, Didi seemed to pull herself together. Once she'd parked, she spent a few minutes swiping at her face with her hands and sniffing loudly.

"You can do this," she said to the rearview mirror just as Remmi pulled her head away from the slit, afraid her mother might see the reflection of her eyes. Within minutes Didi had cleared her throat, grabbed the briefcase and remaining infant carrier, and bustled into the house. Thankfully, she didn't lock the car.

Remmi sprang into action, climbing out of the suffocating cargo space and into the garage. Using the big car as a screen, Remmi stooped low, then, not hearing the approaching click of her mother's high heels, slipped through the side door of the garage, scaring a cat that had been slinking near the garbage cans. The cat hissed, and Remmi startled, bit back a scream before carefully climbing up to the open window of her room, pushing herself through and dropping onto the bed.

Within seconds she'd changed, ditching her clothes beneath the dust skirt pinned beneath her mattress and slipping into her pajamas. She tousled her hair, hoping that it looked rumpled from sleep, then hearing Didi in the living room, decided to confront her mother.

Remmi decided she wouldn't admit to knowing what was happening, would keep up the ruse that she'd been fast asleep all the time. But she would ask about her missing sister.

Forcing what she hoped looked like a just-woken-up demeanor, she padded barefoot from her bedroom and along the hall to the living space with a beige brick fireplace rising to a lofted ceiling. Though she'd taken the time to scrub her face, Didi was still in her Marilyn Monroe getup and was busy pouring herself a martini from the drink cart parked near her favorite chair. The single car seat with a sleeping baby sat on the floor, and Remmi's heart twisted as she thought of the twin girl.

Guiltily, it seemed, Didi looked up as Remmi, yawning, entered the room.

"Oh. I thought you were asleep." Didi took a sip from her drink, and Remmi noted that her hands were shaking.

"I was," Remmi lied. "What's Adam doing here . . . and why is he in Ariel's onesie?"

"Oh, I just grabbed the first thing in the drawer. I, um,

went out for a little while, and when I came in, he was fussing, had messed himself something fierce, so I changed him real quick. Adam ended up in pink. It's not the first time. Probably won't be the last." She took a long swallow from her drink. "You know, honey, you're one of the few people who can tell the twins apart."

"They're not identical, obviously," Remmi pointed out.

"I know, I know. Well, we all know, but . . . they resemble each other and . . . and . . . ," her voice squeaked. Quickly, she knocked back the remainder of her drink, then found her clutch and cigarette case, only to find the glittery case devoid of Virginia Slims. She stared at the empty pack, then crushed it in her fingers.

"Mom?" Remmi asked, concern in her voice. "Are you okay?"

"Yes. No . . . of course." Didi walked to the kitchen, tossed the crumpled pack into the trash can under the sink, then opened the cupboard over the refrigerator and, standing on her tiptoes, fished out a carton of Virginia Slims and found a new, unopened pack.

"What's going on?"

"Nothing."

"Want me to put Adam back to bed?"

"No!" Letting out a long breath of air, Didi shook her head. "Leave him be. He . . . he can sleep in his carrier. He likes it." When she found her daughter staring at her, she said, "What?" then, after tapping the pack of cigarettes on the counter and removing the cellophane wrapper, returned to the living room. "He's fine, really. You know what they say, 'Let sleeping babies lie.'"

"I think that's dogs, Mom. 'Let sleeping dogs lie.'"

"Is it?" She located her lighter and, after cracking a window near the front door, shook out a cigarette and fired it up.

Heart thudding, Remmi decided to push it, force her mother to confess. "I walked by the twins' room."

"So?"

"Both the cribs are empty."

Didi just stared at her. Took another drag.

"Mom, where's Ariel?"

"Oh, Lordy," she whispered on a cloud of smoke. "Look, she's . . . she's with a friend of mine. You remember Trudie?" She managed a thin smile. "Well, okay—the deal is that sometimes I just need a break, you know, from all this—" She motioned to the room in general. Around the perimeter, tucked between the chairs and tables, were bins of folded clothes and diapers and toys.

"You have me. And Seneca."

"I know, I know," Didi said, suddenly squashing out her cigarette with vehemence in the ashtray on a side table. She covered her face with her hands, her polished nails glinting under the lights, and Remmi took note that the one she always colored differently was black tonight. Perfect.

Didi let out a sigh and dropped her hands. "Sometimes, what with my job and all and, you know, no husband or boyfriend, it's all a bit, no, make that a lot, it's a lot for one woman." She carried the ashtray to the kitchen, dumped it, and wiped it with a paper towel. "I'm not getting any younger, Remmi, and to be the single mother of a teenager *and* twins. God, I'm not even thirty-five, and I feel ancient. *Ancient.* I should be out, having fun, kicking up my heels and . . . and . . ." Her voice fell away, and she dropped down into a chair near the table, where the briefcase, still unopened, lay flat. She glanced at the leather case and swallowed hard, blinking as if she were fighting tears.

"Mom?" Remmi whispered, and her mother waved a frantic hand to stop the reproach.

"Just go back to bed. Don't worry about the twins, okay? They're my responsibility. I'll—I'll take care of them. I'll take care of everything." Her smile, faded without the lipstick, faltered a bit. "Don't I always, honey?"

"Sure, Mom." Remmi felt like a heel.

"That's right." Didi glanced at the wall phone hanging over the kitchen counter.

"You can tell me, you know."

"Tell you what?"

Remmi shrugged. "Anything, Mom. You know that."

For a second, Didi appeared to consider the offer, seemed about to divulge the truth, then her gaze shifted to the wall phone again, and she shrugged. "Well, there's nothing to tell, now, is there?" She pinned a bright smile on her face and faced her daughter again. She winked. "Go on, now, honey. You worry too much, you know? Everything's fine. Just fine." Another glance at the phone. "And don't you bother Seneca, okay? She has to get up with the twins . . ." Again, Didi's voice faded out before she cleared her throat and added a little hoarsely, "She has to get up early."

She made little shooing motions with her fingers, and Remmi realized Didi wasn't about to admit to the exchange that had occurred in the desert.

She should call her out, Remmi thought, demand straight answers from her mother, admit that she *knew* what had gone down tonight, but she didn't, and as she slipped between the cool sheets on her bed and stared up at the ceiling, she thought of Noah and her missed opportunity.

It doesn't matter. Not with Ariel gone.

Tears filled her eyes, and over the soft hum of the air conditioner, she heard the sounds of distant sirens as the walls of the house closed in on her.

Didi was obviously expecting a call.

From whom?

Someone with whom she'd been in cahoots?

The "daddy" who had been given a girl dressed up as a boy?

Or someone else?

Remmi wondered if she'd ever know. She barely breathed, listening for the sound of the house phone, but the house remained still, aside from the soft whoosh of air through hidden ducts and her own shallow breathing.

Too many secrets, she thought, as she closed her eyes and knew that sleep tonight would be impossible. *We all have too many secrets.*

Oliver Hedges Junior—or OH2, as he preferred— stood at the windows of his penthouse and surveyed the panorama that was Las Vegas, the lights of the city stretching out to the desert. God, he loved this town. Especially tonight. He smiled and caught his watery reflection in the glass: tall, broad-shouldered, and trim, his hair cut neatly, his beard just visible, a crisp shirt, top buttons open beneath a dark Armani jacket with matching slacks, a drink swirling in his hands.

The picture of health and success.

Everything was coming together for him.

He hoisted his drink to the ghostly image, ice cubes dancing in the short glass. "Here's to you and playing everyone to a T." Then he took a long swallow of the aged scotch.

Perfect harmony, that's what it was, just like the music playing from the hidden speakers tucked into the ceiling panels of the ten glassed-in rooms of his condominium in the sky. Well, make that *near*-perfect harmony. There was that one little hiccup.

He took another drink, letting the taste linger a bit on his tongue as he heard the sound of a baby crying. *His* child. Though not a male child, as he'd been told, but a little girl. Hmmm. That complicated things a bit, presented a new challenge, but he would just have to adjust. Just as he'd accepted many little bumps in the road of life, including the one that hadn't bothered him as a young man but had created a problem later: the simple fact that he was sterile and had been told by several doctors that he would never father his own biological child. A blow. But one he'd finally accepted, and he had found a solution to the problem as his younger brother was very, very virile, as it turned out, and he could almost too easily father a child.

Some things in life just weren't right. He hesitated to use the word "fair," as he'd never been one to complain about his lot in life. Still . . .

He frowned, caught the change in his diluted reflection, squared his shoulders, and told himself everything would work out.

It always did.

Again, it wasn't as if he hadn't made major adjustments in the past. Wasn't that the reason his father was spending the rest of his days at Fair Haven, a nursing facility that took care of the very wealthy? Poor Dad. Spending what remained of his life practically bedridden, needing help from a bevy of nurses and aides for all of his personal needs. Once a titan of industry, now, in his sixties no less, reduced to a mere shell of what he was. All because of an unfortunate skiing accident at Heavenly Valley.

"Too bad," OH2 said, swallowing a smile before finishing his scotch and feeling the slight buzz that came after two drinks. Shifting his gaze to the darkness surrounding the edges of the city, he saw the flash of lights— blue and red, faint, but still visible as the emergency responders, cops and firemen and EMTs, surveyed the damage caused by the incinerated car in the desert.

Good luck, he thought sarcastically. *Try piecing this one together.*

Again, the tiny child let out a whimper, and he glanced to the door of the bedroom, where, he assumed, she was being attended to. For a second, he considered walking inside the bedroom with its makeshift crib, one of those pop-up portable things, and decided against it. Instead, he made his way back to the bar, dipped his empty glass in the bucket of small ice cubes, then poured himself two, or possibly three, more fingers of scotch. Just enough to enhance the euphoric feeling that came with a job well done.

But the other child. The boy, if Didi Storm's story was to be believed, would be an issue. He smiled at that, the double entendre, because, unfortunately, his brother's children would be the only heirs to the estate, and despite the prevailing politically correct ideals of this country, a boy would be preferred.

Of course, his own son would have been better.

But because he was adaptable, his brother's son, or maybe even daughter, would just have to do. Caught young enough, that progeny could be molded.

He took a taste of scotch—cool, as the ice had begun to melt, but warming as it slid down his throat. Sipping steadily, he began plotting his next move. Didi, the greedy slut, was a problem. A major threat. As long as she was alive, knowing what she did, she'd be hanging around, like a wasp that was just out of reach but that you knew, should you turn your back, would sting you. Repeatedly.

Not if he could help it.

Seated at the tiny kitchen table, Didi stared at the money—tens, twenties, and some fifties strewn on the scarred maple tabletop, some in uneven piles, all stacks unstrapped and counted. All two hundred and fifty thousand dollars—yeah, if you were an idiot. Upon close inspection, she'd learned that only about 10 percent of the bills were legit, the others damned good fakes, close to perfect, but not quite. Surely the forgeries wouldn't pass the scrutiny of any bank teller worth his or her salt. They probably wouldn't even get by the cashiers at a quickie mart.

"You bastard," she said under her breath and closed her eyes. What a complete and utter moron she'd been, all the while thinking she was so damned smart. Now, little Ariel . . . Didi let out a pained mewling sound at the thought of her daughter and that fire . . . What the hell had happened out in the desert? Who had been shooting and why? Was it to cause the horrible conflagration, someone out to get Brett? Or her? Letting out a sigh, she flopped back in the spindle-backed chair and pushed her hair from her eyes. Her platinum wig was where she'd tossed it, on the seat of the old rocker, a piece of furniture she'd planned to replace when . . . She eyed the piles of money again.

When your ship came in?

When you scored on the biggest con of your life?

Face it, Didi, you were the one who was conned, and now . . . and now . . .

It crossed her mind again that she should go to the police, to tell what she knew, but what would happen to her then? She'd be arrested and her remaining children . . . No, that just wouldn't work. Ever.

She'd been tricked by Brett, played for a fool.

Double-crossed.

Just like you double-crossed him.

She crumpled a few of the fake fifties and tossed them into the air so that they could flutter up near the pendant

light, then drift back to land on the pile of other bad bills.
How had she been so dumb?

All wasn't lost, she knew. She still had Brett Hedges's
son, and she would be able to exchange him for Ariel . . .
if . . . if her daughter had somehow miraculously survived. She squeezed her eyes shut, refused to believe the
worst. Maybe she could somehow set up another con, get
Ariel *and* the money she was owed or . . . or what? What
exactly could she do to right this wrong?

She'd been a half-wit to make the trade in the desert,
to dress the part of the seductress, to show up in her big
car—all to remind Brett of what he'd given up.

"As if he'd ever wanted it in the first place," she said
and dropped her head into her folded arms, letting her last
cigarette burn out, unattended. What to do? She heard
Adam begin to whimper from the car seat where she'd
left it in the middle of the living room. She'd made a horrible mess of her life, a bigger mess than she'd even
imagined.

She'd burned her bridges in the Midwest, then again in
Hollywood, and now, here in Vegas? How bright was her
future? Not very.

Dear God, she was a moron.

*No, no, you're not. Don't let this get you down. It's just
a setback. Pick yourself up, dust yourself off, and rethink
this . . . situation. It's only a problem if you let it become
one. You're still Didi Storm, still sexy as hell, and smarter
than anyone gives you credit for. You're still young even if
you feel older than your years, and you've still got one
ace up your sleeve, don't you?*

Lifting her head, she spied Adam, looking up at her
with wide, innocent eyes. He was beautiful, with his
shock of white-blond hair, eyes that were crystal blue,
and a button of a nose. Spying her, he waved his little
hands and actually smiled, a big, gummy smile that melted

her heart. "Oh, you," she said, as she reached down, un-strapped him, and held him close. He cooed against her, and she closed her eyes. She couldn't give him up. And she never intended to. Nor had she planned on letting Brett keep their daughter. She'd been certain she could get Ariel back. Now, of course, her confidence was beyond shaken, a hole in her heart.

There had to be a way. Think, Didi, think!

The baby let out another gurgling cry.

"Come on," she said and carried him over to the make-shift changing table near the hallway. She stripped him of Ariel's pink onesie, then changed his diaper and slipped him into blue and white pajamas before making a bottle for him. She was weaning the babies because she had to. No one wanted to see a sexy showgirl with leaking tits, and she'd had to prepare both Adam and Ariel for the event of them living with their father, if only for a little while.

Adam took the bottle hungrily, and she sat on the thread-bare rocker, one she'd picked up from a secondhand store at the edge of town. It squeaked under her weight, but she rocked steadily, gazing down at the miracle of her son.

How could she ever give him up?

Probably just as easily as you did Ariel.

"It wasn't easy," she whispered and fought a fresh wash of tears. What was wrong with her? Probably still the post-pregnancy hormones readjusting in her system. That was it. And what would she tell Remmi tomorrow when it became obvious that she wasn't about to pick up her daughter from her friend Trudie's? Not that Remmi had believed her. The look she'd sent Didi had been total disbelief, as if somehow Remmi had known her mother was lying through her teeth.

That damned girl was too smart for her own good.

Where have you heard that before? Isn't that what

*your father said often enough? And what had been your
mother's response? "You got that right. But there's more.
She's too smart and too damned sexy. It's dangerous,
Frank. You got that? Those raging teenage hormones are
gonna get her into the worst trouble a girl can get in—
you mark my words!"*

Her mother's warnings to her father still rang in her
ears, though they had been whispered over fifteen years
earlier and had, of course, as it turned out, been spot-on.

Willa Maye Hutchinson had not only suspected her
daughter of sleeping around but had known it.

It was all water under the bridge. Didi settled into the
rocker with her baby and started moving back and forth
again. As Adam finished his bottle and drifted off, she
started plotting her next move.

She had to take her emotions out of the situation and
come up with a plan, something that would help her and
her children.

Brett Hedges, dead or alive, still owed her a quarter of
a mil.

Someone was going to pay up. Either him, if he was
yet among the living, or that miserable rich old man of
his.

And this time it would cost them more.

CHAPTER 7

From her bed, Remmi stared at the bedside phone—actually, the cordless extension she'd grabbed from the living room. It had been about twenty-four hours since the events in the desert, and Remmi was still undecided about what to do.

If only Noah would call.

Where was he?

What had happened?

She had so much to tell him.

Biting her lip, she considered calling the police. Again. Just as she had considered confronting her mother for the kabillionth time.

She glanced to the doorway when she heard Didi's distinctive, fast-paced walk along the hall. Her mother rapped softly, then pushed the door open. A bright, false smile was pinned to her glossy lips. "Honey, I'm going out."

Remmi had already gathered as much from the frantic way Didi had gone to her room and started stripping clothes from hangers, tossing her designer costumes onto the foot of her king-sized bed after eyeing each item. It was a routine she went through every night before a performance or a big date. Remmi, or sometimes Seneca, was expected to return the discarded outfits back to the closet. "Stay here, with Adam; wait until I get back," Didi said as she peeked into Remmi's room.

Remmi had spent the rest of last night wide awake and the day dozing off and on; her dreams, when they came, were of fiery blasts and babies crying and Remmi finding herself lost in the desert.

"But you're not going to work?" Remmi asked, sliding into a sitting position against the headboard.

"No . . . not tonight. This is a private appointment." Again, Didi was dressed up in the Marilyn getup. A different dress, tight, black, and cut low enough to show significant cleavage, but the same wig and exaggerated makeup. The spark of excitement that had been with her the night before was replaced by a wariness and a deeper sadness, both visible beneath her forced smile.

"And you'll bring Ariel back?" Remmi knew she was pushing her mother, but she couldn't help herself. She didn't have the guts to admit the truth, to say she'd been there in the desert when all hell had broken loose. She hadn't been able to bring up the fact that she'd been hiding in the Caddy's cargo hold.

Because she was afraid of her mother's reaction.

You're as bad as she is. Just confront her, damn it!

She'd tried, twice, and failed. Had ended up back in her bedroom chewing on her fingernails.

All day, Didi had been wound up, angry, barking orders at Seneca and her daughter. Seneca was used to Didi's moods and secrets, and the tall midwife kept her thoughts to herself, went about her business and questioned nothing. It was so weird. If Seneca thought it odd that Ariel was missing, she didn't question Didi.

Maybe she was in on the plot all along.

With Seneca, you never knew. She kept to herself, especially her opinions. Her hair was long, dark, and curly, tied loosely at her nape, her skin a soft mocha color, her eyes a gold that burned with intelligence. She'd said her grandmother was Jamaican, and that she'd grown up in New Orleans, and she did have a slight accent that Remmi couldn't place. Cajun? Islands? Remmi didn't know. In fact, Remmi knew little about the woman who spent a lot of days and some nights at their house. Seneca had helped birth the twins and never let on to anyone that Didi had borne more than one child. Seneca was ever-patient, and Didi had remarked cryptically once that Seneca "was in it for the long game," whatever that meant.

Now, Seneca didn't question what Didi was up to, just got Adam ready for bed.

It was Remmi who was upset. She'd spent the night worrying about what had happened and the day watching the news, trying to find out what the police knew. Nothing, as far as she could tell. She'd called Noah's home over and over again. No answer. She felt as if she were surely going out of her mind.

She followed her mother into the living room.

"I'll be back as soon as I can," Didi insisted, and she swept her clutch purse from the table and snagged the briefcase from a closet where she'd stashed it the night before. Remmi had sneaked down the hallway a couple of times during the night to peer into the living room and observe her mother's distress. She'd spied the open briefcase and the bills littering the table. It looked like a boatload of money, but it had infuriated Didi, and Remmi had caught the words "son of a bitch" and "bastard," so obviously it wasn't the amount Didi had requested.

For Adam.

She'd sold Adam—that's what it was.

That's why she'd dressed him in Ariel's clothes and put

the little girl in her brother's blue outfit. Didi hadn't just picked up the wrong onesie in the dark. Nope, it was all part of her sick child-selling plan.

"This is an out-of-town appointment," Didi told her, "so I won't be back until tomorrow."

"Where?" Remmi demanded.

"A private residence. Not in Las Vegas. So there's some travel time involved. But it'll be worth it."

She stepped into the hallway, but Remmi called her back, "Mom?"

"What, luv?" She poked her head into the room and gave her a disarming smile.

"Weird stuff is happening. There was that fire in the desert last night. A car exploded."

"Oh, I heard. It was all over the news." Didi, wearing long black gloves, waved off her daughter's concerns.

"A man died."

"Honey, all kinds of awful things happen, I know." She sighed loudly. "But it's nothing to do with us, and though it's sad for the man, we can't let bad things that happen in the world control us, you know. There are always going to be hurricanes and floods and fires and the like, or . . . or that Y2K thing they're already talking about, the computer problem, or the end of the world as some people see it, you know, as if we're all going to vaporize at the turn of the millennium. You can't worry about all those things." She flashed a bright Didi smile. "We have to live our lives. Don't worry. Look, when I get back tomorrow, we'll go shopping or something, have a girls' day." Then, as if realizing something really could go wrong, she hesitated. "Now, listen, nothing's going to happen, but if it does, if I don't come back by tomorrow at this time, seven at night, then . . . Well, I've left some money for you, in the top drawer of my bureau, and there's a piece of paper with a woman's name on it."

"What woman?"

"My friend. Trudie. Her number, too. If, for some unforeseen reason, I don't show up, call her, and she'll tell you what to do."

"What? No! Mom, what is this?"

Didi's face turned to stone. She reached out, grabbed her daughter's arm, and held it so hard that even through the gloves, Remmi felt the points of her fingernails and the strength in her grip. "I don't have time to explain, Remmi. Now just do as I say."

"But . . ."

The tense fingers tightened. "Just do it. We'll be okay. All of us. Just do your part."

"Mom, I don't think—"

"Good." Remmi thought her mother was going to slap her. Instead suddenly, Didi released her, and for a second, tears shone in her eyes, but she quickly pushed them back. "Don't think. Don't worry. For God's sake, honey, just trust me. If only just this once."

And then, before Remmi could bring up Ariel or anything else again, Didi was gone, clipping down the hallway in her high heels, the garage door opening and shutting and the sound of the Cadillac's big engine sparking to life.

Seneca had watched the entire exchange with wide, knowing eyes. "It's best if you just do as she says."

"But . . . what about Ariel? Seneca, do you know what happened to her?"

Was there just a flicker of understanding in the woman's gaze? "I think it would be best if you quit worrying so much. It will do none of us any good."

"You can do this," Didi told herself as she drove through the streets of Las Vegas. Traffic was heavy, and pedestrians clogged the sidewalks, so she couldn't step on the gas. No, she had to be cool, even though the big car, now dusty, caught a lot of attention—something she'd always longed for and now thought might not be a good idea.

She was armed with a plan, and it wasn't a bad one. As horrible as she felt about how things had gone down the night before, she was determined to set things right. She'd been conned. Big-time. And despite the massive, painful hole in her chest, she was going to make certain that, at the very least, she was paid. As agreed upon.

She'd spent the last twenty-four hours unable to sleep, the image of that hellish explosion haunting her, the thought of her missing child crippling, but she was also pissed as hell. And she figured anger trumped sadness.

She had to get what was rightfully hers. Because this was the big payoff. She needed it. Her act was going nowhere, and let's face it, she wasn't getting any younger. It wasn't as if Hollywood had her on speed dial.

This time, she wasn't going to mess around. This time, she planned to go right to the source of all the money. And she hadn't brought Adam for an exchange. At least not yet.

That, if necessary, could come later.

Her heart squeezed a little at the thought of giving him up, but she reminded herself it was only temporary.

Oh, yeah? And what about Ariel? Hmm?

She nearly crumbled inside, then straightened her spine, her gloved fingers clenching over the big steering wheel. "Shut up," she yelled at that tiny, nagging voice in her head. She couldn't be deterred by emotions. Not now. There was a time for grief and regret, if necessary . . . when the time came. For now, she'd hold out hope and onto determination to get what was due her.

For her family.

Jaw set, gloved fingers tight over the steering wheel, she wound her Caddy through a clog of cars, vans, trucks, and buses within the city to join a steady stream of traffic heading west, into the setting sun. A few more hours, that was all she needed, she thought, as she found her sunglasses, replicas from the 1960s, and slid them onto the bridge of her nose. And for security? In case she was walking into the proverbial lion's den, she again had her pistol, though she hoped she'd never have to use it. She'd never shot at anyone in her life.

"Always a first time," she told herself and caught her reflection in the wide rearview mirror. "Always a first time."

Noah opened a bleary eye and blinked.

Where the hell was he?

The room was small, with a window, and he was lying on a bed. Some kind of bed with crisp sheets and—

Holy shit, he was in a hospital room. The underlying smell of disinfectant was barely discernable, but it lingered a bit.

As the cobwebs cleared from his mind, he surveyed his surroundings, a monitor over his head steadily beeping, a tray nearby with an empty urinal on one end and a glass of water with a bent straw on the other. A window with shades at half-mast, a vast parking lot stretching below; his room had to be on the second, maybe third floor. He squinted as he stared outside the window.

Dusk was settling into the city, a few street lamps blinking on, and as the building had an L shape, he noticed the Emergency Room entrance, probably the very spot where he'd been brought in. Elizabeth Park Hospital. He'd been here before as a little kid when he'd broken his left arm after falling from the roof of the shed.

What the hell had happened?

The desert.

The motorbike.

Didi Storm's white Cadillac.

And the explosion that rocked the desert floor and the resultant fire that had burned wildly.

And . . . *the gunman*. That was it, a tall man carrying a rifle and backlit by the conflagration, pointing the end of the barrel straight at Noah. His heart began to race at the memory, and he heard the monitor begin to beep faster. He moved on the bed and felt pain in his right side, then noticed that his arm was bandaged, as was his chest.

How long had he been out of it? He remembered nothing after the gunman had approached. His throat was dry, gritty, and he tried to reach for the glass at the near end of the tray table. Pain shot through his shoulder, and he froze.

At the sound of footsteps and a rattling cart approaching his half-open door, he closed his eyes again, forced his breathing to slow, and waited.

Someone came into the room and puttered around his bed. "Hey, there," she said, a woman's soft, comforting voice. "You awake?"

He didn't move. Didn't so much as twitch. Not even when a thermometer was tucked under his tongue or a blood pressure cuff was placed around his arm or his wrist was lifted by cool, gloved hands.

"Hello," she said again, this time closer to his ear. "Can you hear me?"

When he didn't acknowledge that he'd heard her, she waited, as if expecting him to raise an eyelid or lift a finger. He didn't, but he could feel her presence as he managed to regulate his breathing and, from the sounds of the monitor, his heartbeat.

"Helen?" another woman's voice, lower and raspy. "Is he awake?"

"I thought so, but no. Not responding." A beat. As if both women were looking at him. *Staring at him,* as if they knew he was faking it. He kept breathing normally, or what he thought would be normally.

The second woman asked, "Has the doctor been in?"

"Yes, earlier." Helen again.

Noah strained to hear.

"More surgery?"

More? He'd been operated on? For what?

"No. Not right away. At least Dr. Spears doesn't think so, but it's still early. Take a look at his vitals, Barb. All normal."

"Hmmm. You're right."

He felt someone edge closer, and it was all he could do to lie still as he heard a page from the outer hallway. "Doctor Barrows?" A woman's smooth voice was audible from the hallway. "Please pick up a courtesy phone. Doctor Phillip Barrows."

The second woman, Barb of the deeper voice, said, "I guess we'll just have to wait." He felt her breath on his face, as if she were leaning over him, studying him.

He wanted to swallow hard but didn't. Finally, she must've straightened, her breath no longer warm against his face as she added, "And so will the police."

What? The cops? They were waiting? He almost gasped but stopped himself.

"They're still here?" Helen asked.

"No. Left this afternoon, but they'll be back to speak with Mr. Doe here," Barb said, clarifying. "They're trying to find out who he is."

"Someone must be missing him."

Noah's mind raced. So far, apparently, they didn't know

who he was. That was good, he thought, as the cops had always been trouble.

"They'll figure it out. My brother-in-law's a detective, and he said it's only a matter of time." Barb again. "If they can't figure it out soon, the cops will ask the public for information. Put out his picture, hope to ID him."

That was no good. No good at all. He began to sweat.

"They already have, haven't they? After that car was burned out in the Mojave?"

Oh. Shit.

"I think they're trying to find out who it belonged to. The owner was inside, still behind the wheel, and the license plate was nearly destroyed. Or that's what I heard." Barb, it seemed, had more information. "But the police will want to find out what our Johnnie Doe knows about it."

Johnnie Doe? As if he were five years old? Despite himself, Noah bristled a little and had to fight to keep feigning sleep.

Helen said, "He'll wake up soon, don't you think? It hasn't even been twenty-four hours."

That answered one question, Noah thought, but there were still plenty of others. Plenty.

"I hope. But he was pretty beat up from the accident. Contusions, cracked ribs, concussed. Lucky he's got no broken bones."

"Lucky?" Helen repeated with a snort. "If you call getting a bullet in the neck lucky. I doubt it was an accident."

He'd been shot? In the neck. And didn't die?

Helen continued, "The way I see it, someone tried to pick him off his motorcycle. Unless you think a hunter was out target shooting at dusk and mistook a kid on a bike for what? A wild boar? Or mule deer? Or damned coyote? Was he drunk? A motorcycle makes a loud noise, and it doesn't sound like any animal." Helen wasn't buying the accident theory for a second. "It seems to me someone shot him in the neck, no less, and he lost control of his bike. He's just damned lucky the bullet missed his carotid and his jugular."

"Not to mention his spinal cord."

"Amen to that."

Barb said, "That's what I mean by lucky."

He sensed that they moved away from the bed, on shoes that barely made a sound, with Helen saying, "I'll check on him again after my break . . ." Her voice became soft and muted, as if she'd stepped into the hallway on the other side of the partially open door.

"Good."

Then Helen said, "You heard there was a guy who came asking about him? Someone who didn't look much like a reporter to me."

"The tall man with the moustache? Cowboy type."

Noah nearly pissed himself. Every muscle in his body tightened. The killer. That's who they were talking about. In his mind's eye, he saw the rifleman approach, long gun in his hand, moustache visible in the wicked glow of the conflagration.

He'd been here? Holy crap!

"That would be the guy," Helen confirmed, and he had to strain to hear her, even opened his eye a slit to make sure he was alone. A quick scan, and he saw no one, but the shadow near the cracked door suggested the two nurses were still close. He chanced sitting up, straining to hear the conversation over the escalating beat of his heart.

Barb asked. "Who did he say he was?"

"That's just it. He didn't really. Claimed he was an uncle of a kid who stole a motorcycle and went missing. Wanted to make an ID, but wouldn't give a name the police could cross-check with missing person reports or something like that. Anyway, when the questions got a little too hard, the guy just up and left. Before Ted from Administration could get up here. The whole thing seemed fishy."

Barb said, "But he was caught on camera."

"Not much of him. Baseball cap and sunglasses, two days' growth of beard along with the moustache. The police have the security tape."

As their conversation faded, the shadows in the hallway fell away. Noah let out his breath. He'd survived. Barely. But, obviously, the gunman had come looking for him. Panic shot through him, adrenaline spurting, and it was all he could do to contain himself so that the damned heart monitor didn't give him away. He forced himself to lie back against the pillow and feign sleep again.

He had to leave. Soon. Before the cops started nosing around and before the gunman returned. He'd wait, until the middle of the night, when it was quiet, and then some way, somehow, he'd escape. Not just this hospital, but Vegas, too.

He knew this city, had grown up here, and the hospital was only a mile from his old man's place. His legs weren't broken, so he could walk that far, steal the rest of the money he needed, and hitchhike. Denver sounded good. Or Seattle. Maybe Anchorage. Or . . . Mexico. L.A. to San Diego, across the border to Tijuana, and disappear, a gringo no one would recognize.

Through slitted lids, he glanced out the window again, and for a second he thought of Remmi, wondered what she was doing. Then he closed his mind to her. She was a part of this, if not knowingly, then by association with her mother, who was in the desert last night. His jaw clenched hard enough to ache as he thought about her. Even if she knew nothing, she was guilty because she lived here, and in six short hours, Las Vegas and everyone within its city limits would be dead to him.

* * *

When Plan A doesn't work, then initiate Plan B.

Or so Didi reminded herself as she sped across the desert, the lights of Las Vegas a distant glow behind her. L.A. was in her sights. Around five hours, if she followed the route she had planned, on I-15 across the desert and over the mountains and into the greater Los Angeles area—well, actually a little farther west to Malibu, to an ocean-side home, of course. Nothing but the best for Oliver Hedges, the old bastard.

She clicked on the lighter and, as it heated, found her cigarettes in her purse. She had hours to drive and could smoke as much as she wanted or needed. Cracking the window, she lit up, holding her Virginia Slims in one gloved hand, the steering wheel with the other. She considered taking off her gloves—they were a bit of a problem—but decided instead to stay "in character" and channeled Marilyn Monroe, sitting sexy and sultry behind the wheel.

She glanced at the briefcase on the seat beside her, filled with the phony bills; she'd culled out the good ones. She would throw all those fake fifties and twenties into the Hedgeses' conceited, self-righteous faces! Reignited anger made her grind her teeth at the gall of the con. If Brett had died in that fiery heap, he deserved it.

But not Ariel . . . not precious . . . Her heart twisted painfully. "Stop it!" she growled at herself, then hit the gas with a spiked heel. The Cadillac tore around a slow-moving van that was having a little trouble staying in its lane, the person behind the wheel sleepy, drunk, high, or maybe just terrible at controlling his vehicle. It didn't matter. She blew past and stared through the bug-splattered windshield at the night sky, dark and flung with thousands of stars, the road a ribbon cutting through the desert on her way to the mountains and beyond.

She wondered, not for the first time, if she should have brought Adam as a bargaining chip with the old man, but decided she'd made the right decision in leaving the baby with Remmi. Better to hold back. She'd already lost one child through recklessness and being overly cocky. Her throat closed as her thoughts wandered to Ariel, but she dragged them back from the dark chasm of grief to the reality of the here and now; there would be time enough later for grieving and chastising and feeling downright horrible. Right now, she had to focus on the job at hand.

Oliver Got Rocks—or, more accurately, Oliver Got Stocks—the grandfather of her children, was beyond wealthy, having invested in a fledgling tech company that had taken off and was continuing to soar. And he wanted an heir. She'd learned all this from the private investigator she'd hired, the same P.I. she'd hired to check on her second husband, the magician from whom she'd learned all of her tricks and who had ended up banging his barely legal assistant. The P.I. had provided pictures, glossy full-color shots of Leo in oh-so-many compromising positions with the nubile and nimble assistant; in one particularly clear photo, the assistant, naked as the day she was born, was bent over the very box he used to showcase his tired cutting-a-woman-in-half routine.

At the memory, Didi blew out a last disgusted breath of smoke, then stubbed out her cigarette frantically in the ashtray. No time to think of Leo "Kaspar the Great" Kasparian tonight. The only thing he'd been really great at was being a low-life adulterer. "Jerk," she muttered.

Traffic was light, her tires humming over the dry pavement, the Caddy's engine a smooth rumble under its massive hood. A few red taillights were far in front of her, while a thicker stream of oncoming headlights glowing like hungry eyes approached on her left to speed past.

She settled in, deciding to stop at a gas station once

she crossed into California; there she would reassess her makeup and hair, because no matter what, she wanted to look spectacular for that old goat. Rotating her neck to get rid of a kink, she thought she heard something . . . almost a rattle, a sound she couldn't immediately place, but out of the ordinary, something out of rhythm with the night.

"No," she whispered.

She'd checked the Caddy herself after last night, and other than a few scratches from the cacti she had brushed as she drove like a bat out of the desert last night, nothing had seemed wrong with the car. No broken axle or flat tire or anything. But if something happened now . . .

It was just her nerves, that was it. She was jumpy. On edge. And who wouldn't be? She was going toe to toe with a wealthy and, as far as she knew, unscrupulous old man, bartering with him, challenging him. Deep in her gloves her palms began to sweat. She had heard that he'd declined in health, that some accident had befallen him, but that his mind was still sharp, so despite his frailties, he would still be a sly adversary.

She heard the strange sound again. A click this time.

She eased up on the throttle. What was it? On the outside or . . . ? She glanced into the rearview mirror, and her heart nearly stopped.

Shadowed eyes glared back at her.

Didi shrieked.

The cold barrel of a gun pressed against the back of her neck.

"Drive," he ordered in a harsh, guttural voice.

Didi nearly swerved off the road, the front wheel edging onto the shoulder, bits of gravel flying up as she overcorrected, then straightened the big car. Her heart was a drum. Panic sent adrenaline through her veins. What the hell was this? Who was he? Oh, God, he was going to kill her! Right here in the desert! For a split second, she considered hitting the gas, then the brakes, throwing him off balance or crashing so that someone, anyone would find her. Help her.

"Don't even think about it," he growled in that low voice, as if he'd read her damned mind.

How had he gotten in here? Had he been hiding in the back seat all the time? Sweat blooming beneath her tight dress, she swallowed back her fear and tried desperately to think, to find a way to get out of this mess. With a sinking sensation, she realized he might have been hiding in her cargo hold, the spot she'd used to conceal herself or props or . . . oh, dear God, what did it matter how he got in? The problem was getting him out before . . . before . . .

"Drive," he repeated, his eyes slitting as he calculated her next move. "And keep it under the speed limit."

She did as she was told.

As long as she was at the wheel, he couldn't shoot her, could he? He'd risk his own life if he pulled the trigger and the car sped out of control. No—he needed her. For now. Until he decided to stop. If so, then she'd have to do something drastic. Crash on purpose or something. She glanced at the gas gauge. Half full. What would happen if she ran out of gas and the car slowed to a stop?

Pure terror chilled her blood.

Between now and then, she'd think of something. She had to. Her heart was hammering, and her hands shook on the wheel, her gloves slick on the inside with sweat, her breathing shallow, her mind racing.

She had the pistol. In her purse. If, somehow, she could get the drop on him, maybe claim she had to stop at a rest area or gas station to use the restroom . . . he'd never go for that, though; she sensed it. But if she said she needed a cigarette and instead pulled out her pistol, could she get the drop on him before his finger squeezed the trigger?

She had to try.

She couldn't just let him murder her.

Somehow, she had to outmaneuver him.

But the cold bite of steel against her neck reminded her that she was very quickly running out of time.

CHAPTER 8

As Noah slipped out of his hospital room after the last nurse had been called down the hall, he saw that the clock read 2:45 AM. He stole along the opposite corridor and saw an exit sign, then avoided the elevators and took the stairs, moving silently down the steps. He'd waited for hours, thinking that surely the cops would return and bust him for something, but his ruse of being asleep or comatose, whatever the nurses wanted to think, had worked.

He'd waited until the hospital had grown quiet, the lights dimmed, the parking lot, from what he could see through the window, emptying to the few sparse cars that remained under the security lights. He'd found his clothes in the small cupboard wedged between the small bathroom and the door to the hallway and slipped them on. He hurt all over, especially his neck, where the damned bullet had passed through, and his shoulder, where he assumed he'd landed upon being thrown from the bike.

From the moment he'd woken up, figured out where he was, and his memory of the night before had returned, he'd tried like hell to figure out what had happened in the desert, but only partial images of the events floated through his brain, and he couldn't for the life of him piece together what he'd witnessed.

Hopefully, the gaps in his memory were from the anesthesia, and he would eventually remember what had gone down. Nothing good. And the more he thought about it, the more he'd concluded Didi Storm was involved.

What about Remmi?

Where was she?

Did she know?

The questions had pricked at his brain, but he'd ignored them, forcing himself to concentrate on escaping unnoticed from Elizabeth Park Hospital. As far as he knew, no one had recognized him as he'd slipped through a door from the stairwell to the first floor. No one knew who he was. But that wouldn't last for long. As soon as his picture was circulated, his friends or acquaintances, from school or the jobs he'd held at two diners and a gas station, would recognize him. If he wanted to get out, the time was now.

He felt a prick of anxiety as he passed by a planter filled with fake leafy ferns and headed for the main doors. He had his collar turned up, for he was certain that his image would show up on the hospital cameras. But so be it. He had to get out. Before the killer returned.

He slipped through the sliding doors of the ER when the desk attendant wasn't looking as she concentrated on a phone call and some papers scattered on the counter in front of her. Once outside, he started jogging. His legs worked well, no problem there, but his arms and neck ached. He figured he still had some anesthesia flowing through his bloodstream from the surgery, and eventually it would wear off. Sometime, he'd have to deal with the pain, but so far, so good.

He left the hospital and headed toward the heart of the

city, the Strip, which was in the opposite direction from his house. But if he were caught on some of the hospital cameras covering the parking lot, it would seem as if he were heading south. Once out of clear view of the hospital, he'd pull a U-ey and find his way home. Once there, he'd steal what he could from the rest of the old man's money stash, assuming he didn't realize that Noah had already tapped into it, then he'd start hitchhiking south. L.A. first, then San Diego, before he slipped across the border.

He figured he could make it on his own.

In all reality, he had been for the last few years.

He hitched his jacket tighter around him, ducked across a deserted lot, and wound his way back toward the north, only to spy a police cruiser slipping down the road. He ducked back into an alley and flattened against the wall of a strip mall. Heart hammering, praying the cop car wouldn't turn into the alley, the beams of its headlights illuminating the narrow space, he held his breath and heard a soft snort.

"Hey, boy," a growling voice said, "what you doin' here, eh?"

Turning his head slowly, pain shooting through his neck, he spied a wiry, bearded man with eyes burning deep in his skull. "Nothing," Noah said.

"You got any money?"

"No . . . no, just out of the hospital." Noah was sweating. The cruiser slowed as it passed the alley. He swallowed.

"Drugs? Pills? Y'know, from the hospital."

"No!" he hissed. "Shhh."

"Hey, don't you go shushing me none."

The cruiser rolled by, not turning in.

"You on the run?" the guy asked, and he stepped closer.

"The cops after ya?" In the darkness, his eyes glimmered at the thought of a possible reward.

"I just don't want any trouble," Noah said.

"A little late for that," the man said, and in the darkness, Noah caught a gleam of silver in the man's big hand. A knife of some kind. His guts hardened.

"Leave me the hell alone," Noah warned.

"Just turn yer pockets inside out. Let's see whatcha got."

"Nothin'," Noah said. "I got nothin'." And as the guy lunged, he sidestepped the blow, then hoisted a knee hard in the attacker's groin. For years, he'd been ducking Ike Baxter's attacks, and this guy, smelling of booze, was no challenge. With a hard kick, the bastard went down, sprawling, the knife flying from his meaty fingers. Noah swiped up the weapon, tucked it into his pants, and took off at a dead run, cutting across the street and through a parking lot, to head north again. The guy, if he'd even gotten up, didn't give chase.

He ran through the night, until his lungs started to burn and he had to slow to catch his breath and gather his thoughts. Ike would be at home at least until 6:30 in the morning, when he headed out, first for coffee and smokes with other members of the crew, then onto the job site of the latest building Peterson and Jones Construction was adding to the already sprawling landscape of Las Vegas. Noah would then make his move.

He didn't think of what he was planning as stealing. More like "borrowing" or even paying Ike back for the times he had lashed out and hit him, either with the back of his hand or a fist or even with a belt. That had ended a few years ago when Noah had grown six inches and put on forty pounds of muscle his junior year in high school. He had effectively taken on the older man, to Ike's mortification. But as long as Noah had held a job and "contributed to the family budget," Ike had left him alone. So he figured Ike owed him.

But when he approached the house, not only was it dark, but it seemed empty. Even Roscoe was missing. Noah eased in through a window so as not to wake anyone, and he crept cautiously down the hallway, hardly daring to breathe, but there was no one at home.

Were they out looking for him?

Had he been IDed and the cops called them in for questioning?

Had there been some kind of emergency?

Or had they just packed up and left to avoid the creditors who called day and night?

Had the killer found them? No—they would all be here waiting if that were the case. Right?

He stood in the darkened, narrow hallway and wondered about where they were, the old house creaking around him. He should wait.

For the killer to come looking for you?

"Screw it," he muttered under his breath as he crept into the den. He half expected Ike to be lying in wait for him, the two plastic bags spread on the desk, his expression murderous. But, again, the room was empty, and when he reached into the vent, he found the stash just as he'd left it. This time, he took the rest of the money and left the drugs.

He thought about taking a vehicle but decided it was too risky. He had the switchblade for protection, so he walked to the main road, faced the sparse traffic, and stuck out his thumb. He felt a pang of regret for his mother. She would be worried. He'd have to call. But for Ike Baxter? He only felt a rush of freedom now that he was no longer under that toad's thumb.

Several cars passed, until a guy in an aging pickup

rolled to a stop on the shoulder, his blinker still pulsing amber. Noah jogged to the side of the idling truck and noted that the door was a different color from the rest of the vehicle. As he approached, the driver, a farmer from the looks of him, leaned over and pushed open the door. "Where ya headin'?" he asked.

"West."

"That takes in a lot of real estate." The farmer, wearing glasses, three days' worth of beard-shadow, and a Raiders baseball hat, looked him up and down as the truck's engine idled loudly. "Any particular place?"

"L.A.," Noah said off the top of his head.

A beat. "What happened to yer neck?"

"Car accident. That's why I'm hitchin'. Just got out of the hospital."

Suspicion clouded the farmer's gaze. "Looks like maybe you should've stayed in another day or two."

"Probably. But, y'know, it's damned expensive."

"True enough."

"Just got released."

"In the middle of the night?"

"This afternoon." Geez, what was with the twenty questions? He started to back away. "Look, if you don't want to give me a ride—"

"Oh, hell, hop in." He pushed the door open farther, then straightened behind the wheel. "Just checkin', y'know. You can never be too careful these days."

Noah thought a second, decided the guy was on the up and up, and climbed onto the cracked vinyl of the passenger seat before yanking the door shut.

"Just last night, there was big trouble out here in the Mojave. You hear about that?" He cast a glance at Noah, then checked his side-view mirror as he eased onto the quiet road. "Put on yer seat belt," he ordered. "Don't want no ticket, not fer that. Stupid-ass law, if you ask me."

Noah complied, his shoulder aching with the effort, as he snapped the belt across his chest and lap. The pickup was warm, smelled of chewing tobacco and dust, the heater loud enough to nearly drown out the music, a country-western tune, that was playing through the speakers.

"Anyhoo, last night there was a ruckus out on the desert. Car on fire, people killed, a motorcycle wreck, police all over it." As if he'd finally put two and two together, he cast a sideways look at his passenger, but Noah feigned innocence.

"Y'know, I did hear something at the hospital," Noah said, drawing his eyebrows together as if in deep thought. "It's all kind of messed up in my brain, but now that you mention it, I think I overheard a couple of the nurses talking about some explosion or something."

"That was it." The guy nodded. "Yep."

"I was kinda out of it. Had surgery on my shoulder. Fell off a ladder." God, he hoped the old coot was buying his story. "Anesthesia was still kinda messin' me up. Don't know what I heard and what I dreamed." He flashed a you-know-what-I-mean kind of smile.

"Oh, yeah, that shi—, er, stuff will make you loopy; don't I know it? Must be why you can't remember if you fell off a ladder or were in a car accident." The farmer was nodding to himself, and Noah relaxed a bit. The guy adjusted his cap and just kept driving. "Look, I'm goin' as far as Barstow and you can ride with me 'til I get there; then you'll have to find another ride to take you into L.A. Shouldn't be too tough. Everybody's going to Los Angeles, if y'know what I mean."

"Sounds good. Thanks."

"You want coffee?" He motioned to a silver Thermos in the space between the seats. "It's powerful, let me tell you. Thunder Punch or some such sh—, stuff. The wife brewed it. Always afraid I might drop off and fall asleep."

"I'm fine," Noah lied. For the first time, he felt hunger and thirst, but he thought it best to wait until Barstow or wherever the guy left him off.

"The name's Tuck," he said. "Ned Tucker, but I go by Tuck."

Noah panicked for a second, then said, "Riley Blackstone." He combined two of his teacher's names for the alias.

"Nice ta meet ya. Now, you've had a long day. Go ahead and sleep if ya want. I'll wake ya when we're getting close to Barstow."

It sounded like heaven. Noah leaned back in his seat and closed his eyes, but he didn't intend to sleep as the truck's wheels hummed over the asphalt and he recognized a Garth Brooks song floating softly from the speakers. He didn't know where the hell Barstow was, but it was good enough. For now. Come daylight, he'd figure out the rest.

For now, it was adios Ike Baxter, good-bye Cora Sue, and sayonara Las Vegas.

And what about Remmi Storm? What would you say to her?

She was his one regret, the intriguing girl who had thumbed her nose at popularity, who had been as out of step as he had been. A smart girl. Pretty, but not beautiful. Sassy, but not a smart-ass. He stared out the window. Yeah, he would've liked to get to know her better, even though the truth of the matter was that she was too young for him.

Time to let her go, though.

What would he say to her, if he'd had the chance?

Good night. He wished he could take her on a date and tell her, "Good night," at least once, but of course as far as tonight went? There wasn't a damned thing good about it.

* * *

Two days.

Didi had been gone for nearly two damned days.

The house wasn't cold, but Remmi, chilled from the inside out, had turned on the gas fire, watching the flames flicker and hiss as she rocked in the tattered chair, the baby in her lap. She wanted her brother to fall asleep, but that wasn't happening. Adam was fussy, not taking the bottle she offered, instead staring up at her and gumming the nipple, chewing on the rubbery tip as if he *knew* something was wrong. He was right, of course. Didi hadn't returned. Not yesterday, as she'd promised, nor today. So when? What had happened? As Remmi stared at the flames, she had the eerie and unwelcome feeling that she might not ever see her mother again.

At that thought, the lump in her throat grew, and she swallowed it back and refused to give in to tears. Miserable, her worry inching toward fear, she pushed against the carpet with her bare toe, keeping the motion slow and steady. She smiled down at the baby, hoping to comfort him, while inside she felt a deep, welling fear. What had happened to Didi? She'd flown out of here on a mission, but . . .

Please, please, let her walk through the door, Remmi had silently prayed for hours, but so far, her pleas had fallen upon deaf ears. God wasn't listening.

Seneca, too, had disappeared. Remmi had called her. Seven times yesterday, and ten today. Seneca wasn't answering or returning Remmi's panicked calls. She fed Adam from the store of bottles and watched the clock. Her mother had said she'd return within twelve hours.

She'd either lied or been detained or . . .

Don't even go there; don't think like that! Remmi told herself, as the clock in the kitchen ticked away the seconds of her life; Didi was fine. Okay. Just delayed or maybe . . . distracted. But she'd show up. She always did.

And she always called. Right? So why hasn't she?

Remmi glared at the phone, willing it to ring.

But the house remained silent, the only sounds the tick of the clock, the creak of the rocker, the rattle of the windows as a desert storm kicked up and the wind raced through this hardscrabble neighborhood, and the ever-increasing beat of her heart.

Had Didi planned to ditch her oldest daughter, leave Remmi with the infant for good? No, Remmi didn't believe that, wouldn't believe it, despite Didi's erratic behavior.

But she lied, didn't she?

About the meeting in the desert.

About Ariel being with Trudie.

About so many things.

All of your life, Didi has bent the truth to suit herself. Take, for example, that she's never told you anything straight about your father. Or her own family. It's been lie after lie after lie.

How can you trust her? How?

"Oh, shut up!" Remmi said, startling Adam. The nipple fell from his lips, and he screwed up his face, beginning to cry in earnest. "Oh, honey, no, no, no," she whispered, picking him up and cradling him as she walked—paced, really—in front of the fire. "It's all right. It's gonna be all right." She kissed the downy top of his head.

What should she do?

Call the police?

No. Not yet. Didi would kill her if she found out . . . well, if she ever returned. And then they'd take Adam from her and shove her through Social Services into some strange foster home, a separate one from her infant brother. No thanks.

Call Noah?

What good would that do? Besides, she'd tried several times and had never connected with him. If he wanted to talk to her, he could call or come by. Obviously, he wasn't interested in her, probably never really had been.

Her heart cracked a little, but she ignored the pain. She barely knew the guy. Besides, he was a loser. Otherwise, he would have checked on her when she hadn't shown up the other day.

Unless he thinks you stood him up when you didn't show . . .

For the millionth time, Remmi glanced at the fire. Stared into the flames. Thought of the fiery blast in the desert. And the gunshots. Someone had died last night, Remmi was sure of it. *Died! Violently.* Didi had switched out the babies—that much was certain—and whoever had been in that other car, the man whom Didi had referred to as the twins' "daddy," had expected to be handed a baby boy. Not a girl. That's why the twins had been dressed in the wrong clothes. It had to be. Remmi was almost sure of it—that Didi had switched out the babies on purpose to fool the "daddy" and probably make him pay more for his son. But the guy had cheated Didi, pulled a scam of his own, conning her just as she'd conned him, by leaving her with a briefcase of phony, useless bills.

And he'd died for it.

Someone had killed him in that car. Murdered him and, either by intent or by mistake, had taken the life of the child that was assumed to be Adam.

Oh. No.

She had been so caught up in her own misery, her own fears for herself and her mother, worrying about when

Didi would return, that she had ignored the horrific fact that possibly the murder that had gone down in the desert was about Adam. She stared down at the child in her arms, the innocent baby, a twin without his sister. "Oh, God, no," she whispered when she thought of what might happen to this little one if he were truly at the center of all this, possibly a target himself. "Oh, baby, I won't let that . . ." She didn't finish the thought as the phone rang and she leapt to answer it.

Didi had finally surfaced. Her heart soared and relief flooded through her. She almost cried, "Mom!" as she snagged the receiver from its cradle on the wall, but at the last second, Remmi bit her tongue, found a way to restrain herself, and didn't say a word.

"Didi?" a rough, irritated male voice demanded. "Didi? Are you there?" He hesitated, and Remmi placed the voice. Harold Rimes, her mother's boss at the club. "What the hell's going on? Where are you? Last night, okay, you said you were sick, and fine, Tanya did her thing, covered for you, but what about tonight?" A pause. "Are you there? Damn it all, I'm expecting a crowd tonight. You'd better show, Didi. If you value your job, which apparently you don't." He let out a long breath and, when he spoke again, was more conciliatory. "Tanya's not you, and the regulars, they expect, well, you know . . ." Another pause, and he was furious again. "Oh, for Christ's sake! Just show up, Didi!" He hung up with a sharp click. Shaken, still holding Adam, Remmi replaced the receiver slowly.

Didi hadn't even called Harold to tell him she wouldn't be in. This was not good. Not good at all.

Again, she looked at the baby, and Adam gurgled up at her, all big eyes and innocence. She almost cried. "That's it," she said with finality. She packed him into his carrier, stuffed his clothes and hers into a suitcase, found water bottles and baby formula, a huge box of diapers, some snacks and soda and carried everything, including her brother, out to the Toyota.

Money.

She needed money.

And maybe a credit card or two.

Propelled by the thought, she hurried back inside the house and to her room, where she found the tips she'd saved from Biggie's Burgers, where she worked part-time, coins and bills she kept in a jar. She stuffed the jar into her backpack. It wasn't enough. But she knew where there was more. Without a second's hesitation, not listening to a tiny voice that said she was stepping over an invisible line that could never be crossed again, she beelined to her mother's bedroom and closet, where she found a locked box and dragged it down. After locating the key in the earring compartment of Didi's jewelry display, she unlocked the box that held Didi's money from tips and her few valuable pieces of jewelry. As the lock turned and the box opened, Remmi nearly gasped. Holy moley! She'd found the mother lode! A lot of money in bigger denominations than the bills Didi's fans left in her tip jar.

Remmi decided these were the real bills the con artist had seeded into the phony ones. Didi had culled the good ones out. At least Remmi hoped so. She made sure the extra credit cards were still in the bottom of the box, along with her great-grandmother's diamond ring and a gaudy brooch that Didi had sworn was made of genuine rubies and emeralds. Maybe. Right now, Remmi didn't have time to consider their worth. Then there was a small, spiral-bound address book that had more names crossed out and erased than still existed. But it could come in handy. Remmi decided to keep it. She locked the box again, pocketed the tiny key, then hauled everything back to the Toyota.

She thought about the computer. She'd love to take it, but the monitor was bulky, and the modem wouldn't work without a hookup. The CPU would take up too much space, and as much as she loved the secondhand machine and hooking up to the Net, she just didn't have room for it.

ID. You need ID. Your smiling picture on your high school ID isn't going to cut it.

She slid behind the wheel and told herself that when she got to wherever it was she was going—and she had no idea where that was right now—she'd inquire around and find some way to get some ID that said she was old enough to drive. She glanced at her reflection in the mirror. She looked fifteen, no older. "Fresh-faced," that's what she'd always heard about herself. Well, fresh-faced wouldn't do. "Just a sec," she called over her shoulder to the baby in his carrier, then she raced back into the house, found a suitcase in Didi's closet, and filled it with her mother's costumes, dresses, bras, stockings, gloves, and wigs, then went to work in the bathroom. Beneath the mirror rimmed in lights, she snagged not one, but two, makeup cases and filled them with all of Didi's makeup. Brushes, sponges, and applicators. Mascara, lipstick, foundation, rouge, blush, eye shadow, and liner—all of the feminine ammunition that was in Didi's personal arsenal went into the bags before Remmi hauled them and the suitcase back to the car.

By this time, the baby was wailing.

She ignored him and twisted the key in the ignition. The Toyota sparked to life. Tearing out of the driveway, she told herself to slow down, calm down, and not attract any attention. The last thing she needed was to catch the eye of some cop watching traffic.

Where to? she asked herself as she drove onto the main road. East to what? Texas? Amarillo? Dallas? West to L.A.? She knew no one there, and she would have to contact someone, right? To the south was Mexico, but could she cross the border to a foreign land? Her high school Spanish was good enough for the classroom, though she was hardly fluent. What kind of documentation would she need?

And if you get there, will you ever be able to get back to the U.S.?

Deciding to shelve the Mexico idea, she drove steadily, away from the heart of downtown, where traffic was congested. Her hands were clammy over the wheel, her pulse pounding in her eardrums, her mind racing. She turned on the radio as she came to a spot in the road where she had to make a choice. East or west. Chris Isaak was singing, and she recognized the song: "San Francisco Days."

It was playing as a huge green road sign indicated that San Francisco was many miles away. Far, but far enough? Mentally, she calculated that it would take her all night to get there. So what? She needed distance from Las Vegas, and she also needed time to think, to plan.

Now that she'd left the house and the phone, how would Didi know where to find her? She swallowed hard. There were mobile phones—digital devices that were becoming more popular by the day. Each year, with advances in technology, the phones were becoming smaller, sleeker, and more convenient. Certainly, they were the wave of the future. Remmi could see that, but Didi had been death on them.

"Who needs to be in contact with the world all the damned time?" she'd said on more than one occasion when Remmi had mentioned that one of her friends at school had one.

Once, while seated at her makeup mirror and removing the thick foundation with a cotton pad and some kind of cleaner, Didi had kept her gaze fixed on her reflection as she'd said, "If you ask me, a high school kid with access to a phone day in and day out? That's a recipe for disaster."

"But they've even got small ones that flip closed, kind of like a clam," Remmi had argued, and her mother had laughed.

"What? Why?"

"So you can snap it closed. It fits in a purse or pocket."

"And it comes with a separate bill, something we don't need. We already have one phone bill. Trust me, that's more than enough."

Remmi had leaned a jean-clad hip on the bathroom counter near the sink. "But if I had a phone, you could always reach me and—"

"You?" she'd said, surprised, glancing up at her daughter, her eyes narrowing as if she'd just realized that Remmi might have a mind of her own, one with separate opinions from her mother's. "You think you need a phone?" She'd been shaking her head as she'd plucked a tissue from a box on the counter. "No way. I *know* where you are." She wiped foundation from her fingertips. "At least I'd better." Tossing the dirtied tissue into an overflowing wastebasket beneath the table, she turned back to the mirror and frowned at her reflection. Her gaze had met her daughter's in the mirror, and as if reading the stubborn set of Remmi's jaw as rebellion, she added, "No mobile phone. Not in this house. A computer's bad enough." A pause. "Got it?"

"Got it," Remmi repeated, but inwardly she decided that her mother was just being stubborn, set in her ways, and a bitch to boot. She didn't understand the coming technology and didn't want to. Didi loved to glorify the past, to wear nostalgic clothes, to pretend to be some has-been beauty queen from the fifties and sixties. She lived in a dream world. Also, probably because of Remmi's quiet obedience in school and at home, Didi thought she had complete control over her daughter's life. But she was wrong. Remmi was sick of doing whatever Didi wanted, tired of being the "good girl" who was always so responsible, did what she was told, a stellar student destined for a scholarship to, at the very least, a nearby college.

On the very night of the cell phone conversation, Remmi had turned a corner—maybe, more correctly a U-turn—in her life. No more doing what Mom told her, and it all had started with Remmi slipping onto the Internet, using her mother's credit card to "surf" on the aging computer she'd begged her mother to buy despite Didi's worries about being hooked up electronically to "God knew what." Remmi had also started sneaking out with the Toyota at 2:00 AM, once Didi got home from work and had crashed for the night. From that point on, Remmi had taken the car when she could, always filled it with gas, and defiantly wondered if Didi would ever wise up.

If Didi had noticed the change in her daughter's attitude, she'd never mentioned it, and Remmi had been careful to keep her grades up because she truly believed that her school record was her ticket out of Las Vegas and away from her mother, despite Didi's own wishes.

Because they were at odds with her own.

Didi had insisted no daughter of hers was going to move out at eighteen and make the same mistakes she had, but Remmi thought it was more that Didi would have herself a built-in babysitter; she'd found out she was carrying twins on the night of their last discussion about Remmi's life after she graduated from high school.

"You'll stay here with me and the babies. Live in the house, so there's no rent or utilities to pay, and save money in the process. There are good schools here in Las

Vegas," she'd said, as if her decision were final, not understanding that in the past few months, Remmi had ached to get out from under her mother's thumb. Once the babies had arrived, it had only gotten worse. As much as Remmi loved her tiny brother and sister, she wasn't ready to be a mother or even a handy free babysitter.

Now, she glanced into the back seat.

She would get a cell phone, so that she could call the home number and leave a message or keep trying Seneca.

And Noah? Are you going to try to get in touch with him, too?

"No," she said aloud and surprised herself, the car lurching as she'd been so vehement she'd inadvertently hit the gas instead of cruising steadily at fifty-five miles an hour. She brought the speedometer down. But she was certain she'd never try to contact Noah Scott again.

Everything had changed. Her own life had blown up in the desert two nights ago, as surely as that fireball had consumed the other car. Now she was mother, father, nursemaid, whatever, as well as half sister, to the little boy strapped into his infant carrier in the back seat of this rattletrap car.

Tightening her grip on the wheel, she stared straight ahead to the spot where the twin beams of her headlights illuminated the pavement. There was a steady stream of taillights as she, along with all these other strangers in their vehicles, moved in a red river through the mountains and the dark night. The others, those in pickups, sedans, vans, and SUVs, all had destinations, she supposed, while she was driving blind through the night and heading to a future that was murky and dark.

CHAPTER 9

OH2 stared down at the man lying in the hospital bed. Not even sixty-five years old, but looking ancient with tubes running in and out of his body, his skin milky pale, his pajamas rumpled. A motorized wheelchair with a headrest was positioned near the bed, proof that Oliver Hedges was still able to move around a bit, if only with the help of aides and, of course, the chair, an electric marvel, the best money could buy. Still, he was a pathetic figure, a far cry from the robust, helicopter-skiing, deep sea diving, mountain climbing, rugged adventurer he'd been so recently, a mere shadow of the athlete who forty years earlier had thought he might become an Olympian, a biathlete due to his strength in cross-country skiing and his deadeye aim with a rifle. He'd been edged out of the competition, losing his anticipated spot to the nineteen-year-old son of Norwegian immigrants, who was an inch taller, a bit faster on skis, and a slightly better shot. Losing his chance at competing as an Olympian had been one of Oliver Hedges's few failures in life. And a stinging lesson he'd never forgotten.

And look at him now.

A carcass of his former self.

Wasn't that just too damned bad?

In his firstborn's opinion, the old man lying in room 124 of Fair Haven Retirement Center deserved every moment of pain and mental anguish he experienced—the greater the agony, the better.

Blue eyes glared up at him. Silent eyes. Accusing eyes. His father never spoke a word to his firstborn, but OH2 had heard that he could talk, make his wants known to the staff. Good enough.

"How're you feeling?" he asked, knowing there would be no answer. The old man had been in this facility for over a year, ever since the accident had left him without use of his arms and legs because of a "bruised" spinal cord; the doctors hoped that it would heal.

Not a chance, OH2 knew. Though the cord hadn't been severed, it had been damaged in the unfortunate skiing accident. There were new treatments on the horizon, of course, but they were experimental or, as OH2 thought, iffy at best. The man in the bed was far too compromised. No, this expansive room, with its own gym and private physical therapist, separate nutritionist and personal trainer, wasn't enough to get him to walk again. So he was stuck here in what was essentially a studio apartment, complete with small kitchen, living area, recliner, and small leather sofa. It wasn't so bad, with its view of an interior garden filled with blooming cacti and hardy grasses, succulents, and even a Joshua tree. But it was a gilded cage and one he would never leave.

It was too bad the old coot hadn't died during that unfortunate fall, because his life was probably a torture to him. Well, what goes around, comes around, Old Man.

His father's very own advice echoed through his mind: As ye sow, so shall ye reap.

Well reap away, you pathetic excuse of a man.

He even smiled to himself at the thought while the man in the bed lay still. Who would've thought he'd be reduced to this? Oliver Hedges had once been a titan of industry, the tech industry. But not from any knowledge nor skills of his own, really; he was just an engineer who had gotten lucky enough to pick winners when it came to investing and who had eventually owned 51 percent of a start-up company, supplying the much-needed initial capital for a venture now worth hundreds of millions.

Once awarded Entrepreneur of the Year, he'd been the man who had played rounds of golf with pros and movie stars and politicians, even once getting in eighteen with the Vice President. Heralded as a humanitarian, to boot, because of his donations to a variety of charities, Oliver Hedges was also a lying bastard who had planned to make certain his eldest was disinherited.

So, now, dear old dad was just getting his due. God had found a way to punish the old miser.

"Marilee sends her love."

At the mention of his second wife, his father's eyes seemed to flash with a newfound anger. Marilee, thirty-two years younger than her husband, had divorced him soon after his accident and, in a turn-about's-fair-play move, married his oldest son. It was destiny, of course. OH2 had introduced them when he'd been dating Marilee McIver himself. But the old man had decided to woo her away while OH2 was in his final year at Stanford.

It was a powerful feeling watching the old man suffer in this gilded cage, even while he was attended to by a bevy of private nurses and aides, all of whom knew how to keep their mouths shut.

God, he looked bad.

A thin corpse of a man who had probably given up his will to live.

And yet . . . did one of his fingers move a bit, or was that a trick of light? Afternoon sunlight streamed through the garden and the Joshua tree before slanting past the half-closed blinds that decorated the bed in shadows that reminded OH2 of prison stripes, those he'd seen in old black-and-white movies. Surely, it was his imagination, but, wait . . . there it was again. Just a slight movement on the crisp white sheet.

Startled, head snapping a bit, he met the old man's gaze once more. Oh, Jesus. Was his father actually smiling? His lips hadn't moved in his freshly shaved face, but there was a distinct twinkle in his blue eyes, a malicious spark that indicated he wasn't done yet.

Or was it Junior's imagination? His guilt? He began to sweat in his sharp suit, despite the fact that the temperature and humidity in the room were climate-controlled to a perfect seventy-one degrees.

He studied the old man. No more movement. Good.

Shaken, he decided to end this charade of a family visit. After clearing his throat, he said, "Take care, Dad," without an ounce of warmth.

To his surprise, the old man made a gurgling sound, and his gaze moved from OH2 to the doorway where a nurse, a tall woman he'd never seen before, appeared. Her name tag read SHAWNA. On quiet footsteps, she was at his father's bedside in an instant, and OH2 took his leave. He'd made the dutiful, obligatory visit and gained a sense of renewed power from it. He knew the old man watched his back as he strode out of the room, something his father would never be able to do again, but OH2 was still worried. He glanced over his shoulder, and for a second, he thought he saw his father raise a hand to wave, but that was impossible, and when he blinked, the hand lay where it had been, where it was supposed to be, on the edge of the bed's coverlet.

He was losing it.

He tugged at the knot of his tie, which was suddenly far too tight, but with each step on the carpet, he reminded himself that his father was basically a quadriplegic. He needn't worry. Everything was fine.

Striding down the bright hallway with its windowed view of the garden, a desert landscape, he felt the urgency to do something. For once, he didn't know what. He skirted a woman bent over a walker and breezed past, barely giving her a glance, though she said, "Hello." He didn't have time for any of this. Past the main desk, he made his way to the entry doors and punched in a private code so that the doors to this expensive prison would unlock and he could step out and breathe again. As the glass slid away, allowing him to exit, he slipped on a pair of sunglasses and stepped into the brutal Nevada heat.

His mood was as sour as it had been when he'd driven into the lot of Fair Haven. If he'd thought the visit to his father would restore his sense of power, he'd been mistaken. With a shake of his head, he forced himself to forget the old man for the moment. He had a more important item on his agenda. His latest "project," that of securing his own heir, had turned into his own personal hell, at least according to the phone call he'd taken just before driving here to his prearranged, weekly visit. Crossing the landscaped parking lot to his Mercedes, he unlocked the car, slid into the sunbaked interior, and pounded a fist on the steering wheel.

"Son of a bitch," he said under his breath in frustration.

Maybe the problems with securing the boy child were all of his own making. He had the girl, and that should be good enough. These days, gender didn't matter as much.

To the world maybe.

But not to him.

He wanted a son, damn it. One that was as close bio-logically to himself as possible. Was that so hard? When one was available?

For the right price.

He rammed his key into the ignition and twisted. His sports car roared to life, and he backed out so quickly he almost hit the rear end of a ridiculously long pickup that was parked in the short row behind him. He missed that immense bed by inches, which was just good enough.

Jamming the gearshift into drive and stepping on the accelerator, he wondered if he'd trusted the wrong per-son, made a bad decision, but second-guessing wouldn't help now. They needed to rethink the project. He cracked his window until the air-conditioning kicked in, and at the end of the long, fenced lane of the facility, he headed toward the heart of the city.

Within twenty minutes, he was back at the condo but still tense, his penthouse with its incredible view seeming somehow lacking this afternoon. Yanking off his tie, he glowered through the windows. How could everything have gone so wrong? A second botched attempt to get his son—*his* son. He swore loudly, then punched the air, wishing he could hit something or, more precisely, some-one.

Unwelcome, an image of his father flitted through his brain, and in his mind's eye, he saw the old man as he'd been in the hospital bed, but somehow tossing off the bedclothes and rising, like Lazarus, fully dressed in an expensive power suit, white shirt, and bold tie.

"Stop it," he muttered, just as the door to his study clicked open, and he recognized a familiar but uninvited face.

"You botched it!" he accused, grateful for someone other than himself to blame.

"Complications," was the unacceptable explanation.

"You should have prepared for any event, any 'complication,' any glitch. Instead," he said evenly, trying to hang onto his cool, "you came back empty-handed."

"It won't happen again."

"Of course it won't." OH2 wanted to explode. "Because there won't be another chance." He was furious, his words clipped. How could something as simple as a baby kidnapping go so wrong?

"I'll handle it." The voice was calm and assured as the visitor crossed to the bar to pour a drink.

So damned arrogant.

A glance over the shoulder. "You?"

OH2 hesitated, then thought, what the hell? It had been one lousy couple of days. "Oh, fuck. Fine. Sure." A drink might help. Something had to. This . . . this failure would never do. Never. He heard ice cubes clinking and the gentle *glug* as alcohol was poured.

The visitor turned and offered him a short glass.

OH2 snatched it quickly, and as his guest hoisted a glass, he didn't bother with his own silent toast, just took a long swallow of the cool, calming scotch. It slid down his throat easily, the smoky scent of the alcohol seeping into his nostrils. For a second, he closed his eyes and mind to the madness that had become his life. Yeah, a drink definitely helped calm his tense muscles and tight nerves, but it wouldn't solve the problem. "We have to do something." Opening his eyes, he found his guest staring out the window to the panorama of city, sky, and desert.

"I know. I got it."

"Really? Because it doesn't seem like you 'got' anything." Another cool swallow. "We shouldn't be in this position."

"Just a minor setback."

"Major," OH2 corrected. "A major setback." He downed the remains of his drink, filled his mouth with ice, and,

cracking a small cube, made his way past the visitor to
the bar, where he picked up the uncapped bottle and
poured himself another three fingers. Carefully he sipped,
slowing the alcohol train down a notch. He needed to
think, to plot, to . . .

He blinked.

Felt suddenly dizzy.

Shaking his head to clear it only made things worse.

What the hell?

The world seemed to spin, turn upside down. His
knees buckled, and he dropped the remains of his drink,
ice cubes skittering across the carpet. His fingers scraped
the edge of the bar, but he couldn't catch himself and fell
back against his desk, sending papers and his phone flying.

He collapsed onto the carpet. His head hit. Hard.

Thud!

Pain burst behind his eyes.

Blinking, he still didn't understand. As the desk, book-
cases, and wide windows spun around him, he scrambled
to get to his feet, but he couldn't make his limbs move,
couldn't even get his knees under him. Nausea boiled in
his stomach.

In a lightning bolt of clarity, he remembered he wasn't
alone.

"For . . . for God's sake . . . Help me . . . ," he ordered,
his voice a rasp. He was sweating and writhing, trying not
to vomit, unable to focus. His heart had begun to beat a
wild, frantic tattoo, so fast that he thought it might explode.

That was the first inkling of his problem—that he'd
been drugged. The drink he'd gulped so thirstily had been
spiked.

With what? Oh, Jesus.

Eyes starting to blur, he saw the phone receiver that

had toppled to the floor. He stretched his fingers and reached for it, then watched helplessly as it was kicked away by the polished toe of a boot.

"Not today," his visitor said without emotion, then added, "Well, not any day."

I'm going to die . . . this . . . this maniac is killing me!

His body started to convulse and, rolling onto his back, unable to control his muscles, he witnessed the slow stretch of a smile curve his assassin's lips.

CHAPTER 10

Remmi's trip was cut short.

The damned Toyota's temperature gauge was hovering in the red zone, and Adam had woken up screaming. Dead tired, nerves shot, she was less than a hundred miles from Las Vegas when she spied the gold-colored Star Vista Motel sign mounted high enough to glow over the right side of the freeway. She took the next exit and, nervous as anything, pulled into the pock-marked asphalt and gravel lot that butted up to a single-story, L-shaped stucco building.

After locking Adam in the car and armed with the bills she silently prayed were legit, she hurried to the covered area, pushed a button near the locked glass door, and waited, perusing the offered services posted on the glowing reader board under the gold sign: cable TV, pool, and telephone services, along with 24-hour manager on duty, all as if they were five-star amenities.

She wondered about that as the minutes ticked by, and she hit the button another couple of times before a short man with a ring of graying hair around a bald pate and horn-rimmed glasses appeared from a door behind the desk. Frowning, he switched on brighter lights, fluorescent bars that came on one by one and cast the area under the portico in a watery, unearthly glow. He squinted at her for a few seconds, before seeming to feel satisfied that she wasn't there to rob the place or murder him. He unlocked the door, let it slide open, but blocked Remmi's entrance.

"Yeah?" he said gruffly. "Help you?"

"I'd like a room. For tonight."

He eyed her speculatively, glanced over her shoulder at the near-empty parking lot behind her, his gaze settling on the crappy old Toyota. "You with your folks?" Skepticism colored his words.

"Just my son."

Bushy eyebrows ticked up, arching over the rims of his glasses. "You have a kid?"

"That's right." Setting her jaw, she stared at him, silently daring him to deny her.

"You're pretty young to have a kid."

"So I've been told." She was shaking inside but held her ground.

"I bet."

"Do you have a room?" she persisted. "Your sign says 'vacancy.'"

"How old are you?"

"Eighteen," she lied quickly.

He looked like he didn't believe her. "Got ID?"

Uh-oh.

"You need it if I pay cash?" She nearly shivered under his steady stare and thought all was lost when she heard Adam wailing from inside the car. "And I've got credit cards. Visa. Mastercard. Whatever. My baby needs a warm place to stay. The room has to be clean."

"Oh, you don't have to worry about that—" he said, then trailed off as she waited impatiently.

What if he wouldn't let her book a place for the night? What would she do about the car? The baby? "Look, if you don't have a vacancy," she bluffed, "I'll head farther down the road to—"

"No need for that," he cut in. The man's greed was overcoming his concerns. He looked hardly able to turn down the rent. He held the door open a little wider. "Okay. Fine. Come in and register. Quick." Then, as she passed, "I don't want any trouble."

"I—we won't be any."

"I mean it. You gotta keep that kid quiet. There are other paying guests."

Not many, Remmi thought, by the looks of the empty lot.

Whether he believed her age or not, he took her cash as she registered as Didi Storm, hoping that this guy hadn't seen her mother's act. The credit cards were all issued to Didi, so she saw no other recourse but to use the name. Though she worried he would hold each bill to the light, he didn't, just stuffed them into the register and handed her a key to room 116. "Right down the porch," he said. "Ice machine is around the corner. Soda and snacks, too."

"Thanks." Snagging the key, she couldn't get out of the tiny lobby, with its worn, stained carpet and smells of old cigarettes and stale coffee, fast enough. She drove to the parking slot in front of the door, then hauled Adam, his diaper bag, and her small suitcase into the room, a bare-bones space with one sagging bed, a dresser on which a TV covered the mirror, and two nightstands. A coffeepot and the smallest microwave Remmi had ever seen vied for space on the counter with the sink, which was just outside the small room holding a toilet and tub shower. Not the Ritz, by any means, but clean enough and safe enough for one night.

As advertised, the room did come with a phone, complete with instructions about how to dial "out" and even connect to long distance. She wasted no time, but double-checked the Toyota's trunk to make certain it was locked and that none of her mother's costumes and valuables would be stolen; then she bolted the door to the room, drew the chain, and checked to make certain the windows were latched before pulling Adam from his carrier.

"Sorry, buddy," she said as she changed his diaper, then made a bottle of formula with water she'd gotten from the tap and heated in the microwave. It was far from ideal, but it would have to do, and as she cradled her brother in her arms, watching bubbles form in the bottle as he drank, she worried about the coming days.

After a few hours' sleep, she would go through the changing and feeding routine for her brother again, then drive straight to San Francisco or the area around the city and find a room for rent, then get a mobile phone for sure and leave messages for Didi. And then what? Get a job? Who would care for Adam? The money she'd taken from Didi wouldn't last forever.

You're a smart girl; you can figure this out. Right?

"Book smart, no common sense," her mother had teased, but that wasn't true, Remmi knew.

And what if Didi never called or connected with her? What then? Tears sprang to her eyes, and she paced the short distance between the bathroom and the door, holding the baby until he nodded off and she laid him on the bed. She didn't bother with pajamas, just turned out the light and stared at the ceiling in the semi-dark. Light from a few security lamps outside seeped through the thin blinds, and the traffic noise from the freeway was audible.

What to do?

She was so alone.

The baby let out a soft little sigh, reminding her how wrong she was. She cuddled him close, his breath warm against her neck. She ran through the names of all the people who could help her: Didi and Seneca, both of whom were MIA, so they were out. And then there was Harold Rimes, her mother's boss at the club, with his leering eyes and breath that always had a hint of liquor on it. Didi had warned Remmi about him whenever Remmi had waited in her mother's dressing room. "Avoid Harold tonight," Didi said on one occasion, her forehead pinched in a frown as she'd slid a Cher wig onto her head and adjusted the long strands of black hair around her face. "He's had a little too much tonight, and sometimes . . . sometimes he gets a little handsie, if you know what I mean." She'd met Remmi's gaze in the mirror. "Don't get me wrong; he's a good guy, a little rough around the edges, but . . . well, just be careful." She'd eyed her reflection as she'd stood and surveyed her body in the sequined, flesh-colored unitard. "Sometimes Harold oversteps his bounds." She'd walked to the dressing room door and said over her shoulder as she swept the long hair over one shoulder, "Lock the door."

Remmi had understood, and from that point forward, she always slid the dead bolt into place if she was left in the dressing room, and she was on the lookout for and avoided the mercurial man who, because he had hired Didi, had some power over her. He liked that; it was obvious in the satisfied smile that played upon his lips whenever Didi acquiesced to his ideas of changes in her routine or songs or costumes. Remmi had learned at a young age that Harold Rimes liked power. She'd often enough walked by the open door of his office, where he was forever going over the books, ledgers, and bills littering his desk, a computer monitor filling a wide space, an ashtray overflowing with cigarette butts. Interspersed on the paneled walls were the trophies of the game he'd "bagged." Deer, elk, and antelope horns were mounted, along with his business license and an award from the local chapter of the Rotary Club. A liquor cabinet held several bottles, and on the bookshelf were all kinds of books, everything from "how to" books and a worn copy of the Bible to volumes of Shakespeare to novels by the likes of Aldous Huxley, Ray Bradbury, and Stephen King. She'd even sneaked into the office once, the scent of stale cigarette smoke cloying, and slipped a copy of King's *The Stand* off the shelf, only to have Rimes say the next time he'd seen her in the wide hallway behind the stage, "Hey, Remmi. I know you took the book, okay?"

She'd opened her mouth to deny it, and as he'd taken a step closer, she'd backed away. He was a big man and fit, worked out at a gym. His eyes were wide set and forever watching, his brown hair clipped short, and he made no attempt to hide the fact that he was going bald. He'd studied her at that moment, his gaze sliding down her body and making her skin crawl, before he'd met her eyes again. She'd felt sweat collect at the base of her spine at the hint of lust in his eyes, and her heart had knocked wildly in her chest. She'd realized then that he was thinking about her for the very first time not as a child, but as a girl on the verge of womanhood, with long legs and breasts that hadn't existed eighteen months earlier. Her throat had turned to sand as his eyes had narrowed, and she'd almost been able to see the gears of his mind turning.

Oh, God, why had she snooped and lifted the book?

"I–don't–I mean, I didn't—"

But he knew she'd taken the copy. Harold Rimes

might have been many things, but stupid he was not. So she stopped lying and inched her chin up a fraction. "I like Stephen King," was all she'd said, and that had seemed to surprise him.

"Yeah? Huh." Another appraising glance, but this one hadn't been so sexual. "Me, too." A beat. He'd been rethinking her. Again. Then, "Look. Just return the book when you're done with it. Okay? And no more sneakin' around my office. That's off-limits. If you think I might have something you want to read, just ask. Otherwise, if you take something that doesn't belong to you? I'll have to make your mother pay for it. Get me?"

She did. She left the book outside his door as soon as she'd finished it and hadn't stepped inside his office with the glassy-eyed cougar's head again.

So now, in her hour of desperation, holed up in her room at the Star Vista Motel, she wouldn't call Harold, who, she knew, had loaned Didi money on occasion, but no.

Nor would she try to locate either of her two step-fathers, both men having been the closest thing she had to a father. The first was Ned Crenshaw, a rodeo rider who had taught Remmi a lot about horses and fixing things around his small ranch, but the marriage had lasted less than five years, and he'd moved on, to Montana, she thought. Or had it been Colorado? She hadn't heard from him in forever. The second was Leo Kasparian, the magician now married to his much younger assistant. Leo's breakup with Didi had been brutal. No, Kaspar the Great was out of her life, too, and couldn't be depended upon. She thought of her own father, the grand secret of Didi's life—well, that and bearing twins recently—and discarded the idea. He'd never been around, maybe didn't even know she existed.

Remmi had a few friends she could call, and maybe their parents would take her in, but not with a baby, and not without a lot of questions she didn't want to answer. She didn't want to stare into some mother's concerned eyes and spill her guts, then end up in Child Services or wherever. No sirree. The same went for Didi's friends, the few that she'd collected. Trudie Whoever, someone who smelled of too much perfume and cigarettes, a flamboyant woman Remmi had only met once. She could call Philippe, another friend of her mother's, a handsome black dude whose Diana Ross routine was spot-on. Didi had a love/hate relationship with Philippe, as they had vied for the same jobs in the past. Other than to call him and ask if he knew where her mother might be, Remmi thought it best to leave him alone. What would he want with a fifteen-year-old and an infant? Nothing, that's what.

So that left Noah Scott, a boy she barely knew. Her heart ached even more when she thought of him and the very real fact, she decided, that she'd never see his rugged face again. Maybe that was for the best.

With a sigh, she said to the sleeping infant, "I guess it's just you and me." But she remembered she had relatives on her mother's side tucked somewhere deep in Missouri. As far as she knew, her grandparents were still alive, though she'd never met them. She knew their names, Frank and Willa Maye Hutchinson and, from what Didi had mentioned now and again, had pieced together that they had owned a farm in the southern part of the state. And Didi, born Edwina, was the middle child, with an older sister named . . . Vera, that was it. She was married and probably had kids of her own, cousins Remmi had never met as they lived in California, she thought. The same with Didi's brother, Billy—presumably William, though Remmi wasn't certain. Didi never spoke to or of her family. It was as if they'd done something horrible to her, something unforgivable, but knowing her mother, who probably was the same type of drama queen as Willa, that wrong against her had probably been amplified and magnified over the years. Whatever the reason, Remmi wasn't going to travel to the Midwest and search out relatives who might not even know she existed. The way Remmi figured it, doing the math, her mother had gotten pregnant soon after landing in California, probably by someone who promised to make her the next Demi Moore or Julia Roberts or Cameron Diaz or some other big name, which had all been hogwash, of course. Didi had either never told him he was about to become a daddy, or he'd suggested she end the pregnancy. He was probably powerful, at least in Remmi's fantasies, so Didi, fresh off the farm, so to speak, wouldn't have had the courage or money to fight him for fear of losing her dream of becoming a Hollywood movie star.

"Oh, geez," she said to the dark room as she held the baby tighter. "We're in a world of hurt," and for the first time, she let the tears she'd been holding back drizzle from her eyes and track down her cheeks. How had this happened? What could she do? How would she care for herself, let alone a months-old baby? Where the hell was her mother?

"Mom," she said on a broken sob, and Adam stirred and let out a faint whimper.

This would never do. Feeling sorry for herself wouldn't help her and certainly wouldn't help her brother. If she'd learned anything from her mother, it was self-preservation and how to adapt. Remmi knew she was just as cunning as Didi, maybe even more so, so she would have to use it to her advantage.

Somehow.

Someway.

She finally drifted off to sleep and was awakened by her brother who, squirming against her, started to cry. Groggily, she found the things she needed to make a fresh bottle of formula, then, with her own stomach grumbling, made her way outside and around the corner, where she fed the few single dollars she had into the soda and snack machines, then drank a Coke and ate two packages of small, frosted donuts for breakfast. She snapped on the television and searched through the pathetic menu of channels until she found a news station out of Las Vegas. It was spotty and offered nothing of interest, nothing about Didi's disappearance nor the explosion in the desert.

"We're old news," she told her brother and wondered what she was going to do about the Toyota. It had to be fixed, wouldn't run far without overheating; she knew that much about the car, but where could she drive it to? She could check the yellow pages of the phone book sitting beside the telephone. Or she could find a computer and log onto the Internet with her mother's AOL account; that would certainly make things go faster.

Though it was still early, not even six in the morning, she picked up the phone and, using the instructions, dialed Seneca's number one last time. The phone rang once, twice, a third time. She was about to hang up when she heard a groggy voice on the other end of the line. "Hello?"

Remmi's heart soared. "Seneca?" she cried automatically, though of course she recognized the midwife's voice. "Oh my God, where have you been? It's Remmi."

"Remmi? Oh, thank God! I've been worried sick. Where are you? And Adam?"

"He's–he's with me," she said, fighting a new wash of tears, this time of relief as she glanced at the baby, who was staring up at her. "We're at a funky motel off the Interstate. Star Vista—about, I don't know, fifty or sixty miles out of Las Vegas, on the way to San Francisco."

"I've seen it."

"Oh, thank God. Mom never came back, and I freaked out and, and . . ." She was talking faster and faster, anxious to explain everything, grateful to finally connect with someone, anyone. Seneca would know what to do. "And then the car broke down—not really, but it was overheating, and I was scared to death and Adam was screaming his bloody head off, and—"

"Hey, hey, hey, hey. Hold on. Just slow down, okay? Take a breath, and then tell me," Seneca said in that slightly accented, patiently calm voice.

Remmi did. She explained about waiting and finally deciding to leave and said that she feared Social Services would take the baby away, if they found that Didi had abandoned them, and dump her into foster care. She told Seneca about getting the call from Didi's boss, then packing everything up and heading west, not knowing what to do and landing at this dump of a motel when the Toyota started to overheat.

But she never admitted to knowing what went down in the desert the night before Didi took off, and she left out the part about taking her mother's things, money, and credit cards. Seneca, as it turned out, didn't ask about any of those things and told her to "sit tight. I'm on my way. We'll deal with the car."

Three hours later, she showed up at the Star Vista in her Ford Escort. In a gauzy white dress, clipped tight at the waist, with a wide braided belt and oversized sunglasses, she looked as exotic as ever. Her hair was braided and wrapped into a tight bun, and she was nothing but efficient as she ordered a tow truck to haul the ail-

ing Toyota back to Las Vegas, then drove Remmi and her
brother home. Remmi, though, now that she'd been
"saved," as she saw it, was fit to be tied. Where the hell
had Seneca been? With her back wedged against the passenger door and seat, Remmi eyed the taller woman and
demanded to know why she couldn't reach her earlier.

"I didn't know what to do. Who to call. I couldn't get
hold of you, and I had Adam, and the manager almost
didn't rent a room to us, was nasty and awful, and . . .
and . . ."

"Shhh." Seneca put one finger to her lips while she
drove with the other hand. "I know, sweetie, and I'm so
sorry about that," Seneca said, shaking her head as she
drove her hatchback eastward. She flipped down the visor,
as the sun was already harsh, heat rising in waves on the
asphalt ahead. "Really sorry. My mistake. The phone was
off the hook, and I didn't know. Then when I discovered
it, I replaced it, and then this morning you called. Thank
God!" She sent Remmi a sad smile. "I would've come
sooner. You know that."

"Yeah," Remmi said without enthusiasm. She wasn't
sure. She wasn't sure of anything right now.

"Oh, Remmi," Seneca reproved softly. "I called the
house over and over. Left messages on the answering machine. You'll see. When we get back. You can check."

"Oh, no." Remmi flashed her an uneasy smile. "I believe you." She had no reason to mistrust Seneca, but
everything was topsy-turvy right now, and she didn't
know who or what to trust. So she lied. "It's okay," she
said, forcing a brightness into her voice that she didn't
feel. "We're together now. You and me and Adam."

"Yes. And we'll find your mum."

"You'll call the police?"

A beat, just a second's hesitation, before Seneca

stretched her fingers over the wheel. "Yes, if we need to. But first, I think, considering everything . . ."

Like the exchange of money for a child.

"We'll try to find her ourselves. I know a private investigator. He's very good and very . . . discreet. I, um, I think your mum would want that, don't you?"

"Yeah, I guess. But if he can't find her . . ."

"Then we'll definitely go to the authorities," she said. "We'll have to."

"And . . . and what about Ariel and the money?"

"Maybe we'll find your sister, too. As for the money and how your mum came to get it, well, we'll just have to tell everything we know and let the chips fall where they may."

Remmi thought of the night in the cargo hold of Didi's huge car and what she'd seen. Could she tell the police? Would they believe her? Would they think she was just some weird teenager telling tales?

"Okay," she said, thinking she would feel better with this new plan, but she didn't.

"We'll find her," Seneca said, though she didn't look at Remmi again.

Oh, please, God. Remmi stared out the dusty windshield to the blue, blue sky and the fading line of a jet trail slowly dissipating as a plane soared out of sight. She wondered if she'd ever see Didi again, then closed her mind to that traitorous thought and felt her heart surge a little at the sight of the small house in the cul-de-sac that she called home.

She threw open the car door the second Seneca had parked in the drive and raced into the house, which, of course, was still and lifeless. Not completely convinced that Didi hadn't returned, she ran through all the rooms and ended up in the garage, which was empty, the cement floor stained where the Cadillac had once leaked oil. Her heart shattered. She hadn't realized that she'd held out hope that her mother had returned.

How dumb are you? Didi bailed. It's obvious.

But she wouldn't believe it.

While Seneca tended to Adam and unpacked the belongings, Remmi holed up in her room and flung herself over her bed; she buried her head in her pillow and let loose the tears she'd fought since the night before. She knew it was crazy, that crying wouldn't help anything, but she couldn't stop. Where was Mom? What had happened and why, God, oh, why, couldn't she have a normal mother, one who had married her father and had a couple more kids? One who was content to stay at home or be a teacher or a waitress or anything other than some dumb impersonator, a damned showgirl? How come her mother couldn't stick around and care for her kids?

She didn't hear the door to her room open, but when she looked up, she saw Seneca in the doorway, her smooth brow wrinkled, sadness in her near-black eyes. She didn't ask the stupid, *Are you okay?* question, because obviously Remmi was not. "I'll make you dinner," she said in that calm voice, and for once Remmi wanted to lunge at her, to shake the taller woman and ask her how she could be so serene, so unemotional, so in charge when everything, every damned thing was falling apart. But instead she turned away from her, shunning Seneca as if Seneca was somehow behind that fateful and fatal exchange in the desert, or as if Didi had driven off into the desert in a state of enraged pique the next day when she'd discovered that she'd been conned, as if somehow, Seneca— ever sedate, ever collected and patient, the "cool head," as Didi had referred to her—could somehow have prevented all the horror of the past few days.

That was ridiculous, of course. Seneca wasn't to blame. All of the pain landed squarely at Didi's feet. And yet, as difficult as living with Didi Storm was, Remmi missed her and was worried sick that something horrid had happened to her.

Blinking against a flood of tears, Remmi wiped her nose and rolled onto her back, crushing her pillow to her chest and trying not to wonder what had happened to her mother. It proved impossible, of course, and eventually, from sheer exhaustion, she fell asleep.

When she awoke, the house was quiet.

Too quiet.

She rubbed the sleep from her eyes and checked the bedside clock. Nearly midnight. She'd been asleep for twelve hours. Yawning, she stretched, made her way to the bathroom, used the toilet, and splashed water onto her face. She glanced at the shower, but waited. First, she had to make certain everything was okay. Well, as okay as it had been the night before.

She walked through the house on bare feet, but there wasn't a sound. The living room and kitchen were empty, her mother's bedroom untouched, the babies' nursery as she'd left it, Adam not in his crib.

With each step, her heart sank a little further, and when she went to the room Seneca used when she stayed over, the daybed had not been slept in. "No," Remmi whispered, "no, no, no! Seneca?" She yelled more loudly as she ran through the empty rooms. "Seneca! Are you here?" Of course, she wasn't, and when Remmi went out to view the driveway, the green hatchback was missing, not parked where it had been the night before.

Remmi tried to tell herself that it was all right. Seneca had just needed to run an errand, go to the grocery store, pick up a prescription, buy diapers, whatever, and rather than wake Remmi, she'd taken the baby with her and . . . and . . . It was no use. No matter how she tried to buoy herself, Remmi felt totally abandoned.

She looked for a note, found none. Just some soup that had been congealing in a saucepan on the stove overnight. She went to the phone, frantically dialed Seneca's number, but before the midwife's answering machine clicked on, she knew in her soul that there would be no answer.

Then she noticed the blinking light on her own answering machine. She hit the button and heard a series of ever-more anxious messages from Seneca.

"Remmi? Didi? Please call me."

Three audio messages, each sounding more panicked than the last.

So at least she didn't lie about that.

How do you know? It's not as if the calls are date- or time-stamped.

Stomach in knots, she waited.

For two days.

Nothing.

Just another three harassing calls from Didi's boss. Remmi thought once more about calling the police. She'd even walked to Seneca's house and hadn't been surprised when she, Adam, and her car were missing. She'd walked to Noah's house and had intended on knocking on his door, but when she'd spied the police cruisers, lights flashing at the small ranch, she'd left.

The only good news was that Seneca had left her with all the items she'd packed hastily into the Toyota on the night she'd fled to the Star Vista. She had money, credit cards, and supplies. And the car, too, was returned from the tow shop, a mechanic friend of Seneca's explaining that the temperature gauge had been shot and he'd replaced it. He dropped the car off, said the bill had been "taken care of," and then had gotten a ride with a coworker who had followed him to Remmi's house.

She took it as a sign.

So, burning with a quiet, smoldering rage, she'd repacked the Toyota, this time including the bulky computer as she didn't have need of a car seat, and with her meager possessions and Didi's credit cards and money in her pocket, she drove away from Las Vegas.

PART 2

CHAPTER 11

San Francisco
Now

Sick, Remmi stared at the scene in horror as the thick San Franciscan night seemed to close in on her. The world tilting, she heard the frantic voices as if from a distance. Screams of the crowd and shouts, the *whomp, whomp* of a helicopter's blades as it hovered over the buildings, honks of traffic. People rushed and pushed, some to get away from the horrific, gory scene where the fragile space between life and death had been shattered, others to edge even closer. Remmi forced herself forward, peered over a man's shoulder to the broken body of the woman, and saw that she'd missed the fountain by inches, her wig askew, a dark stain pooling beneath her frothy skirt.

"Oh, God," Remmi whispered as a policewoman ordered the crowd to move away. Remmi was jostled and fell back; she shouldered and elbowed away from the Montmort Tower, now strobed in the lights of fire trucks, emergency vehicles, and police cars. A man, a police officer probably, was ordering everyone to "Get back. Move. Back up! Let us do our job here."

Cameras and phones were clicking, footsteps echoing, and the dull roar of excited voices pounded in her head.

Had she really just witnessed her mother's suicide? After all these years of not knowing what had happened to Didi, had it come down to one last, desperate, and flamboyant act?

Oh. Please. No.

She stumbled away, her boots slipping on the steep, wet sidewalk, her insides nearly frozen. Not paying attention to where she was going, she seemed almost swept away by the throng that crossed the street, some people babbling in excitement, others shocked into silence, one man already wearing a red and white Santa hat. Everything seemed out of sync and discordant, surreal.

When she finally looked up at a street sign, she realized she'd walked blocks away from where she needed to be, which was the parking garage where she'd left her car. Shaking, she wondered if she could drive; as her head cleared, she decided she had no other choice.

It may not have been Didi. It probably wasn't. There are tons of Marilyn Monroe impersonators, even here in the city. Don't freak out. Remain calm. Didi's probably still out there.

She was walking toward the parking structure now, breathing more deeply, as the incline was steep. From the corner of her eye, she caught a movement, and for a second she thought someone was following her. She glanced quickly over her shoulder, saw no one lurking in the shadows, but sensed hidden eyes observing her.

You're imagining this!

Swallowing back the stupid paranoia, she felt her heart knocking a little faster, her skin prickling in apprehension.

There's no one following you. There never has been. For God's sake, Remmi, get a grip.

You're just freaked out because of the tell-all book just published about Didi's life and disappearance, the interest it's stirring up.

The book . . . It had just landed in stores and on the Internet. Why anyone would want to publish a book about a small-time celebrity impersonator, Remmi didn't understand, but there it was, and surprisingly, people were interested in the mystery surrounding her disappearance. Somehow, Didi Storm was achieving the fame she so desperately wanted now, twenty years after she'd walked out the door, never once looking over her shoulder.

Had she died that night?

Been kidnapped?

Or just decided she didn't need the responsibility of a teenager and infant son?

Remmi didn't know, even though she'd asked those very questions of herself a million times over. There were other questions that kept her awake at night, that burrowed into her brain with tiny painful claws.

Why did Seneca leave?

What did the midwife/nursemaid want with Adam?

Did she know where Didi was and return the boy to her?

Were she and Didi in cahoots?

Why—

"Stop it!" she said aloud and startled herself as well as a woman jogging in the other direction. Cell phone in hand, earbuds engaged, eyes flashing a quick anger, the woman made a wide arc around Remmi and breezed by without breaking stride.

Remmi watched her disappear around a corner, then did a quick sweep of the steep sidewalk and street behind her. No one looked out of the ordinary. No one ducked into a doorway to avoid being seen. No one was following her.

She started hurrying uphill again. She had to think, to reason, to figure out if she should go to the police. At that thought, she felt herself shrink inside. Her history with the cops wasn't exactly stellar. Far from it.

She remembered finally going to the police three days after Seneca had left her. She'd hung out at the house. Waiting. Hoping. Praying. But no one had returned. Not her mother, nor Seneca, nor her infant siblings. She was alone. She'd broken down and called Noah again, and that time, she'd gotten his stepfather on the phone.

"He ain't here!" Ike Baxter had growled. "But if you find him, tell him I'm lookin' for him, the worthless piece of thievin' shit. And when I find him, he'd better watch out. I'm finally gonna give that kid what's been comin' to him. Lyin' little prick." Then he'd slammed the receiver down.

Remmi had never called back.

She'd found addresses and phone numbers in her mother's small book and called a number that was just listed as M&D—Mom and Dad, she figured, and dialed, but the number was out of service, and what would she say to the grandparents she'd never met anyway? "Hi, I'm your long-lost granddaughter." What would be the outcome? To move someplace over fifteen hundred miles away with strangers? People who would force her to go to a new high school and try to blend in with kids who had known each other all their lives? No way.

She'd considered her original plan to head to San Francisco, but scrapped the idea and finally, hating herself, had walked into town and to the police station, where she'd found herself talking to Detective Bud Kendrick, who didn't believe much of her wild tales about her mother—not that she could really blame him. If she was being honest with herself, she had held back parts of the truth, though she'd admitted to what she'd seen in the desert through the slit in the back seat of the Cadillac.

Kendrick, a tall man with a shock of coffee-brown hair, thick eyebrows, and a nose that looked as if it had been broken, was built like a football player, and a plaque on the wall had indicated he'd been "All League" at a high school in Idaho. His office was neat, a computer monitor taking up a lot of real estate on his desk, and he surveyed her with cool, calculating eyes as his partner, Lucretia Davis, a thirtyish black woman in a slim skirt and pressed blouse, had hovered near the doorway, as if she expected Remmi to bolt, and listened while Kendrick fired the questions. For some reason, he seemed to have it in for Remmi from the start of the interview. Or maybe he was just one of those perpetually angry men like Harold Rimes, her mother's employer, the kind of guys with a chip on their shoulder that only got bigger as they aged. Whatever the reason, Kendrick seemed to think Remmi knew more than she was telling, which, of course, she did.

"You heard shots and an explosion and saw a 'fireball' from a hiding spot in the *back* of a specially equipped old Cadillac? That's what you're saying?"

"Yes." She'd already explained, saw no reason to go over it again. Tired and worried sick, she glared at Kendrick. "You know that happened. The police and the fire department went out there. I know that. I heard the sirens. So, please, tell me. Did they find a baby? Or a . . ." Her throat had closed. "The body of an infant." Her heart had ached at the thought.

"No baby's body," Davis had interjected, and for the first time in days, Remmi had felt a glimmer of hope.

Maybe Ariel had survived. But how? And where was she?

"But you were there in your mother's car?" Kendrick again.

"Yes! You can ask me a million times, and I'll always tell you the same thing. Because it's the truth." And that part was. Still, she went over her story one more time, told him about hiding in the back of the big car, watching in horror as Didi met another car and she and a man exchanged a baby carrier for a briefcase full of money that turned out to be filled with phony bills. She told him how Didi, feeling cheated, had torn off to go somewhere, but Remmi had no idea where or how far. "She just said she was going to an appointment at a 'private residence.'"

"Whose?" Kendrick had asked.

"I told you, I don't know. She didn't say."

"And she didn't give any indication of how far away it was?"

"No. Just that it was 'out of town,' not here in Las Vegas, and that she'd be back in the morning and we could go shopping or something."

She'd seen a movement in the doorway as Detective Davis had walked out of the office and down the hallway, her footsteps barely audible. Obviously, she'd decided Remmi wasn't a flight risk. Finally. But that meant Remmi was stuck with the hard-nosed, disbelieving senior partner of the duo. Great.

"And she didn't come back or call?"

"No."

"And she left you with a kid, only a few months old, after trying to sell the other one."

"Yes!" Remmi bristled at his tone and what he was saying. She almost came out of the molded plastic chair in which she'd been told to sit, but she forced herself to remain seated. "She . . . she acted like she would get Ariel back."

"After she figured out she was paid in counterfeit bills?"

"No–I mean . . ." What did she mean? "I don't know."

"*Now* I believe you," he said with a snort.

Footsteps returned, and thankfully Davis walked in and dropped a can of Coke and a wrapped sandwich on the desk. "Here," she said to Remmi. "Ham and cheese. Not great, but trust me, it's the best we've got in the machine." Then she shot Kendrick a "back off" look and hitched her chin toward the hallway. Frowning, his desk chair creaking in protest, Kendrick met his partner outside the door that remained ajar, and they got into a heated, but muffled discussion. Remmi, popping the tab on the soda and unwrapping the sandwich, had listened hard, but over the crinkle of the plastic unfolding and the partially shut door, had managed to hear only snatches of the conversation.

Davis's voice: "Back off. Bud . . . she's just a kid."

And the response: "Doesn't matter . . . lying. I'd bet my pension on it . . ."

Davis's answer was low, but Remmi had caught. ". . . scared, and, sure, her mother . . . major flake. Owes money all over town . . ."

"What the hell's all this about selling a baby? Jesus H. Christ, now I've heard everything." Then he'd lowered his voice, as if he'd realized he might be overheard. Remmi'd wanted to walk to the doorway but didn't dare, and so, over the beat of her heart, she'd strained to listen. ". . . probably dead . . . No body, though . . . knows more than she's saying . . ."

". . . give her a break. She's fifteen. Remember what you were like at that age?"

"Oh, hell."

"Yeah, I know . . . don't press too hard. All I'm saying."

Remmi had started nibbling the sandwich, but a bite of bread, cheese, mayonnaise, and ham had stuck in her throat, a glob she had to wash down with the Coke. She should never have come here. They didn't believe her. Maybe they'd arrest her for . . . what? Withholding evidence? Lying to a police officer? They might even think she was some kind of accessory to the crime. And who were they talking about who was dead? Ariel? The babies' father? Maybe even *Didi?*

Her mind racing, she heard Kendrick say, ". . . need a smoke."

"Don't we all?" had been the reply just before Detective Davis had come into the room. Alone.

"This is gonna be okay," she said with a kind smile that didn't quite reach her eyes.

The smile is fake. She knows it won't be okay. It never will be again.

Davis had rested her slim hips against the edge of Kendrick's desk. "Is there anyone else we can call for you? The number for the woman you told us about, Seneca Williams? It's been disconnected. Do you have any relatives?"

Remmi's heart had frozen. Seneca had bailed? Left her for good? Nervously, she'd licked her lips. She had to come up with a name. Someone. Anyone. Or else she'd have to go through Social Services, or whatever it was called, and be put in foster care with strangers.

"What about your father?"

That again. "I told you, I don't know who he is. I never have. I know that sounds lame, but it's the God's honest truth. My mom never told me. And may—" she swallowed hard and whispered a truth she'd always feared, "Maybe she didn't know who he was." Remmi had always suspected that her mother had been eager to please men, and there was a good chance that she'd had more than one lover at a time and so . . .

"Okay," Davis had said without any sign of emotion or judgment. "How about an aunt or an uncle? Older cousin?"

Remmi had been sweating, and her palms were slick as she'd considered her options. In the end, she chose to go for the truth. "All I know is that Mom's from somewhere in Missouri. That's what she said. I don't know exactly where. She would never say. Like it was some big, bad secret or something, you know, as if a really bad thing had happened there. I don't know." Remmi had thought hard. "But I think she mentioned St. Louis a couple of times, and she maybe grew up on a farm. She knew farm stuff, y'know. Like 'bucking' hay, that's what she called it, and 'slopping the pigs,' stuff like that. The kind of thing you don't hear in town."

Davis had nodded, making notes. "Anything else?"

"Just that she was a cheerleader for the high school. I found her old uniform once, a long time ago. Red and white sweater. For a team called the Titans. Her name was Edwina, but the name embroidered on the sweater was 'Edie.'" She met Davis's interested gaze. "I never heard anyone call her either of those names. She always went by Didi."

"Middle name?"

"She never used it, but it was Maria. Edwina Maria Hutchinson . . . but she went by Didi Storm even when she married."

"What are her husbands' names?"

"Leo Kasparian, the magician, Kaspar the Great, was her second." Davis's eyebrows had elevated at that. "Ned Crenshaw was the first. He moved away. Montana or Colorado. Cowboy. A horse guy. Rancher," she'd said, and she felt a little bad. She'd always liked Ned. He'd been kind to her, taught her how to ride, about horses, how to appreciate a sunset. Even how to handle and shoot a rifle, a skill he'd told her he'd learned on a ranch in Wyoming. He'd been a firm stepfather, forcing Remmi to do "chores." He was decent enough, mostly even-tempered, but when he did get mad, it was a slow, smoldering fury that was mainly directed at his flirtatious wife. She'd thought Ned and Didi might actually come to blows once or twice, but they never had, as far as she knew. Remmi remembered him calling Didi "bat-shit crazy," right before she filed for divorce.

Remmi added, "Mom divorced them both." Remmi had never much liked Leo, but he had showed her some tricks and sleight of hand that she thought now might come in handy. Leo had always been out for Leo, first and foremost. As Didi had said on more than one occasion, "Leo could as easily slide a knife between your ribs as make love to you. He could probably do both at the same time and not think a thing about it."

Davis had kept scribbling as Remmi told her the sketchy details she knew about her mother's life before Didi had landed in Southern California and then Las Vegas.

"Mom called St. Louis, 'up north,' so she probably came from south of that, I guess. She never said. It's like she didn't want anything to do with her parents after she moved west." She'd shrugged, trying to remember more.

"You have their names?" she asked again.

"Frank and Willa Maye Hutchinson. And my mother had a sister, Vera, and they had a brother . . . Billy. He's in or was in the service. Army I think. I overheard my mom telling Seneca a little about him, but I only heard that he was a hunter who had gone to the military just after high school. I never met him, either."

"You had no contact with any of them?"

"That's right."

"Not even a birthday present or a Christmas card?"

Remmi had just stared at the detective.

"Okay," Davis had said, finally, it seemed, getting it. She'd ripped off the note with the names. "I'm going to contact them and see what we can do. You have to sit tight for a little while longer because," she'd added a little sadly, "you know that I have to talk to someone at Social Services. You're a minor."

Remmi had sunk farther into her chair, and though she wanted to cry, to break down and sob, she didn't. Her eyes were hot, but dry, her heart heavy, and as she heard Kendrick returning, the scent of his recently smoked cigarette surrounding him, she knew that her life as she'd known it was truly and finally over.

They asked her a million more questions about Didi—what happened in the desert, the twins, Seneca, her job with Harold Rimes at the club—and eventually had shown her a picture of Noah.

Her heart had felt as if it had collapsed in her chest. "Do you know who this is?" Kendrick had asked as she'd stared at the photograph. She'd thought about the short, heated phone conversation with his father, about how Ike Baxter was "gonna give that kid what's comin' to him." But she'd already reacted, so she screwed up her face and shook her head. "He looks kinda familiar. But . . . no, I don't know him."

"You sure? Look real hard," Kendrick pushed, eyes narrowing as if he was attempting to read her mind.

"Who–who is he?"

Davis smiled again, and once more the curve of her lips had seemed forced. "We don't know, but he was in the desert that night. No ID on him. Taken to the hospital."

"Is he okay?"

"Hell, no! He's not 'okay,'" Kendrick interjected, his lips turning down at the corners. "Shot in the neck and crashed his bike."

Shot? In the neck? Remmi nearly gasped, was able to stifle it, but she felt her face drain of color. She swallowed as she remembered hearing a motorcycle revving in the desert while Didi drove away from the exchange. *Pop, pop, pop*—the sharp report of a rifle. Aimed at Noah? What was he doing out there? Her mind had raced, her hands clenching into fists and her fingernails biting into her palms. Someone had tried to kill him? Who? Why? But, more importantly, he was alive. That's what they said, he'd survived. He wasn't "okay," but he'd made it.

"—so, I guess his injuries weren't as severe as the docs thought, because for whatever reason, before he came out of his coma and would talk to us, he decided to take a hike and release himself," Kendrick was saying. "Just walked out of Elizabeth Park Hospital in the middle of the damned night and took off."

She'd felt a drip of relief, forced herself to uncurl her fingers.

"There are security cameras, though, you know, and one of them caught him taking off, but"—he flipped a hand toward the ceiling—"then he disappeared."

Davis sent him another sharp look.

"What?" Kendrick asked her. "I'm not telling anything that isn't gonna be out there. His picture'll be in the paper tomorrow and on the news tonight. We'll be asking for the public's help. So I thought I'd start with her."

The corners of her lips had tightened, but Davis had turned her attention to Remmi and said softly, "Are you sure you don't know him?"

"Positive."

From that point, Remmi had never ever changed her story. She couldn't imagine what Noah had been doing in the desert that night, how he'd ended up in the hospital, or who would want to kill him.

Ike Baxter.

The name had cut through her. But if he'd shot his stepson, he wouldn't be making threats to unknown girls who called, would he? Wouldn't he have acted more concerned, pretended like he was worried?

The police had kept Remmi, prodding her and asking her questions until a willowy woman with dishwater-blond hair and a slight overbite, Miss Evelyn Connors from Social Services, had shown up wearing a prim navy suit, what Didi had called "sensible shoes," a crisp white blouse, and a small silver cross swinging from a thin chain circling her long neck. Miss Evelyn, as she'd insisted upon being called, came with a broad smile and "Praise the Lord," because of the happy news that they'd located Remmi's aunt. Not only that, but Aunt Vera and her husband, Milo, were willing to take in Vera's sister's abandoned daughter and become Remmi's official foster parents.

"It's perfect," Miss Evelyn exclaimed, her long-boned fingers clasped together almost as if she were praying.

As it turned out, not so "perfect," Remmi thought now, as she walked from the wet street into the parking garage, which was near a small boutique hotel and located her ten-year-old Subaru Outback. But she wasn't going to think about the intervening years now, that particularly bleak part of her life she'd endured under Aunt Vera's overly religious thumb, Uncle Milo's cold disinterest, and her two randy cousins' off-color jokes and leering eyes.

She shuddered at the thought as she slipped behind the wheel (long legal now as she'd gotten her license while under her aunt and uncle's care) and reminded herself to forget about them all. If she could. Because now, it seemed, she might have to deal with them again, and the thought gave her a severe case of heartburn.

"No, thank you," she muttered under her breath as she drove onto the hilly, rain-slickened street. No wonder Didi had never spoken to them. She threaded her car through the heavy traffic and headed for the Thomas J. Cahill Hall of Justice on Bryant Street, where investigations of suicide and murder took place.

CHAPTER 12

"Didi Storm?" Detective Jorge Martinez asked when he slid into the passenger side of the Ford Crown Victoria, one of the sedans in the city's fleet. "Who the hell is Didi Storm?"

Dani Settler, Martinez's partner, was already behind the steering wheel and twisting on the ignition. She waited as a uniformed officer removed the barrier so they could pull out of the spot they'd secured at the base of Montmort Tower three hours earlier, just before the Jane Doe had taken a swan dive off the nineteenth-floor ledge.

Settler shivered inwardly at the memory as she'd seen the woman step into the thick San Franciscan twilight, then plummet to her death.

"The victim looked like her."

With a glance up at the tower Martinez prodded, "Again, who is she?"

"Seriously?" Dani snapped back to the present and stared at her partner as if he'd grown horns. "Where the hell have you been?"

"On vacation," he reminded her. At five-seven, he

wasn't quite as tall as Dani, but he had her by about forty pounds of muscle and had been with the department for twenty of his forty-six years. A family man, Jorge had a wife and three kids, all of whom were currently giving him the silver visible in his clipped black hair.

"Well, still . . . you must've been hiding under a damned rock."

He pulled the Crown Vic's door shut. "I was in Cabo. You know that."

She did.

"Wish I was still there," he grumbled. "I hated to come back to this crap."

"C'mon, Martinez, you know you love it."

"If you say so. But I'm gonna retire down there, you watch me. Get a condo with an ocean view, drink margaritas on the beach, fish when I want to."

When pigs fly, she thought, but decided not to argue further. As the officer waved them through, Settler eased into the uneven flow of traffic, the lights of the city swimming through low-hanging November clouds, the streets wet and shimmering, Christmas lights and decorations visible in storefronts, as the season was fast approaching.

Martinez and Settler were heading back to the station. They'd spent most of the day in the hotel room from which the victim, who had registered as D. Storm, had leaped.

"You were saying," Martinez prodded. "About our jumper? Didi, whatever."

"Storm." She took a quick left, beating the light as she headed back to the station. "Didi Storm is, like, everywhere right now, even trending on the Internet, I think."

"Why? Again, who is she?"

"Back in the day, she was a celebrity impersonator."

"I thought guys did that," Martinez said, wiping the condensation from the inside of the passenger window.

"You know what I'm talkin' about, the dudes with the fake boobs and wigs and makeup. I never have figured out how they hide their junk. Can't be easy."

"Well, you're right. It's not easy being a woman," she said dryly.

He snorted, but his lips twitched in his goatee. "Especially for a guy."

"Don't be so sexist." She turned on the defrost to clear the windshield. "Women can be impersonators, and Didi Storm had her own show in Vegas, years back. She wasn't an A-lister, but she did okay, and then she disappeared."

"How do you know that?"

"Because as I said, she's everywhere right now. Not literally, of course, but there's a book out, kind of a tell-all about her life that hypothesizes about what happened to her, if she's alive or dead, that kind of thing. And with the book come articles online and in papers. A buzz." She went on to explain about the unusual case, rumored to have involved the selling of babies, explosions rocking the desert, and Didi Storm's disappearance.

"Okay."

"I have a copy." With her eyes on the road, she reached behind the passenger seat and into her open bag to pull out the hardback of *I'm Not Me,* with the subtitle *The Untold Didi Storm Story*. The cover was a closeup of Didi's face, one side made up to look like Marilyn Monroe, her perfect features appearing to be ripped in half as part of the artwork, the other side a stripped-down picture of Didi Storm.

"You read it?"

Signaling for the next turn, she nodded. "Uh-huh. Finished it last night."

"Good?"

"Kept my interest, and now . . ."

"Yeah. That's weird, isn't it? The book comes out and

then . . . huh." He scratched at his goatee. "I thought for a second when I saw the victim, she was damned Marilyn Monroe—"

"Who's been dead over fifty years."

"Even so, at least I knew who she was. This Didi Storm?" He was shaking his head and lifting his shoulders. "And for sure, I wouldn't buy any book about her."

"You wouldn't buy a book unless it was about fishing."

"Well, yeah. Maybe."

"There's no 'maybe' about it. But other people, like me, would pick it up because her case is interesting. And that's not all, there's even talk of a made-for-TV movie about her."

"How do you know?"

"Because when you were busy wrapping things up with the M.E., I checked the Internet on my phone."

He was finally engaged, his eyebrows drawing together. "So why would she jump now? If she's suddenly famous, why—"

"It's not her," she said. A snarl of traffic was visible ahead, and she cut across two lanes and took a sharp turn to avoid the congestion. The street was narrow and steep, cars parked on either side as huge skyscrapers knifed into the low-hanging clouds.

"I thought you said it was. And there's the wig."

Not only had the victim been dressed in vintage clothes and a short platinum-blond wig, but inscribed within the skullcap of the wig was the name Didi Storm, bold as you like. But there was no other identification in her hotel room, just a small suitcase with a pair of pajamas and makeup. Not even a purse or wallet, though the clerk at the desk swore he'd seen a California driver's license, or at least he thought so, but when pressed, he wasn't able to clearly remember the name on it, nor did he take a copy.

He just recalled that it was busy when she checked in, he was stressed, and the license seemed legit.

"I said it looked like her." Edging into the other lane, she worked her way around a van that was double-parked. Traffic today seemed even worse than normal. She asked, "But how old do you think the victim was?"

"Forty, maybe forty-five."

"Didi would be in her fifties now. Unless she found the damned fountain of youth, she's not Didi Storm."

"Some people age well."

"Not *that* well."

"How could you tell? She was pretty . . . y'know, broken up," he said, frowning as he mentioned the body. "These days there's all kinds of plastic surgery or injections. Botox, whatever. Ten years isn't that much. Some people look twenty years younger than they are."

"Fine. Wanna bet that retirement condo in Cabo on it?"

"Sure."

"Okay. Fingerprints will be in soon. We'll see if the victim is in the system."

"And if she's this Didi Storm?"

She slowed for a stoplight, waiting as pedestrians in coats, hoods, and umbrellas hurried across the street, the crackle of the police-band radio in the background. "If it's Didi, and I'm not saying it is, why would she jump now? Why, when there's a book out about you, when you've always been looking for fame, would you kill yourself?" She couldn't imagine the desperation or the horror of one's life that would make leaping from a tall building seem like the only answer.

"Maybe she didn't mean to jump."

"You mean like a publicity stunt gone wrong?"

He shrugged. "Maybe."

"That would fit. From what I read, she was a drama queen, one who wasn't afraid of much."

"You got that from the book?"

"I read between the lines," she said, turning up the tempo of the wipers as the drizzle turned to a steady rainfall and a trolley, people packed inside, clanged its way up the hill. "It interested me, so I looked her up online."

"And?"

"A publicity stunt would be right up her alley, but this . . . I don't know. Who would stand on a ledge nearly twenty stories over the city just to garner attention? She was flamboyant, always played to an audience. From what I've read, she wouldn't be one to just quietly take some pills; she'd want to go out with a splash." She shook her head. "Then again, she was into self-preservation. A fighter."

"You know a lot about her."

"I hadn't thought about her for years, then I pick up a book and do a little digging and—"

"Splat. She lands at your feet."

She grimaced. "You don't have to be so graphic."

"Just tellin' it like it is."

"But I don't think it's her."

"Just someone who's impersonating a missing impersonator and takes a flying leap to . . . ? I dunno, Dani, doesn't make a lot of sense to me."

"Me, neither," she had to admit.

"Why did she disappear in the first place?"

"The big question. She had a child that year, that much is known, but there're rumors that there were two babies, a boy and a girl, both gone. I read about the case years ago, when I was a teenager. It was in all the newspapers at the time, and so I scanned a few of those articles again, a couple of days ago, after reading the book." Dani Settler had been fascinated with crime and criminals since she was an adolescent and a kidnap victim, one who had managed to survive her cruel captor. Once the trauma of her ordeal had ebbed a bit, she'd decided she'd become a cop, and she'd devoured every true-crime book she could get her hands on. She'd never wavered from that goal, and after college and a master's degree, she'd been hired by the San Francisco Police Department.

The traffic light turned green, and she stepped on the gas, narrowly missing a jogger who'd run against the light. She and the car next to her slammed on their brakes just in time.

"Holy cats!" Martinez braced himself on the dash as their seat belts tightened.

"Lucky idiot," she muttered, carefully touching the gas again. As she turned into the parking structure for the department, Martinez said, "It's your turn," reminding her of the ongoing deal they had about catching a late lunch. Whenever a case called for unexpectedly long hours, one of them picked up sandwiches from their favorite deli. He was right; tonight, it was her turn. "Roast beef with extra horseradish, and don't let them forget I need a pickle. Sometimes they forget."

"Really? In this rain? You expect me to go out?"

"Really. Yeah."

She parked, then tossed him the keys. "Coffee?"

"Two sugars."

"I know. I got it. You just take care of the car."

As he checked in the city's Ford, she walked the two blocks through the increasing rainfall to Sammy's Deli, where she picked up the two sandwiches and heard a little of the local gossip from the small tables crammed near the windows. As she waited for her order, she heard bits of conversation—a couple of women talking about their teenage daughters, two men discussing the San Francisco Giants' future, and a group of four discussing the leaper at the Montmort Tower, though she didn't hear Didi Storm's name.

By the time she'd returned to the police station, her raincoat was shedding water, and the white sacks, holding their lunches were starting to fall apart. She hung her raincoat on the hall tree near her desk.

Water dripped onto the floor, and she caught a glance from one of the senior detectives, Ted Vance, ten years older than she and always ready to impart his great wisdom from years of experience on the job. He also was a neatnik who frowned on any sort of lapse in protocol or etiquette and wasn't afraid to show his displeasure. The tiny pool of water collecting on the floor was sure to get under his skin.

"Are you going to deal with that?" he asked, looking at her over the tops of half-glasses.

"Yeah."

"Someone could slip."

"Thanks for the heads-up." She tried and failed to keep the sarcasm out of her voice, but really, she didn't need a father figure nor anyone looking over her shoulder and pointing out her faults.

"You're welcome." Vance smiled, and his dark eyes glinted. He knew he'd gotten to her. "Again."

She sent him a brittle smile in return. She didn't need this. She was already testy from the long day and lack of food. She dropped one sack and a cup of coffee onto Martinez's desk, then settled into her own chair and dived into a turkey on sourdough. As she ate, she checked her e-mails, and looked for any report on the leaper, whom she still thought of as Jane Doe.

She wasn't buying into the quick ID as Didi Storm, despite the hotel clerk, the registration, and the wig with her name scribbled inside. There was also a suicide angle to consider. It seemed that way from all of the witness accounts, but it was too early to make that call. The police department was looking at footage of the last seconds of the woman's life. It appeared as if she'd been alone in her room, had stepped onto the ledge, and, after waiting until a crowd had gathered, stepped into the thick San Francisco night, plummeting to her death before the rescue workers could storm the room and the surrounding rooms or create any kind of safety device, such as a giant air mattress, on the ground below. Still, Settler wasn't convinced of the obvious conclusion. She had to make sure that Jane Doe/Didi Storm hadn't somehow been helped along in her decision to take a flying leap to her death.

She'd called the Las Vegas Police Department and found that the detective who had been in charge of the missing person case involving Didi Storm had left the force five years earlier. Settler had been told that his partner, Senior Detective Lucretia Davis, would call her back. Davis had been the junior partner on the case, so Settler had left her number, turned to her lunch, and had just finished half her sandwich when she spied Demetrius Brown, a beat cop, walking along the short aisle between the cubicles to her desk. A step behind him, also heading her way, was a woman who looked to be in her early thirties. Around five-six, with brown hair scraped into a ponytail, and green eyes that seemed to take in the entire room at once, she wore slim jeans, boots, a thick sweater, and a jacket with the belt unbuckled. She was tense, lips compressed, and kept up with Brown, who was tall and lanky, with the long stride of the pro baseball player he'd once been.

Her gaze found Dani's before they were introduced, and her expression said that she meant business.

"You've got a visitor," Brown said, motioning to the woman at his side. "Ms. Storm." To the woman, he said, "Detective Settler. She's the one you're looking for." His gaze slid back to Dani, eyebrows arching almost imperceptibly, a silent warning that all might not be as it seemed, silently conveying that this woman might not be a straight shooter.

Ms. Storm? Dani looked the woman over curiously.

He went on, "Ms. Storm claims she might be the daughter of our Jane Doe from yesterday."

Ms. Storm clarified, "The apparent suicide victim. I'm Remmi Storm. My mother is . . . Didi Storm."

CHAPTER 13

"We don't have an ID on the victim yet," Settler admitted, but she was all ears. If Remmi Storm, slim and confident even in these circumstances, had information on the leaper, all the better.

"I figured that when he," Remmi hitched her chin toward Brown, "called her Jane Doe. Maybe I can help with that. I was there. I saw it happen." Remmi paled a bit. "But as I said, I think . . . I think she might be my mother."

"You were there?" Dani asked, more interested. "To visit her?"

"No. That's the weird part—well, one of the weird parts of it. It was totally random."

"Do you live or work nearby?"

"Yes. I moved here about ten years ago," she said. "And I work mainly from home."

"Doing?" Settler prodded.

Remmi hesitated. "I work for Greta Emerson, at her home. I'm her assistant."

"Doing what?"

"She's a widow and owns a large home near Mount Sutro. I keep the place up and handle her books. She rents out rooms in the house as well as other properties in the city, so I collect the rent and pay the bills as well as see that she's cared for by a rotating staff."

"How long have you worked for her?"

"About five, no, now almost six years. Before that I worked in offices, insurance, bookkeeping, technical stuff." She handed the detective her card with her street address, e-mail address, and a couple of phone numbers.

"So you were near the Montmort building because . . ." Settler prodded, pocketing the business card.

"I found out that the agent for the person who wrote the book on Didi actually worked in the city, just a block or two from the Montmort. I wanted to talk to her, to ask about whoever had done all this research on my mother. I was on my way there."

"It was after five."

"I wanted to surprise her as she was leaving, as I had called and she wouldn't see me. On the way, I got distracted," Remmi said, drawing a careful breath. "My mother and I are estranged. I mean, I haven't heard from her in twenty years, and I didn't know if she was dead or alive, and then, then yesterday . . ." She shook her head. "It's all so unbelievable."

"Why don't you start at the beginning," Dani suggested. "Sit down." She indicated a chair near the side of her desk, and Remmi slid into it. "Do you want something? Water? Coffee? A soda?"

"No, no. I'm okay." But she didn't look okay. In fact, she'd paled since approaching Dani's desk.

She took in a long breath, seemed to give herself a quick mental shake. "Years ago, my mother, Didi, worked in Las Vegas; she had had her own act—impressions, singing, a little magic, that kind of thing—and she did a spot-on impersonation of Marilyn Monroe, back in the day."

Settler listened and took notes, though she knew most of the story. She just wanted to hear this woman's rendition of it. She didn't doubt that the woman was Remmi Storm; she'd seen pictures of her as a teen, and yes, this woman was one and the same.

"This all happened twenty years ago." She met the detective's gaze. "But I think you already know that."

"I do. I read the book."

"Oh." Remmi's eyes shuttered a bit.

"I take it you don't approve."

She grimaced. "No one interviewed me for the story, and I think that's kind of weird. I mean, there's always been speculation, and every once in a while, I read something online about Mom . . . do you know she has a fan club now? With a Facebook page?"

"We haven't gotten that far."

"Well, it's true. So there have been articles about her on and off, nothing serious, but then this book comes out and . . . and she's more famous than when she was . . . when she had her act. I tried writing the 'author' through her website and her own Facebook page, but it all looks fake to me."

"Fake?"

"Like the author has a pseudonym or a ghostwriter, I guess you could say. Maryanne Osgoode. Not a real person. At least I can't find a picture or mention of her, other than the studio shot at the back of the book and another more casual photograph on the website with two dogs, French bulldogs. The website itself is very bland, tells you nothing. Says she's from 'California,' but that's pretty vague considering the size of the state, and that she lives with her husband and two dogs, which, by the way, are in the only other picture." She thought for a second, then said, "So when I found out the agent who represents the writer is from San Francisco, I went to meet her, like I said, to surprise her, and then I walked past the Montmort Tower . . ."

"That's a helluva coincidence," Settler said, leaning back in her chair.

"That's what I thought." She swallowed. "The agency is just three buildings down, and since every time I called, I got a recording, and no one responded to my e-mails, I decided to just show up. So I was on my way, and there was this crowd gathered and I . . . I saw her jump."

"Jesus," Brown, who was still standing nearby, whispered.

Settler kept on point. "And you think it was your mother?"

"I–I'm not sure. It would be like Didi, to want to make a big splash and go out with a bang, but not after all this time of being in hiding. And she would have played to the crowd more than . . . than the victim did. So, no, I don't think it's my mom, and I don't want to think it." She squared her slim shoulders. "But I want to see her. The body, I mean. I have to. And then . . . And then I'll know for sure."

"After all this time?"

"Yes." Remmi Storm seemed more certain of that fact than of anything since she'd started talking.

"You have the name of that agency?"

"The Reliant Agency. Jennifer Reliant is the agent of record, but it seems pretty fly-by-night to me," she admitted. "Everything about the book and the small publishing house seems off. And there's not much about Jennifer Reliant or the agency on the Internet that I can find. Seems like a one-woman operation, if that."

"Meaning you're not sure it exists?"

"Meaning I have yet to talk to a real person or get a response from one, just some kind of answering service, I think, so that doesn't say a lot."

Brown had been lingering. His cell phone chirped, and Dani met his gaze. "I've got this," she said and he took the hint and answered his phone as he walked away.

As he left, Remmi reached into the pocket of her jacket and pulled out two pictures, worn and faded, both of which she handed to Dani.

"These are of your mother?"

"Yeah, both of them were taken about a year before she left, I think," she said, and there was a trace of bitterness in her tone. Settler hadn't seen either of the photographs before. There were some black-and-white shots in the book, but not either of these. And she'd seen pictures of Didi Storm on the Internet; these were different, personal.

"When was the last time you talked to her?"

"The night she took off."

"Twenty years ago?"

"She said she'd be back in the morning."

"And she never returned?"

A shake of the head, ponytail bobbing, mouth even tighter. "She just disappeared." Dani guessed the woman sitting so rigidly across her desk was in her mid-thirties. If that were the case, then she'd been a teenager when the mother had vanished.

Settler studied the two photos. One was of a Marilyn Monroe look-alike and the other of a woman of about thirty-five with darker hair and little makeup. With even features, devious eyes, and a little, almost naughty smile, she was staring at the photographer and hoisting a half-full martini glass.

Could this woman in the photo be the Jane Doe who

was lying in the morgue, her body broken from a near twenty-story fall to hard pavement? There was a definite resemblance, but Settler didn't think so.

"So, in the intervening years, you were with your dad?"

A quick shake of the head. "Nope. Out of the picture." Her demeanor suggested the subject of her father was taboo. But Settler left it for now. She knew firsthand how messy family dynamics could be. She had a stepmother and a couple of half siblings to prove it. But if it was important to the case, Remmi and Didi's relationship with Dear Old Dad would have to be put under a microscope—especially if the victim did, in fact, turn out to be the missing Didi Storm.

Which she was still betting against, despite the resemblance of the photographs to the victim. "What happened then? You had to have been in your teens when she left."

A beat. For a second, Settler thought Remmi Storm was going to lie. "I went to live with my aunt. My mother's sister, Vera, and her family. I hadn't even met them before I moved in," she added. "I hadn't met anyone in my family. My mother and her parents weren't close and never spoke, as far as I knew. Same with Vera, but since I was a minor, Social Services located Vera and her husband, Milo. They agreed to take me in, but I only lived with them for a couple of years."

"And the rest of the family?"

"No. My grandparents were still in Missouri, a place called Anderstown; my aunt filled me in. She let me know that they'd passed on a few years ago. I have an uncle, too. Billy. He was in the military, I think, and is probably out by now. But I have no idea and really, no interest. They were all strangers to me."

So far, Remmi's story fit with what Settler already

knew. She'd decided to keep her information on Didi
Storm to herself and let the other woman talk and see if
what she told deviated from what Settler believed to be
fact. So far, Remmi Storm hadn't outwardly lied. When
Settler asked about the baby, her half sibling, Remmi corrected her and said there were actually two, a boy and
girl, who would be going on twenty-one—nearly adults,
if they'd survived. Talk of her infant brother and sister
seemed to sadden her, and she insisted that one, the girl,
Ariel, had been left in the desert with her father, though
he thought he was getting a boy, for a quarter of a million
dollars, which he had paid with what had turned out to be
largely fraudulent bills. The boy had been left with Remmi,
then stolen by Seneca Williams, a midwife who, too, had
disappeared. Remmi feared the little girl had died in the
desert when the car her father had been driving had exploded.

"I don't know exactly what went down that night," she
admitted. "I heard gunshots, saw the explosion, and heard
later from the police that a kid on a motorbike, Noah
Scott, had been shot out there, too. Before they could interview him, he left the hospital. How it all ties in? I don't
know."

"Where's Noah Scott now?" Settler asked.

"I don't know."

"A whole lotta people just up and disappeared back
then."

"Yeah," Remmi agreed. "And now . . ." She let her
voice trail off, then expelled a long sigh. "Look, before
we go any further, I think we should find out if the victim
is my mom. Otherwise, this is all pointless."

"I have pictures."

"I want to see the body." Remmi visibly braced herself, her jaw setting. The determined glint to her eyes

suggested she wasn't about to be dissuaded or even that she suspected Settler or maybe the police in general might try to pull a fast one.

"You sure?"

"Absolutely."

"I have to be honest with you. This won't be easy. The body's not in great shape."

"I get it. I was there, and I did catch a glimpse of her before the cops pushed the crowd back. I assume you need to know if the woman is Didi, and you realize I'll be able to recognize my own mother."

Or not. Settler found several pictures taken at the scene before the body of the Jane Doe had been examined by the M.E. Her gauzy pink dress was bunched around her waist, the blond wig askew, her arms and legs at weird angles, blood pooled beneath it all, but at least this side of the angelic-looking face was unmarred; the other side was crushed by the impact. Settler handed two of the least gory shots to Remmi.

Remmi sucked in a quick breath and visibly cringed. All the color drained from her face, but she gritted her teeth and forced herself to study the pictures. "Why would anyone do this?" she whispered, then said, "I . . . I can't tell. Not from these."

"How about the clothes? Was that dress part of her costume when she impersonated Marilyn Monroe?"

"It looks like it, yes, but there have to be dozens, hundreds of knockoffs."

"What about the wig?"

"What about it? It's a short blond wig. Mom had several."

"Did she put her name in them?"

"I believe so."

Dani handed over another picture, this one a blowup of

the skullcap, with the name Didi Storm scrawled across the inside in her distinctive, loopy style.

Remmi stared at the picture. Her throat worked. "That's her signature. She labeled all of her things herself with a permanent laundry marker, and she'd laugh and tell me that when she was famous, all her things, signed as they were, would be worth a fortune." Clearing her throat, she added, "But someone could have bought it on eBay or in a nostalgia store. She sold some of her things before she left—things she'd quit wearing, you know, when she'd updated her costume wardrobe. She'd sell something or pawn them when money got really tight, which, unfortunately was pretty often." Her lips folded in on themselves as she stared at the photograph of the wig. "You have this—here?"

"Yes. If it's not already in an evidence locker, it will be soon. As soon as the crime-scene techs have processed it. Same with her clothes and personal belongings."

"I'd like to see them."

"When I can get them," Settler promised. "Sure." What would it hurt?

"I need to verify if it's really hers, if I can," Remmi said. "I'd know her signature, and it looks authentic, and—" She shook her head, as if clearing cobwebs, then handed the pictures back, her gaze locking with Settler's. "Why would anyone do this?"

"Dress up as Marilyn Monroe and jump?"

"Dress up as my mother *impersonating* Marilyn Monroe. Not only do the clothes look like they came from Mom's wardrobe, but see, this, the left hand—" She held the photo back so that Settler was looking at it. "The ring finger has one of Mom's rings on it, and more than that, the fingernail is painted black. That was her signature, not Marilyn Monroe's—at least, I don't think so. If Mom

ever wore black nail polish, like for Halloween or something, she'd paint that finger orange or red or something
else. She always kept that fingernail a different color."
She let out her breath slowly and said, "What I really
need to do is to see her. The woman who jumped. For
myself. *I* need to know if she's my mother." She shot Settler a look. "I can handle it," she said evenly, and the detective wondered what else this woman had seen that
made her so certain she could deal with viewing what
might be her own mother's broken body.

Dani nodded, grabbing her phone, though she didn't
believe all of Remmi's story and intended to do a little
checking on the woman herself—who knew what kind of
nut job she could be—Settler's first instinct was to trust
her. As to the mother? Even though Settler didn't person-
ally think that the dead woman was Didi Storm, it was
time to find out.

A pie-in-the-sky condo in Cabo was riding on it.

CHAPTER 14

"**S**he's not my mother." Remmi felt a rush of relief as she turned away from the body lying on the gurney. Most of the blood had been cleaned away from the abrasions on the victim's skin, and enough of the facial features were intact for her to know that the woman lying dead beneath the sheet was not her mother. "It's not Didi."

She walked into the hallway and took a deep breath of air, but still she felt as if the smell of death lingered in her nostrils. It was all in her mind, she told herself, the woman hadn't been dead long enough for any kind of stench to have started, and the body was kept cool.

It was all just too much, and with Detective Settler and her partner, Martinez, following, she made her way out of the morgue and into the night. Her stomach lurched, and she eyed the surrounding shrubbery, but she didn't throw up, just braced herself with a hand on the cool wall of the building as rain misted around them.

"You okay?" Settler asked.

Remmi straightened. "Of course not." What kind of stupid question was that? Now that the shock of viewing the dead woman was receding, she had a million questions. "The woman in there"—she jabbed a finger at the door of the building—"isn't my mother, but she was wearing Didi's clothes and wig. Who is she? Why would she jump off a damned ledge? What does this have to do with Mom?" she asked, the questions pouring out of her. "This . . . this has to be tied to the book, right? I mean, it can't be a coincidence?" The rain was blowing against her face, dampening her hair, but she didn't care. She couldn't imagine why anyone would dress herself up like Marilyn Monroe in Didi's clothes and wig, step onto a window ledge, and leap to the ground below.

"We don't know."

"There's a reason this is all coming out now," Remmi said, brushing rain from her face with her sleeve. "Someone's behind it."

"Do you have any idea who?" Detective Settler asked.

"Probably someone who has something to do with that damned book," Remmi said. "Like I said, that's just too much of a coincidence." She had some ideas, of course, but she had no proof, so she didn't mention them. Until she knew more, she wouldn't give away any of her unfounded suspicions.

As she left the detectives, she walked three blocks to her car through the rain. She flipped up the hood of her jacket and told herself that tomorrow, come hell or high water, she was going to talk to Maryanne Osgoode's agent and find out who the author of the book really was. That was a start. It might lead nowhere, but she had to do something.

She heard footsteps behind her and, glancing back, saw several people through a curtain of rain. Dark, watery shapes following her. Men or women, she couldn't tell; they were all bundled in black, gray, or navy blue parkas or coats.

It's the city. That happens. No big deal. Just other pedestrians.

But she felt a chill that had nothing to do with the cold weather slide down her spine, and she quickened her pace, looking back once more and realizing that only one tall figure was still behind her. A man, she was sure, and he was quickening his pace.

It's nothing. Nothing. He's just hurrying to get out of the rain.

Still, she jogged the remaining half block to the corner, where she had parked her car. She unlocked the door remotely and slid behind the wheel as she yanked the door closed. The instant the door of her Subaru was shut, she locked all of the doors and let out a breath.

Stop being so paranoid.

Ignoring her own advice, she started the Subaru and hit the gas, pulling out just as a truck rounded the corner and blasted her with its horn. Narrowly missing her, it careened down the street, and she hit the gas, one tire splashing through a puddle as she overcorrected, her heart pounding.

"It's nothing, it's nothing, it's nothing," she insisted, but kept an eye on her rearview mirror and watched as traffic closed in around her. If anyone was following her now, she wouldn't be able to tell, but she felt safer in the flow of cars, buses, trucks, and vans than she had walking on the wet city streets.

Rather than taking a direct route, Remmi zigzagged across the city, even going so far as to cut through Golden Gate Park before finally edging up the hill to her home near Mount Sutro. Once or twice, she was certain a black or dark gray SUV was following her, but she couldn't be sure as the vehicle hung back and then disappeared.

Her heart pounded as she made a quick left turn, pulled into an alley, and reversed, heading the opposite direction. No SUV or car or van followed, and she let out her breath. Why was she being so paranoid anyway? So a woman who looked like her mother plunged in a suicide leap to her death. That was upsetting. Yes. Unnerving. But it certainly didn't mean that someone was following her.

It was all just a weird coincidence.

Letting out her breath and checking the mirror regularly to insure no one was tailing her, she drove up the steep, snaking street to a three-story Craftsman home perched near the top of the hill. "Home sweet home," she whispered, pulling into the narrow side driveway and setting the emergency brake before climbing out of the car and dashing up wide steps to a broad front porch, where the skeletal remains of a once-lush clematis trailed along the rail. Her feet rang on the old floorboards leading to a huge double door with leaded-glass inserts. Using her key, she stepped into the grand foyer of the massive home that was constructed three years after the historic earthquake of 1906. It had survived others since then, including the huge tremor of '89.

"Hello?" a female voice called from beyond the parlor as the scent of lavender potpourri reached Remmi's nostrils. "Remmi?" The familiar whirring sound of Greta's electric wheelchair accompanied a surprisingly strong voice for a woman in her nineties. "Is that you?"

"Yeah, I'm home." She hung her raincoat on the hall tree opposite a wide staircase that swept to the upper floors, as Turtles, a slim tortoise-shell cat did figure eights between her feet.

"Hi, to you, too," she said, bending over and petting the cat's mottled head. Turtles was one of Greta's three house cats and was always quick to greet any newcomers.

In her motorized wheelchair, Greta Emerson zipped in through an archway leading from the dining area and whipped across the ancient Persian carpet that had covered the hardwood floors of the parlor for over half a century.

"I heard!" She stopped the wheelchair in the foyer. "Oh, my God, is that woman, the one who jumped from the Montmort Tower, Didi?" Her eyes were bright behind rimless glasses, her cloud of bluish hair sprayed stiffly in place, her pointed chin turned upward. "I was watching the local news, and they said the woman who jumped, she was dressed like Marilyn Monroe, and I immediately thought of your missing mother."

Greta, over the years, had pieced together Remmi's history, partially from what Remmi had admitted, but also from a deep curiosity, lots of empty hours in the day, and computer skills few people of her age had acquired. There was a slim chance Greta knew more about Didi's disappearance, or at least the theories surrounding what had happened to the Las Vegas showgirl, than Remmi did. Remmi suspected, though Greta had never admitted it, that Greta was a member of Facebook groups or Internet chat rooms dedicated to unsolved mysteries and Didi Storm. A smart woman who had defied her generation and become a lawyer, Greta Emerson was a stalwart believer in FDR, Jack Kennedy, and all human rights and wasn't afraid to make her opinions known. An Agatha Christie buff, and a consummate believer in many conspiracies, Greta was keenly interested in Remmi's mother and the question of what had happened to her.

Greta said now, "The newsperson—not the anchor, mind you—was reporting from the base of the tower, near the fountain. She said the body hadn't been identified, but that the woman was dressed as Marilyn Monroe, someone impersonating her."

"That's true."

"You were in the area, yes?"

Remmi nodded.

"Oh, dear Lord, you didn't witness—"

"Afraid so."

"Oh my. Oh my." Another question was poised on her lips.

Remmi answered before being asked, "It wasn't Mom. That's why I'm late. I went to the police station. I insisted upon viewing the body."

Greta was shaking her head. "I can't believe it."

"It was hard. That poor woman . . . Why? I just can't get over why anyone would . . . do what she did."

Greta waved Remmi into a chair. "Are you all right?"

Remmi dropped into one of two floral wingbacks positioned near a massive, mostly unused fireplace, its broad mantel covered with framed photos of Greta and her family. "No, probably not," she admitted, trying to push the disturbing image of the dead woman from her mind, "But I will be."

"Maybe you need some hot tea."

"At the very least."

Greta's eyebrows shot up, and her pale eyes sparkled. "I've got whiskey."

"No, really. I'm fine."

Disbelieving her, Greta whipped over to the portable bar, found a dusty bottle of bourbon, and poured them each a drink.

"Now," she said, balancing the glasses as the liquor sloshed while she rolled back across the carpet to Remmi's chair. "Tell me. And don't leave out a thing." She handed a short glass to Remmi, clicked the rim of her drink to Remmi's, then took a long swallow. "Aaaah. There we go. That's more like it," she said with a happy sigh.

Remmi sipped more slowly, the aged bourbon burning

a trail down her throat as she explained about seeing the woman on the ledge, about hearing the speculation that it might be her mother, how she'd been horrified as the woman had jumped, then decided to visit the police station, telling her story to Detective Danielle Settler and insisting on ending up in the morgue. "And the weird thing," Remmi said, swirling the amber liquor in her glass, "is that the victim was dressed in Didi's things. I know because Didi marked them all, and sure enough, the wig had Mom's signature inside. And this woman—whoever she is—wanted people to think she was Didi, not Marilyn or someone else because she did everything my mom did, down to the fingernail polish; the ring finger on her left hand was colored differently from the others. That was Didi's signature."

"But . . . why?" Greta's features were drawn together as she thought, her glass empty.

"Don't know."

"Does it have something to do with that book? *I'm Not Me?* Good Lord, what a stupid title."

Remmi almost laughed. "I think it must have something to do with the publication. Why else now?"

Her lips pursed, Greta wheeled over to the drinks cabinet again. "Another?" she asked, eyeing the open backgammon board on a nearby table, but for once not suggesting a match.

Remmi shook her head, the alcohol warm in her empty stomach. As Greta poured herself another couple of shots and asked questions, Remmi filled her in as best she could.

"Any chance this woman didn't jump? That she was, you know, helped along?" Greta asked.

"You mean pushed?"

"Yes. Either physically or psychologically?"

"I guess we won't know until she's identified. The police should be able to figure that out if it was physical. It didn't look that way to me, but it was foggy, and there were curtains behind her and . . ." In her mind's eye, she saw that terrible leap once more, and she shuddered inside as she remembered the dull thud of the body hitting the wet cement. Catching Greta watching her, she said, "There were dozens of cell phones taking pictures of the woman. And the hotel has to have cameras everywhere. It's just too early to know." Remmi shivered at the thought and decided another drink might be in order. She pushed herself to her feet and, at the drinks cabinet, poured another shot and took a long swallow.

"It's all so very, very bizarre," Greta said.

What about my life hasn't been?

Greta added, "We just have to find out about this woman, to whom she was linked, how anyone might profit from either her death or from the publicity about it, you know, for the book."

"I know, but I never made it to the agent's office." She finished the rest of her drink, and for the first time noticed two gold eyes peering at her from behind a pillow on the sofa. Ghost. Greta's shy, gray, long-tailed cat that Greta claimed was a Russian Blue and was forever hiding. "Tomorrow I'll go there," she vowed, studying the remaining drop of liquid in the bottom of the glass.

"Yes, tomorrow." Greta finished her last drink as well. "I'm going to do some research." As Remmi turned toward the foyer and the stairs, Greta said, "Wait. Just a minute. Come with me." She buzzed through the dining room and butler's pantry. Remmi grabbed her coat and followed through a large kitchen and past an ancient butcher block island, then turned down a hallway that passed under the stairway and led to Greta's private quarters, a small sitting room, study, bedroom, and bath. Greta was already through the French doors to her den, where she grabbed a book from the corner of a massive desk. The room was large, nearly a library, with floor-to-ceiling bookshelves and a large window overlooking an overgrown backyard.

Handing Remmi a copy of *I'm Not Me*, Greta said, "Here you go. I figured you wouldn't buy this, just on principle, but you need to read it."

"I was going to stop by the bookstore tomorrow."

"Saved you the trouble." Greta poked a manicured fingernail on the cover. "Maybe you can figure out who's behind it without getting a court order." She laughed and glanced at a large framed picture of a stern-looking man that sat upon the desk he'd once used. Judge Duncan Emerson, her late husband, the "love of my life but definitely not my 'soul mate,' whatever drivel that is." Turtles had followed them into the study and, spying Greta, looked up, then leaped onto the old woman's lap.

"Oh, you," Greta said, her eyes twinkling as she stroked him along his neck and nape, and the cat settled, purring loudly, onto Greta's lap.

Remmi thanked her for the book, then walked past Greta's bedroom, with its view of the back gardens, to circle around to the staircase in the foyer. There were two other ways to reach her suite on the top floor, either by the back stairs once used by the servants or by the exterior steps, a winding staircase once used as a fire escape. The old home had no elevator, only a creaky dumbwaiter, which no one had used in this century. She made her way past the unoccupied guest rooms on the second floor and up the final steps to the space she'd occupied for the better part of six years.

She set Greta's copy of *I'm Not Me* on the coffee table and walked to the bank of windows to stare through watery glass that was over a hundred years old. Her view from this third-floor perch was incredible—from the bay on the east, over the peninsula, where the city lights winked brightly, to the Pacific stretching into the dark horizon. This rambling old manor was as much of a home as she'd had since she'd left Las Vegas twenty years earlier. She'd had many apartments in the intervening years, mostly dives, once in a rare while with a roommate, but after living with her aunt and uncle, she preferred to be alone.

CHAPTER 15

Remmi sank onto her couch and thought back about living with the Gibbs family. She'd hated everything about it.

From the get-go, Aunt Vera had forced Remmi to attend weekly Bible study on Wednesday evenings, as well as the Sunday services, where the sermons could not have been more boring.

Once Remmi had made the mistake of suggesting she would rather attend a nondenominational church, and Aunt Vera had nearly come unglued. When Remmi had pointed out that it was all the same God, Aunt Vera had given her a blistering tongue-lashing about sticking with family and faith and the little church they attended, where Reverend Weber, a personal friend, mind you, held services.

One memory rose to the surface. It had been late summer, and Aunt Vera had insisted Remmi learn what she referred to as "the basics," which meant preparing Remmi to be a homemaker like she was—straight out of the 1950s. Remmi was *not* cool with that at all.

Aunt Vera had begun canning peaches one sweltering afternoon. She had been standing at the stove and, as always, was ready to impart knowledge. "Your mother," she told Remmi, "well, she was a hedonist, always all about what made her feel or look good, never giving a thought to anything or anyone besides herself."

"That's not true," Remmi had burst out. She'd been sitting at the battered kitchen table in the kitchen nook, making labels for the jars, and glancing out the window to the cloudless day beyond. The nook had a view of the driveway, twin lines of concrete leading to a sagging garage, where Uncle Milo kept an old sports car that was in pieces all over the cracked cement floor.

As Remmi had tried not to daydream about finding her mother and escaping her life here, Aunt Vera had been sweating over a mottled canner squatting on the largest burner, steam rising. The temperature was over a hundred outside, not a breath of a breeze to be had. The lawn had turned brown, the shriveled blades of grass bleached from the California sun, the tinder-dry shrubs and trees lining the drive having already lost their leaves. The too-small air-conditioning unit had been on the fritz again, and Aunt Vera had been waiting, somewhat impatiently, for Uncle Milo to return from his latest business trip and fix it.

"Mom cares about me," Remmi had continued and swiped at the sweat beading on her forehead. One globule had hit the label she was working on, smearing the wording from her black Sharpie. She wadded the label up in her hand, crushing it in her fist. "And the babies. She loves them. She does! She'll come back. Something just must've happened." But it had already been over a year since Didi had driven away from Las Vegas in a piqued state of fury.

"Oh, honey . . ." Aunt Vera had taken the time to glance

pityingly over her shoulder. "Maybe you should face the fact that she's not—"

"She will!" Remmi had insisted, fighting the sting of tears. She wouldn't break down in front of her aunt. Wouldn't allow herself to. Nor would she think for an instant that Didi might be dead. That horrid thought had seeped through her brain often, but she'd ignored it, wouldn't dignify it. Even at night, when the oozing seemed darker and more foreboding, breeding nightmares that were dark and brutal—explosions rocking the still desert, fireballs climbing into the starlit heavens, blood drizzling over the tufted seats of the white Cadillac, and a baby crying somewhere in the darkness, sobbing loudly, while Remmi, her legs leaden, couldn't find it.

So far, she'd managed to stuff her sorrow and fears deep inside and vowed never to reveal them. Not even when she woke up soaked in sweat from those hellish nightmares, a scream dying in her throat.

"She'll be back," Remmi insisted, repeating herself.

Aunt Vera had sighed over the steaming pot. "I suppose," she'd allowed, though there had been a distinct lack of conviction in her tone. "But what I meant was that Edwina never thought beyond the materialistic, the here and now. Whether you want to face it or not, your mother was a narcissist, her head in the clouds. Where was she when Mom came down with cancer? Hmm? And when Dad was struggling, trying to make ends meet, in danger of losing the farm, was Edie around? No. She wasn't about to give up her wild, showgirl life now, was she?" She stopped to blow her bangs from her eyes and mop a drop of sweat that ran from her hairline to her chin. "Not that your uncle was any better. You didn't know him, of course, but your Uncle Billy was as bad as Edie, always carousing in high school, and then, the minute he got out, he joined up. The army. Ran away from his family. Barely came home when he got leave, let me tell you. Not until he got shot up in Iraq and came back with shrapnel in his hip. *Then* he was interested in the family, or at least what was left of the farm. It nearly killed Mom, let me tell you." With a snort, she added, "Edie and Billy, not a lick of sense between them, and certainly not a drop of spirituality either!"

Remmi had jumped to Didi's defense. "She goes to church on Christmas and Easter, and she even went to a psychic a couple of times."

"Oh my Lord," Vera declared, lips pursed, the silver cross dangling from a chain on her neck, glinting against her cleavage, her skin glazed with a sheen of perspiration. She'd been wearing a sleeveless blouse and shorts, her blond hair pulled into a short ponytail, her feet in flip-flops on the tile floor.

Earlier, Remmi had suggested they wait until a cooler day, and Vera had barked at her, reminding her the peaches were "ready" and that she couldn't risk any of them rotting. "Waste not, want not," she'd lectured Remmi, and the canning had begun.

Remmi had helped by peeling the dozens of peaches, but Aunt Vera was in charge of the water bath, filling the jars with syrup and peach halves, then placing the filled jars carefully on a rack in the huge canner.

She must've realized what she sounded like, so as soon as the jars were settled into the bath, Vera had turned to face Remmi. "I shouldn't have been so harsh. It's amazing to me how you did it—you know, got good grades and held a job—with Edwina as your only parent and her . . . different lifestyle. Even with the babies, you've managed to land scholarships and stay out of trouble."

This was as much of an apology as Remmi was ever going to get, but she hadn't known how to respond. Before she could mutter anything like "It's okay" or "I know you and Mom didn't get along," a loud roar thundered through the open window. A dusty old Jeep with huge tires had careened into the driveway. Half a dozen teenage boys had been stuffed into the open-air Wrangler, all laughing and talking. Her cousins, Jensen and Harley, had been standing in the back of the rig and hanging onto the Jeep's roll bar.

"Oh my," Vera whispered as both of her sons leaped from the back of the vehicle. The second their bare feet hit the ground, the driver rammed his Jeep into reverse and, tires spinning, engine thundering, backed into the street and roared away.

Bare-chested, jeans hanging low on their hips, Jensen and Harley ran into the house, the scents of smoked cigarettes and guzzled beer clinging to them. Blond Jensen was a string bean with peach fuzz beginning to chase away his acne. Harley, a year and a half younger, was built like a spark plug and had wild, curly brown hair, a too-big nose that he might grow into, and squirrelly deep-set eyes that made him always look like he was hiding something, which he usually was. The two teenagers tried to act sober as they walked quickly through the kitchen, but Jensen wove and Harley careened into a cupboard and giggled, then followed his brother down a short hall to the bedroom they'd shared ever since Remmi had moved in. Jensen was right on his heels, yanking the door shut behind him.

"You two, get out here!" Vera yelled. She was still holding the pair of tongs she used to move the jars in the water bath. "You hear me?"

But, of course, they hadn't as the beat from heavy metal music was already thudding from behind their closed door. "Just wait until their father gets back here," she said through tight lips. "He'll skin them alive!"

The timer had then gone off, and after sending one last, withering look down the hallway, Vera squared her shoulders and returned her attention to the jars in the water bath.

"They won't get away with this," she muttered beneath her breath as she reached into the canner with the tongs and touched the side of her hand along the rim of the hot pot. "Ouch! Dear Lord. Oh. Oh. Oh!" Sucking in her breath, she'd dropped the tongs, and they slithered into the steaming water. "Oooh." She'd cradled her burned hand in the other. "Oh, for the love of Saint Peter, Remmi, get those jars out now! Now! You've seen me do it a thousand times!"

Before Remmi had been able to respond, Vera turned to the refrigerator, yanked open the freezer door, and pulled out an ice tray. Her face contorted in pain, she managed to twist some cubes out of the plastic tray. They fell into the sink, and she snagged a couple to hold against the injured side of her hand.

"I'm not sure—," Remmi said, on her feet.

"Just get them out! Hurry, or they'll be ruined." Tears were filling Vera's eyes, and Remmi didn't know if it was from the pain or from frustration that all her afternoon's work would be wasted if her niece didn't pull through.

As quickly as she could, Remmi found a wooden spoon, fished out the tongs from the boiling water, and, after wrapping them in a kitchen towel, worked to pull out the jars without dropping or breaking any.

"Hurry!" Vera said.

Just then a door opened, an ear-blasting guitar riff screaming down the hall before it closed again and Jensen appeared. "Hungry," he mumbled as he made his way to the refrigerator, then for the first time really looked at his mom. "Hey—you okay?"

"Do I look okay?" she threw back at him. "No."

He'd opened the refrigerator. Peered inside. Called over his shoulder, "What happened?"

"Burned myself. It was stupid."

"Oh. Uh. Why didn't you wear gloves?"

"I just said it was stupid. Oh, for the love of Mike! Because I didn't think I'd get burned!" She rolled her eyes and grasped the slippery ice cube even more tightly while Jensen, seemingly unconcerned about Vera's injury, continued rummaging through the laden refrigerator shelves. As Remmi finished removing all the jars intact, he found some lunch meat and jars of mustard and mayo, then located half a loaf of bread on the counter and, with a knife he discovered in the sink, proceeded to make three sandwiches. He slathered mustard and mayo over all six slices of white bread, then plopped several rounds of bologna onto the thick glob of condiments.

"Don't spoil your dinner." Vera dropped the melting ice into the sink.

Fat chance of that. Remmi had kept the thought to herself. Aunt Vera could bad-mouth her husband and sons all she wanted, and that was just fine, but if Remmi even dared to agree with her, Vera would turn on her with a vengeance as swift as a rattler striking. Remmi had learned to hold her tongue as much as possible, and it nearly killed her as she was used to speaking her mind.

"You and your brother are in deep trouble," Vera told Jensen.

"Yeah? Why?"

"You were supposed to be home two hours ago, and you were supposed to be swimming, right?"

"We were."

"Yeah, swimming in alcohol and tobacco." She spat out the words as if they alone were vile.

"Nah, we weren't."

"Then . . . then pot."

"Pot?" Jensen's face split into a grin.

"Weed. Whatever you call marijuana or, um, reefer these days."

"Oh, Mom, you're so . . ." He shrugged his shoulders as he slapped the halves of the sandwiches together. Yellow mustard oozed brilliantly against the crusts. "Melodramatic. Calm down. Chill."

"Are you kidding me?" she somehow shrieked through clenched teeth as Jensen, all three sandwiches stacked in one hand, sauntered down the hall and escaped to the bedroom.

"It's just not fair," Vera moaned, throwing a hostile glance at her niece. "Not fair."

And she'd probably been right, Remmi thought now. But then, what in life was? All that BS parents teach their children about "being fair" didn't add up to much in the adult world, which everyone eventually learned. Remmi was just thankful she'd escaped with most, if not all, of the money she'd saved and squirreled away. Since that time with the Gibbs family, she'd lived in dumps of apartments through college and during her early years after school, sometimes with roommates, mostly without. She'd hated explaining herself, or talking about her past, and as the weeks, months, and years had stacked up without any word from Didi, her hopes of ever seeing her mother again had shriveled and died. Until now. Here, in San Francisco.

How odd. All of the old feelings of abandonment, fear, and anger over having been left had resurfaced. She told herself to push them aside. For now. Since there was interest in Didi's case again, she needed a level head so that she could find out what had happened to her mother, if Didi were alive or dead, and solve the mystery that had clung to her like a shroud.

She glanced around the apartment that was now her home with its fantastic view. It could be drafty in winter and hot in the summer, but it was the nicest place she'd ever inhabited, thanks to Greta Emerson.

Remmi had met Greta years before when Remmi had been a bookkeeper at a small accounting firm where Greta was a client. At the time, Remmi had still been going to college, and over the years, she and Greta had grown closer. Which was a little odd, but Remmi had rationalized it with her absence of a family and Greta having never had children or grandchildren. Sometime after Remmi had received her degree, the accounting office where she worked had changed hands, and "The Judge," as Greta had called her husband, had passed away after years of battling heart disease. Greta then decided she didn't want to manage the upkeep of the house and the rental properties they'd owned, so she'd hired Remmi as her personal assistant. Greta didn't want to be bothered with finding and keeping housekeepers and groundskeepers, so she offered Remmi the job, paying her a salary as well as offering her free rent. Remmi's duties had expanded after Greta's stroke to include finding caretakers and a driver for her, to see that Greta was never alone and could stay in this house she loved. It had worked out well for both of them, and things had gone along quietly until, well, the book and now this suicide . . .

It was unprecedented.

And what about this book? Why were its publication and author cloaked in so much mystery? Did the author want desperately to remain anonymous and hide behind a pseudonym? Or was this some kind of publicity ploy by the publisher to drum up interest in a long-dead unsolved case? And how about the coincidence of the woman jumping just as Remmi passed by the building?

Remmi would force herself to read the book tonight. Greta was right, it might hold answers, a clue to who had written it or why that person had felt compelled to stir up a twenty-year-old mystery, or why some person would pretend to be Didi, even register with the name of D. Storm, then kill herself?

She wondered if going to the police had been the right call.

Possibly not, but she'd *had* to know if her mother had leapt to her death.

Didi hadn't.

At least not today, in San Francisco, from a ledge on the Montmort Tower. But that still didn't answer the question of where she was. Alive? Dead? Remmi checked the meager contents of her own small refrigerator and settled for a dinner of cheese and crackers. She carried the plate into the living room, poured herself a glass of wine, and settled onto the couch with *I'm Not Me: The Untold Didi Storm Story.*

CHAPTER 16

Rain drizzled from the hood on her jacket and down her face as Dani Settler ran up the final two blocks to her apartment, a small one-bedroom unit on the second floor of a building built sometime in the middle of the twentieth century. Beneath the streetlights, the pavement shimmered, and lights glowed from the windows of the surrounding buildings, warm patches of illumination climbing to the sky, some already twinkling with Christmas lights.

She was breathing hard by the time she unlocked the front door of the building, but once inside, still she took the stairs, two at a time, keeping her heart rate up until she reached the second floor, before walking briskly to her front door.

A sharp yip greeted her as she slid through the door, and her dog, a less-than-slim pug, greeted her enthusiastically. "Hey, slow down. Yeah, I love you, too, Earl." The little dog was whining and twirling in circles. She took the time to tell him what a "good boy" he was and petted him before feeding him. Once he'd gobbled every bit of kibble in his bowl, she found his leash hanging by a hook and snapped it, along with his camo-designed halter, over his broad chest. "Now, you're lookin' good," she said, and they set off again, this time on a brisk walk through the neighborhood to a small park; it was over half a mile and enough distance that the dog got his exercise and she could cool down from her run.

"Let's go," she said at each lamppost, tree, or fire hydrant he deemed it necessary to sniff and/or mark by lifting his leg. Usually, she loved this part of her exercise regimen, the time she started breathing normally again, with Earl trotting at her side. The routine was calming after a long day of dealing with death, paperwork, lying witnesses, and coworkers like Ted Vance. However, today, because of the new suicide case, she hadn't been able to leave the job at the office where it belonged.

Well, really, when had she ever? She lived and breathed to be a detective.

Face it, Dani, you're a workaholic with a dog to come home to instead of a husband and 2.5 children.

She didn't even have a steady boyfriend, hadn't since college. Maybe she never would. That thought was a little depressing, but she didn't mind living alone with Earl. At least she didn't have to pick up his boxer shorts or wash the residue of whiskers down the sink. She'd wondered if her lack of being able to hold onto a committed relationship was due to the fact that she'd been kidnapped by a real whack job when she was around twelve—fearing for her life daily, going toe to toe with a killer. Maybe it had molded her into someone who kept serious relationships at bay. Or maybe it was because her father, Travis, who had been single at the time, had ended up marrying Shannon and having a couple of kids with her. Dani had always wanted a sibling, but rather than draw her close, the new family had almost seemed to distance her. At fifteen, she'd been into herself, hadn't been interested in a two-year-old or a new baby.

So she'd never married and had broken off every relationship she'd ever had before it had a chance to get too serious. She knew what the problem was, though. She'd taken enough psychology classes in college to self-diagnose and realize she had trust issues. So, big effin' deal. Ever since she'd been abducted, she'd wanted to become a cop and had focused on a career in law enforcement. Her venture into psychology had been only a temporary diversion during her second year at a junior college.

So here she was, living with a pug who had literally leaped into her life and her heart.

"It's okay," she said aloud, her breath steaming as she glanced down at Earl, who was already gathering himself for the final run up the wide stairs to her old apartment building. He shot forward, jumping up each step, and she had to rush to keep up with him. Then the race was on, up the interior steps, along the short hallway, and through the door to her unit as Earl, little black ears flopping, galloped at the thought of a treat. Once inside, she kicked off her wet running shoes, toweled off the dog, and gave him a biscuit before she stripped down and stood under a hot shower.

Ten minutes later, with the pug's nose visible against the shower stall's glass door, she toweled off and pulled on her pajamas, hoping she was in for the night. With her job, she could never be certain, as many of the crimes she investigated were committed and discovered in the middle of the night.

Though she tried to turn off from work, the suicide case stayed with her. Why was the victim at the Montmort Tower dressed as Marilyn Monroe, or, if Remmi Storm could be believed, as her mother? Why did she jump?

At least the question of who had leaped to her death had been answered. And no, it wasn't Didi Storm. Just before Settler had left the office for the day, the police department had gotten a hit through the fingerprint database. The victim had been identified as Karen Upgarde, forty-seven, of Seattle. A waitress/bartender who had never done an impersonation in her life, as far as anyone knew, Upgarde was divorced, with no kids or siblings, and she had two DUIs on her record.

Martinez had talked to the King County Sheriff's Department and had sent them information on the case via e-mail. An officer with the sheriff's department had been assigned the unhappy duty of informing the next of kin, who in this case was her mother, a woman of eighty-three who lived in an assisted care facility in Kirkland, Washington.

Settler had done a quick check on the victim, but in her first sweep of information about Karen Upgarde, there wasn't a single thing about the woman that linked her to Didi Storm or anyone associated with her. The only reason the police had IDed her was because of her priors. She'd been fingerprinted and was in the national database. Upgarde had also attempted suicide twice during her short-lived marriage, both times with pills that had been pumped from her system in time when her husband discovered her barely conscious. She worked as a waitress, had loved drinks and karaoke, and had been known to wear flamboyant clothes, though she'd never been an impersonator, at least at first look. Tomorrow, the police department would dig a little deeper and get to know the victim. According to police records, the last time she'd been convicted of a DUI had been eleven years earlier; since then she'd been clean. No other run-ins with the law had been found.

Yet.

There was still plenty of time, Settler thought, as she heated a leftover taco she'd picked up from her favorite food cart located between her apartment and the station. The microwave dinged and, gingerly, she carried the steaming-hot plate from her galley-style kitchen to the narrow living room where Earl waited, wiggling his tail in anticipation of at least one bite.

"Glutton," she chided as she sat in her favorite chair—a recliner she got secondhand in college—and picked up the TV remote to click on the news. Her apartment was small, but functional, decorated with hand-me-downs, as rent in this city was sky-high and Settler was saving for her own condo, which she figured she could only afford if some rich unknown relative bequeathed her a small—or, better yet, large—fortune. Nearly burning her lips on the melted cheese, she watched the TV with half an eye and dug into the slightly soggy tortilla.

Earl gave a sharp bark, his bulbous eyes fixated on her plate. She told him, "When I'm done, okay? You can lick the plate."

She'd had the pug a little over two years. While jogging one autumn evening, the chubby little dog, with his curled tail, had nearly barreled into her. She'd tripped, recovered herself, then worried he'd dash into the street, so she'd grabbed hold of him, and he'd licked her face as if they were already fast friends. She'd tried to find his owners, going door to door, checking with local vets and nearby rescue organizations, searching online, at the pound, through the police station, everywhere she could think of, but no one had come forward for him. With no tags and no microchip, the dog was an orphan, and he'd claimed her as his, settling comfortably into her apartment, burrowing his way into her heart. He now slept with her.

She'd sworn she'd never own a dog—too much responsibility—and she'd seen firsthand how much work they could be, as her stepmother raised service dogs.

Nonetheless, Earl was definitely her dog now.

As the news switched from national to local, her cell phone chirped. She snatched it up and checked the screen. Las Vegas Police Department. She answered to find Detective Lucretia Davis on the other end of the connection.

"I'm sorry to call so late," Davis said after introducing herself, "but I'm going out of town and saw that you needed some information on the Didi Storm missing person case."

"Yes, anything you've got."

"Okay. The case about her is old and cold, and I would love to see it finally solved, as I worked it with Detective Kendrick, who retired a few years back. I've already asked that the case files be brought out of storage, and when I get back in a couple of days, I'll send you anything you need. Most of the information is in computer files, though, as we'd just converted to computer data back then, so I'll send you everything I have digitally tonight."

"That would be great." Dani set the plate on the floor, and as Earl started licking any remaining crumbs, she grabbed a notepad and pen from a drawer in the side table nearest the couch.

"The whole thing had us hamstrung. It was a mess. The long and the short of it was that a night or two before she was reported missing, there was a fire, a big explosion in the desert. It lit up the sky, let me tell you. I'd never seen anything like it. Anyway, after the fire department put out the inferno, all we were left with was a burned-out shell of a car—a Mustang—and it had a body in it. Male, probably an inch over six feet, no dental work we could match, never identified. No missing person report that filled the bill.

"The car turned out to be a rental from a small shop in Victorville, a mom and pop operation, but I can't remember the name. It'll be in the file. It was rented to a Brandon Hall. He had a California driver's license and a credit card issued to him—Visa, if I remember right—but other than that, he didn't exist. And the rental car company didn't have cameras at that time."

"That seems strange."

"Yep, a little, even for back then. Maybe it was the reason he picked that rental company."

Settler made a note.

"We found where he'd rented a room, here in Las Vegas, at a hotel months before. The hotel was just off the Strip, and a Brandon Hall using the same ID had been there for a few weeks, and that's where, as far as we can tell, he would have hooked up with Didi. The ID didn't pan out, was phony. The hotel did have cameras, but he kept his back turned and was always wearing a baseball cap and sunglasses, which isn't all that unusual here—no red flags were raised."

"Purposely hiding his identity?"

"That's what we decided. His address was listed as somewhere in L.A., and it was the same address on the fake driver's license. When we checked, it turned out no one by the name of Brandon Hall had ever lived there, and the picture on the license, as I said, didn't match with anyone who'd gone missing. A dead end. But then, the whole case was made up of dead ends. If this Brandon Hall was the body in the car, we could never ID him."

Settler scratched the alias onto the legal pad while Davis continued talking. Losing interest, Earl padded off to his water dish in the kitchen.

Davis said, "So that was mystery number one."

"There were more?"

"What happened to Didi was the biggest one. According to her kid, she took off the next night, or maybe the next—again, it's been a while, and I don't have the details right here, but the kid said her mother was ready to have it out with someone because she thought she'd been scammed. Big-time."

"I heard," Settler admitted. "I talked to Remmi Storm today."

"So she told you about an exchange of money for a baby?"

"And the switch of the babies. The girl for the boy."

"Well, that's just the thing," Davis said, "there was no record of two births, only one. The boy: Adam. Filed with the state by Didi Storm and her attendant, a woman who was supposedly a midwife, Seneca Williams. No second baby was listed or ever reported that we could find. No female named Ariel. Ms. Williams vanished, too, a day or so later, after Didi disappeared. According to Remmi Storm, Seneca Williams took the second baby with her— the boy, Adam—though that's always been a question as we only know of the one. Did Didi really have twins? Did she take the one with her that first night? If so, what happened to the kid? And what about Seneca Williams? What happened to her? She wasn't in any of our records, no driver's license or Social Security number that we could find. Was she an illegal? Or did she have an alias? Witnesses claimed to have seen her, but we couldn't find anyone really close to her, so who knows?"

"And there wasn't evidence of a baby in the car that burned?"

"Nothing to confirm that a kid was even there. Which throws more than a little doubt on Remmi's entire story. Kendrick pointed this out, but Remmi Storm wouldn't back down from her insistence that she was telling us the truth, and she knows what happened, or most of it, because—get this—she was hiding out in a specially equipped cargo space in Didi's Cadillac, a space between the trunk and back seat where Didi used to hide props for her act. Didi was a showgirl who impersonated, sang, danced, and did a little magic, I guess. I never saw her. Never met her. Didn't even know about her until Remmi came in and made the report."

"You didn't believe her? Remmi?"

Davis paused for a second, and Settler heard the distinctive click of a lighter and a long intake of breath, indicating she was lighting a cigarette. "Not completely. I remember we went 'round and 'round about it back then, trying to figure out what was real, what wasn't. We might have had one witness, a kid who was riding a motorcycle in the desert that night and got shot, but he left the hospital before we could interview him. His name was Scott something or other . . . no wait, the last name was Scott. And he was in the wind, too. Never found."

"But he was shot?" This was news to Settler, and she wrote his name down and circled it, to remind herself that Scott would be another witness, just as Earl returned to the living area and cocked his head at her.

"He was lucky to have survived, real lucky. We think he was shot point-blank in the neck."

Dani's attention sharpened. This was serious stuff. "By who?"

"Good question. Still unknown. We think whoever shot him also shot the Mustang and ignited the gas tank or something, which caused the explosion. Shell casings indicate as much. It's all in the report." Frustration edged into her voice as she talked. "To this day, we're not certain what really happened that night or who the real target was. The guy in the car? The kid on the bike? Didi? Maybe even someone knew that Remmi was inside the big car, but, according to her, Didi's Caddy was unscathed, no bullet holes, which, of course, we can't confirm as no one but Remmi saw the car after that night.

"Anyway, that's about what I remember about it. When Didi's daughter came in to report her mother missing, we listened to what she had to say but were never able to connect all the dots. Couldn't tell how much of the truth she was relating and how much she was holding back. Both Kendrick and I had the feeling she knew more than she was saying, but we couldn't get her to open up. Then there was the fact that she was underage, her mother gone. Social Services put her together with someone in her family, an aunt who lived in California, I think, even though Remmi had never met her."

Another audible drag on the cigarette, then Davis continued, "We checked with all of Didi's acquaintances, the ones we could catch up to. A couple of friends, a few people she worked with, her boss, who said that Didi had hinted she was going to come into some money. Big money, and when she did, he could take her job and shove it, or something along those lines. I take it their relationship wasn't all that great."

"Romantic?"

"He said not, but I think he's the kind who could lie to his own mother. At least that's the impression I got."

Settler could tell by her cold tone what Davis thought of the man whom Didi had worked for. "He still around?"

"At a different club in Lake Tahoe. It'll be in the report, too."

"What about romantic interests?"

"Didi Storm had plenty. Men liked what they saw, and all reports suggest she liked them back, though she had trouble sustaining a relationship. Both her marriages were rocky, according to people who knew her. We were hoping to find the father of the baby or babies, but struck out. Her two exes seemed to be out of the picture, but you never know. Anyway, eventually the case went cold. Ice cold."

"Until now."

"Maybe until now. That remains to be seen. As I said earlier, the male body in the car was never identified and to this day remains a John Doe. Four or five people went missing, depending if you believe there were twins: Didi Storm, Seneca Williams, the Scott kid, and at least one baby, Adam Storm. And what was stranger still, or at least an odd part of it, supposedly, according to her daughter: Didi took off in that very unique car. It, too, was never seen again, and a Cadillac built in the fifties—they were immense by today's standards. It would be hard to miss a car like that."

"Or dispose of it," Settler thought aloud.

"Right," she agreed, then, wrapping up the phone call, said, "So, listen, unless you have any other questions, I've got to run. I have a couple of other calls to make before I even start packing, but I'll send you what I can tonight and get the physical evidence to my desk. When I get back, I'll give you a call."

"Sounds good." Settler hung up, and Earl took it as a sign it was okay to hop onto her lap. "This is a tough one," she said, scratching his ears. "But we'll figure it out, right?" The pug cocked his head again. "Okay, *I'll* figure it out." She picked up her plate and was halfway to the kitchen when she heard the ding on her phone, indicating she was getting new e-mail. A glance told her Detective Davis was as good as her word and digital files had been transferred from Las Vegas.

From the size of the file, it looked like she had her evening's reading cut out for her.

* * *

Three hours after picking up and reading Greta's copy of *I'm Not Me,* Remmi snapped the book closed and climbed off the couch. A lot of the narrative was factual, could have been taken off of the Internet, but that part was mostly in the ten or so years before Didi disappeared. Didi's earlier history as Edwina Hutchinson from Anderstown, Missouri, a small farming community ten miles off of I-44 about midway between St. Louis and Springfield, was sketchy, though some blanks had been filled, including the name of the school, Anderstown High School, home of the Terrific Titans; the school colors were scarlet and white. This was old information to Remmi, in a way. She'd just never explored much of her mother's history before she became Didi Storm. Living with the Gibbses had destroyed any curiosity she might have had.

But now, armed with details of Didi's youth, Remmi carried the book into her second bedroom, which she used as an office. There was a daybed pushed under the window, but it had never been used, and her desk, tucked into a corner, was surrounded by books and ledgers, office supplies in baskets and boxes on open shelves, and a desktop computer with a wide monitor. Currently, the screen was obliterated by the hulk of Romeo, a huge Maine Coon cat, another one of Greta's babies. Perched in front of the monitor, his long tail dangling to the keyboard and twitching slightly, he stared at Remmi, tufted ears cocked.

"So who do you think you are?"

He knew who he was: the man of the house. And he wasn't moving. He stretched and yawned, showing his pink tongue and sharp teeth. "Yeah, right, I get it. You've got to go be the boss somewhere else, okay?" She carried him over to the window seat and plunked him on a faded cushion. "Your own private view of the city and . . ." The words got lost in her throat as she stared down at the

street and saw, positioned away from the nearest street-
lamp, a dark vehicle, some kind of SUV.

Her heart clutched.

She knew the cars that regularly parked in the area,
and this one was different. She cut the light behind her
and stared, trying to determine if anyone was sitting in
the vehicle, but she couldn't see into the darkened interior.

*You're paranoid. Why do you think someone's follow-
ing you?*

Nevertheless, gooseflesh broke out on her arms.

The house is safe, she reminded herself. No one can
enter without a key.

Still, she walked to the exterior door that opened to the
converted fire escape and tested the lock.

Secure.

The cat, who had followed her down the short hallway
past her bedroom, let out a low, warning growl, making
the hairs on the back of her neck stand on end. "It's okay,
Romeo," she said softly, and in response, the cat stared at
the door and hissed, then quickly turned tail and slunk toward the main stairs.

After checking that lock as well, Remmi went back to
the study and looked out the window to scan the street
again.

The dark SUV was gone.

And somewhere she thought she heard the strains of
the same old song she'd heard at the Montmort Tower as
the woman had leapt to her death.

This little light of mine, I'm gonna let it shine.

Her blood turned to ice.

Where was it coming from?

But no. She couldn't hear it now. The song must've

just blossomed in her brain randomly. A memory. An earworm. Nothing had triggered it.

But as she stared out the window at the dark, lifeless night, her reflection a pale wraith of her own image, the tune lingered, the refrain repeating and echoing in her mind.

CHAPTER 17

When Remmi got up the next morning, she opened the blinds and checked. No SUV. The space the black vehicle had occupied was empty, dry pavement showing the outline of where a vehicle had been parked. But it could have been occupied by anyone. She stared through the window. Had the driver returned?

"Stop it," she said aloud. She wasn't going to let her nerves get the better of her. She had too much to do.

The day was cloudy and dark, no promise of blue skies, but the rain had stopped for the moment, and Remmi watched a few boats sailing into the bay. Cars were already clogging the bridges as she stretched and told herself today would be a better day.

It had to be.

She'd slept poorly, had had dreams of women dressed in garish clothes, clownish versions of Didi in overdone makeup and ripped, sequined dresses plummeting through the air and whispering, "I'm not me. I'm not me," but never hitting the ground. Instead, all the women dressed as different characters in Didi's repertoire floated, pirouetting, diving, and ascending in the misty air over the bay and Golden Gate Bridge. Didi as Cher or Madonna or Marilyn Monroe, spinning over the tallest buildings and then breaking into that little song she'd heard as a child, all in Didi's high soprano voice, louder and louder, their mouths working choppily, as if they were marionettes.

Let it shine! Let it shine! Let it shine!

She'd woken up with a start, her heart pounding a million beats a minute, the dream fading as she'd realized she was in her bedroom, it was morning, and she still didn't know if her mother was dead or alive.

"Coffee," she said as she stretched. She got out of bed and unlocked her door, and Romeo shot into her room, scaring a yelp out of her. "Lots of coffee," she added dryly.

The nightmare fading, she spent thirty minutes running through the shower, dressing in jeans and a sweater, and twisting her hair into a messy bun. She'd never been much into makeup, so a dash of lip gloss and a touch of mascara did the job. She grabbed Greta's copy of *I'm Not Me* and was down the stairs to the main kitchen, where coffee was brewing, gurgling in a glass pot and filling the air with the warm scent of rich java.

Greta was already up, dressed in slacks, a sweater, and vest, her own makeup and earrings in place. She had her iPad open and was working on the *New York Times* crossword puzzle, which was part of her daily early-morning routine.

"Good morning," she said without looking up as she clicked in the answers.

"Morning." Remmi dropped the book on the table next to Greta's iPad and noticed the coffeepot had sputtered to a stop, the glass carafe full of dark brew. "Coffee?"

"Of course."

Remmi poured two cups, while Beverly, one of the three women who took care of the house and Greta's needs, swept through from the laundry area downstairs. She snatched a couple of wet towels from the counter. "Anything else you need washed today?"

"The sheets?" Greta asked.

"Already through the wash and in the dryer," Beverly said. "New sheets on." She was tall and lithe, fifty-something, with a quick smile, dark eyes, and reddish hair that was cut short and starting to gray. "Towels are next, so I'm talking about load *numero dos!*" She held up two fingers, proud of herself as she was trying to learn Spanish.

Greta played along. "*Gracias.*"

"*De nada,*" Beverly started for the stairs, but Remmi held her up.

"Hey. Either of you know if a neighbor has a new car?"

Shrugging, Beverly said, "Nuh-uh," as Greta shook her head and asked, "Why?"

"Just curious. I saw a black or maybe navy SUV parked out front. Never seen it before."

"Maybe guests," Greta said. "Of the neighbors. Or the kids of the Olsens, there on the corner." She wagged a finger toward the kitchen window over the sink. "Their children are in college now—hard to believe, I know. In high school, they were always coming and going in different cars, parking overnight, a real nuisance for some of us who think street parking belongs to us. Now, one of the kids, the middle daughter, I think, is at Chico State, and always popping in unexpectedly. Has a boyfriend here, you know; the parents do *not* approve, but it's only about a three-hour drive, less if you're under twenty-one and hurrying back to meet a boy, I suppose."

The buzzer went off again. "Better go, don't want wrinkles," Beverly said before disappearing into the hallway leading to the stairs to the basement, where the washer and dryer were located.

"Did you read this?" Greta asked, tapping the cover of *I'm Not Me* as Remmi handed her one of the mugs. She took a sip. "Ahhh. That's better." With a smile, she finished the last word of the puzzle, then glanced up at Remmi.

"Yeah, I finished it."

"Accurate?"

"It meshes with what I heard from Aunt Vera, which, admittedly, wasn't all that much. She didn't talk about Mom if she could avoid it, and I didn't press her. Didn't want to talk to her. From what I understand, they never got along, never had that sister bond."

"So I gathered."

"They never seemed to get over that sibling rivalry and . . . well, all in all, Vera just didn't like Mom much."

Didn't like didn't quite touch Vera's feelings for her younger sibling. Though she'd never said she out and out hated Didi, Vera had carried a deep resentment for her brighter, prettier, and more popular sister, Remmi had realized. Vera clearly placed herself as the "responsible one" or the "good girl," both terms she'd repeated often when asked about her family. Vera's stellar grades had earned her a scholarship, and she'd been the first person in the family to graduate from college, despite the fact that she'd married Milo at twenty and had two children. Meanwhile, Edwina—"Edie" or "Didi," depending upon whom you asked—had bagged out of Missouri and headed for California without once looking back, while Billy had enlisted in the army.

And somewhere along the way, Aunt Vera had found religion and had dedicated her life to God and the church.

Remmi only wanted to forget the two years she'd

spent as an unwanted member of the Gibbs family, but
bits and pieces of her miserable life kept coming to the
fore, even now, years later. How Aunt Vera seemed hell-
bent to beat some Christianity into all of her family.
When her husband, Milo, was in town, she'd drag him to
church, along with Jensen and Harley. Though Milo
might have suffered through the long sermons and even
gotten closer to God, Remmi hadn't, nor had her sons,
both hellions who liked to "party" and were always trying
to hit on Remmi.

She hadn't been able to wait to leave the little bunga-
low in Walnut Creek. The second she'd turned eighteen,
she'd been out the door. Her quick and final exit had only
been possible due to scholarships, grants, student loans,
and the money she'd saved working at the Burger Den
while in high school. Everyone in the Gibbs family had
known she'd been putting her money aside. What they
hadn't divined was that the amount had been significantly
embellished by the remains of Didi's stash, the money
she'd left in Las Vegas after meeting with the guy in the
desert.

Remmi had managed to hide the money, and she'd
been careful, dividing it into two hiding places. Yes, there
was twice the chance of it being found, but half the
chance of the Gibbs family ending up with all of it. If
they did uncover it, they would think they'd found her
entire treasure trove, though she'd silently prayed that her
ill-gotten nest egg would be safe.

She'd tucked half of the money into an envelope she'd
hidden in the lining of her rolling suitcase, behind the
pocket she'd filled with tampons, just to make sure no
one would bother it. They hadn't. The other half she'd
slipped into a manila envelope she'd taped to the back of

a heavy cabinet on the back porch. The old cupboard was used for storage; it held tools and paint cans, even old pieces of tile for replacement, and it was rarely touched, if ever. Dust covered everything on the shelves, and cobwebs draped over the upper corners.

Then, because she knew her sticky-fingered cousins would be looking, she'd seeded a few of the bills in obvious places, which included her purse and underwear drawer. Sure enough, over time that money—nearly a hundred and fifty dollars—had disappeared, stolen, no doubt, by Jensen and/or Harley. The thought of those two disgusting human beings pawing through her panties caused her stomach to churn, but at least they'd thought they'd gotten one over on her.

So . . . fine.

They knew she worked and had cash lying around, even though she had opened checking and savings accounts. She'd hoped they would think she would only leave it in the two obvious places, and when she'd had a hissy fit when twenty dollars went missing, she'd proclaimed that from that point on, she'd keep all her money in the bank. That act had been as much for Aunt Vera and Uncle Milo's benefit as it was their sons'; hopefully, they, too, would think all of her money was in one place. Despite all her professed piety, Vera had never thought twice about "borrowing" from Remmi. She either really believed she was going to replace the money or, more probably, rationalized it as her due for taking care of her missing sister's kid. Pious and God-fearing or not, Vera's soul was tinged by a little bit of greed and a whole lot of resentment. She liked nice things, and though Milo provided for the family, she still had to pinch pennies once in a while but couldn't face the daily routine of a job, not when she had the house, her children, *Didi's* teenager, and her church duties to boot. No, no, no, a job outside the home just wouldn't fit into her already overburdened schedule.

So Remmi had hidden the money, then nearly had a stroke when Uncle Milo had returned from one of his weekly sales trips and decided to fix a few of the shingles on the roof. Aunt Vera had convinced him to paint the fascia board while he was at it, so he'd burrowed around in the cabinet on the porch, searching for enough paint and only a few inches from nearly five thousand dollars.

Remmi's heart had been in her throat, her palms sweaty, but she'd pretended disinterest as she'd carried groceries in from the car for Aunt Vera, who also was nosing around the cabinet.

"I know I have a can of that paint somewhere," Milo had grumbled as he'd sorted through the various cans, looking at the labels or popping off the tops with a screwdriver so he could view the color. "I put it right here." Milo scratched at three days' worth of stubble on his chin. Tall and lean, weathered from years working on his father's Missouri farm, he had sharp, deep-set eyes guarded by bushy eyebrows. His brown hair was kept military-short, and at home he favored battered jeans, cowboy boots, and T-shirts. On the road, he dressed in slacks and a sports coat and sold farm machinery throughout the western United States—mostly in the contiguous Pacific-rimmed states, but sometimes into Idaho, Montana, and even Alaska.

Staring at the paint cupboard, Vera had scowled and fingered her necklace. "Could it have fallen off the shelf and rolled somewhere?"

"Did we have an earthquake when I was gone?" he snapped.

"No, but . . ."

"Probably those damned kids messin' around." He straightened, eyeing the surroundings of the porch, while

Remmi tried not to freak out. She was probably lumped into the "those damned kids" mix with her cousins. Trying to appear uninterested, she passed her aunt and uncle, who were both seriously studying the cabinet and had only breathed again when the missing paint can was discovered hiding behind a larger one and the cabinet was once again left alone.

That had been a close call.

On the night before her eighteenth birthday, Remmi sneaked out of "her" room, had removed the envelope from the back of the cabinet, thought it felt thin and, in the darkness, peered inside. Her heart had dropped as she'd quickly reached into the manila packet and felt nothing but air. Empty. Her stash stolen. *Damn!* Tears burned in her eyes, and she felt bitter disappointment that quickly turned to rage.

Five thousand dollars. Gone.

She thought she might throw up and stepped through the screen door to the dry backyard and stared up at the sliver of the moon as a bat darted past, nearly invisible in the night, the whisper of his wings audible over the sound of a train on faraway tracks.

The thought of staying another second was out of the question, and the money she'd hidden in her suitcase was still there. She could make it. She'd just have to rethink what she was planning, tighten her belt.

So who had stolen her money?

As a warm breeze ruffled her hair, she thought back to the past few weeks. Hadn't it been about a month ago when Jensen, turning sixteen, had put new wheels on the old truck Uncle Milo had bought for him? And he'd somehow outfitted the same truck with a "sick" stereo system with speakers that could be heard from two blocks away.

She remembered his father asking Jensen how he'd paid for the stereo, tires, and rims. Jensen hadn't missed a beat, reporting that he'd worked for a friend's dad in a winery, had been paid under the table, and he got a "great" deal on the equipment. Uncle Milo hadn't questioned him again.

But there was something in the way Jensen told the story, how his gaze slid away from his father to land on Remmi, that suggested he was lying. At the time, Remmi had thought he was just avoiding his father's uncompromising stare. Now she realized Jensen had been silently gloating, knowing she'd hidden the money, happy that he had put one over on her.

"Prick," she'd whispered between clenched teeth as the bat swooped by again. Her fingers had curled into fists, and she wanted to wring Jensen's thick male neck and wipe that knowing smirk off his face. Lying thief!

It was all she could do not to run into the room he shared with Harley and confront him. But he'd just lie. And no one would believe her, even with the evidence of the shiny mag wheels on his beater of a car. And then there would be all sorts of questions about how she'd gotten the money and if she had any more. And Jensen would just end up silently laughing at her. She thought of keying his damned car, slashing those huge monster tires, but she didn't want to do anything to mess up her escape, so she slowly counted to ten as the bat's wings whirred, then kept going to twenty, then thirty, and finally stopped at seventy-five.

Jensen wasn't worth the trouble.

With the money that was left in her suitcase and bank account, she'd departed the Gibbses' home and never returned. She'd left a note explaining that she was an adult and was leaving and that she would let Aunt Vera know when she'd settled somewhere. That was a lie, as it turned out, for she never bothered to contact any of them again.

She'd once overheard Vera say, in a conversation with her friend, Rebecca, the minister's wife, that Remmi was "an ungrateful wretch." Vera had been in a foul mood that day, and Remmi hadn't done a good enough job with the laundry. She had just scolded Remmi, and Remmi had told her, "Oh, bite me!" which hadn't endeared her to the family.

Another time, she remembered Aunt Vera confiding again to Rebecca that her niece was "a poor, misguided thing," which had made Remmi's blood boil, considering the fact that her loser cousins were, for all intents and purposes, juvenile delinquents whose grades were always hovering just above failure. Nonetheless, Vera, whose voice had been low, a conspiring whisper, had added meanly, "Well, you know, what can I tell you? Remmi's mother, you know, Edwina? Or Didi Storm?" Remmi had been in the other room, but in her mind's eye she could see Vera making air quotes around her mother's name. Angry, she almost rounded the corner to confront her, but before she completely worked up her nerve, she heard Vera go on. "You already know Edie was a loose woman, God rest her soul, and, of course, the apple never falls far from the tree."

Meaning Remmi—who hadn't even really started dating at the time. She'd felt her blood pressure rise, and her hands had curled into fists.

"Thank goodness, my parents never really knew, though, of course, I'm sure they suspected. She *did* have that child without a husband, never named him, either. It about killed Mom and Dad. They were God-fearing Christians, let me tell you, and they would have been mortified, absolutely mortified if they knew half the things Edie did when she got to California and Vegas. There's a reason they call it Sin City, you know, and Edie was drawn to it like a moth to a flame."

"You're a saint for taking her in," Rebecca had responded.

"Well, it was the Christian thing to do. You would have done the same."

Remmi had taken one step toward the kitchen when she heard the screen door bang against its frame, and then Milo's voice filled the kitchen. "Hey, there, good-lookin'!"

"Oh, dear. Milo! I didn't expect you 'til tomorrow or Friday," Vera had cried, startled.

"Got the deal done early. It came together slick as can be. Three combines and five—count 'em, *five*—tractors to a dealer in Boise!" He sounded excited, and when Remmi gave up eavesdropping and walked into the kitchen, he was swinging his wife off her feet near the table where an open Bible and lesson plans were spread next to the salt, pepper, and napkin holder. Rebecca, whom Remmi called Mrs. Weber, was still seated, a glass of iced tea in one hand, her expression one of surprise as Uncle Milo set his wife onto the floor and Vera, rosy-cheeked, fanned herself with one hand.

He'd even tossed a rare smile Remmi's way, then winked at his wife. "Big bonus for this one." Cocking his head, he'd added, "Tell ya what: Dress up. Let's go out for dinner tonight! Just you and me. Remmi can be in charge of the boys."

Oh, sure. Like they would do anything she suggested.

But Aunt Vera looked almost girlish for a second.

"Okay!" she'd agreed, and Mrs. Weber had found her large bag and stuffed the lesson plans into it.

"You two have fun," she'd said and bustled away.

The moment had passed for Remmi to mention her own upbringing and defend her mother, so she let it slide, but she never forgot the conversation.

Never.

CHAPTER 18

"So what have we got on Karen Upgarde?" Settler asked from behind the wheel of one of the department's Crown Vics as she and Martinez drove to the Montmort Tower. The morning was gray and gloomy, clouds low enough to wisp around the higher buildings, the upper stories of the tower itself seeming to disappear. They parked on the street, as the valet was confused about what to do with a police vehicle and the hotel management did *not* want any signs of police presence on the premises. The brass had agreed, and Martinez found a spot within one block and nosed the Crown Vic into it.

"Nothing much more than we knew last night," he'd told her as they climbed out, the chill of the day seeping through her raincoat. Threading their way through pedestrians hurrying in the opposite direction, they found a coffee shop adjacent to the Montmort. Though it was early November, the windows facing the street had been decorated with tiny Christmas lights. Inside, the small establishment smelled of roasted coffee. Settler and Martinez stepped into a line of customers that curved around small café tables, where a few patrons were sipping from steaming cups while reading their handheld devices. One older man actually had a newspaper spread in front of him, while a millennial with a man bun and thick-framed glasses worked a laptop in the corner. Christmas music played as background to the conversation, rattling silverware, and a hissing espresso machine. The "to order" line moved quickly, and within minutes, they were seated at a table in the back, near the hall to the restrooms, Martinez, as always with his back to the wall, watching the front windows and glass door.

She, too, had a view of the front door and the big windows, but also of the walkway to the back hallway. "When will we get the tox screen?"

"Autopsy's today. Pushed up," he told her. "Because of public interest."

"Fast."

"Uh-huh." He was eating a breakfast sandwich—egg, ham, and gooey cheese tucked into a croissant. He washed it all down with coffee doctored with cream and sugar while she worked on a skinny latte, the foam artistically formed to look like the Golden Gate Bridge.

She asked, "Can we get a tox screen ASAP?"

He sent her a look with a quick shake of his head. "Takes time."

"I know, but I sure would like to know what was in her bloodstream." She tapped the table, wishing she could push the investigation faster.

"We will. And we'll get a prelim, at least for alcohol."

Not good enough, but she had to curb her impatience, which was always a challenge. "Anything from King County?"

"Not yet. They're sending pictures and reports, have got a laptop, are checking her social media platforms,

Facebook and Snapchat or whatever, but they haven't found her phone yet. Probably had it on her.

"They did locate a cell phone bill—she had no landline—and so they've contacted the phone company. We should have records within the week. Maybe sooner. Find out who she's been in communication with." He was talking to Settler, but his gaze was still taking in the restaurant, especially the door as it opened and shut, letting in customers who rubbed their hands from the cold and surveyed the glass case of pastries as they inched their way across the tiled floor to the barista.

Martinez had been shot once, while a beat cop. On the scene of a convenience store robbery, he'd taken a bullet to the gut and spent a week in the hospital, along with several weeks' recovery. Luckily, he'd only lost part of his spleen, along with a lot of blood. He, along with almost everyone on the force, was always on the lookout for danger.

"I hope they put a rush on everything," she said as she sipped from her cup, hot milky coffee warming her from the inside out. "I'll push them."

"Every case is a rush."

"I know. But . . . I have a friend who transferred up there. I'll see what she can do. I'd like to find out if Upgarde bought the clothes and wigs online. Maybe there's a credit or debit card receipt that will lead us in the right direction."

"Anyone can pick up that junk—celebrity paraphernalia—online. Craigslist, eBay, whatever."

"Yeah, but they don't usually put the 'junk' on and leap from nineteen floors up."

"Okay. See what your friend can dig up ASAP," Martinez said, but it was just an automatic response. Martinez believed that the more you pushed people, the more they pushed back, and in some cases, she supposed, that was true. But not in this one. Her friend and ex-partner, Rosamie Ugali, would do what she could.

She let it drop and said, "I talked to Detective Davis from the Las Vegas P.D. She worked the Didi Storm missing person case with a partner who has long since retired."

"You still think Storm's connected?"

"The daughter nearly convinced me yesterday. And come on, she registered under D. Storm."

"Well, there is that."

"Yeah, there is that." She was certain there was a connection. "Obviously, she was using Didi Storm as her alter ego, at least for the time she was in the hotel. She was pretty meticulous about keeping up the Didi image by dressing in her things, down to the signature fingernail, so she knew this woman inside and out. And here's the thing. Not a lot of people did. Not twenty years ago, and certainly not now. But the daughter's right. There's a new book and a Didi Storm fan club online. I checked the Facebook thing and Twitter feed last night. Her 'fans' are all talking about the fact that Karen Upgarde was dressed like her. Why would anyone care? The woman was a second-rate impersonator at best, and it's been twenty years."

"But there was the mystery of her disappearance."

"Again, a generation ago. So, yeah, I definitely think the suicide has something to do with Didi Storm. I just don't know what. When we get into Upgarde's computer and phone, maybe we'll get some answers." She told Martinez about her conversation with Davis, about the explosion, the unidentified man in the burnt car, and the twin babies. He nodded, finishing his breakfast and wiping his mouth, brushing off a few crumbs that had stuck in his dark goatee.

"So why here? Why would Upgarde choose San Francisco and not Las Vegas to make her splash? Because the daughter's here?" Martinez asked.

Settler finished her latte. "I'll ask Remmi what she thinks. Come on, let's go." She pushed her chair back, bussed the table, and Martinez followed suit.

They planned to interview the hotel employees again and walk through the room Upgarde, as D. Storm, had rented, figure out who had occupied the rooms on the same floor, check on the security tapes from the cameras, and make certain they had been sent to the department.

Already they'd asked the public for anyone with film, digital images, or video of the leap. The request had been made through the public information officer. Settler believed there would be dozens, if not hundreds, of images submitted. She only hoped that the public would send the police the pictures rather than try to sell them to the tabloids or whatever questionable online news source would pay, but she'd learned not to underestimate a person's greed.

In the kitchen of Greta's big house, Remmi heated a bagel in the toaster oven, while Greta sipped coffee. "Remember, the Christmas lights are supposed to go up today."

Greta nodded. "Big job. Usually takes two."

"I know, but call me if he doesn't show, okay? I'll get on them. Kris Kringle's Christmas Lights is kind of flaky. Last year, they didn't come until mid-December."

"No one wants to climb up to the roof."

"Do you blame them?"

"No, but Santa and his reindeer have been mounted by the chimney for fifty years, and as long as I'm alive, the children in this neighborhood will see them. Duncan always insisted upon it, and I'm carrying on the tradition."

"I know." Remmi had heard this same story every year since she'd moved in. "But if they don't come, text me or call me. Okay?"

Before she could answer, Beverly, a little breathless, poked her head through the archway from the back corridor and said, "I'll get the paper! I think it's here." Before anyone could answer, she hurried outside to the front stoop. Remmi heard the door open and close just as the toaster oven dinged. Careful not to burn her fingers, she slid the hot bagel halves onto a plate as Beverly returned.

"Here ya go!" Beverly dropped the folded paper onto the table next to Greta just as the sound of the dryer buzzer emanated from the basement again. "Duty calls," she said, then turned to Greta. "Have you ever thought of fixing the dumbwaiter? I'd be less likely to trip carrying up the laundry."

"Nothing wrong with it," the older woman stated.

"What? Why don't we use it, then?" Beverly asked.

"Well, I don't really remember." Greta thought for a second. "It's creaky, and I'm not sure the ropes are still strong, but it has to be filthy and filled with cobwebs, dust and spiders, mice . . . maybe even rats." She gave a little shudder and, as Beverly was still staring at her, added, "I suppose it could handle something not too heavy. But you might want to clean it before you give it a try."

"I will," Beverly said, just as the dryer squawked again. "I'll be right back. With the laundry. Poached egg day, *si?*"

"*Si.* And a muffin, er, *mollete*," Greta said. "Or is it *magdalena?* I get them confused. But yes, please." She kept to a strict morning schedule and wouldn't eat until she'd had two cups of coffee and finished the puzzle. Three days a week, she ate a poached egg and a muffin, on the other days oatmeal with fruit. It never changed, not even for holidays.

"*Bueno!*" Beverly was off again, nearly tripping over Turtles, who trotted across the tile floor to duck under the table and rub her mottled, furry back against Greta's leg.

"She hasn't improved much, you know," Greta remarked.

Remmi was slathering peanut butter on one half of the bagel when Greta snapped the paper open. "Who?"

"Beverly. Her Spanish, such as it is, wouldn't get her as far as Tijuana. And she's been at it for months. If she's really serious, she should take a class at . . ." Her voice faded away for a second and then, "Uh-oh."

"What?"

"I think you'd better take a look at this."

Remmi dropped the bagel onto a small plate and turned to see the front page lying open on the table. The first headline that caught her attention was:

SUICIDE VICTIM IDENTIFIED
Leaper Said to Be Dressed as 1950s Icon

Heart in her throat, she skimmed the article about the identity of the dead woman. "Who's Karen Upgarde?" she asked, rereading the few paragraphs more carefully.

"I'm sure I don't know."

"I've never heard of her."

"We are bound to find out a lot more about her," Greta said. "It'll be all over the news, at least for a couple of days, until something more dreadful or sensational or scandalous or whatever comes along."

Remmi tried to read between the lines, but the article was short, straightforward, and didn't give a lot of details. "The police didn't call me."

"Why would they?"

"Because I'm involved. Didi is my mother. This woman was dressed like *her*, not some '1950s icon,' meaning Marilyn Monroe, for God's sake."

"You already told them the victim wasn't your mother, but I do suppose they will call to see if you know of any connection." She thought for a second. "I'm surprised you didn't already see this online this morning."

"I didn't check my computer, and my phone is charging upstairs. I was just about to do that." Remmi read the article for the third time and frowned. "All this gives is her age, and that she's from the Seattle area. Divorced. No children. Mother is next of kin. Mind if I take this?" She was already scooping up the paper and heading for the stairs.

"Just save me the puzzle," she said. "Oh, Remmi, your breakfast—"

But Remmi ignored her rumbling stomach and raced up the back staircase so quickly that her heart was pounding as she reached her apartment. Unhooking her phone from its charger, she caught her breath, then dialed Detective Settler's number, one she'd memorized, only to hear it ring on the other end, then go to voice mail.

She hung up, wanting to throw the phone across the room. What good were the police if you couldn't reach them when you needed them?

Stop. Slow down. You know about the cops. You've dealt with them before.

A little calmer, she punched in the numbers again, and when the phone again went to voice mail, she left a message. "This is Remmi Storm. Please call me back." Then she left her number and clicked off.

She'd wait. For now. First, she'd do some checking on

Karen Upgarde, then she'd visit Jennifer Reliant, that damned agent for Maryanne Osgoode, and find out who the hell the author really was.

So far, Settler's phone calls to the agent for Maryanne Osgoode had gone unanswered, and she'd gotten the runaround at the small press that had published *I'm Not Me*. Currently, still in a suite where she'd conducted interviews at the Montmort, she was waiting for the editor of Stumptown Press, a small publisher located in Portland, Oregon, to return her call. Said editor was conveniently "out for a few days," which seemed more than a little suspicious, given the fact that the book on Didi Storm was getting a lot of attention and was certainly Stumptown's biggest seller.

As for the interviews with the hotel staff? Most had been a bust.

But not all.

After spending nearly three hours with employees and guests, Settler and Martinez hadn't learned much more than she had the day before. The detectives had again examined the room occupied by Upgarde as D. Storm, noting that there were doorways on both sides to connecting rooms; both, it had been reported, had been locked. They'd reviewed the security tapes of the outer hallways, elevators, and common areas with the hotel security manager and spoken to room service, maid service, and the front desk staff, but no one had experienced much interaction with Karen Upgarde aka D. Storm.

The only point of interest came when they'd been able to speak to one of the janitors who worked the night shift.

Al Benson, a portly man with a thin moustache, told them: "Saw a guy I didn't recognize using the service elevator. About three in the mornin', maybe three-fifteen or so, you know, on the mornin' of the day that woman jumped? Anyway, I got on at the tenth floor and said, 'Hey,' and he said it back then real quick-like punched the button for fourteen and got off. I rode up to twenty-one. But the strange thing about it was, the car stopped on the nineteenth floor. Doors opened. No one got on, so he probably was headin' that way, but then decided to get out on fourteen. Or else someone on nineteen decided not to wait and took the stairs, y'know."

Settler had felt that little buzz at the back of her neck that warned her she was onto something. "And you didn't know him?"

"Never seen him before, I don't think, but he was wearin' tinted glasses and a baseball cap, had a bit of a beard going, three days' growth or so, I'd guess. Which probably should have made me sit up and take notice." He'd shrugged. "I guess I was payin' more attention to my cell phone. Had a call from the parking garage attendant, who was havin' trouble with the electronic gate." Al frowned and scratched his chin. "But the more I think about it, I don't think he was wearing a badge, y'know, like this one." He'd wiggled his name tag, pinned to his shirt pocket. "But sometimes people forget. They're s'pose to wear them, but they don't always. And once in a while, guests, they hop on the service elevator; it's not locked or nothing, so it's really not that big of a deal." But his eyes had clouded. "You don't think he had anything to do with that poor gal on nineteen's death, do you? I mean it was a suicide, right? She jumped."

"We're just investigating all possibilities," Settler had said, but the sensation that she'd just found a fissure, a crack in what had, at first, seemed like an open and shut case of suicide, stayed with her. Now the door leading to homicide was definitely ajar.

"Anything else you can tell us about this guy?"

"Wish I could," he'd said, but despite more questions and prodding, Al had told them all he remembered. They had double-checked the security tape for the time listed but didn't find anyone on the nineteenth floor between three and four in the morning, though when they viewed the film of the service elevator, they saw that Al's memory had been spot-on, and now there was a black-and-white image of a man who appeared to have pushed a button on the panel of the elevator car when he'd gotten on in the parking garage. When Al Benson had stepped onto the car, he'd immediately pressed another button. In the footage, she couldn't read the floor numbers, but he'd made a quick exit on floor fourteen.

They reviewed the videotape of the stairs, and sometime later saw the same man in the stairwell, his face hidden by the baseball cap, hurrying down to finally exit into the parking garage.

From that point, they'd lost him.

And they hadn't seen him in any of the footage of the nineteenth floor, though, unfortunately, the camera on the floor had been working only sporadically for the week before the tragedy, so it was possible someone could have slipped into D. Storm's room without there being any footage of his or her entrance.

Coincidence? Bad luck?

Or had someone purposely fiddled with the camera?

But how? An inside job? Was someone on the hotel staff compromised?

Or was all of that conjecture just too damned far-fetched?

Maybe Karen Upgarde, who was known to be a flamboyant dresser, got a wild hair to leap off the building as a celebrity, possibly Marilyn Monroe.

But there was the fingernail—the damned signature of Didi Storm.

Dani had stared at the image of the man who had fled the elevator on the fourteenth floor.

Who are you? she'd wondered. *And how are you involved in all of this?* One way or another, she intended to find out.

CHAPTER 19

The Reliant Agency didn't exist. At least, it didn't exist in the context of an office within a building with a front door and four walls. The "suite" in the building was actually a post office box within a mail annex, and Remmi suspected the telephone number she'd found online and left messages on was never answered. The whole agency was a scam. "Someone must pick up the mail here," she said to the twentysomething worker behind the counter.

"I can't give out information about our customers," the clerk said primly, with a certain amount of relish. He was a string bean of a man, with thin shoulders and hips and a feeble, sparse attempt at a Lincolnesque beard.

"Someone pays for that space," she said, pointing to the box in question. "Or else you mail it somewhere else. But someone pays the bill."

"The box is registered to the Reliant Agency," he told her. "That's all I can tell you. Next." He looked over her shoulder to a woman in a pink coat and gloves who was balancing three packages in one hand while dealing with a toy poodle on a leash with the other.

"If you'll excuse me," she said pointedly to Remmi as the woman pushed past her and let her packages tumble onto the counter with a scale. She declared, "I need these to be insured, and they have to get there by the end of the week!"

Sensing she wasn't going to get any more information from the guy, Remmi left the building and walked onto the street. Nearby, rising higher than its neighbors, the Montmort Tower knifed into the gray sky. She counted up to the nineteenth floor and studied the window and ledge from which Karen Upgarde had leaped to her death.

As Didi Storm.

Why?

She turned her gaze to the base of the hotel, where potted plants had been decorated with festive garlands and lights. Cars, vans, and taxis pulled into the curving drive in a steady line, moving around the fountain to drop off or pick up patrons of the Montmort. And on the pavement, just to one side of the illuminated, bubbling water feature, Karen Upgarde had given up her life.

Remmi felt cold inside as she remembered the horrid fall and then the body crumpled on the pavement.

The suicide leap would have been the kind of splashy, front-page exit so like her mother, except that Didi Storm had never had a death wish. No matter how bad times became, Didi always worked up a way out. *If Plan A doesn't work, then go to Plan B.*

Ending her own life didn't seem like either.

But could Didi really still be alive? Would she have existed twenty years and never so much as contacted Remmi? The same cold sense of abandonment she'd felt as a teenager wrapped an icy blanket over her heart. She'd almost come to grips with the fact that her mother had died somehow, that whatever she'd planned to do to the father of the twins had backfired and she'd disappeared without a trace.

How odd that Didi's ghost was rising now. First that damned book—*I'm Not Me*—and now this? A stranger dressed in Didi's things to look like her leaping to her death? If she were a God-fearing person, she might think she was being given a sign. Surely, her aunt would believe that God was talking to her . . . well, or maybe Satan. For a second, she stopped in her tracks to stare at the fountain and hotel doors where people were going about their lives, unconcerned about the tragedy that had unfolded only steps from this very spot.

"Excuse me!" A woman in knee-high boots and a long coat that billowed behind, quickly stepped around Remmi. She was holding an umbrella and shot Remmi a perturbed look. A man in a business suit and raincoat, his collar turned up against the persistent precipitation, followed after her, and only then did Remmi realize she was standing in the middle of the sidewalk, caught up in her thoughts, holding up pedestrian traffic. Hastily, she continued toward the parking structure where she'd left her car, the same garage she'd used before.

She spent the rest of the day waiting for Detective Settler's call while running errands and checking on two of Greta's rental properties. The first was in Sausalito, across the Golden Gate Bridge, and as she drove over the wide span high above the neck of water linking San Francisco Bay to the Pacific, she thought about her half brother and sister, wondering if they were alive and where they might be. She'd registered years ago on several websites that were supposed to connect people with missing loved ones, but so far, she'd had no responses, which was not surprising. She'd known the chance of finding either

Ariel or Adam was a long shot. If they had survived, they probably knew nothing of their birth or family.

From the bridge, through its cables, she caught a glimpse of the island of Alcatraz, its famous prison and lighthouse visible, a ferry churning toward its rocky shore. Usually the drive was uplifting—freeing, somehow, as she left the city behind, but not today. The weather was as gray as her mood, and by the time she'd stopped at the triplex, a sprawling older home that had been converted into three large apartments with water views, she couldn't shake the feeling of doom that had been with her for the past two days. She found a PowerBar in the console, unwrapped it, and ate the stale mixture of oats, peanuts, chocolate, and God-knew-what-else just before she pulled into the short driveway of the rental.

The property was in good shape, but one of the tenants had reported a water leak in the bathroom, so Remmi met with the single mother who lived there and saw that, sure enough, the ceiling in the bathroom showed water damage. She promised to have a repairman out to fix it. The second property was a six-plex, basically a shoebox of a building with three units up and three down, located in Berkeley, not far from the university, where Remmi had eventually gone to college. (Even with her scholarships, she still had the debt to prove it.)

One of the six-plex tenants had quit paying. When she arrived at the apartment, she found that the front door was unlocked, the unit empty and smelling of filth. Left-over trash littered every room, and the plumbing was obviously not working, the sinks, tub, and toilet filled with garbage. Remmi was completely disgusted. "Not going to get the security deposit back," she muttered grimly, as if the delinquent renter could hear her. She locked the mess up for the moment. The neighboring tenant didn't answer the door, so Remmi called the handyman she used and explained the situation. Once he'd agreed to clean, disinfect, and paint the apartment, along with making repairs to the triplex in Sausalito, she wiped her hands with sanitizer she kept in the car and backed the Subaru out of the shared, oversized driveway to join the traffic heading south toward Oakland and the Bay Bridge on her way back to the city.

Detective Settler contacted her just as she reached the western shore of the bay. Remmi took the call through her speakers via Bluetooth, so she could keep both hands on the wheel as she exited the freeway.

"Got your messages," Settler said. "I assume you heard that the victim was IDed."

"It's all over the news."

"Do you know of any contact your mother would have had with Karen Upgarde?"

"No," Remmi said, having trouble hearing Settler over the sounds of her car's engine, tire noise, and the road noise from the other vehicles crowded around her. "I've never heard of her before. And I tried to go to the Reliant Agency today. It doesn't exist, not like you'd expect. It's just a mailbox."

"Yeah, we checked that out, too, but we're looking for the owner."

"Jennifer Reliant."

"Maybe." Settler didn't seem convinced. "Did you ever hear from the author? Osgoode?"

"No."

"Huh."

"I told you, she's a phony." Remmi was following a delivery truck that was gearing down for the steep hill. Hoping for a way around the lumbering behemoth belching diesel smoke, she glanced over her shoulder. The cars in the neighboring lane were inching forward bumper to bumper, headlights glowing, as dusk had already descended.

"Okay, so then who would write the book? Who would know everything in it? Some of those details were pretty specific."

"Anyone could find out, I suppose," Remmi said as she, too, had wondered how the author had gotten her information. "But they'd have to talk to someone from Missouri who knew Mom."

"Someone in Anderstown."

"I suppose. Or nearby, and we're talking, what? Fifty-some years ago?"

"What about your aunt? You think anyone talked to her to get the info on your mom?"

"Maybe." She'd already been considering the possibility of Aunt Vera being somehow involved. She would have loved being able to tell someone about her semi-famous sister with her loose morals. There was a break in the lane next to her, and she nosed the Subaru into the open space, only to hear an impertinent beep from a red Toyota when the driver looked up from her cell phone and realized Remmi was squeezing her. *You snooze, you lose,* Remmi thought and gave the blonde a quick nod. For that she was rewarded with another sharp honk and a rude finger gesture.

Too bad.

Settler was asking, "You talked to her?"

"Vera? Not in a while." Not since leaving at eighteen, to be exact.

"Do you have a number for her? Address?"

"Old information, but when I get home I'll send you what I have," Remmi promised and hung up. She thought of the address book she'd taken when leaving Las Vegas, the names and numbers her mother had written in her strong, loopy handwriting. Maybe she should turn it over to the police. Over the years, Remmi had called every number in the book and reached about half of the people listed; the other half of the numbers had been disconnects or had been reassigned. She doubted many of them were good now, as people used cell phones to communicate. But still, the police might be able to find something in the notebook and the remainder of Didi's things that might help. Remmi had been so paranoid about dealing with cops she'd never confided in any, and now she was pinning her hopes on the idea that Detective Settler could help her find her missing mother and siblings. What were the chances of that?

"About zero," she told herself, then took a call from Greta, asking her to pick up a couple of prescriptions and groceries. The rain had started again, and her wipers began slapping away the cold drops as she drove to a market next to the pharmacy off Clayton, lucking out by getting a parking spot in the nearby lot.

As she was climbing out of her car, a dark SUV passed on the street nearby. She thought again of the vehicle that had been parked on the street in front of Greta's house the night before. This one looked identical, but it was out of sight down the hill before she caught any numbers on the California license plate. A tiny frisson of anxiety slid down her spine, but she ignored it.

There have to be hundreds, more probably thousands, of them in the Bay Area. Dashing through the rain, she stepped inside the brightly lit store just as the automatic door was closing.

The market was busy, and it seemed no one was inclined to hurry. As she swept down the aisles, she was invariably stopped by a cart clogging the passageway, its owner caught in the dilemma of which product to purchase and totally unaware anyone else might be in a hurry. She did manage to grab a pre-made tuna salad at the deli without too much trouble but was hung up again at the pharmacy, having to wait impatiently in line as all the clerks at the prescription counter were dealing with customers who chatted with the clerk and asked either about their medications or the possibility of getting a flu shot.

By the time she had carried her bags to the car, nearly an hour had passed, and the rain was coming down in a torrent, wind snatching at the hem of her coat as she threaded through puddles to her car. The windows were fogged, making visibility difficult; her wipers streaked the windshield as she backed out of the parking spot. The lot was crowded, and two cars were vying for her space. She eased around a white Chevy Impala that was forced to wait, and before she put her own car into gear, a Mini Cooper darted into the spot she'd vacated, causing the woman at the wheel of the Impala to pound on her horn and shake her fist.

The whole ordeal only added to her tension as Remmi melded her Subaru into the flow of traffic. Turning on the radio, she heard Burl Ives warbling "A Holly Jolly Christmas." She hated that song. She changed stations only to hear:

> *Rockin' around the Christmas tree*
> *At the Christmas party hop—*

She snapped the radio off even though the lyrics echoed through her brain. *Ugh!*

"You're just a grinch," she told herself, fogging the windshield as she turned onto Stanyan Street. Then she glanced in the mirror. Her fingers tightened over the steering wheel. For just a second, she thought she noticed a dark SUV a few cars back.

Don't. Be. Paranoid.

But paranoia had seemed to be Remmi's middle name in the last week or so, and though she kept one eye on the mirror, nearly rear-ending an older Volkswagen in the process, she didn't catch a glimpse of the vehicle again.

For the first time in her life, she wondered if Aunt Vera had been right after all. Maybe Satan really was always close by.

CHAPTER 20

Settler stood up and stretched, cracking her back. The department was quieter than it had been earlier, many of the employees already having left for the day. She'd been at her desk for hours. Lunch had consisted of a California wrap sandwich that had been primarily avocado, tomatoes, and sprouts and a Coke, consumed while she stared at her computer monitor and tried to piece the case together.

She hadn't discovered any links between Didi Storm and Karen Upgarde other than the obvious—Upgarde had been dressed in Storm's clothes and makeup when she jumped. Nor had the book publisher been forthcoming on the author of *I'm Not Me*. Yet. But even vague threats of abetting a killer or impeding an investigation had gotten the powers that be at Stumptown Press to scramble around. She expected a call from someone higher up, or an attorney, soon.

Though she had located some of the people associated with Didi, she wondered if she was spinning her wheels. There was a chance that Upgarde's leap to her death had not much more to do with Didi Storm than a wig the impersonator had once worn.

As she raised her arms over her head and bent over, she caught sight of Ted Vance as he walked by carrying several reports and, as ever, wearing a crisp suit, white shirt, and tie, the only person in the department who took the trouble. He looked over the top of his half-glasses and thankfully didn't say a word, just radiated disapproval with his tight-lipped expression.

So what else was new?

She returned to her desk chair, where after rotating the tightness from the back of her neck, she settled back to work. She'd located several people associated with Didi. Didi's first husband, Ned Crenshaw, and his wife lived on a ranch just outside of Sacramento, less than two hours away. Her second husband, Leo "Kaspar the Great" Kasparian, divorced from wife number two, had moved to Reno, where he now performed his act in one of the casinos. Reno was around four hours distant. As for Harold Rimes, who had once employed Didi, he now lived near Lake Tahoe, just east of the state line, so still in Nevada, where gambling was legal. Rimes had a club there, even seedier than the one he'd owned in Las Vegas years earlier. None of them were all that far from San Francisco.

Did any of these men know Karen Upgarde? she wondered. So far, she hadn't found a connection, but the phone records from Upgarde's cell were on their way, and the lab had cracked into her computer, so links, if there were any links to the people in Didi Storm's life, were about to be uncovered.

"Good," she told herself.

She heard someone approach and saw Martinez round her desk. "Take a look," he said, "I just sent you a picture you need to see."

"Okay." She clicked into her e-mail account and saw

the new message from her partner. She clicked on the attachment, and a grainy picture came into view.

"Right there, see that?" Martinez said as he stood next to Settler at her desk. Martinez pointed at her computer screen, which showed a somewhat fuzzy image of the window from which Karen Upgarde had stepped out onto the ledge of the Montmort Tower. The window was open, a curtain inside visible, Karen seeming to teeter upon the ledge. "There, behind the curtain." She saw a dark shadow evident behind the gauzy fabric. Was it just a trick of light, or was a man standing just beyond the focus of the camera's lens?

"I see it. Kind of. Can't the lab enhance this any more?" She used her mouse and enlarged the photo, but it only became more blurry and pixilated.

"They're working on it," he said, "but there's only so much you can do. This was just from a bystander's phone."

"I can't tell if there's anyone in the room or not." She moved her mouse around, studying the image from different angles before bringing the picture back to its original size. "Damn it." She glanced up at Martinez. "Any other pics?"

"None any better than this one. At least none that have been sent in. The PD has made pleas to the public through the local news stations, and we've received tons of shots, and videos, too. The lab is sorting through them."

Once more, Settler tried to increase the clarity of the image, but it didn't work, so she still wasn't certain what she was seeing.

"We have no footage of anyone in the hallway going in or out of her room or the rooms that connected to hers."

"But the camera wasn't functioning properly," Martinez reminded.

"I know. But what are the chances that someone walked into her room, convinced her to jump, or somehow helped her along, then fled off camera before rescue workers got the hotel staff to let them in?"

"I'm saying it's possible," Martinez said, straightening and scratching absently at his goatee.

"Well, yeah."

Her cell phone rang, and she glanced at the screen: King County Sheriff's Department. "Gotta take this," she said. It was likely her ex-partner, Rosamie Ugali, who was returning the call she'd made earlier in the day. She traded places with Martinez, who took over the mouse and tried to enhance the computer image while Dani walked several feet away.

"I did some checking on your vic, Karen Upgarde," Rosamie started in after identifying herself. "There's not a lot I can tell you that hasn't been sent down via e-mail. Upgarde tried to commit suicide a couple of times already. I interviewed the ex-husband, who was here in Seattle when she leaped. Seemed pretty broken up about it. Talked to her mother, too. Her response was 'I've been expecting this for years' when she heard about Karen, I was told."

"Okay."

"Karen was never all that mentally steady, that's what her ex said. She was always up and down, possibly had some kind of condition that was never diagnosed. The mother, Irene, said she was grateful Karen didn't take anyone else with her and, when questioned, wouldn't elaborate, but the upshot was that Karen wasn't stable. No current boyfriend or roommate, not tight with any girlfriends. Her boss said she was a 'capable' waitress. Not friendly but could do the job. Didn't hang out with other workers, and that's it. Said she'd been at that restaurant for four years, before that a diner that went out of business."

"Was she a drinker?"

"No record of it—no evidence of bottles in the home, no drugs, no suicide note. Nothing. Her apartment was a little messy, but I've seen a lot worse. I looked for more celebrity paraphernalia and clothes, but there wasn't anything that I could label as belonging to anyone but her. She wasn't a conservative dresser. She was kind of edgy—for a woman her age, you might say on the flashy side. She did karaoke down at the local club near her apartment, but we didn't find anything out of the ordinary. And no wigs. You asked if she had anything with Didi Storm's name inscribed in it. Nothing. Nada. Not even a picture of the woman, so it doesn't appear she was obsessed with her."

"So no connection?"

"Not that we've found so far. We also talked to the people at the karaoke bar, and the bartender—his name is Chuck—said she was better than most. Could sing, and really got into it but usually came in alone."

"No friends?"

"None that he could name. He called her a 'loner' and remarked that she seemed to come out of her shell on-stage, but that was it. She drank diet soda or sometimes sparkling water, usually a Diet Coke or something like that. No alcohol."

"Did she attend AA meetings?"

"We think so, but you know that's hard to say. They take both the alcoholism and the anonymity pretty seriously. Tight-lipped organization. That's the whole point."

"But people talk. Even people who go to meetings." Settler re-took her chair as Martinez stood up. She held up a finger, indicating she needed to talk to him, and he rested a hip against the edge of her desk and eavesdropped on her end of the conversation.

"The only thing of interest was that there was a guy who came in about two weeks ago," Rosamie added.

"Someone the bartender didn't recognize, not a regular. According to Chuck, the guy ordered a beer and nursed it while he watched the show. At that time, Upgarde was on stage belting out a Madonna number that was her favorite—'Papa Don't Preach'—along with some others, which he didn't remember. She always sang songs with a moving beat, not much for ballads like some of the more serious karaoke-ers. Anyway, Chuck noticed because this guy walked over to her table after she'd been onstage a couple of times and struck up a conversation with her. Karen kind of brushed him off—at least that's the way it seemed to Chuck. But soon after she left, the stranger did, too. Didn't wait for his tab, just left enough money to cover the drinks and took off."

"In a hurry to go after her?"

"Maybe. The guy didn't use a debit or credit card, just cash, and Chuck is pretty certain he'd never seen him before or since. He couldn't give that great of a description of him except that he was probably in his late forties, maybe early fifties, and dressed like we all do up here, in a dark sweatshirt and jeans, jacket with a hood. The only odd thing about him was that the dude was wearing tinted glasses and the bar is pretty dark, which is the reason Chuck noticed him. Oh, and even though he had a hood on his jacket, he wore a baseball cap instead. Mariners. Which eliminates no one in this town."

"Any footage of the bar that night?"

"They have cameras, but they're on a forty-eight-hour loop, and this was several weeks ago."

Damn. What was it with the cameras on this case? Settler thought as she glanced at the computer monitor with the poor-quality image. Either they weren't working, the film had been erased, or the pictures weren't clear.

"E-mail me Chuck's full name and contact info," she said to Ugali.

"You got it."

They talked for another ten minutes, and Settler asked about Rosamie's twin daughters who were six now— "going on thirteen; let me tell you they sure grow up fast." Then, with Rosamie's promise to let her know if she found out anything else about the victim, she ended the call and turned to Martinez.

"Any chance there's a Mariners baseball cap in that photo?"

He snorted a laugh. "I can't even tell if there's a person in the shot, let alone determine what's on his head."

"I know, but . . ." She was squinting at the image, and he was right, she couldn't tell if she was looking at a man, a woman, a shadow, a ghost, or nothing at all. "Ten to one, that's a person. We need to double-check anyone on that floor."

"Got a junior on it already."

"Who?"

"Mina Camp."

"Okay." Camp was new to the department, fresh out of college, but eager and efficient, as well as a tech wizard.

"What did your friend up in Seattle say?"

"That we don't know enough about Upgarde. Yet. And there's an unidentified male we need to find."

"One wearing a Mariners baseball cap?"

"Yep." Settler filled Martinez in on the conversation as an e-mail from Ugali arrived. It included the bartender's name, cell phone, and place of business: Buford's Bar and Grill, Chuck Buford, proprietor.

The Marksman loaded up, stowing his equipment in his vehicle. He'd cleaned and oiled his weapons, a rifle for long distance and, if needed, a pistol for close up, then made certain he had an adequate supply of ammo. Now he placed the guns and extra clips in their respective cases in the back of his SUV.

He had another job to do, so he'd stay another day or two, but it would feel good to leave the crappy fleabag of a motel in Oakland and get to work again. As he climbed behind the wheel, he rolled his shoulders to release some tension, then fired up the Ford. The engine caught almost instantly, a good sign.

He had to be careful, he thought, as he backed out of his parking slot and eyed the brightly lit reception area where that kid, barely twenty, was working the counter and chatting up a woman with a roller bag who was registering.

No one else was loitering on the porch in the rainy dusk, not even someone out for a smoke. No one would be able to tell when he'd come and gone, and he knew that this particular "no-tell/motel" had only one surveillance camera, and it worked only part of the time, due largely to his own efforts. He knew his way around technology, had kept abreast of the latest security devices as well. It all came in handy. But this was his last night at the Baysider, which wasn't anywhere near the bay. He never stayed anywhere too long, didn't want anyone to get a good look at him, needed no one remembering him, or pointing to him, or even wondering about him. He had to be a ghost, nothing more substantial. At least when he was working. He would return back here after the job to clean up, then wait to come down from the high that followed a killing, maybe grab a little shut-eye, if possible, then handle the next job and check out of the Baysider for good. He would never return. There were enough cheap motels that he never had to occupy the same space twice.

As he drove out of the lot, he whistled under his breath, and the songs of his youth, ingrained in him from dear old granny, played through his brain again. The "lit-

tle light song," as he thought of it, was one of his favorites, and it rolled easily through his gray matter. He
tingled a little inside. It felt good to be working again,
and he felt more than a little elation at the thought of taking care of some old loose ends.

He crossed the bridge and turned on the GPS tracker
he'd placed under the bumper of Remmi Storm's Subaru.
Seconds later, on the screen, a blinking dot told him exactly where she was. Not only did he know where she
was, but someone else did as well. This particular bug
could be accessed by an app where more than one user
was able to view the location.

He smiled to himself. Wasn't technology great?

CHAPTER 21

Just to be certain she wasn't being followed on her way home, Remmi made a quick turn off the main artery of traffic, then cut through a neighborhood with narrow streets and cars parked tightly on either side. As she did, she watched for a tail but saw no dark vehicle keeping her Subaru in its sights while hanging back and maintaining its distance.

"You've seen one too many horror flicks," she told herself. She was in the city, *her* city, not some lonesome private dirt road winding deep in the woods leading to a haunted house or cemetery or whatever. She passed the UC San Francisco Medical School before reconnecting with the main street and driving her Subaru up the hill to the house. She parked in her usual spot in the driveway and, with a last look over her shoulder, swept her gaze over the wet street but again noticed nothing out of place, nothing suspicious, no lurking dark vehicle. Good.

Get a hold of yourself.

She locked the car. Laden with grocery bags, she dashed up the front steps.

The porch light flipped on just as she reached the front door.

"Saw you coming." Jade, Greta's caretaker for the evening, shut the door behind Remmi as she slipped inside. "Thought maybe you could use a hand."

"At least one."

"Got two." Jade, a woman in her late forties, was tiny and lithe. Part Asian, Jade boasted often enough that she had earned a black belt in karate *and* tae kwon do. And she looked the part: Tough. Compact. Supple. Her black hair was twisted into a neat bun, and she wore yoga pants and a tunic as well as a woman half her age. Remmi believed Jade's accomplishments, though she'd never witnessed any martial arts display. "Let me take those," Jade insisted and, before Remmi could protest, removed the soggy bags from her, allowing Remmi to hang her coat on the front hall tree.

Ever vigilant, Turtles noticed she was home and trotted out to greet her.

"There you are," Remmi said, feeling a little better now that she was inside the warm house, with its mingled scents of Greta's lavender potpourri and something Jade was simmering in the kitchen, something tangy with onions and garlic, she guessed.

"Mongolian beef," Jade said as if she could read Remmi's mind. Her stomach rumbled as she bent down and Turtles lifted her front legs off the floor to receive the proffered petting a little more quickly. "Greta's in her room"—Jade was already hurrying around the staircase toward the kitchen—"and I think she wants to talk to you."

"Got it."

Remmi found Greta dressed as she was this morning, but with a fresh sheen of lipstick. Seated in her favorite reading chair, her feet propped on an aging ottoman, she looked up at the sound of Remmi's footsteps. "I thought I heard you come in," she said, shifting slightly and wincing a bit as she set the book, her copy of *I'm Not Me,* next to a box of tissues on a side table. "Damn this arthritis." With a sigh, she adjusted a pillow propping her back, then added, "It's hell getting old," something she confided to Remmi at least once a month. "There we go. Now," she said, her attention back on Remmi again, "tell me. What did you learn today?" She was always eager for news, and this evening was no exception.

"We've got some work to do." Remmi started explaining about the repairs needed to both the buildings she'd visited today in Sausalito and Berkeley, but Greta swatted the air impatiently.

"Not that! For God's sake, I know you'll take care of whatever needs to be done. What I want to know is what you learned about that Upgarde woman. Sit down, sit down." She pointed to the corner of her antique four-poster bed, but Remmi settled on the window seat instead.

"I don't think Mom knew Karen Upgarde. At least not that I remember, and I spent hours trying to research her before I left this morning. I searched the Internet as best I could. Unfortunately, I came up empty."

"Huh." Greta scowled in disappointment as Turtles finally waltzed into the room and hopped onto the ottoman, curling into a ball at Greta's feet.

Remmi explained about the Reliant Agency being nothing more than a post office box with an answering service, and Greta let out a snort.

"What about the police? They must know something."

"If they've found out more, they haven't told me. I'm not exactly on their 'need to- know' list. I think they're going to try to find Aunt Vera, check on the validity of the book, see if she was interviewed."

"Or, if she's behind the whole thing, including the book," Greta suggested. Over the years, Remmi had confided in the older woman, whose view of Aunt Vera had been colored by Remmi's stories. Though Remmi had originally been reticent to say anything about her family, she'd let the story out bit by bit, due, in part, to Greta's intense curiosity and constant, if gentle, prodding.

"I've thought of that," Remmi admitted. She wouldn't put it past her aunt to try to find a way to make some money off her missing sister.

"Well, who else?"

"I don't know. Someone from Anderstown, Missouri? One of Didi's—or Edie's, I should say—friends? Or, maybe someone who didn't like her? A relative I don't know about? Or someone else she confided in?" She thought of Seneca or Leo Kasparian or Ned Crenshaw, or several of the other men who had come in and out of Didi's life, men Didi had dated but hadn't married. And then there was the mystery man, the twins' father. Or maybe a random person. Someone unknown.

"Frustrating," Greta said.

"Agreed."

Remmi's phone rang, and she pulled it from the pocket of her jeans and glanced at the number. She didn't recognize it and almost hung up, but then decided it could be important. "Hello?" she answered.

"Is this Remmi Storm?" a gravelly male voice asked.

"Yes."

"Good." He sounded satisfied. The voice was starting to sound familiar, and it struck a chord, not a good one.

"Who is this?"

"Harold," he said. "Remember me?"

Harold Rimes. Her mother's boss. She tensed. "How did you get my number?"

"Like that's hard." He didn't reply, and she wondered if he could be the person in the dark SUV she'd sensed was following her. "You got any idea where that mother of yours is?" he asked. "Didi?"

"Nope."

She'd never liked Rimes, and the feeling hadn't changed over the years. "She still owes me money. Over twenty grand, and I figure with interest it's more than double that."

"Why are you calling me now?"

"With all this stuff that's going on? That book? I'm startin' to see it everywhere, and now with the new publicity, y'know, with that woman killing herself all dressed up like Didi or Marilyn? There's all kinds of chatting about it online, did ya know that? Somebody's cashing in big time, and I bet it's Didi."

"So . . . you think my mother's alive?" she asked.

"'Course she is!"

From the corner of her eye, Remmi saw Greta's head snap up. "Have you heard from her?"

"No . . . but she's too ornery to die . . ." When Remmi didn't immediately reply, he added, "Isn't she?"

"I don't know," Remmi admitted. "I haven't seen or heard from her since she left Las Vegas."

"Seriously?"

"Seriously."

"You're bullshittin' me."

"Have you seen her? Heard from her?" Remmi asked again.

He let out a derisive snort. "If I had, would I be wasting time with you? No, Remmi," he said, and the way he said her name made her skin crawl. "But she wouldn't be lookin' me up, if ya know what I mean. Remember: twenty grand. But, believe you me, it would take more than a fireball in the frickin' desert to kill that woman. She's like a cat. Just one difference, though. Instead of nine lives, she has ninety-nine."

"Look, if you have any information—"

"No, listen, if *you* have any. If you're just shinin' me on and you know where she is, tell her that I want my money back, and I'm going to come lookin' for her."

She expected him to threaten her as well, but he hung up then, and Remmi, more angry than scared, thrust the cell into her pocket.

"Who was that?" Greta asked.

"Didi's old boss. A real bottom feeder. He wanted to know if I knew where she was or if I'd heard from her."

"I gathered that much."

Remmi told her about the rest of the conversation and how she felt about Harold Rimes.

"Do you think he's dangerous?" Greta asked.

Remmi made a face. "I've always had the idea that he was more bark than bite, one of those guys who likes to throw his weight around and threaten but is really a coward inside." She remembered the incident at his club when she'd been caught "borrowing" the Stephen King novel, and she felt that same old slimy feeling she had had when his gaze had traveled up and down her body. "He's a pig, but I don't think he would do anything."

"If you say so." Greta didn't sound convinced, but Remmi managed to turn the conversation away from Didi's lech of a boss.

"What's been going on around here?"

"Nothing earth-shattering or even interesting." Greta explained that the company she'd hired to string the Christmas lights would finish the task either tomorrow or, more probably, the next day. "Yeah, real exciting around here." She frowned and asked Remmi if she wanted to have dinner with her. "It's Mongolian beef."

"I heard, and it smells great, but not tonight." She was beat and didn't want to answer any more of Greta's endless questions. "I'll see you tomorrow." Retracing her steps, she retrieved her battered sandwich from her coat pocket, then headed upstairs, nearly tripping on Ghost, who'd been hiding on one of the risers. "Oh—geez."

The cat hissed, displaying his needle-sharp teeth, his ears pinned to his head, before he scurried down the steps to slink into the hallway and out of sight.

"Nice," she muttered, then, more loudly, "Back at ya, Ghost," before climbing the remaining stairs to the third floor and unwrapping her dinner, such as it was. Her stomach rumbled again, as it had been hours since the Power-Bar. She took a bite of the sandwich before actually putting it onto a plate and uncorking a bottle of Chardonnay she found in her fridge. Romeo appeared and hopped up on the counter as if he owned the place. "You leave this alone," she said as he looked with interest at the sandwich. She wasn't about to share tonight. "Hear me?"

The big cat sat on the edge of the counter, his long tail draping over the cupboards and twitching slightly as he eyed her dinner.

She didn't trust him. Not for one second.

She carried her plate and glass into the living area, plopped down in her favorite chair, then found her remote, clicked on the TV to turn on the news, and hoped for more information about Karen Upgarde, but she was disappointed as the anchors were already talking about the weather; a storm was predicted, and they were leading into sports. The Seahawks were favored in Sunday's game against the 49ers here in the city at Levi's Stadium.

Between bites of tuna, pickle, and rye bread, she channel-surfed but found nothing on the woman who'd leaped from the nineteenth story of the Montmort Tower.

Yesterday's news.

She tried her iPad, as she had earlier this morning, but again discovered no more information than she'd had before leaving the house. After she washed the dishes, she put on her pajamas and spent another hour doing a little digging on the computer to see if she could uncover any information on the people Didi had listed in her little notebook, but she came up dry.

Muttering to herself, she watched Romeo curl into a ball at the end of the couch. She stretched. It was too early for bed, and she wasn't interested in television. Maybe she'd pick up that book she'd started three or four times, a mystery that couldn't quite grab her attention.

Getting to her feet, she glanced out the window. Her heart nose-dived. Parked in the very spot as the night before was the dark SUV.

He was back?

The guy who she was certain had been following her?

She snapped off the light so she wasn't visible, then squinted through the glass. Was there someone in the driver's seat?

Maybe. But she couldn't see. Heart in her throat, she decided she had to find out who owned the car and why it had suddenly taken a spot right in front of the house. She'd just go down and take a picture of the vehicle and license plate, that was all. If the vehicle belonged to anyone nearby, or a guest, no big deal. But at least her curiosity would be satisfied.

She threw on her clothes again, found her purse in the kitchen, grabbed the tactical flashlight she always carried, her phone, and her remote Subaru key, then grabbed her short jacket from the bedroom closet. Stuffing everything into the pockets, she started for the exterior staircase, steps that had been converted from the original ladder-type fire escape. The key could be used to hit a panic button on the car and cause the horn to blare and the lights to strobe to scare anyone intent on harming her or to alert the neighbors that she was in danger. The flashlight was powerful enough to temporarily blind an attacker if she pushed the right button as she shined the beam into his face, and the jagged, metal edges around the flashlight's lens could cut deep and wound an attacker should she unexpectedly end up in close proximity to him.

She certainly hoped it wouldn't come to that. She told herself again that she was overreacting, that, as Greta had suggested, a neighbor just had a different vehicle or rental car or guests or something. Kids home from college.

Fair enough, she thought, her pulse skyrocketing.

She'd take a picture of the SUV and license plate and find out who it belonged to.

And hopefully she could do it on the sly. There would be no confrontation.

As she headed through her small kitchen, she said a quick prayer under her breath.

The killer set up.

The rifle would do. He stroked the barrel with a caress, then eased along the path, careful not to make a sound. Lights were burning in the house, but he checked the road.

Quiet.

No traffic right now.

Good.

All he had to do was wait for the exact moment.

A dog was barking closer than he liked, but he forced himself not to react. He took a calming breath of the cool night air to center himself. He closed his eyes for the briefest of seconds.

Then he was ready, every muscle tense.

Go time.

He slipped his night-vision goggles from the top of his head to the bridge of his nose and *voila* . . . dark night became a colorless day.

Perfect.

And the familiar song from his youth rolled on through his brain.

Flipping her hood over her head, Remmi peered through the window cut into the back door that opened off her small kitchen. Nothing. No boogeyman lurking on the top landing. No ghost of Didi lingering just outside the door near the vine-covered wall. Just darkness on this side of the house. Gripping the flashlight, she headed outside and started down the steps.

Rain was beating steadily, the November air heavy and cold, the streetlights dimmed by low-hanging clouds. So far so good. No . . . wait.

She'd just stepped onto the second-floor landing when she felt a vibration. She froze, straining to see through the rain, trying to hear over the continual plop of drops and gurgle of water in the downspouts.

A noise.

A footfall?

Her throat constricted.

One soft thud, then another. More vibrations. In rapid succession.

No doubt about it now. Someone was climbing steadily upward.

Every muscle in her body tensed as she peered through the open stairs to the level below, where a dark figure of a man was ascending from the first-floor landing.

For a second, she panicked, thought of fleeing upstairs, back through the door of her apartment to safety. She could throw the dead bolt and, if he kept coming, dial 9-1-1 and alert Jade and Greta. That would be the sane move. But then she'd never know. *Damn*. She clicked on the flashlight. The harsh beam illuminated the staircase. She rained that sharp light straight down on the man's upturned face. "Jesus!" he exclaimed, throwing an arm over his forehead to shade his eyes.

"Who are you?" she demanded shrilly, heart stampeding. He'd stopped dead in his tracks. "What're you doing here?"

"What the hell is that? Turn it off!"

In that second, she recognized him.

The breath died in her throat. She couldn't breathe. Shocked, her heart pounding frantically, she found herself staring into the chiseled features of Noah Scott.

The boy from Las Vegas who had stood her up, then nearly died in the desert.

The boy who had haunted her dreams for two damned decades.

For a second, time seemed to stand completely still. Her throat turned to dust. Unexplained tears suddenly burned the back of her eyes. No words came, though a thousand questions spun through her mind. Somewhere, not far away, an engine started.

"For the love of God, Remmi, are you trying to burn out my retinas? Turn that damned thing off!"

"Noah?" she whispered, still disbelieving, raindrops splattering around her.

"Yeah, Remmi. It's me," he said, his voice deeper than she remembered. "Do you mind? You're gonna blind me."

"But why?" she asked in disbelief. "What are you doing here?"

His head had turned to the side to avoid the glare, and she saw it then, the scar at the base of his throat, evidence of the bullet that had nearly taken his life. Letting out a breath, he squinted upward again. "I came here looking for you."

CHAPTER 22

Noah winced. Damn, that light was harsh.

"Looking for me?" Remmi repeated in a voice that brought back memories of hot summer nights two decades earlier. For a second, she seemed stunned. He wasn't sure she believed him. "Looking for me? Are you kidding me? After all this time?"

"Yes. Now, can we get out of the rain? And turn off that damned light."

"Go *inside?* Are you crazy? I don't even know you anymore!"

"Sure you do—" Rain was seeping under his collar, and still she kept that garish, painful flashlight trained on him. He closed his eyes for some relief and was vaguely aware of the start of an engine, a car driving off.

"It's been twenty years, Noah!" Her voice was tight. "No, we're not getting out of the rain. What the hell are you doing here?"

She certainly was the girl he remembered, full of piss and vinegar, a smart, pretty girl who'd been sassy and intellectual and ready to take a dare at a moment's notice. He surmised she hadn't changed all that much.

"I saw you on TV," he explained. He could rush her, of course—the illumination wasn't completely crippling—but he didn't want to scare her any more than he already had. "You were in the crowd at the Montmort when the woman jumped."

"So?"

"I was looking for you anyway. I'd just found out you were in San Francisco. Then there you were, on TV."

"You expect me to believe that?" she scoffed.

"It's the truth, for God's sake. Now, can you switch that thing off!"

She hesitated, said something unintelligible under her breath, but snapped off the flashlight, the staircase becoming immediately pitch dark, no image visible for a few seconds as his eyes adjusted.

"I don't appreciate being stalked," she said.

"What? *Stalked?* I'm not—"

"You could have rung the bell downstairs," she argued, cutting him off. "You know, like a normal person? I mean, how did you even know I was up here? On the third floor?"

"I saw the lights go on."

"There it is!" she said. "What I said: *stalker.*"

He held up a hand as his vision returned and he saw how angry and scared she was. He hadn't meant to frighten her. "Look, I know other people live in the house." She started to argue again, accuse him, but he broke in, "Yes, I did check that out."

Her scowl deepened, and she still held the flashlight as if it were a weapon, clutching it tightly in one fist as if ready to strike.

"I didn't want to bother them."

"Even though it's not that late, other lights are on, and again, it's the *normal thing to do*."

"Okay, next time I'll do it the normal way. Even though there's not much normal about us," he said dryly, looking up at her, icy drops of rain running down his face.

"Us," she repeated. From the higher landing, he could see her glare down at him. "You show up here, out of the blue, after seeing me on TV . . . after twenty years."

Noah's pupils returned to normal, and the lights of the city, low and muted by the rain, came into his vision again. "I didn't mean to scare you."

"Then use the front door."

"Okay. Okay. Should I go down there now and ring the doorbell?"

She didn't appreciate his sardonic tone. "Maybe."

"Meanwhile, we're getting wet out here," he pointed out.

"Oh, hell." She let out a long puff of air and started back up the stairs. "Fine. I guess. Come on in." At the top landing, she threw open the door and stormed inside, with Noah a few steps behind.

"Lock it," she ordered. "There are all kind of crazies out tonight."

"Like me?" he asked.

"Very possibly."

Her running shoes leaving a trail on the kitchen floor, she led him to a small living area with a broad bank of windows offering a panoramic view of the bay. The room was cozy and lived-in, an architectural throwback to a previous century, filled with furniture that had seen better days and a patterned carpet covering part of the battered hardwood floor. On one wall, a bookcase was crammed with paperbacks, hardbound books, a few knickknacks, and a stack of magazines. An iPad had been left glowing on the couch. He could see the remains of a sandwich on the table. "Maybe you should start over," she suggested, and he noted she hadn't put down the flashlight with its sharp-toothed bezel surrounding its lens.

"You've been following me for days, nearly giving me heart attacks," she charged, her lips compressed into a thin, angry line, her eyes, as green as he remembered, narrowed as she glared at him. She was peeling off her jacket, water dripping on the rug. She scarcely noticed as she struggled with one sleeve because of the weapon she still held.

"What are you talking about?"

"I saw you."

"Following you?"

"Yes! Your SUV!" Finally extricating herself, she tossed her jacket over the back of a worn chair as he unzipped his. "Yesterday. Last night . . . you parked out front and . . ." Her voice fell away as she read his expression. "Right?" she asked, some of her anger dissipating. "In the dark Explorer or Pathfinder or Tahoe or whatever? You were following me earlier today, while I was—"

"Not me. I drive a pickup. Silver."

"But . . ." Brow furrowed, she walked to a window and looked outside, then let out a harsh breath. "But it was right there." After one more glance at the street in front of the house, she shot out of the room and down a short hallway.

He hurried to follow.

She was standing at her bedroom window, staring into the night. The room was small, dominated by a twin bed and a battle-scarred dresser: the pictures on the wall were black-and-white cityscapes, nothing personal. "It was just there," she said from the far side of the bed. "Right there." She pointed a stiff finger and tapped the glass. "It's gone. But I saw it. Not ten minutes ago."

He stood behind her, looking over her shoulder at an empty space near the darkened curb.

"You're talking about the SUV."

"Yes! The one that's been following me! You're saying it's not yours?"

"It's not mine." From behind her, he dropped his hands on her shoulders. He felt her flinch as he rotated her body slightly to an angle where she was looking farther down the hill to the final ess curve. "That's mine down there." He pointed over her shoulder, his right arm nearly brushing her ear. "The pickup. Chevy Silverado 4x4." The grill and windshield of the vehicle caught in the vapor glow of the streetlight.

"That's yours?"

"Yes."

Twisting her neck, she looked directly in front of the house again. "It was there," she repeated, staring at the empty space. "Last night and, again, just a few minutes ago. That's why I was coming out of the apartment."

"To confront the guy? Blind him?"

"Whatever." She didn't find his joke the least bit funny. "This"—she held up the flashlight—"can also be used as a club or attack weapon."

"I'm aware. But again, whatever vehicle you saw wasn't mine."

"Then whose?"

He still had one hand on her shoulder, noticed the warmth of her body beneath her sweater. Then, as if she realized he was still touching her, she tensed and slid away from him. "I don't know. Maybe it belongs to . . ."

"The neighbors? Some friend dropping in on someone who lives nearby? I've heard the theories. And I don't have any idea if they hold water. But even so, even if the SUV's legit and belongs to someone or their friend, why was it, or one like it, following me?" She turned and faced him, her face only inches from his, the warmth of her body radiating from her.

"You're certain it was—"

"Yes!"

"I don't know, Remmi," he said honestly.

She regarded him belligerently for a moment, then sighed heavily. "Oh, hell. Am I going crazy? Imagining all this? Because of what happened? Because of the woman who looked like Didi and jumped."

"I don't think you're certifiable yet."

"Come on," she muttered, walking into the living area again. Dropping into a corner of the worn couch, she pointed to a faded chair and said, "Why don't you sit down and take the time to tell me why you're here. Everything. Why now?"

"Because," he said, "I have a feeling it's all starting again."

"What?"

"Whatever we were caught up in that night in the desert."

From her expression, he guessed she felt the same. "Because of all of this sudden interest in Didi Storm again?"

"That could be a part of it," he allowed as a huge furry cat appeared from behind the couch. Without any effort, the cat hopped onto the cushions, then the back of the couch. Once perched, he focused gold, unblinking eyes on Noah.

"This is Romeo," she said as he finished taking off his jacket, laying it next to hers on the back of the chair. Leaning forward, she took their coats and, in a swift motion, tossed both onto a parson's bench near the bookcase. "Sorry, cat hair," she explained. "This guy here is one of my landlady's pets. She has three cats, and they're allowed to wander throughout the house. Romeo likes to hang out up here when I'm home." Absently, she stroked Romeo's wide head as Noah dropped into an oversize club chair. Leather, no fur visible.

"So he's a guard cat?"

The corner of her mouth lifted in a way he found as intriguing and sexy as he once had. He hadn't expected that.

"This guy?" She gave the cat another pet. "Uh, not so much." She got the conversation back on track. "You were telling me why you happened to show up tonight. If only part of it is about Didi, what's the rest?"

"I wanted to see you again."

She laughed. "Okay, sure."

"No, really. I saw footage of the crowd surrounding the building, and I was pretty sure I caught a glimpse of you. I couldn't believe it, and I wanted to reconnect."

"Again—why wait so long?"

"Because I've been on the run. At least in the beginning. I was a scared kid. Someone tried to kill me that night in the desert, and I don't know who. I remember him approaching, with the rifle, backlit by the fire, and I have the sensation that I might have known him, but then everything went blank until I woke up in the hospital, where I overheard nurses saying that someone came to visit me, a guy without ID. And the police wanted to question me, too. It all sounded like trouble, so I ran, as fast and as far as I could. Stole some money from my old man and hitchhiked to L.A." He stopped then, and she just stared at him.

She slowly shook her head. "Fast-forward and you're here? In my living room? What the hell happened during all those years in between?"

"A lot. I joined up. Army. Believe it or not, I became an MP." He caught the surprise in her eyes. "Yeah, I know. The kid who always bucked authority."

Again, her lips twitched in a hint of a smile, probably remembering his run-ins with the law back in the day.

"Anyway, I got out two years ago. Didn't last the full twenty for a nice pension, but I was done with it. And finished looking over my shoulder. Always thinking that someone—I didn't know who—could be that bastard who blew up the car and shot me point-blank. He left me for dead, then tried to finish the job, I'm sure of it, when I was in the hospital. So I ran. For a long time. But I was sick of it."

She was listening, petting the cat again, the shaggy beast having slid onto her lap, but it didn't seem as if she believed Noah. At least not completely. When she looked up, there were still doubts clouding her eyes. "So why are you in San Francisco?"

"Because of the book. The agent is in the city, so I thought I'd start there."

She started to say something and seemed to think better of it. Instead she said, "But you never returned to Las Vegas?"

"No. You were gone. Ike and Mom split. She lives outside of Reno, closer to Carson City, really, in a mobile home park. She says she's dried out." He shrugged. "Who knows if that's true, but she sounds okay and gets by. As for Ike the Spike? I don't know where he is. Don't care." Noah met her eyes. "He's one miserable, mean son of a bitch."

"No love lost?"

"None to lose in the first place."

"What about your mom?" she asked.

"I just told you."

"You don't see her?"

He shook his head and then said, "When I got out of the army, I found out she lied. My dad was never in prison. He just didn't want to be saddled with a wife and kid at eighteen. I met him. He sells insurance in Boise. Has a wife, three grown kids, one still in college, and a granddaughter."

"You have a relationship with him now?"

"That's overstating it . . . we know of each other. That's about as far as we've gotten. I confronted Cora Sue about her lies, and she said she thought it was best if I thought he'd been rotting away in prison, but I think it was easier for her." He shrugged. "I talk to Mom once a month, and the guy I'm supposed to think of as my dad every so often. He's a stranger. His kids—my half siblings? Strangers. I guess if I ever got around to sending Christmas cards, we could do that. But we won't. At least not in the foreseeable future."

"If I could see my mom again, I'd want to."

"After what she did to you? To your brother and sister?"

"Yes. Absolutely. Because I want to know what happened, why she left me, and where the twins are."

"And then—?"

"I don't know," she admitted. "I never get that far, I guess. I'd like to think we could start over."

Noah scratched his chin thoughtfully, his fingers scraping on the stubble of a day or two's growth of beard. "Sometimes it just doesn't work out, wasn't meant to be."

The silence stretched between them for a few seconds before she let that subject die. "So, what about you, Noah? What do you do? You know, for a living."

"I'm a P.I. now, got my license as soon as I said goodbye to the military."

She stopped petting the cat. "Really?"

"Yep."

"Where do you live?"

"L.A. But I'm between cases, so I thought I'd do some investigating on my own. Just for me." He held her gaze and got to the point. "And maybe for you, too. I figured you'd like to find out what happened to your mother. I would, too. Whatever she was caught up in that night in the desert nearly cost me my life."

One of her eyebrows arched. "I was there, too."

"You?"

"In Didi's Cadillac. Special cargo space. I was going to sneak out and meet you, remember?" she charged. He'd seen mention of the fact in the news about Didi's daughter making claims about a baby exchange and that both she and her mother had been in the desert that night. He'd known about Didi, had remembered seeing the huge white Cadillac, but Remmi's story had been sketchy, from a distraught minor, and there had been no proof, that he'd seen, of any baby being a part of the explosion and tragedy in the Mojave.

There had been a murder, he knew, a man shot and killed, burned in the conflagration of the Mustang. And someone had definitely tried to kill him. Absently, he rubbed the scar on his neck.

Remmi went on. "That night, Didi came home earlier than I'd expected, and I had to hide. I crawled into the space in the Caddy's trunk, not knowing what she was planning. I hoped to get out as soon as I could, but she unwittingly took me with her, and I watched through a peephole in the back seat as she drove the twins into the desert. You know about all that, right? Her giving one of the babies to a guy who was supposed to be their father? For money?" She turned a little pale at the memory, and her features had hardened.

"Yeah, I read about it in the papers." The truth was he'd devoured every bit of information he could find about Didi Storm, the explosion in the desert, and the hunt for a murderer. He'd run away back then, yes, but now it had become his mission to find the bastard who was behind it all and haul his sorry ass to justice.

She asked, "So why were you out there that night?"

"Rebelling against Ike and Cora Sue and the whole damned world, I guess. Ike had laid down the law, so I took his bike behind his back. I was mad. You didn't meet me, and I was disappointed and pissed. Ended up being in the wrong place at the wrong time."

"Like me." She eyed him. "I suppose you read the book?"

"About Didi? Yeah."

"I think the author's a fake. I haven't been able to reach her. The agent sure is, just a P.O. box and an answering service. I checked."

Now, it was his mouth that smiled. "Well, that's where I come in."

"What do you mean?"

"I already talked to her."

"Who? Maryanne Osgoode?" she said, surprised. "Like she's a real person?"

"Pseudonym."

"I knew that name was a fake!" She jumped to her feet, and the cat, caught off guard, leaped to the back of the couch and arched his back to glare at Noah. "She's an actual human being? An author? Where?"

"Lives in Sacramento," he said.

"Where did you get this information?"

"Research. There's a lot on the Internet if you know how to get through a few barriers, and I have a tech who works with me who"—he lifted his hand and tilted it—"is a bit of a hacker. I found out that 'Maryanne' even went to Lake Tahoe and interviewed Didi's old boss."

"Harold Rimes?" Her stomach turned sour. "Funny. He didn't bother mentioning that he was interviewed by her when he called. He's such a *slime*."

"He phoned you?"

"Oh yeah. Just tonight. Claimed Didi owes him money and he wants it back. Even threatened me."

"Nice guy," he said dryly.

"What about Aunt Vera—Vera Gibbs? Was she interviewed, too? Someone had to have been to get all that old information on her when she was a kid in Missouri."

"Oh, yeah, she was interviewed," he said. "But here's the kicker: Maryanne Osgoode's real name is Gertrude Crenshaw." He waited a beat, then saw her putting it together.

"Trudie?" she whispered, dumbfounded. "My mother had a friend . . . and . . ." Her eyebrows drew together. "Crenshaw? As in Ned Crenshaw?"

"Uh-huh. Your mother's biographer just happens to have married one of Didi's ex-husbands." He let that sink in for a second, then said, "So I'd say that Maryanne Osgoode had some pretty good sources of information."

"I guess. But I thought Ned was in . . . Montana or—"

"Boulder, Colorado. He was. Until a couple of years ago. Now he's living in Sacramento."

"You talked to him?"

"Not yet. I got all this from—"

"Your hacker friend," she said, standing. She picked up both wet jackets, tossing his to him. "Let's go."

"Now?"

"Yeah. Right now. It's been long enough. Sacramento? What is that? Two hours away? Maybe an hour and a half, if we push it?" she asked, glancing at the digital clock tucked into a corner of the bookcase. Was it really only seven-thirty? It was so damn dark. "We can be there by ten, maybe even nine-thirty if we're lucky. I'll drive."

"I'll drive," he insisted, patting his jacket pockets, then his jeans. "Wait a second. I must've dropped my wallet. It's not—"

She reached into her own pocket and, to his amazement, pulled out his leather tri-fold before tossing it to him. He caught it on the fly. "But—wait a sec," he said, then understood. "You *picked my pocket?*"

She slid him a sly look. "Kaspar the Great was my stepfather. One of them."

"The magician," he said, realizing there was still a lot to Remmi Storm he didn't know. "But how did you do it?"

"I never reveal my secrets," she said, and for the first time that night, he caught a glimpse of the teenager who liked to tease him, flirt with him.

"Okay. Then why?"

"I needed to check you out. See if you were being honest." Her expression turned a little harder. "As I said, I don't really know you."

"Did I pass the test?"

"You got a 'C.' But it's good enough."

Meaning she hadn't caught him in an outright lie.

Yet.

"When did you have time to check?"

"You were standing behind me, right? In the bedroom?"

"You're fast."

"Yeah. And good. Come on." She snagged a bag from a nearby chair. "I'm still driving." Her eyes met his as if she was expecting him to challenge her. He lifted his hands in surrender. "And I'm taking my flashlight."

He didn't argue.

Didn't need to.

He had a gun.

CHAPTER 23

"We should never have gotten involved in this. It was a mistake from the get-go." Ned Crenshaw forked hay into the manger and talked to his wife as he worked. They were in the stable, and he was feeding the horses, the front half of the building illuminated, the back still dark, as he'd only flipped one switch. Tonight, he planned to cut his chores short as there was a big football game on TV, and he'd already missed the first half.

Nova, his favorite mare, a bay with intelligent eyes, was in her stall and watching his every move. Nova was due to give birth in the late spring, and her body was just a little heavier than normal, her coat shining under the lights of the stable. She nickered at him, impatient, as he was later with the feed than usual.

"Hey, it's coming, it's coming," he told the mare as the others, Frida, a paint mare in the next stall, and a buck-skin gelding farther down the line looked at him expectantly, their ears forward as they snorted to gain his attention. The stable could hold eight horses, four boxes built along either side of a concrete walkway that ran the length of the building. Currently he owned these three, along with a small herd of cattle and a coop full of chickens. Oh, and one dog, a mix of lab, pit, and possibly shepherd, who was currently outside in the woods that cut through these fifty acres and was barking his fool head off.

Probably caught scent of a rabbit or skunk or . . . whatever, but it worried him a little. There were coyotes in the area, and six weeks ago, Bob Hanson, who owned the place just up the hill, had spotted a cougar.

"You worry too much," Trudie said.

"Maybe. But we'd better get Copper inside."

"Precisely my point. He's just doing his dog thing. But now back to the book." She was currently sitting on a stack of sacks of grain, watching him as he fed the horses. A split bale lay open, most of the hay already fed to the horses, a second bale ready to go.

The book. "It's nothin' but trouble, especially since that woman did the flying leap in San Francisco. What the hell, Trudie?"

"That's nothing to do with us."

He shook more hay into the manger. Nova snorted her approval as dust motes swirled and strands of hay fluttered in the air. Boy, the dog was really going at it. "Jesus God," he said, looking out one of the open windows. "What if Copper tangles with a porcupine, or a coyote or a skunk?"

"When's the last time you saw a porcupine around here?"

"Okay, but we've both seen plenty of coyotes."

"I suppose. But Copper can hold his own, I think. He's smart and tough. Like you."

He rolled his eyes and threw the last of the bale into Nova's manger, the tines of the pitchfork scraping against the concrete floor.

Trudie was one of the reasons he'd left his first wife, Didi Storm, though he hadn't stepped out on Didi, hadn't hooked up with Trudie until after he was divorced. Long after. He'd only fantasized about his wife's taller, leaner, and more grounded friend. Didi had married the magician before Trudie had even moved in with Ned. In the meantime, Trudie had traded in tight dresses for tighter jeans, swapped an abundance of flashy jewelry for a simple gold band, and opted for a warmer, honey shade of blond rather than the near-white platinum she'd sported in Las Vegas. Trudie had even toned down her makeup, though it still took her nearly an hour to get her look just right. And he loved her.

But the main reason he'd left his first wife is that Didi had been freakin' nuts. Beautiful and sexy as hell, but a stone-cold kook. Insane. He couldn't count how many objects, from ashtrays to frying pans to books, he'd had to duck when she got mad. Boy, howdy! He'd left without looking back but had felt a pang of regret for her kid. The daughter. Remmi. He'd liked her but had no claim to her, so he'd left her with her loco mother.

When he'd heard about the leaper the other day, Ned had half believed Didi had actually jumped from that hotel in San Francisco.

And here he and Trudie were, eyeballs deep in that damned book. A huge mistake, no matter how much money they were paid. So far, it hadn't been all that much, but with sales soaring, Trudie had stars—or at least diamonds—in her eyes.

Nova let out an impatient snort.

"Okay, I get it . . . hold your hor—," he heard himself, saw Trudie smother a smile, and corrected, "Hang on a sec, Nova. I'm getting there. Sheesh. Pregnant females!"

Trudie actually giggled, even though she'd never, to his knowledge, been pregnant herself.

The dog was still going crazy, though the sound was a little closer now. Ned tossed another forkful of hay into the manger, then walked to the open door and whistled loudly enough that Diego, the buckskin, let out a sharp whinny. "Copper! Come!"

Trudie said, "He'll come in when he's good and ready."

"I know, but . . . he's not usually out this late."

"Neither are you. We. It's our fault," she said, and she wasn't wrong. They'd had dinner in town, and traffic had been slow. A two-hour trip to Kate's Steak House had lengthened to well over three. Darkness had fallen in the meanwhile, but at least the rain had stopped, leaving the air smelling fresh.

Ned always enjoyed this time with the horses, doing a familiar job he'd started when he was eight or nine, feeding the stock in a warm stable that always smelled of dust, hay, oiled leather, and horses.

However, the last few days, he'd been tense. Worried. And he didn't need a shrink to know why.

It was all because of that damned book.

"Come on, Copper, knock it off!" he yelled again, with a little more bite than usual. He pulled the wire clippers from his back pocket, cut open the remaining bale, and, after pocketing the clippers, restarted the feeding.

Trudie didn't move a muscle to help him with the chores, but that was their arrangement. He dealt with the outside stuff, keeping up the livestock, outbuildings, and exterior of the house. Roof repairs, painting, raking and mowing, gutter cleaning—those were all his jobs. She took care of the inside of the house. Period. But she was a helluva housekeeper, and she never nagged him about his filthy clothes or leaving things lying around. They shared cooking, but only because he was better at it than she was, something they both understood but never mentioned. All in all, they were both happy, or at least he was, and she said she was, until she'd got that wild hair about the book—that had come unexpectedly, out of the blue, and she couldn't be talked out of it. He knew. He'd tried.

"I wish this whole thing was over," he said, meaning the book. She knew what he was talking about. "We should never have agreed to be a part of it. Anything to do with Didi always turns into a disaster." He looked at her. "I'm talkin' from personal experience."

"I know, but it's a little too late for cold feet."

"It's gone too far. That's all I'm sayin'." He tossed hay into the next manger. "That woman is dead."

"She jumped," Trudie said. And then again, "Nothing to do with us."

"Hope you're right."

"I am."

He took a break, leaned against the pitchfork. "So, why would she do that? I mean even if you wanted to take yourself out, fine, okay, as long as you don't take anyone with you, but why make such a big show of it?"

"Some people are like that. Didi was."

He pronged another forkful and dropped it into the last stall, where the buckskin nickered and shook his head, halter rattling, his black mane shimmering nearly blue under the fluorescent lights.

"It doesn't feel right. Too much of a coincidence with the publication of the book."

"I know, honey," she said, and there was a hint of empathy in her voice. "But you know, there's nothin' you can do about it now. And really, nothin' you could have done about it before, right?" She climbed off the grain sacks and closed the distance between them. "Let it go, cowboy," she advised in her sexiest voice as he hung the pitchfork on a hook near the door. "Are we done here?" She wound her arms around his neck and pushed her hips into his. A small smile played upon her lips. "Because I have plans for you."

"You think you can turn around my thinking with your body, is that it?"

"I know I can." She stared into his eyes in that way that turned his brain to mush, to the point where all he could think about was one thing: sex. She had always known how to silently convey the fact that she was ready, and to prove it, she kissed him on the lips so hard, his heart immediately started knocking and he felt his damned cock begin to take notice. Man, she could turn him inside out.

Still.

After all these years.

"Okay, okay, I get the hint . . ." He walked her backward, never breaking the embrace, bits of hay fluttering in their path until she fell onto the very stack of bagged oats upon which she'd recently perched.

"What?" she giggled, her eyes bright. Her voice was breathy, her eyebrows arched coyly. "Right here? With everyone watching?"

"Everyone?" he asked, noticing the cleft between her breasts, visible in the open collar of her blouse.

"Nova, for one." Trudie was teasing him, but he looked over his shoulder at the row of stalls and noticed the buckskin had stopped eating. His ears were flat against his head, and he was backing up, snorting, and shaking his big head.

Ned started to laugh, was going to chide the horse for being a prude, but its change of demeanor registered. Something was wrong. Was it a full moon? First the dog, and now Diego—

Frida, too, had turned her head, ignoring her feed, and Nova let out a nervous nicker, her coat quivering, her nostrils flared.

Ned froze.

Trudie was still giggling, nibbling on his neck while, closer now, Copper was still barking. *Sounding an alarm.*

Ned had a quick premonition of danger. The hairs on his nape stood at attention. "Shhh."

"Why?" she said and laughed. That glorious sound he usually loved. He placed his finger over her lips, and she started to nibble on them.

"No," he whispered, and she stopped just as he heard the creak of old hinges. The slider door at the rear of the stables.

Shit. A damned intruder? Thief? What?

"The horses don't—"

He placed the flat of his hand over her mouth and stared at her hard. Every muscle in his body tensed.

She got the message. Beneath him, her eyes rounded.

Was that a footstep? Was someone actually in the stable? He strained to hear or see anything out of the ordinary, as he moved all but one finger from her lips. He told himself he was overreacting. That he'd been tense lately. Jumpy. But he'd been around animals all his life, and the horses were spooked. By something. Maybe something as insignificant as a rat slipping through the straw, but he didn't think so. They'd all stopped chewing, and three pairs of equine eyes were studying the back of the building, all looking deep into the umbra where, behind a half wall, equipment, including the old John Deere, was stored.

He saw nothing but the shadowy images of the machinery.

Half lying over the stack of feed sacks, Trudie was staring up at him.

Slowly, he removed his finger from her lips.

Her eyes rounded in newfound fear, she mouthed, *You're scaring me.*

Nodding sternly to indicate she should be alarmed, Ned whispered, "Phone," and hooked his hand to his ear, thumb and pinkie extended, middle fingers curled to indicate the silent "call me" message. In this case, he wanted to phone the police.

She shook her head and mouthed, *in the house*.

With his. Charging on the desk, side by side. He remembered.

He heard it distinctly then. Definitely the pad of a footstep on concrete. *Inside* the stable. But the intruder hadn't yet come into the light, was still hidden in the back, as Ned had only hit one switch when entering the building.

Who the hell would be trespassing?

No one with any good intentions.

Maybe it was just a kid, but he didn't think so. Should he yell at the person? Demand for him to show himself?

Something told him that would be a grave mistake.

The stable was open air, no glass in the windows. There was nothing worthwhile to steal except maybe the horses, but then a person would need a truck and a trailer and . . .

Another footstep.

He couldn't take a chance. Not with Trudie's safety.

Silently he motioned for her to get up.

"Ned—"

A quick shake of his head cut her off. Ned could flip the switch, turn on the lights at the back of the building, but if the intruder had a weapon . . . no, better to even the playing field.

He took Trudie's fingers in his and pulled her to her feet. With his free hand, he slipped the pitchfork from its hook, and with one eye focused on the darkened back of the stable, he pulled Trudie to the door and hit the light switch.

Immediately, the stable went dark.

The horses snorted, hooves stomping, and the damned dog was barking continuously, still sounding the alarm. He pulled Trudie tight for a minute, then whispered in her ear, "Run," he said as he edged her to the door. "To the house. Lock it. Get to a phone. Call 9-1-1."

"But what about you?" she whispered back.

"I'm right behind you. Leave the slider open 'til I get there. And get the gun."

"What?"

"The pistol, out of the box. Ammo is in the case next to it in the closet."

"I know where it is!"

"Call the cops first."

"No—"

"Just do it!" he hissed. "Run! Don't stop!"

She did, took off through the door, the rush of night air sweeping into the stable as she flew out. She was running full bore, long strides eating up the yard separating the stable from the house, staying on the straight path.

No, no, no. If the intruder were a hunter and determined to do harm . . .

Ned yanked the door closed behind him, hoping to stop whoever was inside the stable, then sped up after Trudie, taking off at a dead sprint, holding the pitchfork like a medieval lance. All the while he told himself he was being foolish, that he hadn't heard anything, that he had no reason for overreacting like this and scaring Trudie half to death.

But something was off. Something was definitely not right.

The damned dog was still howling.

Jesus—

Crack!

Trudie, halfway to the open back door, stumbled in front of him.

No! Oh, God. No!

She went down. Crumpled onto the grass.

No, no, no! This couldn't be happening. Not to Trudie. Not his Trudie!

Crack!

Bam! His legs buckled, and he fell to his knees before he felt the pain of the first bullet. On the ground, he propelled himself forward, still scrambling on pained knees to his fallen wife.

The back of her white blouse was blooming with a dark, horrifying stain as she lay prone, her face turned, blood in one corner of her perfect lips. *No, no, damn it, nooo!*

Blam!

The gun went off again. So much closer.

His body jerked, and his ears rang from the sound. He felt a rush of air escape his lungs and was aware of the smell of fresh blood tinging the cool night air. The dog, Copper, was still barking, but hiding in the bushes near the house, or somewhere, and Ned could barely hear him as his ears felt as if the drums had shattered. It seemed like he was swimming upside down and . . . and . . . he was starting to fade. Was that a car? Did he hear a car's engine over the echo of the blast that was still reverberating through his brain?

Oh, Lord, his ears and his legs . . . Everything hurt . . . His wife—beautiful, sensual Trudie—wasn't moving, just lying on the grass in front of him, not thirty yards from the breezeway and back door of the house. On his knees, he reached out to her. "Trudie," he whispered, his voice cracking, "Don't . . . don't leave." But, in his heart, he knew she was already gone.

Footsteps.

He sensed the heavy tread and twisted his head to look over his shoulder. He was vaguely aware of grass tickling his nostrils and the scent of damp earth and the menthol smell of the eucalyptus tree Trudie had refused to let him cut down, but those were fleeting thoughts that came in and out of his head.

He thought he noticed a movement in the shadows.

Ned squinted, his heart pumping wildly, his fingers gripping the slick pitchfork as if it were a lifeline.

As he focused, lying still, he saw the monster, a hulking, faceless shadow that swam before his eyes as it approached.

To find out if you're dead.

Now the assailant was close enough that Ned saw the rounded toes of the killer's leather boots, then the barrel of a rifle, so close, so damned close and smelling burnt, of gunpowder, pointed straight at his heart. He played dead and hoped the night veiled the movement of his left hand, half tucked behind his body as he slid the wire cutters out of his pocket. They slipped and fell to the ground beside him.

"Let it shine, Crenshaw," the killer said cryptically as he aimed, "Let it shine."

Ned was never one to give up without a fight.

Give me strength; this SOB killed Trudie!

Throwing his weight forward, he grabbed the barrel with his left hand, yanking the killer off balance. With his right, using all his strength, he swung the pitchfork in an arc that sliced through the air and landed hard on the stunned killer's face.

"What the—"

Whack! Whack-whack!

"Oooawwa, shit! You stupid cocksuck—" His words

were cut off by a howl of pain as Ned swung again, the sharp tines cutting through clothing and scraping across raw skin.

Whack! Whack!

Sharp metal spikes hit hard again, bounced a bit, then sliced across the attacker's chest, ripping through clothing and slicing skin to the bones of his ribs.

"*Aarrrgh! You stupid fucker! You're gonna pay for that,*" the attacker yelled, jumping back, jerking hard, the barrel of the rifle sliding from Ned's sweaty, bloody fingers.

Ned, fading, swung again, and the killer caught the weapon on the neck, where the metal was attached to the handle. Gloved hands gripped hard. With a sharp pull and twist, he yanked the pitchfork from Ned.

Furious, the attacker flung the pitchfork toward the house.

Ned rolled to one side, agony searing through his body, his fingers grappling through the grass as the killer took aim again. The tip of his index finger touched metal, and he swept up the wire clippers. With the barrel of the gun pointed at his chest, Ned flung himself forward and lunged at his attacker, the sharp point of the clipper jabbing jeans and flesh to bury deep in thigh muscle. Ned hoped to heaven he might somehow sever the bastard's femoral artery.

The assailant screamed, another satisfying, primeval howl. "*Arrrggghweee!*"

Ned clung to the clippers, using his weight, and twisted the grips as blood poured through the ripped fabric.

"You stupid ass-wipe!" Kicking forward, the killer connected with Ned's chest, and he heard a rib crack with the blow. He lost his grasp of his makeshift weapon and went down, no longer on his knees, but flattened to the cool ground.

The killer fired.

Craaack!

So loud! So damned loud!

The shot went wild.

Another blast.

Blam!

Ned's body jerked again.

Agony spiraled through his body.

The ooze of blood was warm against his skin.

His strength gave way, and the world spun.

He seemed to be floating from a body full of pain, and he saw himself on the grass, his body at a grotesque angle, blood blooming through his shirt, his arm outstretched and only inches from Trudie's still form. He wanted to reach out and touch her just one last time, and he tried to stretch out his hand, but nothing moved, not even a finger.

Thud! The hard toe of a boot landed hard against his ribs and forced him onto his back. Pain screamed through every inch of him, radiating from the point of impact. Bringing him back. Sharply. No longer floating above, he was back in his broken, bloody body. In agony, he tried to focus. His vision blurred as he stared at the night sky. Tried to focus.

Stars. He saw the stars.

He blinked and recognized a slice of moon like the pale smile of the Cheshire Cat.

And in the foreground, bending over him to see if he was dead or alive, was the killer. His face was bleeding, bruised, and scraped raw from the attack of the pitchfork, but he was still recognizable. "You prick," he said, before hocking blood and spittle onto Ned's upturned face. "Die! And do it slowly. Feel it. Know that Trudie's dead."

Ned felt the warmth of ooze running down his face and knew, in that moment, the mind-numbing wrench of heartache.

Trudie. Sweet Trudie. What did we do?

In the next instant, Ned Crenshaw's entire world went black.

CHAPTER 24

"It's just up here. Right there. Right there. On the left," Noah said, pointing through the windshield of the Subaru to a break in the split-rail fence.

Remmi slowed to turn into the lane, the Subaru's headlights washing over the row of oak trees flanking the drive.

Her fingers were tight on the wheel, knuckles showing white, as she'd driven with an urgency she couldn't name. If she could talk to Ned, to Trudie, to find out what they knew about Didi, maybe some of the questions about her past could be answered.

The rain that had poured in San Francisco subsided once they were off the peninsula. They'd crawled through Oakland, but traffic had finally become lighter, and Remmi was able to push the speed limit. The sky had cleared, clouds no longer blocking the moon or the thousands of winking stars.

During the drive, she and Noah had discussed the mystery surrounding Didi, caught up on their own lives, and speculated about how Gertrude Melborn, Didi's one-time best friend, had ended up becoming the second Mrs. Ned Crenshaw before assuming the alias of Maryanne Osgoode.

Remmi planned to find out.

The drive sloped steadily upward and opened to a wide parking area with several outbuildings huddled near the gravel skirt. A low-slung ranch-style house dominated the rise, and two vehicles, a battered pickup without a tailgate and a red sedan, were parked in front of a garage connected to the house by an open breezeway.

Her heart was pounding at the thought of seeing Ned again, the one positive, if short-lived, father figure in her life. And Trudie? Didi's once-upon-a-time best friend? The woman who was supposedly taking care of Ariel that night, though Didi had obviously lied. Still, Trudie knew about the twins, she'd even mentioned them in the book, though only that Remmi had insisted to the police that she had a half brother and sister.

Remmi had a million questions for both Ned and Trudie. Finally, she hoped, she'd get some answers.

Whether she liked what she heard or not.

"Go time," she said, parking behind the red car and cutting the engine. She took one deep breath, then was out of the Subaru and heading up a gravel walkway to the front porch. A dog was barking wildly, and in the distance toward the back of the property and farther away, she thought she heard a car's engine turn over.

She was near a wide front porch when a caramel-colored dog, part lab mixed with something shaggier, bounded through the breezeway, leaped onto the porch and started barking wildly at them.

"Hey, boy," Noah said, but the dog just backed up, racing to the breezeway and back again. Finally, he didn't return. Just kept up his ruckus.

Remmi pressed the doorbell as Noah stared after the

dog. They'd agreed that she would take the lead on this. It was her show.

No one answered.

She pushed on the doorbell again.

She listened for sounds of life but could hear no footsteps, especially over the excited, frantic barking now coming from the back of the house.

Nothing from within.

"They gotta hear us," Noah said. "Their dog's loud enough to wake the dead in the next three counties . . ."

Remmi rang again, but a cold premonition had crept over her. Noah stepped closer, reaching around her to pound on the door.

Again, nothing but the sounds of the night: the sough of the wind, rustling the dry leaves still hanging onto the branches of the surrounding trees, and, farther away, the hum of traffic. The dog was baying now.

"They have to be home, their cars are here . . . ," she said, half expecting someone to start yelling at the lab to pipe down. It didn't happen. Even though she told herself that Ned and Trudie could have other vehicles, or that they could have caught a ride from friends and gone out, she was starting to get a bad feeling about this. A very bad feeling.

Noah tried the knob, and the door swung open. "Hello?" he called loudly into the interior, but no one answered. Remmi felt the hairs on the back of her neck raise. "Hello?" Even louder.

Nothing.

No sounds of life from within.

She peered inside, where the lights glowed against the honey-colored wood floors of the living room. Remmi saw the flicker of a television, muted and tuned to a football game, mounted over a fireplace cut into a wall of brick that rose to a soaring, beamed ceiling. Furniture was clustered around a rug, positioned to view the TV or fire, but all of the chairs were empty, and the house felt as if there was no life within its walls.

There was no point in standing on the porch. "I'm going in."

"Wait! No," he said. Then after a beat. "Hear that?"

"The dog. Yeah. I know—" But there was more. Beyond the barking dog and the sough of the wind, she heard a low moan, barely audible, seeming to emanate from the same spot as the dog's constant noise.

"It's outside." Suddenly Noah was grim, all business.

Turning toward the breezeway, he withdrew a pistol from his pocket. "Stay here."

"You have a gun?" she whispered, surprised.

He nodded. "Yeah. It was in my truck." He had stopped by his Silverado, "to grab a dry jacket," before they took off. "Just wait here." He was already walking, skirting around the corner of the house, bending to keep his body low as he kept close to the shrubbery that edged the grass.

No way was Remmi staying put. Inching her flashlight out of her pocket, she was only one step behind Noah as he slipped through the dark breezeway. Then, as the backyard opened to him, he sucked in a breath and whispered, "What the hell?" Then, over his shoulder: "Call 9-1-1!"

"What?"

But he was already sprinting forward. Clicking on her phone, Remmi saw the bodies stretched out in the grassy area that stretched from the house to a barn of some sort. Her hand flew to her mouth. "Oh my God."

"Just call! Now!" he ordered, reaching what appeared to be a woman.

Remmi was already punching in the numbers, her fingers shaking.

"Get to the car! Lock the doors!" He was bending over

the woman, while the dog, crouched in the shrubbery, howled mournfully.

Neither of the two people were moving, not an inch, and there was blood, on the grass, on their clothes, every damned where. Remmi thought she might be sick. She didn't recognize the couple in the dark, but they had to be . . . Oh. God. Oh. God. Ned? And Trudie? Oh dear—

"9-1-1," a female voice said, bringing her out of her panic. "What is the nature of your emergen—?"

"We need help! There are two people injured here. Badly. We need an ambulance! Do you hear me? An ambulance. EMTs!"

"Please identify yourself and give me the address."

"Yes. Oh. My name is Remmi Storm and . . . and . . . Oh, God, um, we're at the Ned Crenshaw place, about four or five miles outside of Sacramento." She blurted out the address and the fact that two people appeared dead or near dead. When the operator told her to stay on the line, that an officer was being dispatched, Remmi clung to the phone and, on shaking legs, hurried closer.

"Stay back. Crime scene!" Noah barked as the officer on the line said something Remmi didn't comprehend. It, along with the dog's yowling, was just noise in a shrinking, horrible world. Her gaze was riveted to the bodies. Unmoving. Close together. On the ground where they'd been attacked. Her heart twisted painfully.

"Didn't I tell you to get into the car?" he demanded, startling her back to the present. "Whoever did this could still be here."

Remmi couldn't stand it. She had to know for certain. She turned on her flashlight with her free hand, and the blood-soaked yard was instantly illuminated. Her worst fears were confirmed as she saw, first, Ned's upturned face, his eyes closed, his body battered and bruised, his clothes soaked with blood.

Nearby, Trudie was lying prone, except her neck had twisted, her pale profile visible against the grass. Her eyes seemed fixed, her face ghostly pale, the blood showing through her blouse, a large, dark, and spreading stain. Noah caught Remmi staring down at the body. He'd been feeling for a pulse, listening for a breath, while still holding the gun in his free hand. He shook his head. "Gone," he said quietly, and she heard the operator squawking, hadn't even realized she'd let her hand slide away from her ear.

Disbelief nearly strangled her. She remembered Trudie's laughter with her mother, Ned telling her to trust a rambunctious colt in a dusty paddock.

"Turn it off!" Noah ordered, hurtling her back to the here and now. "Remmi! Can you hear me? Turn the damned thing off! The killer could be in the barn or anywhere around here. Jesus! Don't make us an easier target than we already are."

She clicked off the high beam.

Remmi thought she'd prepared herself, but as she looked down at the still form of Trudie Melborn, she knew she'd been kidding herself. From a distance, it seemed a woman was talking to her.

The 9-1-1 operator was speaking through the phone. Trying to clear her head, she brought the cell back to her ear.

"Still here."

"An officer has been dispatched. He should be there within three minutes."

Remmi barely noticed as Noah moved on his knees to the next body. Ned. Lying still. So close to his wife. But no movement.

Please, let him be alive . . . But there was so much blood. Too much. Pooling beneath the bodies, staining their clothing, and trailing off through the grass toward the back of the large building, where now she heard the sounds of horses.

The dog had finally given up barking, was whining as he lay in a fringe of trees near a fence line surrounding the property.

She surveyed the scene. Why was the trail of blood leading behind the stable? Obviously, Ned and Trudie had fallen here, where they lay, where most of the blood had collected. Unless one, or both, of them had been shot farther away, run, then been shot again, and finally dropped to the ground? Or was it someone else's? She heard the first siren wailing far in the distance, and then, within seconds, a second, lower siren, bleating through the night.

"He's still with us," Noah said, a little hope in his voice and once again bringing her back to the present. She looked down and met his gaze. "Just barely. He's the one who's been moaning, but . . ."

"He stopped." Remmi's heart felt as heavy as if it were made of stone. Ned's face, like that of his wife, was colorless, not a hint of movement. Remmi felt tears in her eyes and fought them.

Ignoring Noah's warning about the crime scene, she walked forward and dropped to her knees, grabbed Ned's hand in her own. "Hang in there," she whispered. "No matter what happened, you hang in there." His hand was still warm and smeared with blood.

"Remmi, don't," Noah said, but she twined her fingers through Ned's. This was the man who had once shown her how to load a shotgun and saddle and ride a horse, told corny jokes, and swore that he could make the best chili "north of Texas." He'd probably been right. And now . . .

"Stay with me, Ned," she whispered, "You just stay with me."

The sirens screamed louder. Looking past the house,

she saw flashing lights as emergency vehicles raced ever closer, but they were still far away. She silently prayed that they would make it in time to save Ned Crenshaw's life.

What a mess!

Settler surveyed the scene at the Crenshaw farm, now illuminated by temporary lamps as well as exterior lights they'd turned on from switches inside the back door of the house. The victims, identified as Ned Crenshaw and his wife, Gertrude or "Trudie," had been carted off, she to the county morgue, he to the nearest hospital. His life was hanging by a thread, but Settler hoped to high heaven he hung in there, survived, and was able to tell his story. To her. She planned to head to the hospital the second they were finished here, and she'd cut with a razor through whatever red tape might surround the victims.

Settler didn't have to be Sherlock Holmes to know that the carnage here was somehow linked to Didi Storm. The two people who found the bodies, Remmi Storm and Noah Effin' Scott, one of the myriad of people missing from Las Vegas twenty years before, assured her of that. Now, not long out of the army, Scott had apparently become a frickin' P.I. in Los Angeles.

Just what she didn't need.

She'd already given them the talk about the attack being police business and warned them to "let the police handle this." She'd also reminded each of them that they could inadvertently screw up a case, destroy evidence, but judging from their reactions, she figured they'd each heard the spiel before, maybe multiple times, and most likely had ignored it in the past.

They would again.

She'd read it in their gazes.

Great. Just frickin' great.

Now Storm and Scott were in separate squad cars, being interviewed by different officers who were taking their preliminary statements. Though she'd been fooled before, Settler didn't think either one had actually fired the missing rifle. No, she believed their story that they'd come here when they'd figured out that Trudie Melborn was not only Mrs. Ned Crenshaw but also the fictitious Maryanne Osgoode. Even so, there was a chance that they knew more than they were telling or were, in some way, even unintentionally, complicit.

They'd already screwed up the crime scene, whether inadvertently or intentionally. Settler was betting on inadvertently as Remmi Storm appeared shell-shocked. Noah Scott, not so much. But he'd had a lot of time in the military, had served in war zones. He'd seen it all.

"The blood trail ended at an access road just on the other side of the Crenshaw property, where it butts up to federal land," Martinez informed her. "Crime guys are typing the blood on the ground, making matches to the victims and taking tire prints."

"Any good ones?"

"Too many. Looks like it's a place kids might go from the trash littering the area. Broken beer bottles, condoms, sacks from McDonald's and In-N-Out and Burger King, and all the rest."

"Wash your Big Mac down with a Coors Light."

"Bud," he corrected. "Bud seemed to be the beer of choice."

"Okay."

"Anything else up there?"

"Not that I can see, but it's dark; they're putting up lights, going over everything with a fine-tooth comb. And the lead—you've met her, Anna Lee? She's pissed, says the whole scene's compromised by Scott and Storm trying to revive the victims."

"What were they supposed to do, just stand in the driveway and wait?"

"She would have preferred they stay off the property altogether. Maybe park on the road. Or in the next county."

Settler nodded. Anna Lee was precise and good at her job, but she was intense, and if anyone screwed up, or made her job harder, they heard about it. "Well, too bad. It is what it is."

"God, I hate that saying. It's almost worse than 'What goes around, comes around.'"

"No, that's worse," Settler thought as she studied the Crenshaws' backyard and noticed the strips of crime-scene tape that roped off the killing area and what was assumed to be the escape route of the wounded killer. That was a bonus. The fact that the murder had occurred here, in the county, not her jurisdiction, wasn't. But the detective in charge, Brian Ladlow, was efficient and, rather than look at Settler and Martinez as adversaries who were butting in to his case, actually welcomed them.

He was approaching now, a big man who had played pro football for one season before an ankle injury had taken him out permanently. He was a foot taller than Settler, probably double her weight, and everything about him, from his close-cropped hair to his perma-press clothes, screamed efficiency, no nonsense, and definitely no frills.

"Getting anything from the witnesses?" she asked, hitching her chin toward the two squad cars where Remmi Storm and Noah Scott were giving their preliminary statements.

"Not so far." His voice was deep, rough from a cigarette habit, judging from the pack visible in his shirt pocket and the slight scent of smoke not quite covered by a breath mint. "Just what you'd expect. And they jibe. They're clean."

"But connected," Settler reminded him.

"Uh-huh. That business about the woman who jumped from the Montmort? Heard all about it. But I gotta tell you, I don't see how. So this guy, Crenshaw, was married to Didi Storm for what? Like two minutes? I think it's stranger that these two"—he motioned toward the squad cars—"show up here like minutes after the attack went down."

They'd found rifle shells here, near the victims, and some farther away, near a large eucalyptus tree in the yard between the stable and the house. It appeared that Crenshaw and his wife had been in the stable and had come out, most likely with a pitchfork that had been found discarded in the bushes surrounding the house, its long wooden handle smeared with blood. Had the killer been hiding behind the tree and ambushed them as they left the stable, or had the victims been chased from the building and the killer, behind them, taken cover by the tree and fired?

Still unknown.

"They showed up pretty damned quick after the vics were shot," Ladlow said, the fingers of his right hand delving into his shirt pocket and extracting a cigarette. "Kind of a coincidence, if you believe them."

Settler nodded. "Lucky for the Crenshaws they got here when they did."

"Not so much. She's dead. He will be soon if he isn't already." Ladlow fiddled with the cigarette, didn't light up.

Settler said, "Let's hope not. I want to hear what he has to say."

"You and me both." Ladlow stared at the bloody

ground, watched the techs for a second. "Helluva thing. Double murder."

"Not yet." He was starting to irritate her by writing off Crenshaw when Settler felt talking to the rancher would be key to the investigation. Sure, they could analyze phone records, computer data, e-mail accounts, and the like, but that would take time and wouldn't fill in all the blanks. Hopefully, Ned Crenshaw, if and when he regained consciousness, would be able to complete some of the missing pieces that linked this attack to the woman who had jumped from the Montmort and, yes, back to what happened to Didi Storm.

From the corner of her eye, she witnessed the interior light of one of the squad cars wink on, and Remmi Storm got out, slamming the door shut behind her. She was still talking to the officer who'd been interviewing her and now appeared to be waiting for Noah Scott.

What was their deal?

When she'd talked to Remmi the other day, Settler had gotten the impression she hadn't seen him since leaving Las Vegas. She made a note to check that out, if the officer interviewing her hadn't already gotten a satisfactory answer.

In the other car, Noah Scott was still being interviewed. That was going to take a while. There was a lot more to question him about—if not this case, then the other one, when he'd walked away from the hospital in Las Vegas as a kid. For the first time, the police could question him about what had happened in the desert that night, see if he could ID the would-be assassin who had shot him in the neck and left him for dead. Or possibly the man who'd died in the Mustang, even whether he'd seen a baby exchange or whatever the hell it had been.

Las Vegas PD had been notified. They'd want to talk

to Scott as well as Ms. Storm about each of their parts in that very old, very cold case.

So far, the two seemed to be cooperating, and Settler's first instinct was to think neither of them was the murderer. But you never knew. She'd learned that sometimes the least likely suspect was a stone-cold killer—the most boring guy who was forever mowing his lawn or walking his dog or helping a neighbor fix his fence. Once in a while, behind an everyday mask was the face of a monster. How many times had she heard shocked statements from those who had known a killer—a man who lived in the neighborhood. The remarks had varied from "Helluva nice guy" to "He kept to himself most of the time, but he was friendly enough" or "I can't believe it; he seemed so normal." There were the crazies who went on killing sprees, of course, the killer everyone knew was "a little off" or "odd" or "a loner," the one about whom someone always said, "I always wondered about him." But, often as not, a killer turned out to be the guy in the neighborhood who was least expected to be so violent.

Settler eyed the crime scene once more. Blood still everywhere on the grass, the house itself spotless—or it had been before they'd arrived and started dusting for fingerprints and searching for evidence. Then there was the stable, with its three horses, and the barn where twenty or so head of cattle came and went. The animal control people would see that the animals were cared for through a neighbor they'd interviewed; Joe Pastiche had come to the scene out of curiosity and, realizing what had happened, had been shocked and distraught and then offered to see to the stock and the dog. Animal control was considering letting Pastiche take the job once he was checked out and it was determined he was in the clear, hadn't been a part of the attack.

Good.

She watched as the techs went over the ground, taking pictures, covering the area in the grid, looking for the tiniest bit of trace evidence. The blood, though, if any of it was from the killer rather than the victims, that would be the best. If the killer was in the system. If not . . . well, first things first, and what she wanted to do was interview Ned Crenshaw if he ever regained consciousness. She was heading to the hospital as soon as she was done here. Already, she'd ordered a comparison between the bullets from the body of Mrs. Crenshaw and those extracted from Noah Scott twenty years earlier, as well as the one found in the dead John Doe who had been burned beyond recognition in the rented Mustang in the desert.

Maybe, just maybe, the two cases could be linked, and she would find some clue to what happened and the reason Karen Upgarde had jumped and Didi Storm had disappeared.

He was fucked.

Big-time.

The Marksman had left the Crenshaw place in a hurry, nearly peeling out. He'd been parked on the access road facing out, for a quick exit, but that's about the only part of his plan that had worked as it was supposed to. He'd been bleeding like a stuck pig from the wound in his leg and knew he'd left a trail of blood. That wasn't supposed to have happened.

He'd gotten too close, wanted to taunt the cocksucker.

He checked his face in the rearview mirror once he'd put Sacramento behind him and didn't like what he saw. His visage spoke of violence. It looked like he'd gone ten rounds with a damned grizzly bear and lost. How the hell

was he supposed to hide that? Wear a mask? That fuckin'
son of a bitch, Ned Crenshaw!

Driving, mindful of keeping his speedometer right at
the speed limit, he rethought the plan and decided he'd
underestimated Crenshaw. The killer should have expected that the cowboy wouldn't die like a normal human
being. The Marksman had been a fool to let himself get
so close, to taunt the man. He knew better, damn it. Shoot
from a distance. Hit in the heart or the head and get the
hell out. That was his forte. He was good at long distance—the best, he'd told himself; it was the very reason
he'd been hired in the first place, back when this all
started so long ago. And tonight he'd fucked up. He had
the pistol, here in the Explorer, locked in its case, and he
hadn't even taken it with him to the killing site to finish
the job. All in all, the job had been a major cluster-fuck,
and ultimately, he could blame no one but himself.

He pounded the steering wheel. Why the hell had he
gotten so sloppy? Why the hell had he let his emotions
get the better of him? Why the hell had he let Ned Crenshaw take a damned pitchfork to his face and a pair of
wire clippers to his thigh?

*Because you'd wanted to gloat. Don't you know that
pride goeth before a fall?* He heard the words as if
Granny were speaking directly to him, as if her damned
ghost were seated in the passenger seat, lighting a Pall
Mall cigarette, the black kind that she'd smoked on the
sly. *Pride is a sin, you know. One of the seven. And so is
murder, but there's no talkin' you outta that. I know. I saw
how you were, even at ten, maybe eight, how you loved to
hunt. To kill. Why do you think I tried so hard for you to
find the Lord? Do you remember your Latin? Do you? Do
you remember how to atone? God will catch up with you,
boy. You know he will.*

Not tonight, not tonight. He'd make damned sure of it.

He let out his breath, tried to calm himself as he bled all over the interior of his vehicle. The lights of Oakland appeared, shining upward, obliterating the stars, and he reminded himself that he was a survivor. He'd get through this and finish the job. He just had to center himself.

Despite the late hour, more cars were on the road, taillights glowing red. He kept his speed steady, couldn't risk being pulled over by a cop, not now. He had an emergency first-aid kit with him, and he'd use it as best he could in the dingy little motel. He could feel the blood flow slowing, and that was good. Damned good. No artery nicked by those needle-nosed cutters. Good thing. Otherwise, he'd be in far worse trouble than he already was; he'd be forced to go to an ER, and then he'd be exposed.

He took the exit for his motel, and when he finally turned into the bumpy, worn asphalt lot of the Baysider, the reception area was still lit brightly, and the kid behind the counter was alone, playing on his cell phone, not paying the least bit of attention to who was coming or going. Good.

After parking in his usual spot, he grabbed the softsided pack that held all the essentials for treating wounds, burns, bug bites, and the like. He found his room key, hurried inside, and tried his best not to track in any blood. Once in the doorway, he hit the lock button on his key fob. Yeah, there were some red spots on the dusty cement, but he'd be gone before daylight and would disappear into the city.

Inside the bathroom of the locked room, he stripped off his pants and saw the ugly gash in his leg. It was deep, still bleeding slightly, and would probably need stitches. Several. But not tonight.

That ass-wipe Crenshaw!

It's your own stupid fault. Why did you have to get close and taunt the bastard? He was down. You were lucky to have run out of the stable and set up quickly behind the tree, so you were able to nail the wife. Crenshaw would have bled out, or you could have taken another shot from behind the eucalyptus. But you had to get cocky, try to rub it in.

He'd hoped to catch them in the stable, but somehow he'd given himself away.

That damned dog.

Barking his fool head off.

You should have shut the yapping mutt up. That was your first mistake. One of many. You had to get close, didn't you, like before, with the kid in the desert. Couldn't be satisfied to shoot from a distance. What's wrong with you?

"Nothing!" he said, louder than he'd expected, then clamped his teeth shut and decided not to listen to the nagging voice in his head or the ghost of Granny or any other unwanted recriminations. He had work to do. With the barest of supplies.

Inside the zippered pack, he found a packet of antiseptic wipes and another of antibiotic cream, some large sterile gauze patches, gauze roller strips, and tape. Not the quality of a hospital ER, but good enough. For tonight.

He washed his hands under hot water, using soap from a dispenser, then tore open the sterile paper envelopes so he could extract the gauze the second he needed it. After cleaning the raw flesh with hot water and the antiseptic wipes, he was able to view how deep the snippers had cut. All the way through muscle to the bone—his damned femur. "Bastard," he muttered again with another dark thought for Crenshaw; then he focused on adding antiseptic and antibiotic ointment before binding the wound with a compress and two of the largest sterile pads. He hoped to hell he didn't bleed through.

As soon as he was finished, he tested the leg.

It worked. He could walk and bend, without too much trouble. And if the pain was great enough, he had pills he could use, but those painkillers were trouble; they dulled him, and he still needed that razor-sharp edge. Nor did he take the aspirin in the kit. He needed his blood to clot, couldn't risk thinning it.

He tested himself again, stepping on the leg and walking. It hurt like hell, but he'd suffered through worse. For now, it would hold up if he didn't strain it too much.

How the hell was he going to accomplish that?

Somehow, he'd have to figure it out.

He had more work to do. First his chest. He tore off his shirt and saw four large, evenly spaced scrapes running across his chest, higher and deeper on his left side; the merciless tines had cut through hair, skin, and muscle and driven down toward his gut. At least the wounds were no longer bleeding. He cleaned them as best he could, bandaged where he needed to; then he looked at his face in the mirror.

Ugly gashes.

Bruising and deep scrapes.

One nostril in tatters, the eye above swollen. He hoped that wound was superficial, but he couldn't be certain as he couldn't see out of it.

The bastard had nailed him, but good. Going out during the day would be a problem. He couldn't cover the damage. From this point forward, he'd have to go out only at night, then come up with some logical accident to explain what had happened when he finally had to face people again.

But the current job was far from finished.

There was still Remmi Storm to deal with.

He felt a slow, cold smile crawl across his face as he realized that finally he would get some revenge.

Some of his own back.

He couldn't wait to kill Remmi.

CHAPTER 25

Trudie was dead. *Dead!*

And Ned . . . he probably wouldn't make it, either.

Remmi was sick as she and Noah drove away from the hospital where her ex-stepfather was clinging to life by a dwindling thread. At least that's the feeling she'd gotten from the staff who had surrounded him. They hadn't been allowed to visit him, of course. He'd already had emergency surgery, was slated for more, and would end up in the ICU, possibly under police guard.

"You okay?" Noah asked as they'd walked out of the brightly lit hospital and into the parking lot to the Subaru.

"No," she said. She never would be. Seeing Ned and Trudie, two people close to her mother long ago, shot, covered in blood on the lawn of their own home—Trudie shot in the back, gunned down; Ned, battered and beaten, his eyes never opening. Was Remmi okay? No way. She hadn't been "okay" before, and she certainly wasn't now.

She stared through the windshield and felt cold to the marrow of her bones, despite the heater blasting warm air from the vents. Noah was driving. She hadn't put up much of a fight after the interviews at the station. They'd been kept apart, been driven in separate vehicles from the ranch to the sheriff's department, where they'd been questioned more intently, each in a private room with detectives from Sacramento and San Francisco. The ordeal had taken hours before they were taken, together this time, back to the Crenshaw ranch to pick up Remmi's car; crime-scene techs were still working there, and a deputy was guarding the scene, while two news crew vans circled the end of the drive. A reporter and cameraman had been poised to talk to them as they left, trying to flag down the car, but they hadn't stopped. Noah, who had snagged the keys from her, had shaken his head at the dogged blond reporter and sped onto the main road. Remmi had been thankful for his sudden lead foot. No way had she wanted to discuss anything with the press.

However, she had insisted on visiting the hospital, and Noah had agreed. Then, after they'd been denied access and any real information on Ned, they'd left, and Noah had swung the Subaru into an In-N-Out Burger, where they'd picked up hamburgers and fries before the place shut down at one in the morning.

So now he was at the wheel, and they were driving across the dark waters of the bay, the lights of San Francisco glittering like jewels on the hilly peninsula.

They'd tried to talk, to discuss what had happened, but after spending hours being grilled, they hadn't spoken much since leaving the hospital, each engrossed in their own unsettling thoughts, left to wonder why this had happened.

Tired as she was, the questions kept running through Remmi's head: Why were Ned and Trudie killed? Was it because of the book? Had to be, right? The timing couldn't be ignored. And what about that book? Why had Trudie decided to write it, or at least publish it, now? It would have taken a year or more to put together probably. Who had helped her? And what about Ned and Trudie—her mother's first husband and once best friend? How had they gotten together? And Noah, why in the world had he turned up now, in the middle of all of this?

She glanced at him again. He looked serious, his profile thrown in relief when cars driving in the opposite direction passed, the beams of their headlights flashing over the interior. For a second, she closed her eyes and thought how her life had changed in the few, short days since Karen Upgarde had taken that fateful leap.

From then on, her life had been turned upside down.

Oh, who was she kidding? Her life had always been in some kind of turmoil.

They reached the house, and Noah parked the car in her usual spot. Out of habit, she checked the street. No unfamiliar SUV. Noah's Silverado hadn't moved. Nor were there any Christmas lights blazing from the rooftop. Greta was sure to be in a state about that, as one of the neighbor's eaves was aglow with a string of lights, and Greta liked to be the first to welcome the season.

With Remmi leading the way, they climbed the exterior staircase, walking up the steps where they'd met less than eight hours before.

Had it only been that long? It felt like a lifetime. Then, she hadn't been certain she should allow Noah into the house, had suspected him to be an intruder, but now it felt natural that he was with her.

Did she trust him?

Not completely, of course. She still barely knew him, but at least most of the story he'd told her he'd reconfirmed with the police, and it had seemed to be the truth.

Funny how time changed everything.

Inside, Noah unwrapped the burgers and fries and packs of condiments, then spread them onto the coffee table.

Remmi found the bottle of wine she'd been working on and, without asking, poured the remains of the Chardonnay into two glasses. "You game?" she asked, offering him one.

His smile didn't quite touch his eyes, but he tried to joke, "I prefer a merlot with my Animal-Style Double-Double, but this'll do in a pinch."

She tried and failed to grin just as Romeo strolled in. "Not yours," she said to the cat as they dug in. Romeo took his usual spot on the back of the couch, switching his tail.

Food helped. Though she'd been dead tired and depressed, she felt a little more energy as she finished her burger and sipped the wine.

"You're wrong," she said.

"About what?"

Holding up her glass, she said, "I think this is the perfect pairing. If you don't believe me, Google it."

He laughed for the first time since they'd reconnected, and the sound touched her, almost brought tears to her eyes, as she considered the terrible ridiculousness of the situation.

"God, what's happening?" she asked, suddenly struck anew by the spiraling events that had led them to this point.

"We'll find out."

"You sure? After all this time? When some kind of madman is on the loose mowing down people with a rifle?"

"A madman connected to Didi. Yeah, we'll find him." He took a bite of his burger and chewed.

"How can you be so confident?"

"He'll show his hand. They always do."

"Do they?" she countered. "Then how come it's been twenty years?"

"We haven't been looking."

"The police have."

"A long time ago. As I said, he'll show his hand. Maybe tonight was it." Another bite and a swallow of wine. "Pretty bold move, killing the author of the book and trying to take out her husband, who happens to be Didi's first husband." He frowned a little. "But unless there's something we don't know about the Crenshaws—like they owe money to the mob, or whatever—it sure looks like the hit was connected to the publication of the book."

"Or Karen Upgarde's death."

He nodded. "Probably both."

"So how do you think they're connected to Karen Upgarde?"

"Million-dollar question. What we have to figure out. That techie I told you about is already on it. I texted her before we left the hospital."

"It's the middle of the night."

"She doesn't exactly keep regular, nine-to-five hours."

"Handy."

"Very." He was finishing off his fries.

"So she can get into bank records and phone records and e-mail? That kind of thing, like hackers do on TV?"

A slow grin slid across his face. "Why, Ms. Storm, are you suggesting I've asked her to do something illegal?"

"Never." They both knew that was a bald-faced lie. She was desperate to get at the truth, to learn the fate of her mother and the twins, to put the whole mystery of her past behind her. "I just want to find out what happened to Didi. And what happened after she left. Was the dead guy in the car that burned really the twins' father, and who was he?" She could feel her long-simmering anger burn brighter.

"I don't know."

"What happened to Ariel? I saw my mother hand my sister over to the man she swore was the twins' father, Noah, but the police insist they didn't find any evidence of a baby in the burned-out car. So, is she alive? Where? How'd she survive?" Remmi couldn't stop the dozens of unanswered questions that had piled up in her mind from rushing out, faster and faster. "And what the hell happened to Seneca and Adam, huh? Why did she take him away? To be with Didi?" She tossed back the last of her wine and set her glass down on the coffee table. "It just seems the more we learn, the less we know."

"Sometimes that's the way it works," he admitted. "A case seems to get murkier before it finally clears."

"It's been two damned decades. How much murkier can it get? I'm tired of living my life not knowing, maybe never knowing. And now . . . and now all that's happening: the book, the suicide, the murder . . . there's a reason, Noah. And the way we were going to find out was by talking to Ned and Trudie."

"Maybe," he interjected.

"Not maybe. She was Maryanne Osgoode."

"You don't know that she was killed because she wrote the book."

"It's a good bet. And they took her out before anyone had a chance to talk to her."

"To shut her up," he said.

"Yes!"

"But the book is already out there, the damage done."

"Maybe they had something in their notes, something they didn't realize was dangerous or whatever. Or they were going to write a sequel, or promote the book and then it might come out. I don't know." She let out her breath and stood, unable to sit a second longer. "Then there's the money. What about the payment she got for the book? There has to be some money involved. If Trudie as Maryanne Osgoode is the author of the book, then she gets paid for it, right?"

He nodded. "But how much are we talking about? It couldn't be a lot. A small Oregon press that no one's really heard of?"

"But the book is taking off. There's a buzz around it. All weird, I know, but some people are into that true mystery thing, possible crime, a little glitz thrown in. I don't know. There's money there."

He nodded again, thinking over her words.

"But what about after she dies, like now?" Remmi pressed. "Who gets the money that the book earns?"

"Ned, probably."

"And if he dies?"

"Her heirs, I suppose. Or whatever the agreement, the contract with her publisher, says."

Remmi was pacing, walking from one end of the living room to the other. From the windows and bookcase to the archway leading to the interior stairs. "As near as I can tell, she doesn't have any heirs, if Ned doesn't survive. She didn't have kids, I don't think, but I suppose there could be a sister or brother, maybe even parents still alive."

"You're saying you think the killer's after the book's royalties."

"Yes, I . . . I don't know. Maybe. I'm just thinking aloud."

"Maybe we're getting ahead of ourselves," he said, as he crumpled the wrappings and stuffed them into the white In-N-Out sack. "Tell me what you know about Ned and Trudie's relationship."

"There's nothing to tell," she said, stopping her pacing near the bookcase. "I never thought either one of them was interested in each other or . . . you know, making a buck off of my mother." She just couldn't see it.

"Seems like they did."

"I know, but why? From the looks of things, it seemed like they were doing okay." The ranch house had been clean before the police started going through it, the furniture up-to-date in that retro mid-century modern style that had made a comeback. They had acreage and horses, two older vehicles, and in the garage, she'd learned, a Porsche, only a few years old and in great condition.

"Appearances can be deceiving. You know the old saying, 'Big hat, no cattle.'"

"Except they had cattle," she reminded him.

"I know. Maybe a hat or two, as well." He smiled again, and it touched her deep inside, caused her heart to do a traitorous little flip, and reminded her again of how infatuated she'd been with him. But that had been eons ago, she told herself. He was different now. A man. Battle-scarred from life. Yet she still found him innately sensual, probably because he seemed so unaware of his own sexuality. Was that even possible? She considered the beard shadow darkening his strong jaw, the creases near deep-set eyes that sparked with intelligence, the way he could stare into the distance thoughtfully.

"You think Trudie or Ned or the two of them together were working with Didi?" he asked, bringing her back to the present.

"I don't know. Some of that stuff in the book, about when she was a kid, they might know from being close to Didi, but no, I don't see Mom having anything to do with Ned. She was pissed when he left, and they never reconciled. That's the way she is. Once you burn her, she never forgives."

"What would she think about Trudie marrying Ned?"

"Oh, man. No way she would like it. She would see it as a betrayal on both their parts." She leaned against the bookcase and viewed a shelf where she'd kept a few favorite pictures. Didi was there, front and center, her black-and-white head shot dominating the smaller pictures.

The very picture that had been used for the cover of *I'm Not Me*.

Damn. The old pain bloomed, feelings of desperation and abandonment emerging. Setting her jaw, she fought them as she stared at the photo.

Dear God, Mom. Where are you?

She was so lost in thought she wasn't aware that Noah had climbed out of his chair and crossed the room to stand next to her. He slid his arms around her waist, and she tensed before he pulled her so close she felt his breath upon her neck. "Give it a rest," he said. "Go to bed."

"I can't," she said. "Seems as if I've got company."

"The company can take care of himself."

"I was talking about Romeo."

He chuckled. "I'll crash on the couch."

She thought about that. "You don't have anywhere else to go?"

"We just came back from a disturbing homicide scene, with people linked to you."

"So, what're you saying? You think I need . . . a body-guard?" She let out a soft chuckle. "When I've got a guard cat and a flashlight guaranteed to rip an assailant to shreds, if you use it right."

"Okay, okay, you've convinced me."

"Hope so."

She waited for a rejoinder, but suddenly the strong arms slipped away from her. "What's this?" he asked, picking up a small framed picture that had been partially hidden by the bigger head shot of Didi.

"Oh." Remmi studied the picture. "It's the only picture of the twins I have."

Noah studied the snapshot. "Okay, that's Didi, I rec-

ognize her, holding one of the kids." He was pointing to
Remmi's mother, who was standing under the awning
shading the back patio of their house in Las Vegas.

"I took the picture, not long after the babies were
born." Wearing sunglasses and slacks and a T-shirt, Didi,
still hanging onto some of her pregnancy weight, was
holding her son.

"She's got Adam."

"You said twins, but there's only one kid here," he
said. "Oh, I get it now. There, just inside the patio door."

"Uh-huh. Seneca's got Ariel, but she was still in the
house. Didn't realize I was taking a picture, and I really
didn't notice that she was in the shot as I was concentrat-
ing on Mom, and Didi was death on anything proving
that there were two babies. She'd admitted to one, but she
didn't want anyone—not the public, not her boss, not
anyone—to know there was a second one. I didn't understand it at the time, but she was obviously planning the
baby swap from the time they were born."

"Maybe before."

"Yeah, possibly when she found out she was going to
have twins. She wasn't very happy but got over it."

"So that's Seneca." He walked to a table lamp as if to
get a better view.

"Uh-huh. Why?"

Noah was studying the snapshot, his brow beetled.
"Do you have any other pictures of her?"

Remmi shook her head. "I don't have many pictures
period." She motioned to the bookcase. "What you see is
what you get. These just happened to be in some of Didi's
stuff I took that night. Why?"

"I've seen her before."

"Recently?"

"No." His eyes narrowed. "Back then. With Ike. But I
don't think that was her name." He glanced back up at

Remmi. "She had this exotic look about her, and she was at the house. Mom wasn't there. She and Ike were in his little shop, and she was talking about a bike . . . no, a moped."

"A motorized scooter."

"Essentially, yes. Ike had one, and she was asking about it, but it was just conversation. There was something else . . ." He thought for a moment, staring at the photo again. "She wanted him to fix something that was not his usual thing, and he was saying he could do it." Noah shook his head. "It'll come to me, but I'm sure Ike didn't call her by Seneca."

"What then?" Remmi asked.

"I can't remember right now," he said, drawing the picture closer to his face, "Something like . . . Shelly or Shirley or something." He squeezed his eyes shut. "God, it's right on the tip of my tongue, but it's not there," he said, staring at the picture.

Shelly or Shirley . . .

She yawned, all of a sudden weary to the marrow of her bones.

"Go to bed," he ordered, and this time she didn't argue when he pointed her in the direction of her bedroom.

Settler couldn't sleep. Couldn't shut down. She'd stayed at the hospital until 2:00 AM, returned home, taken Earl out again, and even managed a short run. By 4:00 she should have been exhausted but was still keyed up.

Who had attacked Ned Crenshaw and his wife?

Had to be because of that damned book, right?

What was the thinking when trying to prove collusion in a presidential election? Follow the money?

The department was already on that, as well as trying to figure out the blood at the scene. Tomorrow, they might have a hit with the blood typing. They would be able to see how many wounded victims and/or attackers had been at the crime scene. Phone and credit cards and computer records might link the Crenshaws to Trudie Crenshaw's killer. The bullet casings and any other trace evidence would hopefully provide a link to the murder in the desert, or not. The same killer could have used a different weapon.

Maybe, too, there would be something more on a tox screen for Karen Upgarde. She doubted it. Those things, like DNA, took time, but the lab could do miracles if motivated.

She drank a banana, strawberry, spinach, and yogurt smoothie, usually her go-to for breakfast, but what the hell? It was early in the morning, right? Just very early. After the smoothie, she fell into bed. Earl whined, and she gave in. "Up," she said, and that was all the encouragement the dog needed to hop onto the bed, lick her face, then burrow under the covers.

Staring at the ceiling, Settler tried once more to put the pieces together. Noah Scott was back, claiming he wanted to clear up his past and find Remmi Storm again. True? She didn't know. She filed that into the "maybe" category.

She glanced over at the book lying on her bedside table. The torn picture on the cover did look a lot like Karen Upgarde. So why had that woman jumped? Or had she been pushed? Still a lot of unanswered questions there, and the unfocused photograph of the hotel room hadn't provided a clear-cut answer. Who would encourage a woman to leap off a nineteenth-story ledge?

The thought that it could have been Didi Storm herself floated through her mind.

Who else would profit from the publicity? But would

the aging, B-level impersonator go to so much trouble after hiding all these years? Would she drive a mentally unstable woman to end her life? For what? Publicity? To create "a buzz" about Didi? To try to make a comeback to a career that wasn't that great to begin with? For a few bucks? Or maybe a few hundred thousand bucks?

Settler rolled over, drew up the covers, listened as rain started to fall again, slanting against the windows.

She just didn't see that angle.

I'm Not Me had been pretty detailed about all of Didi's life, and the Los Angeles and Las Vegas parts of it were pretty much known to all of her friends and coworkers and other people she'd run across in her life. There had been some newspaper and magazine articles about her— not national, but still available.

But her growing-up years? Who would know about those besides her family and close friends in the Midwest? Her parents were dead, but Settler intended to talk to Vera Gibbs and Billy Hutchinson, Didi's sister and brother, if she could locate them. Maybe they could shed some light.

Then there was Remmi's father, the mysterious man without a name. And Noah Scott's father, whom Scott claimed his mother had told him was in prison and hadn't been. Instead, he'd left Cora Sue and her son and raised another family. And, of course, Didi's twins' (if they existed) father who probably died in the conflagration in the Mojave that night twenty years ago. Lots and lots of daddy issues in the case. Lots of missing people, including Didi and her infant children.

And now, with Karen Upgarde and Trudie Crenshaw, two more victims.

So far.

Settler had requested info on everyone Remmi Storm

had mentioned when she'd first come to the department. Tomorrow a lot of that information should be waiting. Maybe then she'd find some answers. Perhaps she'd even catch a killer.

She finally drifted off to sleep somewhere around 5:00 with a final thought that she should call her own dad, forgive him for finding happiness with a woman who wasn't her mother, and try to kick-start their once tight father-daughter relationship. Could they repair the fences she'd tried so hard to knock down?

She hoped so.

The Subaru hadn't moved.

Not in the last two hours.

According to the Marksman's GPS, which recorded information for up to two weeks, Remmi Storm had returned after spending hours at the Crenshaw place in Sacramento, arriving there soon after he'd finished the job. He only wished he'd been able to stick around. He would have finished her off, too. Wouldn't that have been tidy?

But because of that prick Crenshaw and the damage he'd inflicted, the Marksman had been forced to leave.

And you left your DNA there. What about that? Unless the cops are complete idiots, they'll have proof that you were there.

He needed to end this.

Soon.

Tonight?

Before dawn?

No. He didn't have cover. And he needed time to recuperate, at least a little time. His entire body felt as if it had gone through a meat grinder and back again, and tomorrow it might not feel a hell of a lot better; then he'd take some over-the-counter painkillers, but nothing too strong that would push him off his game. How hard could it be to kill one woman?

Tomorrow night. Under the cover of darkness.

He'd take care of her.

For good.

CHAPTER 26

"Guess who was flat broke?" Martinez said as Settler was hanging up her coat on the rack in the department the next morning.

"You?" she said. She was dragging a bit from her interrupted sleep. She'd finally gotten about an hour's worth of shut-eye before her alarm blared at her; her eyes felt like sandpaper, and she was dying for a cup of coffee. Martinez, damn him, looked like he had slept a solid eight hours and was ready for a marathon.

"I mean besides me," Martinez said, teeth white against his goatee as he flashed her a devilish grin.

"Let me take a guess: You got the bank records on Karen Upgarde."

"That I did, and man, that girl was drowning in red ink," he said.

"You can fill me in when we get coffee. Just let me check my e-mail and snail mail. I wanna see what's come in." She was already heading toward her desk, catching the evil eye from Vance, who, as always, looked as if he'd just stepped off the cover of *GQ*. The whole damned department was making her feel as rumpled as Columbo, the detective from the old TV show. Her phone buzzed, and she looked at the screen, recognizing the cell phone number of the most persistent reporter from a local channel. She didn't answer; the calls had been coming in steadily, and so far, she'd referred everyone to the public information officer. She'd already called the hospital in Sacramento. Ned Crenshaw was still alive. Still unconscious. Nonresponsive. She'd also tried to reach Detective Ladlow in Sacramento and, when he hadn't picked up, left a message asking for any updates.

The department was already noisy, phones ringing, keys clicking on keyboards, conversations muted but audible, and behind it all the rumble of the heating system circulating warm air on another gloomy San Francisco day.

She'd woken up late, taken Earl outside, and connected with her next-door neighbor, whose ten-year-old daughter always checked in on Earl when Settler was working long hours, like yesterday. Addie was desperate for a puppy of her own, and her single mother hoped that having to deal part-time with the responsibilities of the neighboring pug might cool the girl's ardor for a dog. The reverse had proven true, and now Addie was begging her mother for a puppy for Christmas. "I may need Addie's help with this guy, here," Dani had said as Earl had wiggled and tried to jump up when he spied Addie, dressed in the uniform of her private school, coming up behind her mother in the doorway.

"No problem."

"I love him." Addie was already on her knees and giving the dog all her attention, while Earl danced in circles and washed her face, causing Addie to collapse into giggles.

"I'm doomed," her mother had sighed, and Settler

thought she was right. Like it or not, Addie was going to end up with a puppy. If not this Christmas, soon.

Settler slid into her desk chair, cracked her neck, and started going through her e-mail—reports, no autopsy yet on Upgarde, but yes, the bank records, phone records, and computer information. Martinez hadn't been kidding. Upgarde's credit cards were maxed, her checking account about nil, and there was a string of past-due notices in her e-mail. But in the past two months, she'd made two cash deposits of five grand each, most of which had been eaten up by her bills, which included payments to the retirement home in which her mother, Irene, resided.

"So where did you get the money, Karen?" Settler asked. "And for what?" More precisely, from whom? Had she sold something, like a car, something big? Cashed in some savings bonds or . . . Was she blackmailing someone? Was someone paying her off? She made a note to check the bank records of Ned and Trudie Crenshaw to see if they had taken out any significant amounts of cash in the last couple of months.

Her cell buzzed and she answered. "Detective Danielle Settler."

"Hey, yeah, this is Chuck Buford." A rough voice, deep. "You left me a message yesterday, I think it was. Maybe the day before."

Buford. The guy who ran the karaoke bar where Karen Upgarde performed.

"Hey, look," he said, "I told that other officer—Ugali, or something like that—everything I knew about Karen. She was really just a sweet kid who liked to sing, y'know. No friends, a mom who was failing and costing a lot of bucks. If you ask me, what happened was a damned shame."

"It is," Settler agreed. "Do you have any idea why she would want to take her own life?"

"Nah . . . Her life sucked, but, well, not bad enough to, you know, off yourself."

"Was she drinking?"

"Not here. Not around me at least. And I think I'd know. Been around it a lot in my line of work, y'know."

"What about drugs?"

"Hey—whoa, I don't know anything about any of that."

"Weed is legal there."

"Yeah, yeah, I know. But really, I have no idea. If I had to guess, I'd say no, but then, what do I know?"

"You said that she was a loner."

"She was."

"But that she left with a guy once."

"Oh, whoa, whoa. She didn't leave with anyone, not like you're saying. I think it was more like the guy followed her out. He paid for his tab the second she left and took off after her. But that's all I know about that. It didn't seem like she knew him, but I could be wrong about that. Look, I don't know what happened to Karen, and I don't know who she hung out with."

She asked him a few more questions but got no more answers beyond the guy was wearing a baseball hat and dark glasses, and seemed only interested in Karen.

Martinez—taking pity on her, it seemed—showed up within the hour with a double-shot espresso from the nearest coffee shop. She accepted it gratefully. "I owe you," she said as he took a seat near her desk.

"I know. Hey, look what the lab came up with."

She took a sip from a paper cup imprinted with the name of the shop in red and green. "What?"

"Early Christmas present. Check your e-mail."

She turned to her computer while Martinez looked over her shoulder, saw the new e-mail, and clicked on it, opening the first of two attachments. The same picture of the hotel window appeared, only this time it was sharper, the shadowy image clearer. Definitely a person, just behind the veil of the curtains. "So someone was with her."

"Yup."

The second picture was from a slightly different angle, but sure enough, the image was there.

"This one came in yesterday," Martinez said.

"There's no way you could recognize anyone in this shot."

"Agreed. But that sure looks like a Mariners baseball cap . . ."

"Bingo," she said, the espresso forgotten as she tried to zoom in on the last person who saw Karen Upgarde alive. That little buzz tickled the back of her neck again, the thrill of uncovering the truth and potentially nailing a killer.

He added, "The lab's comparing this image to the video of the guy in the elevator who is unaccounted for, the one who ran into the janitor that night and hopped off the car on another floor."

"Let's have the lab give us a clip of that, send it to the news stations, and see if anyone recognizes our person of interest. They've been calling me nonstop since this all started."

"I'm way ahead of you," he said.

"Aren't you always," she threw back at him and was rewarded with a wide grin. She took another drink from the festive paper cup and enjoyed a moment's satisfaction; she felt as if, at least now, they were making some progress. She couldn't help but think that, if they identified the person in these photos, they would find a link to the murderer of Trudie Crenshaw, aka Maryanne Osgoode, and possibly, just possibly, a clue to what had happened to the missing Didi Storm and her reported infants.

Settler had checked with Clark County and the state of Nevada, hoping for records of the twins' birth, but so far hadn't gotten a response. According to Remmi Storm and the book, Didi and the attending midwife had only recorded the birth of a son, but Didi had borne both a son and a daughter. Records showed the live birth of Adam Brett Storm. Nothing for a girl born on the same day or at any time. No Ariel Storm.

She stared at the information a second and wondered about the babies' names. Ariel and Adam, both A's. A twin thing. Did the girl have a middle name? And why Adam Brett . . . A. B. Storm.

She spent the morning again talking to people who had known Upgarde, and everything Ugali had sent her was confirmed. The ex-husband, coworkers, a couple of "friends"—everyone agreed that Karen was troubled but had given no signs of intending to kill herself. The same went for her social media pages, which were rarely used or viewed and were mainly dominated by her musical interests, new albums from her favorite artists, a few fad diets, and some funny cat videos, though she owned no pets. She was a member of the Facebook page for the Didi Storm fan club, and as Settler scrolled through the posts, there was some mention of her imitating Didi during the leap. The posted comments ran the gamut from sad and kind to downright mean:

RIP. Heart emoticon. Thirty-two likes.

What a great tribute to dress as Didi for your last act. Bless you. Kiss-blowing emoticon. Fifty-six likes. Four dislikes.

Who do you think you are, impersonating her? No emoticon but fifteen likes.

Shame on you for trying to eclipse Didi and Marilyn. You were a loser in life, and you're a loser in death. No emoticon. Twenty-seven likes.

You're ugly. You didn't even look like her! Thumbs-down emoticon.

And so on. Settler would have someone check out the people who made the comments, but it looked like the regular kind of stuff followers wrote.

Remmi slept fitfully, images of Ned and Trudie on the blood-soaked grass invading her waking thoughts and dominating her dreams. She'd fallen asleep after 3:00, and now, as she glanced at the clock, she groaned. Nine-thirty, well after her usual time to rise. With an effort, she rolled out of bed, walked into the living room wearing only her night shirt, and discovered Noah sitting on one end of the couch, laptop open on the coffee table, Romeo curled at his side.

"Traitor," she said around a yawn, but the sleeping cat didn't so much as open an eye.

"Mornin', sunshine." Noah glanced up and smiled, making her aware of her uncombed hair and state of undress.

"Not so sunny," she said, stretching and wondering why she wasn't irritated to find him already up and at 'em "You're up early."

"Years of training. Military," he said, flashing her a smile.

His hair was still damp. And his beard shadow was gone. He was even in what appeared to be clean jeans and a T-shirt covered with an unbuttoned flannel shirt, the sleeves rolled up. Had he really showered, shaved, and dressed and she'd slept right through it?

"There's coffee in the kitchen," he said.

"So, make yourself at home, why don't you?"

"I have." He grinned.

"I see that. Great."

"It is great. You're a lucky woman."

"Funny. I don't feel so lucky."

"Then you need to change your attitude." He glanced up at her, really looking at her for the first time that morning.

"I'll take that under consideration. Well, maybe." For the first time, she noticed the steaming cup of coffee sitting on a side table. He'd made coffee? That definitely improved her mood.

She made her way to the kitchen, found the carafe of coffee and poured herself a cup, and asked him, "What're you doing?"

"We're out of cream."

We, she thought, rolling that over in her mind as she took a long swallow.

As she started past the living room again, he said, "You asked what I was doing."

She paused. "And?"

"Research. Looking over what Emma sent me."

"Who's Emma?"

"The techie who works for me. Emma Yardley. I told you about her."

"Just not her name," she said as Romeo finally deigned to open his eyes and stretch, extending his paws so that his claws were momentarily visible. "Anything important?"

"Don't know. Possibly. Just going through it now."

She thought about taking a seat next to him and trying to decipher whatever he was studying so intently, but, remembering her state of dress, said, "Brief me in fifteen. I'm going to get dressed."

"Okay," he said, and if she'd expected at least some acknowledgment that he'd heard she was going to be naked, if only for a second, she was disappointed. He kept staring at the computer monitor and typing quickly, ignoring his barely touched coffee. Whatever he'd found, it certainly held his attention.

She grabbed a pair of jeans and a sweater, bra, panties, and socks, then went into the bathroom, where she thought about locking the door, hesitated, then pressed the button and turned on the shower.

Stripping out of the nightshirt, she felt a little strange. Noah Scott was in the next room, after all this time, seated on her couch, while she was stark naked and stepping under the steaming spray of the shower. She lathered herself, and in a ridiculous but quick feminine fantasy, she imagined him rushing into the room, the mist parting as he, naked, threw back the shower curtain and spent the next hour kissing her neck, soaping her breasts, splashing water over her nipples, and lifting her onto—

She shut her brain down. "What're you thinking?" she asked herself, turning the water several degrees cooler and rinsing off. He still was essentially a stranger to her.

"Remember that," she told herself as she toweled off and dressed. She swiped the condensation off the mirror and combed her hair into a ponytail. A touch of lip gloss, a little mascara, and done, in under fifteen minutes.

She stepped out of the room and saw Ghost slithering down the stairs. "Curiosity kills cats like you," she reminded him as his tail disappeared around the open landing.

"What?" Noah asked.

"Just talking to one of Greta's 'babies.' Ghost isn't very friendly."

"Gray cat?"

"That would be the one."

"He seemed fine to me," he said. "Hopped right up on the couch and started batting at my fingers as I typed."

"No way. You're kidding."

"Yeah. I am," he said with a laugh. "He came to the top of the stairs, took one look at me, and did a one-eighty."

She grinned back at him. "That sounds more like it. What've you got?"

"Nothing yet, but Emma says she's sending something important. We've been e-mailing."

"In that case, I'll be right back."

She hurried down the back stairs, past the empty second floor, and into the kitchen, where she found Greta seated at the table finishing a crossword, the breakfast dishes stacked neatly in the sink. Dressed in a pink vest and white turtleneck, along with slacks and pearls that matched her earrings, she said, "Well, good morning!" and pushed her iPad aside. "That one," she said, pointing to the screen where the puzzle was still visible, "was a doozy, let me tell you. A little trick to it today." Then she added, "I've been hoping you were coming down this morning. Dear Lord, I saw on the news that Ned Crenshaw's wife was murdered! And he's injured?" She was shaking her head. "He was Didi's first husband. Yes?"

Of course, Greta remembered Ned's name. She had that damned book memorized. No way was Remmi going to get out of confiding in the older woman, and she owed Greta the truth.

"We found the bodies, called the police. Noah and I."

"Noah?"

"Noah Scott."

"The boy . . . I mean, he was the one on a motorcycle that night in the desert. Right? Oh, my!" Her eyes were bright with excitement.

"Yeah. He's upstairs now."

"Is he? And, of course, he's not a boy any longer." Greta's eyebrows shot over the rims of her glasses. "Are you going to bring him down and introduce him?"

"Not now. Maybe later. We'll see."

"But why is he here? I mean, did he just show up out of the blue? I thought he was missing."

"He was."

"So . . . what's going on?"

Remmi didn't have time for long explanations, so she filled the older woman in quickly, without too many details, sketching out what she'd done the day before, starting with discovering that Trudie Melborn was married to Ned, but also that she was the author of *I'm Not Me.* She explained about going to Sacramento with the intention of finding out more about the writing of the book and to learn if Trudie'd had contact with Didi or had any idea of what had happened to her and how she'd gleaned all the information she'd published about Didi's life. She explained about finding both Ned and Trudie shot, Trudie dead, Ned ending up in a Sacramento hospital.

"Oh, my goodness!" Greta exclaimed, a hand to her throat, fingers twisting her pearls. "I just can't believe this. You were probably in danger yourselves!"

"I don't think so," Remmi said, stretching the truth a bit as she remembered Noah, stern-faced, eyes dark, holding his pistol, ready to shoot if he saw the killer, while the dog barked crazily in the dark night. Had they been in peril? Possibly. But there was just no reason to worry Greta. "Anyway, we got home late."

"Are you all right?"

"Yeah, I'm fine. I mean it's upsetting, and I wasn't great last night, and it took hours explaining everything to the police, but I'm okay." That was probably another bit of a lie, too, as the events of the night before were more than disturbing. Her own nightmares were proof enough, but again, why worry the older woman?

"And poor Ned . . . will he make it?" Still grim-faced, Greta finally quit twisting her necklace.

"I don't know. I think it's touch and go. I take heart in the fact that he's tough, you know, a real cowboy, but he was shot and . . . well, I just don't know." She felt an overwhelming sadness at the thought and turned to the refrigerator. "I just came down to borrow some cream for coffee."

Greta made a shooing motion toward the refrigerator. "Anything you want, you know that." She let out a breath as Remmi opened the fridge's door and pulled out a small carton of half-and-half. "While you've been out chasing criminals, the most excitement around here is that the Christmas lights will finally be up today." She motioned to the window, where a string of lights was swaying in a stiff breeze, yet to be hung. A ladder and a man's torso and legs were visible as the worker attempted to secure the lights. "Nasty day for it, too," Greta observed, "but I've been promised by the owner of the company that the lights will be tested tonight for the first time and should be spectacular even if it takes all day to string them." She paused and gave her head another little shake. "But with what you're telling me, it all seems so . . . small. So unimportant." As if to add emphasis to her statement, the string of lights clattered against the window, and outside a man swore loudly.

A whirring noise caught Remmi's attention just as she heard footsteps ascending from the basement. Turtles trotted into the room and rubbed against Remmi's legs. A few seconds later, Beverly appeared, her face flushed slightly, her short hair a red mop. Spying Remmi, she said, "*Hola. Buenos dias!*"

"Good morning," Remmi responded just as the whirring stopped and Beverly went back out to the hall.

"What's that?"

"The dumbwaiter. Jade and Beverly cleaned it up and found out it was still operational." She looked surprised herself. "Now they play with it, haul everything up and down with it. Beverly's pretty proud of herself."

"I sure am!" Beverly yelled from the hallway. "And it's not play. It's a lot of work. Man, this thing was filthy!"

"Hasn't been used in about twenty years," Greta whispered as the mottled cat hopped onto her lap and she automatically began stroking Turtles's head.

Beverly said, "I'm telling you, it's going to make my job a lot easier. Unless you find a way to put in a stacked washer and dryer on the first floor. That would be the best."

Greta snorted. "I'm not giving up my powder room," she insisted under her breath.

Remmi headed for the back stairs, carrying the cream, passing Beverly, who had opened the dumbwaiter door and was pulling out a basket of clean dishtowels. "This is the best," Beverly declared. "*El majore.* At least that's how I think you say it."

"It is," Greta called from the kitchen. "*Buen trabajo.* Good job."

On the third floor, Remmi found Noah still engrossed in his computer. "Anything yet?" she asked from the kitchen, where she reheated her coffee in the microwave and added some cream.

"A couple of things."

"Tell me." Cradling her cup, she took a seat next to him on the couch, in Romeo's spot, from the looks of the long hair left behind. The cat had now somehow climbed to the top of the bookcase, where he surveyed the living room like an emperor.

"Okay. I asked Emma to go back through old records and find out if anyone was reported missing in Las Vegas around the time of the explosion in the desert."

"Didn't the police already do that?"

"Yeah, to try and ID the guy in the Mustang, and they came up empty."

"And you found someone?" She couldn't believe it. Was it possible that the man might finally be identified?

"I expanded the search a little, that's all."

"More than the cops did?" She found that hard to believe.

"Right."

"And?"

"Some possibilities. She's still looking to see if any of them were later located," he said, "but she found out something else. Something a little more interesting."

"What?"

"Phone records. For Gertrude Crenshaw."

Trudie. Remmi felt a little tremor of trepidation. Something in his tone was worrying.

"Take a look. These numbers, all the same?" He was pointing at the screen to a list of incoming calls from different phone numbers and was picking out many that were the same. "Emma tried to track down who owns this number, but she couldn't. It seems to be for a disposable phone, you know, one of those prepaid and untraceable burners."

"Yeah."

"Well, here's a cluster of them." He scrolled back through the digital pages. "They all happened about a year, a year and a half ago."

"Meaning?"

"I'm guessing that was the time Trudie was doing research on the book. These calls are to numbers around Las Vegas. This one, closer to us, belongs to Harold Rimes, and this one," he pointed to another, "belongs to Leo Kasparian. Looks like she was getting stories and checking facts for putting the book together. She calls them, and then they call back, or she re-calls them. You can tell by the duration of the calls."

"I get it."

"So. Here's one." He pointed to another number. "And the call lasts less than half a minute. Like a pocket dial. Wrong number."

"So?"

"So, almost immediately, that number is called again, only this time from this same burner number. See?"

She compared the numbers. "Yes."

"What if whoever made the first call goofed. Called on his mobile phone, then, realizing his mistake, hung up and phoned back on the burner, to make himself anonymous."

"Or it really was a pocket dial."

"Could be. Or a mistake, and the burner call is a coincidence."

"Or it's just as you say . . . Who does that number belong to?"

"Jensen Gibbs."

"Jensen?" she repeated, feeling a distinct shock. Her cousin's surly image swam to view in her mind. "But what would he have to do with Trudie and the book? He wouldn't know anything about Didi."

"Maybe not, but he still lives with your aunt and uncle. I checked. Works for a towing company. A driver. He could have been calling Trudie, I suppose, but what if he was, say, charging his phone, left it on the kitchen counter or somewhere easily accessible, and then someone—your aunt, maybe, as she's the one with background information on your mother—what if she picked up the wrong phone by accident and, realizing her mistake, cut the call short to talk on the untraceable phone?" He scrolled through the numbers once more as Remmi's mind raced through scenarios. "And here's the kicker," he added. "There's not a single call listed between Trudie and Vera. I double-checked. And Emma has Vera's phone number. Don't you think that, in researching the book, Trudie would want information from Didi's sister, the one person who knew her growing up?"

Remmi put down her coffee cup. "Absolutely, she would. And Vera would be more than interested in talking to her. She hated Didi."

"So, maybe she'd enjoy making a buck off her? There are a few calls on Trudie's phone to Anderstown, Missouri, but they were short, to different people. Nothing that stands out. It's possible also Trudie got her information from Billy, Didi's brother."

"I don't even know where he is. I don't remember ever meeting him."

Noah looked at her directly. "One more piece of information. The Gibbses' house is pretty full. Not only do your aunt and uncle live there, but also their oldest son, Jensen, and good old Uncle Billy."

"Uncle Billy? Truly?" She was stunned. "Are they all in it up to their necks?"

"There's something there. That's all I'm saying."

"Then, let's go," she said, shooting to her feet, her mind spinning ahead.

"Wait a minute." He grabbed her wrist, and she spun back to face him. His fingers tight around her forearm, he said, "Slow down. Trudie was murdered last night, remember? And Crenshaw might not make it. Someone involved is a killer."

"And you think it's Vera?" She thought about her aunt, with her intense Christian beliefs. "She raised me, Noah. At least for a few years after Didi took off. If she'd wanted me dead, she had ample opportunity to knock me off. I'm not afraid of her, but I sure as hell want to hear what she has to say for herself."

"What about the others?"

Jensen and the uncle she'd never met.

She gazed down pointedly at his hand, which still held her tight. "I want answers, don't you?"

He loosened his grip and said succinctly, "I'll drive."

CHAPTER 27

The publisher caved.

Or at least the lawyer for the Stumptown Press in Portland called, talked to Settler, and promised to send, via e-mail, a copy of the publishing contract for *I'm Not Me*. He'd been reticent and full of bluster, but in the end, facing a subpoena and with the publisher's consent, the lawyer was mailing the contract to Settler's account at the station.

"It's a start," she said to Martinez as they climbed into the department-issued Crown Vic. Settler got behind the wheel as Martinez flashed his hallmark smile and said, "We may catch the fucker yet."

Actually, they had more than a start.

Though it would take weeks for blood analysis to determine what kind of psychotropic drugs may have been in Karen Upgarde's system, the trace evidence had been examined, and a partial tablet containing Rohypnol had been discovered in the fibers and dirt vacuumed from Upgarde's hotel room. No one who knew her thought Karen would ever willingly take a roofie, the common name for the date-rape drug, but it could have been slipped into anything she drank. Time would tell when the blood analysis was complete.

And then there were the pictures of the shadows in the room. With increased enhancement, the second picture they'd received showed that there had definitely been a person in the room with Karen when she "jumped." It was only a matter of time before they found the son of a bitch.

Better yet, they'd discovered a glitch in the phone records: Jensen Gibbs had stupidly or maybe by error called Trudie Crenshaw over a year ago, then hung up. A prepaid phone, a burner, called her seconds later. The department was trying to ID it or the person who had bought it at the store from which it had been purchased.

And Jennifer Reliant, the agent on the Didi Storm tell-all book, had contacted the police and was due to meet them at the station just as soon as they were finished with Robb Quade, the lying bellhop, whose story had changed quite a bit since his original interview.

But Ned Crenshaw still hadn't roused to consciousness, and according to the doctor she'd spoken with earlier, there was no indication that he would awaken soon. Detective Ladlow in Sacramento had echoed the doctor's words but had promised to call her the second he heard of any change in Ned Crenshaw's condition.

Once Martinez was inside the Crown Vic, the door slammed shut, and all buckled in, Settler drove them out of the lot into the gray San Francisco morning. The sky was silvery, and though it wasn't quite raining, there was enough moisture in the air that she had to use her interval wipers. They were heading back to the Montmort to interview Quade, as apparently the bellboy's conscience had gotten to him, and he now had more information on the person whom he'd let inside the room next to Karen Upgarde's, the room with the connecting door.

She was caught by a red light and drummed her fingers on the steering wheel as pedestrians—some with umbrellas, others with shopping bags, others on cell phones—flowed in both directions within the crosswalk. The skyscrapers surrounding the street knifed upward into the overcast sky, and Settler fought her impatience.

They were getting close to cracking the Upgarde case; she could feel it, and it made it hard to sit idling, the first car at a light. As the signal turned, she was about to step on the gas when a young businessman, carrying a computer case, his coat billowing behind him, flew in front of her car, racing to reach the opposite curb. The car beside her started, then hit the brakes and banged on his horn, while Settler's heart beat a little faster.

"Guess he's late for a meeting," Martinez drawled.

"Could've been way late."

"Remmi?" Aunt Vera said from the other side of the screen door. She seemed about to faint at the sight of her niece on the doorstep of the same cottage where Remmi had spent most of her less-than-happy high school years. The house was now a gun-metal gray that matched the morning sky. Though the loose board Remmi remembered on the step had been fixed, the yard was still untended, a crow picking through the tufts of grass, dry leaves, and dozens of walnuts still in their oversized green skins.

Even through the battered screen, Remmi saw that Vera, like the house, had aged. Her dishwater-blond hair was now turning gray, her eyelids sagged a little, a few more wrinkles had formed around her mouth, and her

waist was a bit thicker than it had been. In jeans and a
long-sleeved T-shirt, she forced a smile. "What a surprise!" she said, reaching for the delicate chain of gold
with its tiny cross that still dangled from her neck.

Remmi didn't waste time with pleasantries. "I want to
talk to you about the book."

Her gaze moved from Remmi to Noah. "The book?"
she said, as if she didn't know what they were talking
about.

"About Mom. *I'm Not Me.*"

She visibly started, then inhaled slowly as if trying to
pull herself together. "Didi," Vera said flatly. "Always
Didi."

"This is Noah Scott," Remmi introduced.

Vera's body stiffened. Obviously, she knew the name.

The sound of a truck's engine cut through the morning
air, and Vera looked up sharply as a small tow truck
wheeled into the driveway, startling the crow. Cawing
loudly, it flapped wildly to perch on a branch in the walnut tree.

Jensen Gibbs cut the engine and, after throwing open
the door, hopped down from the cab. He, too, was heavier
than she remembered, his blond hair thinning, a cigarette
hanging from the corner of his mouth.

He spied Remmi and he grinned. "Holy sh—," he
started but caught a warning glance from his mother behind the door. "Remmi? Criminy, I never thought I'd see
you again." He actually broke into a smile as he tossed
his cigarette into the grass, stomped on it, then strode up
the cracked cement of the walkway. "What is this? Some
kind of freakin' family reunion or something?"

"Watch your mouth," his mother warned.

"I said 'freakin.' Holy crap, girl, what're you doing
here?" He actually appeared glad to see her.

"I wanted to talk to Vera. About the book."

"The one about your mom?" he asked, bounding up the steps. "I read it. It was pretty good."

"You read it?"

"Hell, yeah. I wanted to find out all about that 'mysterious' aunt who disappeared." Smelling of smoke, he actually gave Remmi a hug when he reached the front porch, then stuck his hand out to Noah. "Jensen Gibbs."

Noah introduced himself, and Jensen's eyes narrowed. "You were in the book, too. Well, come on in. Ma, watcha doin' standin' in the doorway?"

"I was going out to church."

"When you're supposed to be watchin' Monty? No way." He strode inside and held the screen door open for them to pass.

Reluctantly, Vera backed up a step.

Jensen explained. "Monty's my son."

"You have a kid?" Remmi was surprised.

"Sure do. Didn't you tell them?" he asked his mother as Remmi and Noah followed him into the living room, with Vera bringing up the rear. The same worn furniture and pictures of Jesus were in place, just as Remmi remembered, though now, along with pictures of Jesus on the mantel, there were several photos of a smiling, bald baby. An overflowing basket of toys sat near the recliner facing the television. "Where's Monty?" Jensen asked his mother. "Napping?" Before she could answer, Jensen waved Remmi down the hall.

"Don't you dare wake him!" Vera hissed. "He was fussy, just went down." She hurried after Remmi and her son down the hallway.

Remmi's stomach tightened as she peeked into the room where she had once spent those miserable high school years. The room had been painted a soft blue, while the bed, wall posters, and awful carpet had been stripped away and replaced by new carpeting and a crib with a mobile of Disney characters mounted over it. Within the crib, sleeping soundly, was a chubby baby of about nine months. With only a bit of blond fuzz for hair, Monty lay on his back in a gray onesie that announced in bold blue letters: *I love Grandma.*

"He's the best," Jensen gushed as he ushered them back into the hallway. "Already pulling himself up. Probably will start walking soon. He's getting ready."

"He's adorable," Remmi agreed, though she never in a thousand years would have thought the surly teenager Jensen had once been would morph into a doting father. What were the chances? And yet he seemed a new person. Remmi found it nearly impossible to believe that the boy who'd belittled and made fun of her in high school and who, she was certain, had stolen the money she'd hidden behind the cupboard on the back porch, had grown into this new version of himself. But a long time had passed, and Jensen had matured somewhere along the way. Probably in large part due to Monty's birth. Fatherhood must've been the making of him.

Jensen was waxing on about how great his kid was, revealing that even though he and Monty's mom had never married, and had since split completely, they were "cool with each other."

Back in the living room, he asked Remmi and Noah, "Can I grab you a beer or Coke? Oh, I think we only have diet—Mom's vice of choice."

Noah said, "I'm good." Remmi shook her head, and Vera looked absolutely apoplectic as she sat down heavily into her favorite rocker.

"I don't think they're staying," she said while her son disappeared into the kitchen and returned with an open can of Pabst Blue Ribbon.

Remmi said, "We won't be long. We just have a few questions."

"Yeah, you said so. About the book, right?" Jensen asked. "Fire away." Again, he made waving motions suggesting they all sit down. For himself, he grabbed a dining room chair, twisted it around, and straddled it. Remmi took the hint and sat in one corner of the same couch she remembered from her high school years. Noah stood by the fireplace.

For her part, Vera looked guilty as sin. Not so her eldest son.

"So, where's Harley?" she asked.

Vera stopped rocking. "In Alaska, working on a fishing boat."

"He'll probably stay up there," Jensen added. "Loves all the huntin' and fishin'. The big outdoors, you know. Got himself a girlfriend, and they're talking marriage, I guess. We haven't met her. Wonder if we ever will."

"Of course we will. When they get *married,*" Vera said, giving Jensen the old stink eye, one Remmi suspected he'd received often, since her son had become a single father who had never bothered to walk down the aisle. As ever, Jensen appeared impervious to his mother.

"And Milo?" Remmi persisted.

Vera was quick to answer. "He's not here. Working."

"On the road," Jensen said. "Supposed to be home in a couple of days." He grinned through his blondish beard stubble. "Can't wait. Dad and me're takin' Monty to his first monster truck rally."

Vera sighed, long-suffering, and for once, Remmi agreed with her aunt. She couldn't imagine a baby under a year old at an event filled with huge trucks on massive wheels with excruciatingly loud engines.

"I said I'd take care of him," Vera reminded. "Monty doesn't have to go with you."

Jensen waved her off. "Forget it. You do enough." He took a big slug from his beer, then said, "Mom watches

Monty while I'm workin' at the tow company or sometimes at night when I take a class out at the junior college."

Jensen. Work. College. A father. It was still hard to
fathom.

"Billy lives here, too, right?" Remmi asked.

Vera sat up straighter. "Billy?"

"Your brother. The uncle I've never met. We know he
lives here."

"Out in the garage," Jensen said, hooking a thumb toward the back of the house. "Him and Dad built a kind of
bachelor pad out there. It's cool. Has a bitchin' monster
flat screen. Great place to chill, have a few brewskies,
and watch the Niners play."

"It's temporary," Vera said quickly and threw her son a
dark look. "Bill's just getting on his feet after a bad
breakup and . . . financial problems."

"He went banco," Jensen said. "What, twice? Maybe
three times?" he asked his mother.

"That woman's fault," Vera said defensively. "Until
Bill gets back on his feet, Milo and I said he could stay
here."

"Is he working now?" Remmi asked.

Jensen answered, "Yeah. Down at Tiny's Tackle Shop.
But he got a couple days off."

Remmi absorbed that. "Do you know where Uncle
Milo is now, specifically?" Remmi asked.

"Of course, I do!" Vera acted as if Remmi had im-
pugned her somehow. "For the most part, he has a schedule. It's pretty routine, only changes a little around the
holidays and sometimes in the summer. This week he's in
Montana." She got out of the rocker in a hurry and bustled through an open archway to the kitchen. She paused
near a calendar hanging on the wall next to the back door.

Muttering under her breath, she leaned closer, then snagged a pair of reading glasses from the windowsill over the sink and plopped them onto the end of her nose. "Yes. Western Montana and Idaho."

"Still selling farm equipment?" Remmi asked.

"Is the pope Catholic?" Jensen responded, finishing his beer and squashing the can in a meaty fist. "But that's the kicker, isn't it? He's never farmed that I know of." He tossed the can over his shoulder, and it landed in a trash can. "Another trey!"

From the kitchen, Vera said, "Milo knows farming inside and out. Grew up with it, long before you were born, Jensen. He worked his dad's place before going into the service."

"That's in Anderstown, Missouri," Noah said.

"Well, near there. Milo's family lived to the south of town, my parents' place was to the west." Folding the reading glasses, she returned to the living room, stopping to pick up a red block and toss it into an overflowing basket of toys. "I don't know what this has to do with anything." She focused her judgmental gaze on Remmi. "You know what your uncle does for a living. You lived with us. We put a roof over your head when that fly-by-night mother of yours bailed on you."

Remmi couldn't help but feel a sting at that barb, and she saw the anger, maybe even pain, in her aunt's eyes, the same emotion that was always there just under the surface whenever Didi's name came up. Of course, Remmi understood how Aunt Vera felt about her younger sister; Remmi had been told enough times. Vera saw herself as the responsible daughter to her parents, while Didi, who was *slightly* prettier and sexier and *a lot* more hedonistic, had left her parents and Anderstown to seek her fame and fortune under the bright lights of Hollywood, and it had all devolved to a sad and tawdry tale of another fame seeker whose big dreams had never been fulfilled.

"What the hell's going on?" Buzz O'Day demanded as he climbed out of his truck, jammed his hard hat onto his head, and crossed the gravel lot to the construction site. The wind was kicking up, sand and dust swirling, the winter sun beating down. Nevada in winter. That was the trouble with this place—warm enough during the day, for sure, but cold as a witch's tit at night. Freezing. But he could deal with the weather; it was the other stuff that got to him.

He'd had a bad night at home, his teenage daughter sneaking out to be with her boyfriend and showing up at five-damned-o'clock in the morning, rumpled, her top on inside out, looking like she'd been making out all night. Did she even know about condoms? Would he have to be the one to offer them up? O'Day's wife was a wreck about the whole thing and looked to him for help, for God's sake, so he sure as hell didn't need any problems today at work.

But it looked like he was getting his fair share.

"We struck something," his assistant, Ramon Valdez, said. "In the pit. Something big."

"Big like a boulder? Big like an elephant? Big like a casino? What?"

"I think you need to see for yourself."

"Just tell me. Don't keep me in suspense, for crying out loud. I'm not in the mood today, Ramon." He'd had enough melodrama for one twenty-four-hour period, catching his daughter trying to sneak back into the house while that douchebag of a dropout boyfriend had driven off. God, what a scene. His wife had never quit crying, nor had his daughter.

That's what he got living with two females, he told himself as he passed through the makeshift fence surrounding the excavation. The job was already behind schedule, and he didn't need any further delays on this project about a mile from the outskirts of Las Vegas. A new "planned community" was in the making. Three hundred homes in five "unique" models, two clubhouses, a golf course, a spa, and three restaurants. Just what Las Vegas needed.

If they could ever get the project moving. Right now, the backhoe was idling loudly, the operator appearing frozen at the controls, the scoop of the articulated arm filled with debris that slowly trickled from beneath the bucket's teeth.

O'Day was already sweating as he reached the edge of the area where the machinery had scraped the land, a layer of raw earth exposed in a deep hole.

"What the hell is that?" he asked as he squinted against the sun glinting on what appeared to be the metal fender of a huge car.

"I think it's a 1957 Cadillac," Ramon told him.

"A Caddy? And you can tell the year?"

Ramon shrugged. "I'm a classic car buff."

"For the love of Christ, I don't care what it is. What the hell's it doing there?"

"Beats me."

"Well, get it out of there." He hooked his thumb and thrust it over his shoulder, to indicate yanking the car out. Classic or not, it had to go.

"That's another problem. I don't think we can."

For the first time, O'Day noticed that the younger man seemed worried, his dark brows drawn together, the edges of his mouth curved down. "Why the fuck not?"

"Because I went down and dusted off the windshield. The car's not empty."

O'Day's anger seeped away in an instant. Oh . . . shit. "What?"

"There's a driver behind the wheel," he said. "Probably a woman. Hard to tell. Except for what's left of the clothes. Just . . . just a skeleton really."

He let out a long breath, took off his hard hat, and rubbed a hand through the buzzed hair of his head. "Okay. Call the police."

"Already did," Ramon said. "They're on their way."

"The damned site'll be closed for who knows how long."

Ramon shrugged and shot him a *what're ya gonna do?* look.

"I'd better take a look." He did not need this. Not today. Well, not ever, really. Dreading the task, he tightened his hard hat back on his head and, girding himself, made his way down the steep grade of sand and dust to the bottom of the pit, where the car rested under a thick layer of grit. As Ramon had said, the windshield had been dusted off. As he peered through the streaked glass, he damn near jumped from his skin. His heart trip-hammered, even though he'd expected what he was seeing.

But it was different seeing a skeleton with bits of hair poking out from a toppled blond wig. Her visage was hideous. Macabre. Black eye sockets in a ghoulish skull. Straight teeth, some showing fillings and a bit of gold, were set in a gruesome, blood-chilling grin.

A clavicle and parts of her spine and ribs showed dingy white beneath some kind of black sequined dress. Gloves covered the bones of her hands, which were gripping the wide steering wheel.

His skin crawled as the wind whispered over the pit, dust flying around him.

Every ghost story he'd heard as a kid about the dead rising rushed through his brain, and for a second, he imagined one of those gloved, fleshless fingers reaching out to caress his cheek.

And then he noticed the baby carrier, strapped into the back seat.

Oh . . . no . . . The interior back there was so dark. He'd need a flashlight or more grit wiped from the windows before he could tell for certain.

"Jesus, Mary, and Joseph," he whispered, stepping back, feeling cold from the inside out. What the hell was she doing seated at the steering wheel, as if she were out for a Sunday drive, a baby with her?

The back of his mouth turned dry, and for a second, his stomach clenched, threatening to turn inside out. He backpedaled up the hillside of the pit, sweating despite the iciness around him.

It was all he could do to maintain his composure. "Tell everyone to stand back from the pit," he told Ramon. "And, uh, we, um, we may as well let the crew take their breaks." He was rattled, no doubt about it, and though it was only eight in the morning, he planned to get back to the office, reach into his bottom drawer, and find his bottle of Jack. He needed a drink. But it would have to wait. He was in charge here and had to remain cool, so he hitched up his pants and said, "Until the cops get done with whatever the hell they're gonna do here, there ain't a lot we can do."

"Could take a while for them to process everything," Ramon said just as O'Day heard the sound of the first siren wailing in the distance.

"Let's hope not."

He waited, most of the crew standing around the pit, while the first cruiser arrived. The deputy took a look in the car and called in to the station, and within the hour, the place was crawling with cops, crime-scene tape strung across the fence, news vans parking outside the gates.

"Swell," he said under his breath. "Just terrific."

Two detectives showed up, the lead a tall, African American woman in a pair of sleek sunglasses, who was all business. "Show me," she said to a deputy, who walked with her down into the pit. They examined the body behind the wheel without touching it. She and her partner discussed the situation and talked on their cell phones before climbing back out of the hole, and O'Day wondered how she could scramble up and down the sides of the pit and not break a sweat.

Cool as a cucumber came to mind as she approached again and asked him the basics: What was the job? Who discovered the car? When? Simple stuff that either he or Ramon answered. She and her partner seemed about to drive off and leave the site in the hands of a crime-scene crew, but O'Day followed her to the car.

"So how long will we be shut down?"

"As long as it takes," she said.

"I've got a schedule."

"And I've got a murder investigation." She flashed him a patient smile that he suspected didn't quite reach her eyes, but he couldn't tell with her reflective shades. All he could see was his own distorted face in the mirrored lenses.

"We'd appreciate you speeding this through."

"We will, but we'll be thorough. You understand that."

"Absolutely." He was good with the cops. A couple of the guys on his bowling team had been with the Las Vegas P.D. Retired now. "Hey, tell me. There was only one person in that car, right? I mean I saw a baby carrier in the back seat . . . but I didn't see any kid." God, he prayed that an infant hadn't died there.

"Just one body, it looks like to me. But you know I can't discuss the case."

"Right, right, but, do you think . . . I mean did the driver . . . was she buried alive?" He had to ask, had to know.

She reached for the door handle, signifying the end of their conversation. But she hesitated and said under her breath, "Twenty years. What the hell?" To O'Day, she said, "I don't think so." She flashed a cold smile. "There appears to be a bullet hole in the back of her skull, so I'd guess she was dead before she was put into the car, or at least driven into the pit. But, really, that's all I can tell you now."

"Wait a sec." He was putting it together now. Hadn't his wife and kid just read that book . . . the one about the woman who went missing here, what? Twenty years ago? And hadn't she last been seen in some kind of tricked-out Cadillac? What the hell? There had been lots of talk about it lately, and now the press was here, Johnny-on-the-spot.

He stared into those mirrored glasses and said, "Are you telling me that we just dug up fuckin' Didi Storm?"

CHAPTER 28

Vera was struggling. It was obvious. She started rocking again, pushing against the carpet with the toe of her tennis shoe. "I didn't read that book, even though Jensen wasted his money on a copy. Didn't need to. I can't imagine why a book on Didi would even be published. She was just another woman with loose morals who slept around and never made it big."

Remmi wanted to argue but held her tongue when she caught Noah's eye and silent message: *Let her talk.*

"She's been gone what—?" Vera threw out a hand. "Twenty years or so? But she's right here, isn't she?" She pointed at the carpet and said bitterly, "Right here in this room. With us now. She's like a bad smell, you know. No matter what, you can just never get rid of her!"

"Maybe you didn't want to," Remmi said, and she saw Jensen's total look of bewilderment.

Vera shook her head. "Trust me, I never want to hear her name again."

Remmi wouldn't let it go. "Even if you could make money off her?"

"Are you kidding?" Vera actually recoiled.

"What're you talking about?" Jensen asked, but a light seemed to be dawning in his eyes.

Noah said, "We know you were in contact with Trudie Crenshaw."

"Trudie who? Oh—wait, the woman who was killed?" Vera tried to act innocent, but it didn't quite come off. "I just saw it on the news. She was supposedly the person who wrote the book, right?"

"Wait a sec," Jensen said. "This doesn't make any sense." He reached into the top drawer of a small table and pulled out a copy of *I'm Not Me*. "It was written by—"

"Maryanne Osgoode," Remmi said. "It's a pseudonym." When he didn't seem to get it, she added, "An alias."

"Oh. Why?"

"Anonymity," Noah interjected. "But it didn't work. The author's dead. Murdered."

Jensen looked from Remmi to Noah and back again. "What do you mean murdered. Like killed?"

Jensen had improved, but he was still no Rhodes scholar.

"Gertrude Melborn Crenshaw. She was my mother's best friend, and she married Mom's first husband, Ned Crenshaw," Remmi explained.

"Whoa . . ." Jensen was processing slowly.

"They were attacked at their ranch near Sacramento last night. She's dead, and he's in ICU, critical condition," Remmi added.

"Holy shit, why?" Jensen asked and stared at his mother.

Noah said, "We're hoping you can tell us."

"Me?" Jensen asked, seeming incredulous, as from the hallway the sounds of a baby cooing reached their ears. "How?"

Noah said, "Your phone."

"What?" He gazed at Noah blankly.

"Somebody might have used it by mistake. Say, when it was being charged?"

Jensen's eyebrows drew together, and he looked over at the recliner and the phone chargers attached to an outlet nearby. "What do you mean?" he asked.

Vera broke in, "This is ridiculous! Jensen obviously has never even heard of Trudie Crenshaw. And I never met her. Or her husband, not even when Didi was married to him." She stood abruptly and turned to Remmi. "I don't even know why you're here. On some kind of wild-goose chase. Trying to punish me because I wouldn't let you run wild like your mother did. Let me tell you," she said, winding up, "you're lucky I raised you during those formative years when you were a teenager. It was me." She thumped her chest with her hand, and the little cross danced. "I was the one who saved you from a life of sin and debauchery."

"Mom, whoa," Jensen said, half-embarrassed.

Remmi'd had enough. "How? With your pseudo-Christianity? Your holier-than-thou attitude?"

"Shame on you!" Vera declared. "Shame on you, Remmi! Who put a roof over your head? Who cooked for you, cleaned for you? Saw that you found the Lord? And did we get a dime for our trouble, or even a 'thank you' from you for taking you in when you had no one? *No!*"

She was nearly spitting now, the venom that had been seeping through her veins for years finally spewing.

"Someone helped Trudie write that book," Remmi pointed out calmly. "Someone who knew my mother inside and out. Someone who grew up with her."

"Not me. I never wanted to think about Didi again!"

Remmi said, "When I lived here, you brought her up all the time. Just so you could tell me how awful she was. You never missed a chance to put her down."

"No."

"Yeah, Mom. You did," Jensen broke in quickly. "You still do. You've always hated her."

"Not hate." Vera shook her head rapidly. "No, no, no."

"Well, what do you call it then?" her son demanded.

The question stopped Vera cold. "You didn't know Didi! You don't understand what it was like for me. I was the one who was responsible. I was the one who got good grades. I didn't lie or smoke or drink, do drugs, run around, or anything. Mom and Dad could depend on me, but Edie—that's what we called Edwina back then, before she adopted that ridiculous name!—Edie just took everything she wanted, did what she wanted, it didn't matter who she hurt. Mom. Dad. Me. Billy. Her best friends. She was just *horrid!*"

Gathering herself, her face a mask of disgust, Vera went on, "Edie stole other girls' boyfriends and never thought a thing about it. Didn't matter if it was her best friend. How she was so popular, I'll never know. Well, with the boys, that was a no-brainer. They *all* loved fun-loving Easy Edie. But the girls? Why in the world she was popular with the girls when she was forever stabbing them in their backs, sneaking out with their boyfriends, doing . . . doing immoral things . . ." Vera glared straight at her niece. "It's time for you to take off those rose-colored blinders and see your mother for what she really was: a wicked, wicked girl. Pure evil."

"Wow." Jensen just stared at his mother.

Vera's eyes sparked with pent-up hatred and jealousy. "Okay. So it's out there. No, I didn't like her. She is a . . . a Jezebel!"

"Was," Noah said. "Not 'is.'" He stared hard at Vera. "Do you know what happened to her? If she's still alive?"

Remmi didn't move. Held her breath. For a second, it seemed as if the air had been sucked out of the tiny room.

When Vera seemed to be at a loss for words, Remmi whispered, "She's dead, isn't she?"

"I don't know," Vera said, coming back to herself. With a little less fire, she added, "I really don't. But I would assume that since no one has heard from her in all this time, she's gone." She let out a slow breath as if trying to find her equanimity again. "You shouldn't grieve too much if she is gone, Remmi, because she wasn't a good person, I think you know that. It's not for me to judge, of course, I leave that to the Father, but . . . oh, well . . . it doesn't matter."

"It does. It matters a lot," Remmi argued, unable to sit still and listen, to just take it about Didi.

Now, the baby was no longer babbling but starting to cry.

Jensen was on his feet in an instant and heading down the hallway.

Remmi wasn't finished. "And don't lie to me about you not judging her. You judged her every moment of her life, just like you do everyone."

"I–I do not!"

"What do you have to do with the book?" Noah asked her, apparently trying to get the conversation back on track.

"Nothing—I don't know anything—"

"Give me a break." Remmi jumped to her feet and crossed the faded carpet in two strides, kicking a plastic puzzle piece out of the way. "You talked to Trudie, gave her information on Mom, and—"

Vera gasped and shook her head. She, too, was on her feet, apparently determined to stand toe to toe with her niece rather than cower in her chair. The empty rocker swayed as Jensen, carrying his son, returned to the room.

The baby was in full-fledged wail, and he said loudly, "I need a bottle."

"In the fridge," Vera snapped, turning back to Remmi. "I already told you I didn't even know the woman. This Trudie. Never met her."

"What about you, Jensen?" Noah called out. "Your cell phone connected with Trudie's. A little over a year ago."

Through the archway, Remmi saw Jensen as he opened the refrigerator, the now whimpering baby on his hip. Deftly, he placed a premade bottle in the microwave. "I don't even know who you're talking about," he said over his shoulder.

Noah pressed on. "The trouble is, we've got the phone records, and I'm sure the police do, too. So it looks like you, or someone who had access to your phone, dialed Trudie Crenshaw, then hung up when they realized they'd used the wrong phone and called back on a prepaid phone, a burner, supposedly untraceable."

"Supposedly?" Vera repeated as Jensen returned and sat in the recliner. He tested the bottle, dripping milk on his wrist, then, satisfied the formula wasn't too hot, let his son start sucking from it.

"There are ways to trace burner phones based on where the phone was purchased," Noah said, and Remmi guessed that he was bluffing a bit. "The police will know."

Vera was wagging her head, but Jensen, holding baby and bottle, glared at her from the recliner.

"Mom?" he said. "You know it's a sin to lie."

"I never—"

"That's what Jesus told us, right? Isn't that what you always say? Ten Commandments and Psalms and Proverbs . . ." He was looking at her, daring her to lie. When she opened her mouth, he said softly, "God and Jesus, they're watching," and, at that moment, Remmi realized he'd been waiting for years to throw his mother's admonishments back in her face. He was actually enjoying watching her squirm, a part of the old Jensen surfacing.

"Proverbs 12:22, 'Lying lips are an abomination to the Lord,'" Vera said, as if the words were torn from her soul.

"Yeah, Mom, that's it. God doesn't like liars."

To Remmi's amazement, a tear rolled down Vera's cheek as some of her anger slid away. "It just wasn't fair," she squeaked out. "Edie had so much and I . . . we . . . we were the good ones, and we had so little."

A muscle worked in the corner of Noah's jaw. "So how much was it worth to you?" he asked.

Vera closed her eyes.

"Jesus, Mom. Tell me this isn't happening," her son said. He stood up abruptly, the baby crying in his arms again. "Tell me you're not the biggest hypocrite on the planet. That you didn't have anything to do with those people getting shot!" His face was a mask of horror, and even though Monty started to cry again, Jensen didn't pay any attention.

"Of course not." Vera walked to the front door, wrapping her arms around herself. "I don't know anything about that. But . . . but the money." She weighed her answer as Jensen waited, and finally she said, "I did get some money. Twenty-five thousand dollars. That might sound like a lot, but it's really not, now that the book is doing so well . . . I got a pittance for all the trouble I went through." She sighed and shook her head.

Was it regret?

Or an act?

Noah asked, "So that's it? You got twenty-five grand?"

Vera looked at the floor. "I worked out a deal with Ned and Trudie."

"And now that Trudie's dead?" Noah pressed. "What happens to her royalties from the book?"

"I don't know. Probably her heirs, I would guess."

"What if she doesn't have any? What happens if Ned dies?" Noah pressed.

She shrugged, but not convincingly, and she changed the conversation. "It's terrible, the poor woman. I've told you everything I know. Yes, I worked with Trudie. Yes, I told her all about Didi's life, the Missouri growing up part, a bit of sibling rivalry, but that's it. I figured Edie owed me." She met Remmi's gaze. "Believe me, it wasn't enough. Not near enough. All the money in the world wouldn't make up for the pain Edwina put our family through."

"Did you kill her?" Noah asked.

Her hand flew to her throat. "Goodness, no. Of course not. She was out of my life. I already told you, I have no idea what happened to her. Now, please. Leave. I've told you everything I know. That's all there is."

The kid looked scared out of his mind. Barely nineteen, in the crisp uniform of the bell staff for the Montmort Tower, he was seated at a table in an empty conference room and drinking from a plastic water glass. Sweat had beaded on his forehead, and he licked his lips constantly as he answered Settler's questions.

His name was Robb Quade. He was a skinny nineteen-year-old, going to college part-time, and was pale as a ghost, his hands shaking on the glass, his already large eyes wide, the pupils dilated in fear.

Yes, he'd taken money to let a guy into the room next to Karen Upgarde's on the day of her death.

No, he didn't know the guy. Didn't know that he was going to open the connecting door or that the woman in the next suite would do the same. He just couldn't even believe it now.

Yes, he'd lied to the police the first time around because he was scared about losing his job, scared the police might arrest him for abetting a crime, even though, he swore over and over again, he had no idea what was about to go down, and now, oh, God, that woman had *jumped*. He'd witnessed the fall.

Why had he decided to come forward now?

Because several people knew about it, and he figured it was best to come clean himself.

"Do I need a lawyer?" he asked, looking as if he might break down and cry.

"That depends; do you think you need one?" Settler asked.

"No! I'm telling you everything I know," he insisted, blinking. "I was stupid and should never have done it. I'm going to lose my job over it, won't even get a decent reference, but, I swear, I had no idea the guy would do . . . well, whatever he was gonna do." His face crumpled, and he had to strain not to cry.

"Is this the man?" Dani asked, and they showed him still shots from the security footage of the elevator that they'd gotten after the statement by Al Benson, the Montmort custodian.

Quade stared down at the photographs and swallowed hard. "Yeah," he said. "Same guy, but he was dressed a little different. Sunglasses, yeah, okay, they look the same, but his hair was longer, and I thought it looked fake at the time. Don't ask me how I knew; I just thought so. Too blond or something. And he was wearing a Mariners baseball cap. I remember because I come from Seattle. I'm a fan." He swallowed again. "I'm so fucked."

"What do you think he wanted to use the room for?"

"He didn't say, and I didn't ask. I figured maybe a hooker might come up, or he wanted to get high privately, or"—he shrugged, lifting his thin shoulders—"whatever."

"Did you give him a time limit?"

"Yeah, oh, yeah. Two hours. That was it."

"Fifty bucks an hour?" Martinez said.

Quade looked miserable. "Yeah. I did it for a cool hundred. Jesus, I'm a moron."

She didn't argue. He was. They asked more questions but got no new information. "If you think of anything else, let us know," she reminded him at the close of the interview.

They were heading to the car, just stepping through the glass doors of the Montmort, when her cell phone buzzed. She picked it up, didn't recognize the number, but answered, "Detective Settler," just as a gust of cold wind blew along the street. Quickly, she tugged her collar closer.

"Hey, yeah. This is Leo Kasparian."

The elusive Kaspar the Great. She pressed the phone to her ear with one hand, found the keys in her coat pocket with the other, and tossed the ring to Martinez. He caught them deftly on the fly.

"I've been wanting to talk to you," she said.

"Yeah, I got your message and figured it must have somethin' to do with Didi. She's everywhere now these days; it's kinda like she rose from the dead, if you know what I mean."

"Is she dead? Do you know that?" She and Martinez were skirting other pedestrians, heads bent against the wind. She had to hold one hand over her opposite ear to hear Kasparian.

"Just a figure of speech, since no one's seen her for years. It isn't like Didi to hide under a rock. Not her style. So, if she's not struttin' her stuff, I figure she must be dead. But a shame about that Upgarde girl. What do you figure happened there?"

She ignored the question and, as they reached the car, slid into the passenger side as Martinez adjusted the driver's seat. "You didn't know her?"

"Never heard of her before. Didi and I, well, it wasn't all that friendly when we split up, if you know what I mean."

"I do."

"I married someone else. That didn't work out so well either. Now, I've got me a nice little act in a casino in Reno. You should catch it sometime."

"You heard about Trudie Crenshaw?"

"Aw, yeah. A shame there. But Ned, he's gonna be okay? He's an all right guy. Just got mixed up with Didi, like me. Can't hold it against him."

"We hope he recovers. Your cell number came up several times on Trudie's call list, about a year ago, when Trudie was probably doing research for the book."

"Oh, yeah. Sure, I talked to her. Even met with her a couple of times. She was writing the book and needed some information on the year me and Didi were together, y'know. We did parts of our acts together and . . . well, it was a good time until it wasn't."

She asked him more questions about Trudie and Ned, but she seemed to have drained him of information about them. And he swore again that he'd never met Karen Upgarde, never even heard of her, and he had solid alibis for the day she jumped. He started growing distracted, talking to people around him, and when Settler tried to get his attention, he admitted he was trying to rehearse. The club owner, a couple of waitresses, and an audio tech were in the building.

"Just a couple more questions," Dani assured him.

Martinez had driven down the hill, and they were skirting the waterfront on the Embarcadero, the San Francisco–Oakland Bay Bridge stretching across the churning

waters of the bay. White caps formed and the surface of
the water rippled with the storm that was brewing. Quickly,
Dani asked, "So what do you know about Didi's disappearance?"

"Nothing."

"Did you know she had twins?"

"No. I mean that hasn't been proven, has it? There
were rumors she had a baby, but she wouldn't tell anyone
who the father was. Kind of her MO, y'know. She never
revealed who her older daughter's dad was, either. That
always bugged me, and I'm sure it bothered Remmi. It
had to. But as flamboyant and out-there as she was, Didi
could zip her lips when she wanted to."

"So you don't know who she was dating about the
time the babies were conceived."

"Nah . . ." Then a pause. "Well, there was one guy. I
heard about it from Rimes—Harold, y'know. We both
used to work for him. What was his name? . . . She
bragged about him. Like he was this big high roller. Let
me see, I remember because his name was like some TV
personality, like . . . no . . . oh, maybe a game show personality that had been around for a while, kind of an icon,
if you know what I mean. Not Downs . . . or Trebek or . . .
you know, I think his last name was Hall. Yeah, that was
it. Brandon Hall. Shit, where did that come from?"

Settler slid a glance at Martinez. "Hall. You're sure."

"Pretty damned sure," Kasparian said. "Yeah."

Brandon Hall. The guy who had rented the Mustang
that burned in the desert. The unidentified body. She
asked Kasparian a few more questions, then told him he
would have to make an official statement to a cop from
Reno. Groaning about Didi still invading his damned life,
he reluctantly agreed. "I'll go down to the station today,"
he promised before disconnecting, but the guy had a reputation for being as slippery as an eel, so Settler called

the Reno P.D. and gave them a heads-up. If he didn't show up, they promised to track him down.

She filled Martinez in as he found a spot to park near Fisherman's Wharf. It was noon, so they grabbed fish and chips at a restaurant with a view of Pier 39, where they watched the seagulls land and sea lions bask on the floating docks.

Through bites of fried halibut and thick salty fries, they were discussing the case when Settler's phone went off again. She read the screen—Las Vegas Police Department—and answered. "This is Detective Settler."

"Lucretia Davis. I'm going to cut to the chase, okay? This morning at a construction site, an old white Cadillac was uncovered, buried in the desert. License plate indicates it belonged to Didi Storm." Davis's voice was grim, and Settler waited for the next bit of information, but she still felt a bit of a shock when she heard, "Looks like Didi was at the wheel."

"In the car?"

"Yep. The body was reduced to a skeleton, but there was a sizable hole in the back of her skull and what looks to be a bullet where her brain used to be. So, I guess one mystery is solved: Didi Storm was definitely murdered."

CHAPTER 29

"You did what?" Remmi demanded as they drove away from the cottage in Walnut Creek where she'd grown up. She was at the wheel, heading toward the freeway, when Noah had dropped the bomb that he'd bugged Aunt Vera's house.

"It's a very small camera, complete with audio."

"In Aunt Vera's *house?*"

"Yep, on the mantel of the fireplace when you, Vera, and Jensen went in to look at the baby. A tiny spot between a picture of Monty and Jesus, right in the center of the room, panoramic view."

"Isn't that illegal?"

Shrugging, he said, "Whatever we get wouldn't be of any use in a court of law, but I'm a private citizen, and so are you. We're not the police, so any information we collect can't be used as evidence. But we could use it to steer the police in the right direction."

"What if she finds it?"

"She might, but it's hidden in a pair of sunglasses, no wires. I'm talking small, but effective."

"What if she finds them?"

"Hopefully she'll just think we or someone else left them there. Several people live in the house, and presumably they have visitors, so why not?"

"It's sneaky."

"Very. But necessary."

"You're right," she agreed as she'd felt Aunt Vera was holding back, that she knew more than she was saying. The cell phone call from Jensen's phone to Trudie Crenshaw was damning enough.

"Then let's head to a coffee shop, someplace that has Wi-Fi, and see what we find out. The images and audio will show up on my phone as well as being recorded."

"You've got an app for this?"

"At least one. We'll be able to see and hear whatever happens in the living room and part of the dining area leading to the kitchen, even down the hallway."

She didn't care about the legality any longer. It was a means to an end. "Find an all-day diner or coffee shop that has Wi-Fi, and we'll head there."

"Already on it." He clicked on the keys. "Okay, here's a good one. The Bellwether Café. They advertise 'cutting-edge coffee,' whatever that means, and 'wine and beer starting at four PM.' Better yet, 'free, fast Wi-Fi.'"

He gave her the address, and realizing she was heading in the wrong direction, Remmi found a place for a quick U-turn, one tire skimming the curb, then drove south till they found the café, an A-frame building that she remembered from high school. At that time, it had been a burger and ice cream takeout spot with limited seating. Now, it had been redone in an industrial motif, with black and silver vinyl, vaguely space-age, chrome light fixtures, a stainless-steel counter, exposed pipes, and the smell of freshly ground coffee mingling with the sweet scent of baked goods.

Tables were scattered over a cement floor, and only a few were occupied. Two women were chatting loudly at a table near the counter, while a twenty-year-old with a beard and close-cropped black hair stared at his open laptop, watching some kind of video, his coffee forgotten while he stared at the screen and chewed on an already flattened stir stick.

Instrumental versions of classic rock songs played but could barely be heard over the buzz of conversation, the clatter of cups, and the hiss of an espresso machine.

They found a corner booth in the back of the eating area, and while Noah set up shop, connecting his phone and laptop to the Internet, she ordered them each a cup of coffee. "Want anything else?" she asked when she returned with the cups, and he looked up.

"Maybe," he said, and when his gaze touched hers, she felt an unbidden rush warm her blood. "Let me think about it." She handed him his cup, then ordered two scones. The barista placed them on a plate, which she set on the table before sliding into the booth next to him.

"I figured if we're going to hang out here a while, we'd better order," she said.

"Good idea." His phone rang, and he answered quickly. "Emma," he mouthed and then listened, his expression growing grim.

"When?" he asked tersely. "No, I hadn't heard . . . when? . . . no foul play . . . well, yeah, other than that. But I meant at the hospital . . ."

Hospital? Oh, no. Ned!

". . . Okay. Yeah, thanks." He clicked off, and Remmi slumped on the bench.

"Ned died," she said, and he nodded.

"Just a while ago."

She squeezed her eyes shut. She'd told herself she'd been expecting to hear this, that no one could survive the attack he'd been subjected to, but deep down she'd hoped for a miracle, had felt that if anyone could make it, Ned, the rough-and-tumble cowboy, could. He would be able to beat the odds . . . but no. She felt Noah's arm reach across the back of the booth and pull her close.

"I'm sorry," he said, his breath ruffling the hair at her crown. "Really." He kissed her softly above her temple, and she nearly broke into a million pieces.

"I haven't seen or heard from him in years," she whispered. "But still . . ."

"He was the one guy you looked up to back then, I know." He squeezed her, and she melted into him, let go for just a second.

A kaleidoscope of memories assailed her—short, colorful pictures flashing through her mind of happy years with the gentle cowboy. For a second, she remembered the scents of horses and dust, the feel of his hands helping her into the saddle, the way he showed her how to aim a .22 and how to quiet a frightened mare in the throes of foaling.

"He was a good guy," she said. "He deserved better than this. And I know that, somehow, he was involved in all of this, that he was compromised, I guess, but he didn't deserve to be gunned down, Noah." She wiped her eyes and swallowed back her tears.

"You're right."

"So let's get this guy, okay?" She felt her jaw harden and pulled herself upright, away from his embrace.

"That's the plan."

"Good." She took a swallow of her coffee just as his laptop gave off a soft ding, and he glanced at the screen.

"Bingo," he said, his gaze touching hers. "We're in."

She leaned in to view the interior of Aunt Vera's small living room. "Now what?" she whispered.

His eyes narrowed on the screen. "Now, we wait."

* * *

Just outside of Las Vegas, Settler viewed the construction site, where the huge car was being winched out of a pit. Sand and dirt and litter fell away as it slowly rose from the earth.

To cut down on red tape and delays, Settler had called a friend with a private plane and a pilot's license. Always interested in being a part of an investigation, Stinson had flown both her and Martinez to Las Vegas and had agreed to fly them back, all for the price of fuel and dinner.

The only hiccup had been the interview with Jennifer Reliant, which had been pushed back until tomorrow after Settler found out about the extraction of what was believed to be Didi Storm's Cadillac.

She and Martinez had arrived mid-afternoon, rented a car, and met Detective Davis at the construction site as the big Caddy was being hauled onto a tow truck that would take it to the garage, where crime-scene techs would go over every inch of it and take it apart.

"It's Didi Storm's, for sure," Davis said, "Not only licensed and titled to her, but also the cargo space that the daughter described? Yep. It's there."

"Body's already been taken to the morgue?"

"Yeah. It was in the clothes the daughter described in the missing person report, the last thing she'd seen her mother wearing, a black, low-cut dress that had seen better days, matching gloves, and a Marilyn Monroe-type wig. Platinum blond, or it had been. Didi's name scrawled across the inside. We're checking dental records, for official ID, but it's a done deal, I'm thinking. And the cause of death is pretty evident, what with the big hole in her skull."

"Anything else?"

"Nothing out of the ordinary. Her purse and ID, cosmetics from that era, and a small gun. Looks like she came prepared, but it didn't help."

"No other body?"

"None. And no baby, either. There was an empty infant car seat, but no baby."

Settler felt a little bit of relief at that.

Davis assured her, "The lab is all over this, checking for fingerprints and DNA, if there's any to collect. Time will tell."

"I want to see the body. Didi."

A dark eyebrow lifted over the edge of Davis's mirrored glasses. "Not much to see, but okay. You got it." She hitched her chin in the direction of Settler's rented Toyota. "Got a GPS in that thing?"

"No," Martinez said, "but I'll use my phone."

"Okay. If I lose you, the phone's directions should get you there." Davis rattled off the address of the morgue and told them to follow her, which they did, though Davis turned out to have more of a lead foot than Settler, and Martinez held onto the safety bar for dear life.

"Sin City," he said, eyeing the flashing lights of the casinos and the throngs of people on the street, with an envious eye. He rolled down the window and took a big lungful of air. "Ahh. The smell of money. You know, I could retire here, get myself a sweet penthouse on the Strip, play poker for walking-around money."

"What happened to the condo in Cabo?"

"Oh, that's in the budget, too." He stroked his goatee as they drove away from the Strip, with its mega-storied hotels and casinos, and onto streets flanked by low-lying buildings. "Margaritas in Cabo and straight shots here, in Vegas."

"Your wife and kids, they're into this?"

"Oh, yeaaaah."

"I've met Maria, remember?" Maria Martinez was a

schoolteacher who aspired to be an administrator in the district where her kids went to school. "I don't see her in this scenario. Don't think she wants to uproot your kids."

"She's on board," Martinez insisted as Settler threaded her way through the traffic, while keeping Davis's car in sight. "You gotta admit that this weather, it's better than what we got."

"Today," she said, eyeing the blue sky that stretched forever. A few clouds were visible, along with a jet trail, but the sun was shining, as opposed to the gray day they'd left in the Bay Area.

"All damned winter."

"Okay, okay, but you've got a few years until retirement."

"You hope," he said. "Who else would partner up with you and always be saving your sorry ass?" As they turned a final corner onto Pinto Lane, she spotted Davis's vehicle turning into a lot, sunlight reflecting off the windows of her car.

"A man can dream, can't he?" he asked.

"No harm in that." She eased into the large parking area, a wide stretch of asphalt surrounded by a landscape of rock, sand, and some well-placed desert-friendly plants, cacti and other succulents. Settler located a spot near Davis's vehicle. The Las Vegas detective was already out of her car and lighting a cigarette.

"Ready to meet Didi?" Settler asked Martinez as she parked and pocketed the keys.

"Can't wait." He was already out of the car.

As they approached, Davis exhaled a long stream of smoke. "I'm down to two a day," she said, as if she had to explain herself. She slipped her lighter into her jacket pocket and started walking them toward the long, low building that housed the Clark County Coroner's Office. "My kids are all over me to stop completely, even want me to use the patch or e-cigs, because vaping is supposed to be so much healthier, you know, but when I'm working . . ."

"I hear ya." Martinez nodded. "I quit fifteen years ago, when my wife was pregnant with the first one. She accused me of fouling the air for her and the babies, so eventually I quit."

"And you still have the craving?" Davis sighed dispiritedly.

"It's not so bad now," he said.

Pausing near the entrance, she took a final drag on the filter-tip, then squashed the butt into the sand of an ash-can set not far from the main doors. "Let's go." She led them inside, where the air-conditioning had cooled things down.

Davis knew her way around. She found an officer who was working the case and guided them to an even colder room, where three toe-tagged bodies covered in tarps were stretched out on gurneys.

"Over here," the officer said, and they entered a smaller examination room where a single stretcher was waiting. It, too, was covered by a plastic sheet.

"Let's do this," Davis said.

"Okay." The officer pulled off the tarp of the single body lying face up.

Settler wasn't squeamish, but she always braced herself.

"Jesus," Martinez said and crossed himself, as he always did upon first viewing a dead person.

The body on the table was little more than a skeleton, bones hung with bits of leathery flesh, eye sockets dark holes, ribs covering a chest devoid of internal organs. A few tufts of hair were still attached to the skull, but for the most part, twenty years of being buried in the desert hadn't preserved the body as much as Settler had hoped. It seemed completely decomposed.

"This is Didi Storm?" Settler asked.

"ID isn't a hundred percent. There's a chance someone else was dressed in her things, with her purse, in her car, but unlikely." She met Settler's gaze. "And the bullet hole, you see that?"

"Uh-huh." Through an eye socket, past the empty brain cavity and hole in the back of the skull, the top of the gurney was visible.

"I think we've seen enough," Settler said, "but I'll need pictures of the body, the car, and all of her personal belongings, her purse and what was in it, and the baby carrier, although I'm not certain that Didi's daughter will be satisfied with pictures. She may want to view the body herself, not that she could identify these bones, but I can't say."

"We've got Didi Storm's dental records on file, ordered out when she went missing. We'll check, but it's a pretty done deal."

Settler nodded.

"Let me show you what we have," Davis suggested.

The other officer brought all of the personal items that were discovered with the corpse in the buried Cadillac. The items were bagged and tagged, but Dani viewed them through the plastic and was convinced that, yes, they'd found Didi Storm. The wig, dusty and dull, had been short and blond and was labeled with thick black ink that had faded but had been written in Didi's distinctive hand.

They drove to the police station and found a private room. Over cups of black coffee, Davis said, "We've already done some preliminary work, just since the car was discovered, strictly by chance, by the construction firm.

Wellsley Construction is totally legit, good company, building a subdivision on the property for R&D Homes, a company that also checks out. R&D stands for Richard and Diana Duvall. They're divorced but still run the company together. It's a strong business, no money problems. They've done several large projects in the city. R&D bought the property about three years ago and started working to develop it, but because of their other projects, and the time it takes to draw up plans, take care of all the environmental impact stuff, get approval and the permits to build, they didn't get started on the site until about three months ago."

"Who'd they buy the property from?"

"A company by the name of Morgan Investments, which is under the umbrella of a larger company, OH Industries, a California-based business located near L.A. OH had done some work on the site back in the day. They'd planned to develop it as well, years ago, but all that happened after the permits were received was that a ravine was filled."

Settler asked, "The ravine where they found the car?"

"Bingo."

"So why did Morgan Investments and OH Industries abandon their project?"

"Still looking for answers. Should know something soon. We'd better," she admitted, glancing toward a window with a view of the parking lot. "The press is already all over this. All the interest in the book, then the suicide, and now the murder of the author of *I'm Not Me*. Reporters have been calling me day and night."

Martinez said, "We're getting them, too. The public information officer is inundated, and the last I checked, the book is already hitting some of the best-seller lists."

Davis nodded. "The publisher admitted they're going into more printings."

"Wait until the public finds out that Didi's been found," Settler thought aloud.

"They'll want all the gruesome details," said Davis. "Just watch, there will be a film or made-for-TV movie in the works."

Settler was already way ahead of her. If the scenario they were discussing played out, whoever owned the rights to the book stood to make a small fortune. She thought of Karen Upgarde and the increased buzz that began after her suicide leap dressed as Didi Storm.

They ended the meeting with each department promising to keep the other informed. Then Settler and Martinez drove to the airport to meet Stinson and fly back to San Francisco.

On the way to the airport, Martinez was on his iPad looking for information on OH Industries, while Settler thought over what they'd learned. First, she wondered about Didi Storm's infant son and daughter. The baby carrier discovered in the Cadillac convinced her that Remmi Storm had been telling the truth, at least in part— that Didi Storm had given birth to at least one child and had been trying to barter it off to its father, trying to scam him.

And because of it, Didi had paid the ultimate price— with her life.

Assuming Remmi was credible and there were two children, where were they? Had they survived? Were they together, or had they been separated, perhaps raised by different families? Did either of them, assuming they were alive, have any inkling about their biological mother, their own history? Unlikely, since neither of them had ever come forward, and especially now, with all the publicity about the book.

The questions churned in her mind, and she expelled a breath of air in frustration.

"What?" Martinez asked, looking up, just as she saw a sign for the airport.

"Nothing. Just thinking." She turned on her blinker and changed lanes.

During the investigation, they'd discussed the money trail, and once again, she ran through it.

Who would profit most from Karen Upgarde's death?

The obvious answer was Trudie Crenshaw, now dead.

Next in line? Her husband, Ned. But he was hanging onto life by a thread and might not recover. Who would benefit from his demise?

One answer: Vera Hutchinson Gibbs, sister of the deceased Edwina, "Edie," aka Didi Storm. Vera was a known contributor to the book. Legally, the succession of rights and money wasn't clear to Settler, not yet, but she sensed she was on the right track with Vera.

She thought about the photographs of the hotel window and elevator car, of the blond man in the Mariners baseball cap. Could "he" have been a "she?" It didn't seem so, by all accounts from Al Benson, the janitor, and Robb Quade, the frightened bellhop. Or had Vera hired someone else? A proven assassin who'd then knocked off Trudie Crenshaw and tried to kill Ned, the only people Settler knew of who stood between Vera Hutchinson Gibbs and a fortune? Or had Vera set her husband or brother or one of her kids up for the job? Who had been in that room with Karen Upgarde in her final moments? Did Vera know what had happened to her sister and the babies?

Was there someone else in the wings?

The airport tower loomed closer, and Settler drove to the rental car lot where they were meeting Stinson. His promised dinner would have to wait as she had to get back to the city.

First, she'd give Remmi Storm the bad news in person.

Then Settler planned to drive to Walnut Creek for a tête-à-tête with Mrs. Vera Gibbs.

As she wheeled into the parking lot for the rental car company, her cell phone blasted. Martinez picked up the phone. "Sacramento P.D."

"Answer. Put it on speaker phone."

He punched the appropriate buttons.

"This is Detective Settler," she said, loud enough for the phone to pick up her voice as she parked and took the cell from Martinez's outstretched hand.

"It's Ladlow." The ex-jock detective from Sacramento. "Hey, look, I'm gonna cut right to the chase."

A premonition of dread slid through Settler's brain. She knew what was coming and exchanged looks with Martinez, who'd stopped working on his tablet and was listening in. "Okay."

"It's Ned Crenshaw," Ladlow said. "He died about an hour ago. Never woke up. Just lost the fight." A pause. "It's a real pisser, but he had a poor chance, being shot at close range like that. I'll send you the autopsy report once we get it."

Settler stared out the window to the row of cars being checked in, suitcases and bags and strollers and laptops hauled out of vehicles, paperwork exchanged with attendants. For a second, the scene seemed a little surreal, just as it always did when a person died. Reality shifted. What was important and what was trivial were almost indefinable.

She gave a slight shake of her head, and the world righted itself, as it always did. It was up to her to make certain Crenshaw's killer came to justice.

On the saggy bed of his room at the Baysider, the Marksman stared at his computer screen and swore under his breath. He was going over the path recorded by the GPS locator he'd planted beneath the bumper of Remmi Storm's Subaru. From the map on his screen, it was obvious Remmi had driven all the way to Walnut Creek and the very street where she'd lived.

He knew the address. No doubt, Remmi had made a visit to dear old Aunt Vera. It had been inevitable, he supposed, wishing he'd taken out Didi's daughter earlier. The fact that she was talking to Vera was worrisome; that woman didn't know how to keep her damned mouth shut. What was worse was the fact that after visiting Vera, she hadn't left Walnut Creek.

Agitated, he shifted on the bed, feeling a painful twinge in his thigh where the wire clippers had ravaged his flesh. He should never have let that happen; the pain was an impediment. One he'd have to overcome. At least mentally.

He slid the laptop onto the bedside stand, stood, and found he could walk without too much difficulty. The pain, though, was a problem. He couldn't allow himself to limp, couldn't draw attention to himself.

Already naked, he hobbled to the bathroom and twisted on the shower jets, then located a strip of gauze from his first-aid kit and, using the flimsy little shower cap to cover the patch on his leg, anchored it with the gauze and tape. Then he stepped under the not-quite-hot-enough spray.

Weak as the shower was, it helped loosen his muscles, and once he'd stepped out and toweled off, he found he could walk almost normally, although his stride was a bit shorter.

With his towel, he took a swipe at the moisture collected on the mirror, then glowered at his image. The tines of the pitchfork had done their job, no doubt about it. His face was black and blue, the deep scratches clear, but with the weather being as cold as it was, he could cover most of his face with a scarf and hat, even use the fake hair, he supposed.

He surveyed his chest and swore mightily. He considered shaving the whole area and slathering his pecs and abdomen with antiseptic again. The wounds were deep, but, for now, they would have to wait. He'd clean them later.

His body felt as if he'd been thrown from a high building, then run over with a bulldozer. He was used to a certain amount of pain. Had learned mental toughness over the course of his life. He'd get the job done. For now, he couldn't risk a trip to the hospital, and he knew that as soon as this part of his job was finished, he'd be able to have a nurse tend to him. A private nurse.

He turned on the TV and located a cable news station, hoping to hear that Ned Crenshaw had let go of life, but he couldn't find any update confirming the rancher's death. He then looked online, Googled Crenshaw's name.

And there it was.

A gift from heaven.

Ned Crenshaw had expired in the last few hours.

Hallelujah.

The Marksman smiled. Looked like Ned hadn't woken from his coma to shoot off his mouth.

Praise the Lord.

Even tough-as-old-leather Crenshaw hadn't been able to survive the point-blank attack.

Now, he could concentrate on Remmi. He checked on the GPS and saw that finally it appeared that she was nearing that monster of a home owned by the old lady, the shingled house on the hill.

At least she was back in the city.

Good. He'd already checked out the old house where she lived and had come up with a plan to get rid of her.

A damned good one.

Stretching his bad leg again, he walked from the bathroom to the bed and back again. Yeah, it would hold him.

Tonight, Didi Storm's nosy daughter would die.

CHAPTER 30

Even if she felt a little like a voyeur in the corner booth at the Bellwether, Remmi was mesmerized. The camera hidden on Vera's mantel worked a little like a baby monitor, only with a clearer picture and a wider range of vision. She and Noah had kept their eyes on it for several hours, switching from coffee to soda and water, replacing the scones with a small pizza they'd picked out.

Vera had come and gone through the rooms without incident, following what was probably her normal routine. Nothing of import happened until after Jensen headed out. Then Vera checked the front room windows, as if to make certain she was alone, put the baby onto the floor with some toys, and made a phone call. Both Remmi and Noah focused sharply on the screen.

The conversation was one-sided, but chilling.

"She was here, damn it," Vera said when someone answered. "Who? Who do you think? Remmi. And she was with that boy she knew back in high school. Noah Scott . . . Remember Ike Baxter, the mechanic? His stepson . . . yeah, that's him, and guess what? He's a P.I. now . . . what? . . .

No, no . . . you heard me right, a *private investigator*.
They know that I helped Trudie with the book . . . Huh? . . .
I told you we should never have gotten Karen involved!
That was your idea, and it backfired . . . yeah, yeah, I
know . . . but you'd better fix it. We can't be linked to
her, you know . . . Why? . . . Are you crazy? She jumped
off that ledge and brought all the spotlight on us!" Vera
was on her feet, pacing from one end of the room to the
other, from the dining room and archway to the kitchen to
the window to peer outside, then back again.

Noah and Remmi exchanged glances. So, Vera knew
Karen Upgarde but seemed confused as to why she
jumped.

"Now I'm going to have the police at the door! If
Remmi figured it out, how much longer before the cops
are here?" She glanced over at her grandson. "I know, I
know. That girl has always been an ingrate. After all I did
for her! She was no picnic, after being raised by that
slut."

Remmi bristled. She'd known her aunt had always re-
sented her, had done her Christian duty, but had wrapped
it all in a blanket of martyrdom.

"And they were asking about everyone. Even Harley.
Oh, this isn't going to end well, I just know it . . ." She
shoved her free hand through her hair, obviously upset.

"This is all because of Didi, you know," Vera said with
a lot more heat. Then a pause, while she stood at the window and stared out at the yard and street beyond, listening, her lips drawn into a deep frown. "I know . . ."
Nodding. "Finally, I'm going to get a little back, but no
matter how much I get off that book, it's not enough. Not
worth it. Not for all the heartache she put me and the
folks through. Uh-uh. Look, I'm just letting you know
that because Trudie was killed, Remmi thinks I had some-

thing to do with it . . . I'm telling you . . . what?" A pause
and a swift intake of breath. "He died? . . . No, no, I hadn't
heard. Well, God rest his soul . . ." Another long pause.
". . . Uh, what? The money for the book? Really? I'll
check the contract . . ."

Phone to her ear, she disappeared from the screen and
hurried down the hallway, returning less than a minute
later. She was carrying papers, and she sat at the dining
room table and flipped through them. "Let me see, this is
so wordy . . . here it is." For a few seconds, Vera went
silent as she read, then she sucked in a deep breath.
"You're right. It says right here . . ." A wide smile broke
out across her face, and she jumped to her feet, joyous.
She was transformed. "I can't believe it, this is such good
news. The best!" She was deliriously happy, on her feet
and doing a little dance. "I guess every cloud does have a
silver lining, doesn't it? God works in mysterious ways . . .
yes, I know. Jennifer called, said the book is doing spectacularly, that's the word she used—*spectacularly!*—and
she's taking calls about a possible TV movie about Didi,
or so she said. And now . . . Wow!" She was beaming, but
suddenly her smile faded a bit. "Still . . . it's a shame.
About Ned and Trudie. Good people. When I got into
this, I never thought anyone would die . . . I mean, they
were killed and it could be because of the book." She was
pacing again, listening. She stopped where the baby sat
on the floor, toys spread around him, his gurgling voice
audible as she found a truck in the basket of toys and put
it within his reach on the carpet. "Yes, yes, I know."
Straightening, Vera said, "Of course. What's done is done.
And . . . yes, there is the money to consider."

She turned to stare straight at the mantel, and Remmi's
heart dropped, thinking they were about to be discovered.
But Vera's attention was solely on her conversation.

"Yes," she was saying. "I'll light a candle and say a prayer. Okay. Okay. I'm just worried, that's all . . . Yes. I'll talk to you then. Bye."

She cut the connection and clutched the phone to her chest with both hands. Then, after seeing that the baby was amusing himself with some toys, walked directly to the mantel and stared up, her eyes nearly level with the camera. Her lips trembled a bit, and tears filled her eyes. "Thank you," she whispered. "Thank you, Jesus." She started to walk away, then looked directly at the camera and, in an almost inaudible breath, added, "And please, please forgive me."

Remmi's blood turned to ice. "She's involved," she said to Noah.

"To her eyeballs."

"But she just learned about Ned. Was surprised."

"I know. Doesn't quite fit." He thought aloud as a waitress carried two salads to a trio of women who were talking animatedly at a table near the door.

Noah and Remmi had been in the booth for hours.

Remmi got up and stretched, noticing how long the shadows in the parking lot had grown. What was Vera's part in all this? Did she know what happened to Didi? Had she lied about that, as she'd lied about so many things? But it seemed, listening to her side of the conversation, that she hadn't been part of the attack on Ned and Trudie.

"Who was she talking to?" Remmi asked. "Uncle Milo?"

"He's my first bet," Noah said, nodding. "But there's Billy. He could be involved."

She agreed; her uncle was never around, always MIA.

"Or Harley. We don't know that he's in Alaska. Or even Jensen."

"Except he just left. She didn't have to talk to him on the phone, and as awful as he was as a teenager, I didn't think he was faking us out." She remembered his pride about his baby. "He's getting his life together, and neither Harley or Jensen were around when Didi went missing."

"Doesn't mean they couldn't be involved in the book and Karen Upgarde."

She nodded. Any of them—Harley, Milo, Jensen, or even Billy—could have been disguised and involved somehow. She'd seen the grainy picture of the "person of interest" the police had released to the public, but the photo had been unclear and could be nearly anyone.

From the booth, Noah said, "Uh-oh."

She slid in beside him again and glanced at the screen to see Vera's face up close. The camera wiggled and grew dark, then was suddenly focused on the tip of Vera's nose.

"What the devil—?" Vera said. "Whose are these?" She must've held the glasses away from her face because all of her face came into view. Her lips were twisted in confusion, lines creasing her forehead.

Remmi's stomach tightened, and she bit her lip as Vera examined the sunglasses with their minute camera.

Finally, Vera sighed. "Bill's." She carried the sunglasses to what appeared to be the dining room table. "He'd lose his head if it wasn't screwed on."

She left the room and Remmi let out her breath. "She thinks they're her brother's."

"Until he comes home."

"So what do we do now?"

"Head back to your place. We know where we stand. We can set up the reception there. The camera will keep recording, so we'll fast-forward to the action when we get there."

Remmi looked at the monitor again and saw her aunt

make her way to baby Monty. Vera picked her grandson off the floor and spun him around. Monty giggled and clung to her.

She said, "Oh, baby, did you hear? Gramma's going to be rich! Richer than I ever thought." The baby laughed, and so did Vera, a joyful moment for both, while Remmi felt a newfound disgust as she stared at her aunt. Breathlessly, Vera said, "Whee!" as she spun and held her grandson tightly. Finally, she wound down, but any sadness or regret she'd felt about hearing that Ned Crenshaw had died seemed to be forgotten.

"Okay," Remmi said, digging in her purse for her keys. "Let's go. I think I've seen enough."

"I need a rain check. For that dinner I promised," Dani told Stinson after she'd climbed out of his Cessna and into the rain. Darkness had fallen, evening seeping into night.

"You always need a rain check." He was standing on the tarmac beneath the nose of his plane, the stiff wind ruffling his windbreaker and messing his hair, lights from the terminal illuminating the darkness.

"I'm a busy woman."

"A busy woman who always seems to need a favor."

"Yeah, well . . ." She couldn't argue the fact, and he knew it. She'd known Mark Stinson since college, when he'd married Celia, one of her best friends. In the past few years, Stinson, with his plane, had been her go-to guy for quick, short flights when she needed one. Though he was always paid by the department, he had to adjust his schedule on a dime to accommodate her.

So far, he'd never failed.

She flipped up the hood of her jacket and heard the

loud roar of a jet as it sped down a runway off the main terminal.

"Throw in a drink," he yelled as she started walking away.

"You got it. At least one!" But her words were snatched by the wind and another jet that roared into the black, cloud-covered sky.

Once in the car and on the road again, she said to Martinez, "First stop, Remmi Storm's house." As soon as they'd landed, they'd received a call from Detective Davis in Las Vegas with the news that the dental records for Didi Storm were a match with the corpse now lying in the morgue. No question. No dispute. Next of kin would have to be notified.

Settler hated this part of the job, informing family members that a loved one had died, and violent deaths were the worst. Even in the case of a mother gone missing for twenty years, the loss would be painful.

Switching on her wipers against a heavy dousing of rain, Settler wove through a clog of traffic and got onto the 101 heading north. "I just hope we reach Remmi Storm before she hears that her mother's body was found."

Though Davis had promised to keep Didi's identity secret until after Remmi had been notified, it would be a difficult job. The press had been at the construction site, and the Las Vegas P.D. had been inundated with phone calls.

As if he'd read her thoughts, Martinez said, "The press is gonna have a field day with this."

"Yep. Next of kin for Didi Storm is public knowledge." She'd considered calling the information into the station and asking for someone in the department to contact Remmi, but she felt it was her responsibility as Remmi had come to her, looking for her mother.

"Gun it," he suggested, eyeing the GPS road map as he scrabbled in his pocket for a nonexistent pack of cigarettes. When he realized what he was doing, he stopped. "Lights and siren. But stay off the 280. Looks like it's clogged. At least, according to my app."

She considered turning on the lights, then just hit the gas. Her cell phone rang, illuminating the interior.

"Got it," Martinez said. He hit the speaker button, and a woman's voice came through.

"This is Jennifer Reliant," she said. "I'm sorry, I can't meet with you today. Sick kid, but I heard you wanted information on the contract between my client, Gertrude Crenshaw, and Stumptown Press. You know I can't give out that information, of course."

It didn't matter. They were getting the contract from the Portland lawyer for the publishing company. Still, Settler didn't like letting the agent off the hook; the whole mailbox/answering service "office" seemed a little flaky. "If you can't come down to the station, an officer can come and take your statement."

"If he's not afraid of the flu," she said a little huffily.

"Ms. Reliant, the officers of the San Francisco Police Department aren't afraid of much."

"Fine. Let me know!" And she ended the call.

"I take it she's not happy?" Martinez asked.

"Probably not ever, unless I miss my guess."

They headed due north. The storm was coming in, rolling off the Pacific and across the peninsula. She caught glimpses of the black waters of the bay whipped to a froth, rippling with white caps.

Finally, Settler got out of traffic and turned up the steep incline to the house where Remmi Storm resided. She parked a little too close to a mailbox, risking the wrath of the owner and the USPS, although it was past normal delivery hours. Some of the houses lining the street were decked out with holiday wreaths on their doors, a few with Christmas lights glowing.

"It's not even Thanksgiving," Martinez complained, eyeing a van that advertised Kris Kringle's Christmas Lights, which was parked near the Emerson house, a huge manor dominating the hill.

"Getting a head start," she said automatically, though her thoughts were deep on the case. She couldn't care less what time of year it was. In tandem, they climbed the wide front steps of the home. Christmas lights were already strung along the rail.

Martinez rang the bell.

For a second, no one answered, then she heard sounds from within. Moments later, the door was opened by a small Asian woman in a tunic over yoga pants. Her black hair was twisted onto her head, and she held the door only open a crack. Settler gave her name, introduced Martinez, and showed their IDs, which the woman studied intently before handing them back. "We'd like to speak with Remmi Storm," Settler said.

"She's not here." She was still eyeing them warily.

"But she lives here," Settler clarified, and the woman nodded. "When do you expect her back?"

"Soon."

"Jade? Who is it?" a female voice demanded over a humming sound.

"The police," Jade called back over her shoulder. Moments later, an elderly woman seated in a motorized wheelchair came into view.

"The police? Here? Oh, dear." Wearing a cable-knit sweater and gray slacks and earrings that glittered beneath her short, coiffed hair, she looked up at the detectives inquisitively, without the intensity of Jade. A cat in varying hues of black and orange sat comfortably on her lap.

Settler made introductions, complete with flashing their IDs again. The woman studied their wallets as if they were long-lost, ancient scrolls that contained the secrets of the ages. Finally, she seemed satisfied that the badges were genuine and handed them back. "You're here on official business, I take it."

Martinez nodded. "Yes."

"I was afraid of this," she said on a sigh. "Well, come in, come in, and close the door behind you; you're letting in the cold." Waving them inside with one hand, she deftly turned her chair around.

"Wait." Settler felt a hand on her arm, and Martinez said, "She's here."

Sure enough, a car was pulling into an open spot on the street.

Remmi Storm was at the wheel, Noah Scott in the passenger seat.

Settler waited until the two dashed through the rain and up the porch stairs. Remmi was already looking up, recognizing the officers and taking in their grim expressions.

"You're here with bad news," she guessed as she reached the porch. "We already know about Ned."

"He's not the one," Settler said, her stomach clenching a bit. God, she hated this. "It's your mother. We believe she is deceased. Her body was located in Las Vegas at a construction site."

"What?" The color drained from Remmi's face. "Are you sure? I mean, everyone thought Karen Upgarde was her and . . ."

"Dental records match," Martinez broke in.

Settler said, "I'm sorry for your loss" and watched as the other woman's knees threatened to give way. They probably would have, but Noah Scott quickly wrapped an arm around her shoulders.

"God, Remmi," he said softly. "I'm sorry."

Tears starred her eyes, and she blinked them back. "Me, too." And then as if she thought the detectives would leave without telling her everything they knew, she sniffed, and said, "Please come in. And tell me . . . tell me how you know and what happened."

Shell-shocked, Remmi walked on rubbery legs into the parlor and, with Noah, dropped onto Greta's couch. The world seemed to spin and distort. She'd always thought Didi was alive, no matter what anyone said.

She was aware of people joining them in the room, but the voices came from a far distance, and all she could really concentrate on was the fact that her mother, the woman she'd wondered about for two decades, was gone.

A small part of her had still held onto a slim thread of expectation that she would see Didi Storm again, have a reunion of some kind.

No longer, if the detectives were right, and she believed Danielle Settler wouldn't have delivered the devastating news if she weren't 100 percent sure of her facts.

She blinked. Someone, Jade, was stuffing tissues into her hands, and she realized her tears had tracked down her cheeks. Noah was seated behind her, his arm around her. She was still wearing her jacket, and it was speckled from the raindrops that had splashed against it as they'd hurried from the car to the house to hear that her mother was dead.

A thousand memories of her childhood threatened to cripple her, but she wouldn't think of them now. Not when she needed to hear the truth, to find out what had happened.

Noah whispered into her ear, his breath warm against her skin, "Hey, you okay?"

She nodded. She knew she was in shock, but that she would get over it. Today wasn't that much different than yesterday, right? She wouldn't see Didi again, but then she hadn't for a long, long time, and now, at least, some questions would be answered. "What happened?" she asked the detectives.

Greta was insisting they take a chair before she asked Jade to get everyone some tea or coffee or maybe something "a little stronger."

"How do you know it's my mother?" she asked.

The detectives explained about visiting Las Vegas, seeing the car, license plates, and body, that the female behind the wheel was wearing Didi's clothes, had her ID, and that the dental records matched.

"There's really no doubt," Settler said from one of the wingback chairs.

"You said there was a baby carrier?" Remmi braced herself.

"Yeah, the kind that can be strapped in as a car seat, but we found no trace of a child or any other person in the car. The techs went over it with a fine-tooth comb. They searched the cargo hold and trunk, all of the interior. No trace of a baby, and no blood other than that in the area surrounding the driver."

That, at least, was a relief. It didn't appear Adam had died in that car. But it didn't mean he'd survived, just that he hadn't been killed at that time.

There was a chance he and his sister were alive.

Don't get your hopes up.

Could she believe it? After all this time?

"Where was she found? Where was this construction site?"

"Outside of Las Vegas," Settler answered. "A new development's going in. The land was bought several years ago, but the company who held it about the time your mother disappeared was OH Industries, and the owner was Oliver Hedges. There wasn't as much sprawl then, so the city wasn't as close as it is now. You ever heard of OH Industries? Or Oliver Hedges?"

"No." She was certain of that much, but her head was spinning. The thought of her mother dead in the car all this time . . . hard to believe. Was there any chance they were wrong? The expressions on the detectives' faces and the raw evidence of the dental records suggested not, but Remmi wasn't completely convinced. "I want to see her," she said.

Greta said, "Oh, dear," as she moved her wheelchair closer to the bar.

Settler said, "She's . . . very decomposed."

Martinez, standing near a window, added, "There's nothing left but bones, really. A skeleton. Might be better to remember your mom the way she was."

"I need to see," Remmi insisted. "At least a photograph."

"It's not a good idea," Settler said.

"I still want to see."

Martinez was shaking his head, but Settler seemed to finally get it. "Okay." She opened her phone, found the images, sat in the vacant seat next to Remmi on the couch, then said, "But I'm giving you fair warning. These aren't going to be easy to see."

And she was right. There were shots of the car and items that had been located inside, including Didi's clutch purse, a once sparkly pink cigarette case, and the car seat, all of which brought back memories.

But the reddish-brown stains on the driver's seat were horrifying.

Oh, Mom, what happened?

She must have blanched because Settler, who had been showing each of the pictures, stopped. "You want to go on?" she asked.

No. "Yes," she heard herself say, and then recoiled at the first shot of the corpse, a grisly skeleton with an obscene grin and black holes for nose and eyes.

Her stomach clenched. Could this horrid, lifeless, desiccated body really be the once-vibrant woman who had been so full of life? The woman who had danced with her babies, laughing and throwing her head back in delight, only to plot and scheme and even sell those very infants? She forced herself to keep her eyes on the picture, taking in the macabre image. How could anyone know . . . and then she saw it, noticed the slight flair of one of the skeleton's eye teeth. Remmi remembered Didi at her makeup mirror, tilting her head and studying that tooth.

"I'm gonna get that fixed one of these days," she'd promised, catching a nine-year-old Remmi watching her in the mirror.

But, of course, Didi never had fixed the tooth.

Remmi swallowed. "It's Didi," she said, pulling herself together as she handed the phone back to Settler. Noah's arm tightened around her. "She was murdered, wasn't she?"

"Yes."

"Then we have to find out who did it. And you might want to start by talking to her sister." She had to bite her tongue to keep from spilling the beans about what they'd seen and overheard on the tiny spy camera.

"Vera Gibbs. We were going to visit her next," Settler said.

"Good," Remmi said with feeling.

CHAPTER 31

As Settler drove away from the Emerson home, navigating the steep streets of the Mount Sutro neighborhood, she sensed they were closing in, the pieces of this fragmented puzzle starting to fit together. But she wasn't quite there yet. It was almost as if she was trying to force a piece that was in the wrong spot, and she would have to shift around her thinking and figure it out.

Finding Didi Storm's body had been a lucky coincidence. Who would have guessed that, at the very time the book about her was being published, twenty years after her disappearance, her body would be discovered?

Or had someone planned that, too? How?

"Ready for some overtime?" she asked Martinez, who was riding shotgun again. Once more, it was raining, pouring, and her wipers were having trouble keeping up with the onslaught, the city lights a blur.

"Sure. I'm already on the clock."

"What about Maria and the kids?"

He shrugged. "They're used to my hours." He slid her

a look, "And it's getting near Christmas, so Maria will appreciate the overtime."

"So let's go have a visit with Gibbs."

"In Walnut Creek? It'll take a while to get there." He checked his traffic app. "Well, about forty-five minutes, maybe less. Traffic's not that bad on 80. But it's pretty late."

"All the better," she said, her hands gripping the steering wheel as the Bay Bridge came into sight, its thousands of LED lights illuminating the spans and cables. "Maybe the whole family will be there, and we can have a chat with Milo, Billy, and Jensen. Four for the price of one."

He grunted. "Fantastic."

"You're in?"

"Oh, yeah."

"Punch in the navigation to the Gibbses' house on my GPS, then start digging into Morgan Investments and OH Industries."

"Waaaay ahead of you, partner," he said. "I've already got Camp working on it."

Mina Camp, the tech wizard of the department.

"She'll be able to access more information, more quickly," he added as he put the address into Dani's GPS. "By the time we're finished with Gibbs, she'll have everything there is to know about OH Industries and Morgan Investments uncovered, organized, tied with a red bow, and attached to an e-mail. You watch."

"I believe you." She passed a large truck piled high with baled Christmas trees. When she reached the exit for Walnut Creek, she peeled off the freeway. Fifteen minutes later, they were on the street where the cottage belonging to Milo and Vera Gibbs stood, and as she pulled into an empty space, Martinez's iPad dinged.

He looked at the screen. "What did I tell you? Preliminary information from Mina the Marvelous." He opened the attachment and scanned it as Settler cut the engine. "Holy shit," he said under his breath.

"What?"

"OH Industries?"

"Yeah?"

"It's owned by Oliver Hedges, which we knew. But the man has an interesting history."

"Tell me."

"He has—no, wait—*had* two sons. Oliver Hedges Jr., or the second, called himself OH2, and a younger son, Brett, who is fifty-five now. But the second Oliver Hedges, the son who called himself OH2? He took over as head of the company when the old man had some kind of accident, doesn't say what. The old man survived, but that son, OH2, died at age thirty-seven."

"From what?"

"Let's see." He was scanning the information. "Doesn't say. But the upshot is that the old man, Hedges Senior, improved somehow and took back the reins of the company. And here's the kicker. Both father and son were married to the same woman."

"What? Not at the same time?"

"Nope. OH2 married his much-younger-than-daddy stepmother, Marilee McIver, not too long after the older Hedges was placed in a care facility and—" He paused, then gave a low whistle. "I was wrong. Here's the real kicker. The date that the younger Hedges died?" He was scratching his goatee and studying the screen. "Less than a week after Didi Storm was reported missing."

"Coincidence?"

He barked out a laugh. "Seems unlikely."

"We need to know what the younger Oliver Hedges died from. Natural causes or not so natural."

"Mina is doing more digging." He tapped the screen.

"This report is just the beginning. She says she'll have more later."

"Good." Settler reached for the door handle. "Let's see what the Gibbs family knows about Karen Upgarde, Ned and Trudie Crenshaw, Didi Storm, and Oliver Hedges Senior and Junior."

Greta wasn't going to be satisfied until she knew everything. And she wanted details.

Remmi brought her up to speed as best she could, but the truth was that, other than believing Vera was somehow involved and accepting the finality that her mother was dead, she didn't have a lot more information. She had no idea who had murdered Didi or Ned and Trudie. The same person, or another player? She believed that, somehow, Aunt Vera was involved at some level but didn't know how. She suspected that one of her uncles, or maybe both, were involved, though were they really cold-blooded killers? Could either of them have been involved in Didi's death and, now, the recent homicides?

And what about Karen Upgarde? What had driven her to take the final step that precipitated a nineteen-story fall?

Remmi was too exhausted tonight to rehash theories and speculation with Greta. The older lady would just have to wait, though she'd cornered Remmi while Noah was on the phone, motioning her into the kitchen. The minute they were through the doorway, Greta had killed the motor on her chair so that she could whisper, "I assume he's still here."

"It's been a whirlwind. He showed up last night. I thought he was an intruder and . . . he convinced me he wasn't."

Greta's eyebrows arched speculatively, but Remmi

didn't elaborate or try to explain that Noah had camped
out, that they hadn't slept together, and that it wasn't any
of the older woman's business anyway. "He's very handsome," Greta pointed out.

"Yep."

"If I were twenty years younger . . ."

Remmi shot her a look but held her tongue.

"Well, thirty . . . or . . . forty . . . or . . . ," she conceded.
She caught Remmi smothering a smile. "For the love of
Mike, Remmi, I'm *not* going to say fifty! That's half a
century."

"I wasn't going to say anything."

"All I'm saying is you're young and single, and presumably he is, too, so . . ."

"So . . . ?" Remmi said dryly.

Greta let out a huff. "You're being purposely obtuse."

"And you're being purposely nosy."

"He's pretty handsome, and he looks like he's . . . in
love with you."

"That's a leap, Greta. We reconnected twenty-four
hours ago."

"Well, it sure didn't take me twenty-four hours to fall
for Duncan, I can tell you that. One look at him, and I
thought, 'He's the one. He's the one I want to wake up
next to every morning,' and I never looked back. He felt
the same way, and we were engaged in three months and
married in six." She hoisted up her chin. "So don't you
lecture me about love."

"Was I lecturing?" Remmi said but laughed, her first
of the day, she thought.

"Sounded like it to me," Greta said with a smile, then
grabbed Remmi's hand. "I'm sorry about your mom,
Remmi, I really am. I know that you hoped she was still
alive. I saw that, and I don't blame you, so this is a hard
day for you."

Remmi nodded, not trusting herself to respond.

"But I just want to remind you that you're young, you have your whole life ahead of you, and that man in there"—she jabbed her finger toward the doorway to the dining room and beyond—"he's into you. So give him a fair chance. That's all." She squeezed Remmi's hand, then spun her chair back toward the dining room and rolled past the table, her wheelchair humming.

Though Greta's story was sweet, Remmi wasn't going to fall in love in one damned day, not even if it was with the boy she'd been pining about for twenty years. She was a child back then, but she was a grown woman now, and she hoped she'd gained some sense along the way. Besides, her life was chaos now, upside down. She'd just found out Didi was dead, and other people she knew were dying . . . no, this was not the time to fall in love. She'd been a rebellious teenager when she'd imagined herself falling for Noah Scott, the bad boy, but now, she was a grown woman.

And he's a man . . . who straightened out . . . who seems to care for you.

"Forget it," she told herself. She had to keep a clear head. Yes, it was a stone-cold fact that Didi was dead, but her sister and brother, now nearly adults themselves, could still be out there. Somewhere. She had to find them if it was at all possible.

She'd been on her way toward the stairs when she heard Noah end his call. Greta had buzzed his way, so Remmi changed her mind and headed into the parlor. Greta was near the bookcase, just bending down to pet Ghost, who'd been hiding on the lower shelves. That didn't work, of course, and Ghost, true to his nature, gave a quiet hiss, then slunk out of the room and disappeared into the shadows.

"You're such a naughty boy," Greta said and looked up

to find Noah staring at her as she rolled back across the room. "What?"

"The chair," he said, then met Remmi's gaze as she approached. "The woman who was in the picture we looked at earlier? Seneca Williams?" His eyes narrowed, and he stared into a space in the hallway, but Remmi guessed he was somewhere else, lost for a moment in a distant memory.

"What about her?" she demanded.

He snapped his fingers. "That's why she was talking to Ike!"

"Who's Ike?" Greta asked.

"My stepfather." He turned to Remmi. "I couldn't remember why Seneca stopped by his shop."

"You said they were talking about his moped."

"But that wasn't it. He was a mechanic and fixed small engines and motorcycles, messed around repairing lots of different things. But she came in and asked him to fix a *wheelchair,* like that one." He pointed at Greta's chair. "She said she worked in some kind of care facility, and she needed an electric chair or scooter, or whatever she called it, fixed. Ike sent her on her way, said he didn't work on those things, but it was Seneca, I'm sure of it. Only she said her name was . . . Shelly . . . no, *Shawna.*" He paused and rubbed the back of his neck. "Shawna . . . Whitman! That's what it was, because I remember thinking about the Whitman Massacre and the fact that, to me as a kid, her name sounded exotic, kind of Native American, like a shaman."

Remmi's pulse quickened. "You remembered."

"Yeah. Shawna Whitman is Seneca Williams." He got to his feet. "Now, all we have to do is find her."

> *This little light of mine*
> *I'm gonna let it shine . . .*

The familiar tune whispered through his brain as the Marksman yanked hard on the thin wire of Christmas lights that he'd wrapped around the handyman's neck. The guy was struggling and fighting like a wildcat, but he was smaller and older than the Marksman, and his fight was futile. He flung one hand back, trying to claw at the Marksman's already mutilated face, but he failed and soon was trying to force his fat little fingers between the wire and his windpipe.

It was no use.

The wire was digging into the guy's skin, deeper and deeper, cutting off his air. Still he wrestled around, gasping until he couldn't. The Marksman could visualize the man's eyes already starting to bulge from their sockets.

He gritted his teeth and tightened his grip even further, pulling the man from his feet. His victim—an unlucky handyman for Kris Kringle's Christmas Lights who had been hired to decorate Greta Emerson's house—was losing the battle, his frantic attempts at freeing himself beginning to slow.

Hide it under a bushel? No!

Another twist of the wire, flesh splitting. His dangling victim went limp. Just in time. The Marksman's leg was pounding in pain from the strain on his thighs as he'd hoisted the man from his feet.

Dead, probably. No reason to take a chance, though. He held the wire taut, despite the fact that the man wasn't moving.

Hide it under a bushel?
No!
I'm gonna let it shine . . .

A last twist of the wire.

No fight. Zero response. Dead weight.

Still the Marksman waited. If he'd learned anything from the killing of Ned Crenshaw, it was to not take a death for granted. He had to remember he was not invincible and that a victim could sometimes respond with almost superhuman strength.

So he held the man off his feet as his own thigh pulsed in angry pain. Rain poured from the dark skies, and the wind blew harshly, rattling the branches of the shrubbery around the Emerson mansion. The Christmas lights winked brightly from the eaves and peak of the roof, but still the Marksman held fast until at last he was certain that the man, whose clothes and keys he was going to use, was surely, without a doubt, dead as the proverbial doornail.

Satisfied, he let his victim sink down to the soggy ground. His plan was to change into the handyman's Kris Kringle jumpsuit, grab a string of lights, and use the man's access to the basement garage and electrical panel. Then he would sneak into the house and up the interior, back staircase to the third-floor apartment.

First, though, he planned to stuff the body into the back of the Kris Kringle's Christmas Lights van and then, using the handyman's ladders, peer into the windows of the house to orient himself with the layout. He should be able to pull it off. Even if he was seen, it was dark and gloomy. No one would suspect he wasn't the regular guy.

Carefully, he rolled his dead victim onto a tarp he kept in his SUV.

He didn't really have anything against Remmi other than that she was nosy and poking around where she didn't belong, but she had to go. There was a chance she could challenge the authenticity of the book or start making noise about wanting to get paid for any royalties or movie deals or whatever.

So, good-bye, Remmi Storm.

He lifted the body over his shoulder in a fireman's carry and then cautiously, quietly, sneaked within the curtain of rain to the empty street and stuffed the man into the back of his Kris Kringle van. There was enough room to climb inside. Just enough. So he followed after the body and around the spools of lights, small ladders, staple guns, and the like, stripped the worker of his jumpsuit, ripped off his own clothes, and in the cramped space, his leg screaming in pain, he zipped up the ill-fitting suit. It didn't exactly fit like a glove, but it would have to do. Once outside, he quietly closed the back doors and locked the van, then returned to the house, where he repositioned the ladder and climbed up it, still checking every window as he passed, keeping himself oriented with the inside of Greta Emerson's huge home.

He hadn't counted on his leg aching so badly—pain was radiating from the wound in his thigh—but he'd deal with it.

Once he'd scoped out the place, he would leave in the guy's van for a few hours, then return later. If anyone looked out, they'd see the same handyman's vehicle that had been parked on the street, off and on, for several days. Once he was certain the neighborhood was asleep, he'd sneak inside and finish this job.

The plan wasn't foolproof, but it should work.

It was long past time for Remmi Storm to join her mother in eternity.

CHAPTER 32

"Didi's dead? For certain?" Vera Gibbs whispered, her hand over her mouth as she stood framed in the doorway, backlit by the interior lights, a screen separating her from the detectives.

She'd answered when Settler had rung the bell. She and Martinez had introduced themselves, shown their badges.

"I'm sorry for your loss," Settler said.

"Dead? You found her? After all this time. I can't believe . . ." Turning her head, she called, "Jensen. It's the police. They found your aunt."

Behind her, a tall man in his twenties appeared. "They say Didi's dead," Vera whispered, and though she seemed a bit shaken, she didn't fall apart.

"You'd better come inside." Jensen pushed the screen open farther, and they entered. "I'm Jensen, Vera's son," he said. "Have a seat." He motioned to the living room, and as Vera took refuge in a rocker, Jensen stood in the open space between the living room and dining room, his arms crossed over his chest. "What happened?" he asked.

Settler and Martinez took turns explaining about finding the body in the car in the desert, that it was obvious that Didi had been dead for two decades and that she'd been murdered.

"Murdered?" Vera repeated. "I guess I'm not surprised. But who would . . . ?" She let the question fade, and Settler noted that though she appeared surprised and was obviously processing the news, she certainly wasn't sad about her sister's violent death.

Jensen ran a hand over his short-cropped, blond hair. He swung a dining room chair around and sat on it, while Settler and Martinez, at his urging, took seats on opposite ends of a couch that had seen better days. A recliner angled toward a flat-screen TV remained unoccupied. Milo's chair, Settler thought.

"Is your husband here?" Martinez asked.

Vera shook her head. "Working."

Jensen said, "It's just Mom and me, and my son, who's sleeping." He brightened a bit at the mention of his boy, but then added, "Dad's on the road. Sales. Farm equipment. And Uncle Bill, who lives out in an apartment in the garage, he's gone, too, for a couple of days. Vacation from work." He paused, then looked at his mother. "You know, Mom and I, we'd talked about coming to see you. You aren't the first people to show up today." He explained about Remmi Storm and Noah Scott showing up unexpectedly, and as he did, Vera seemed to shrink farther into the rocker.

Though irritated that Remmi and Noah Scott had been here already and hadn't bothered to mention it, Settler managed to keep an outwardly calm facade. Why couldn't people just leave police investigations to the investigators?

". . . they left a few hours ago," Jensen finished, staring at his mother as she seemed to shrink into the well-worn cushions of the gently swaying rocker. "Mom?" he said, encouraging her.

"Oh, no . . . this isn't a good time." She was shaking her head.

"There's never a 'good time,' Mom, and you know it. So, if you don't tell them, I will. At least I'll tell them what I know." He turned his attention to the officers. "Look, I was a screw-up as a kid. Did a lot of things I'm not proud of."

His mother made a little snort of disdain.

"I even stole from my cousin."

"Which you didn't tell her," Vera popped out with. "You had the chance today."

"I will. And I'll pay her back." Jensen appeared sincere. "I'm a father now, and I've got to set a good example for my son. But this doesn't have anything to do with me." Once more his gaze landed on his mother. "Mom?"

She sent her son a furious glare.

He pushed. "We talked about this. You said you needed to do the right thing. The Christian thing."

Silence stretched between them, and for a second, Settler thought Vera would stand firm, but she finally exhaled on a long, weary sigh. "Fine." Gathering herself, she faced the officers, her pointed chin lifting in a bit of a challenge. "I think . . . I mean I'm not sure, but it could be that my husband is into something very bad."

"What do you mean by that?" Settler asked.

"I don't really know," Vera said as she rocked slowly and fingered the cross at her neck. The room was tired-looking, the lamps dim.

"Mom," Jensen said, urging her. "You know it's a sin to lie, and worse yet—"

"Don't lecture me!" She held up a hand to him, her lips moving silently as if she were giving herself a mental pep talk or maybe praying. With all the pictures of Jesus decorating the room, and the huge Bible lying open on the dining room table, that seemed the most likely.

"Milo's a good man," she whispered.

"What did he do?" Martinez asked.

"I don't know that he did anything. I'm not really certain. I mean . . . I don't know for sure, but there's a chance he was involved somehow in that poor woman's death." She blinked and looked at the floor.

"Whose death?" Settler asked.

"Karen Upgarde's. The woman he—we—hired to dress up like Didi."

"You hired her?" Dani asked. "Why?"

She was wringing her hands now, her voice shaky. "For publicity. For the book."

"*I'm Not Me,* the story about Didi?" Martinez jumped in before Settler could ask.

She nodded. "It was my idea. I thought it might add a little interest in the book if there were 'Didi sightings' like there are Elvis sightings, and it was a good idea." She glanced at Settler. "She wasn't supposed to die!"

"What went wrong?" Martinez asked at the same time Dani queried, "Did you run this by Trudie Crenshaw?"

"Trudie knew. She even had some of Edie's . . . Didi's old things. She was close to her, when they both were in Las Vegas, and sometimes Didi would crash at Trudie's, you know, if she was too drunk or too stoned to go home, or if she had a fight with her current boyfriend." Her face pulled into an expression of disgust.

"Did Ned Crenshaw know, too?" Dani asked.

"Yes, he was a part of the book, of course. Edie's first husband."

"And Trudie, his second wife, was the author," Martinez clarified.

"Whose idea was the book itself?" Dani asked, but she suspected she already knew.

"Mine," Vera said with a bit of remembered pride, but then her face fell. "But Trudie was a better writer, and I didn't want anyone to know that I was connected. I'm a respected member of my church and . . ." She shook her head and sniffed. "If anyone found out who Maryanne Osgoode was, it was better if it wasn't me. I'd tried to sell the idea years before, but nothing had happened, and Trudie knew this agent who was connected to an editor at Stumptown, who bought the book. The advance was small. They thought that, other than a few true-crime buffs, who would buy it? So, we decided to stir up some interest. Since no one knew if Didi was alive or dead, why not create a publicity buzz?" She looked at Settler as if she expected the detective to understand. "The only way to make a lot of money was if the book's sales really got going."

"How did you find Karen Upgarde?" Dani asked.

"Milo had seen her in some bar in the Seattle area. He'd gone in for a beer, and she was up on stage, and he thought she looked a lot like Edie. He was right. With the right makeup and wigs, and dresses, she could pull it off. It turned out she could use the money—well, who couldn't? So they struck a deal."

Vera's lips started to tremble, and she swallowed hard. "She was just supposed to walk through a crowd, hope someone would see her, catch someone's eye. Even though Didi Storm wasn't exactly a household name, Marilyn Monroe still was."

"How did you expect someone to make the connection? That she was really trying to act like Didi, not Marilyn?" Martinez asked.

"The book was just out. We thought if we called some reporters . . . you know, nudged them in that direction, someone would get interested in what had happened to Didi. But Karen wasn't supposed to commit suicide. No, no, no! It was supposed to be kind of a guessing game. She'd show up at a mall. Or a bar. Or walking through a hotel, y'know. It's the holidays, and TV cameras are filming events everywhere. Karen was supposed to show up; then one of us would call the television stations anonymously and say we thought we saw Didi Storm, and the reason we thought she was Didi was because of her hands, the fingernail thing that Edie always thought was so cute, one nail different from all the others." Vera pressed a finger to her trembling lips. "We thought we might be able to make some real money from it."

"From your sister's disappearance."

"I didn't know if she was really dead. I expected it, of course, but . . . well, I figured Edwina, she owed me."

She glared at Dani, her deep-down jealousy, rage, and moral superiority on full display.

There it is, Dani thought. *The true motive.*

Vera went on. "We knew my sister as Edie, short for Edwina. She and I never got along. She was always so . . . outgoing. She always got the attention. Edie thought the world revolved around her, even as a child. She was beautiful," she added grudgingly. "And, of course, she caught the eye of every boy in school, but she did terrible things. Smoked, drank, and did drugs, I'm pretty sure. Anything for a good time. And she had the loosest morals of any girl I knew! We were brought up by good Christian parents, but it just didn't take with Edie." She glanced at her son, who had listened silently to his mother's take on her sister. "She even went out with your father, did you know that? Milo and I were nearly engaged, and she and he . . ." She shuddered. "Well, anyway, it was a short period, and he begged me to come back to him, *begged.* So I forgave him, and we got married not long after. Moved away from Anderstown."

Dani silently questioned whether the philandering Milo had ever been truly forgiven but kept her own counsel.

"You think your husband might have done something bad?" Martinez reminded her.

"Well, yes . . . I mean, I really don't know. But . . ." She glanced back at her son for encouragement, and Jensen, sober, nodded. Vera's eyebrows drew together, the lines on her forehead deepening, the turn of her lips downward. "A friend of mine was in San Francisco the day Karen jumped, and . . . Milo was supposed to be in eastern Oregon, selling hay balers, or tractors, or whatever. I just wanted to make certain he was where he was supposed to be, so I checked with a couple of equipment dealers in Bend and Prineville and Baker City, stores on Milo's sales route." She began to wring her hands, unconscious of her actions, Dani was pretty sure. "And no one had seen him. So I checked a little farther east into Idaho, but no . . . and he wasn't in Washington, either. Everywhere I called, they said he wasn't scheduled for another month or two weeks or whatever. It was obvious he'd lied to me. And then . . ." She blinked rapidly, her expression even more pained. "I checked his cell phone. He was definitely in San Francisco."

"You think he was with Karen Upgarde?" Settler asked.

A whimper escaped her throat. "I don't know! But he did say once that she was unstable, had tried to commit suicide or something like that, and, you know, with the right urging . . . Oh, sweet Lord." Tucking a lock of hair around her ear, she added, "I thought he was joking, you know, just kidding around."

"And now?" she pressed.

"I don't know. We're kind of in a bad way. A lot of bills, and we paid Karen a lot of money to impersonate

Didi, so . . . I don't know what to think. And now . . ."
She squeezed her eyes shut. "I just know that he lied.
Again. Just like before. When I was in college and he
cheated on me."

Martinez asked, "Do you know where he was when
Ned and Trudie Crenshaw were killed?"

"No . . . ," she said weakly. "But when I called and we
talked about it . . . he pointed out that, with them gone, all
of the royalties for the book would fall to me."

"Does he own a rifle?" Martinez asked.

She didn't answer immediately, seemed somewhere
else, so Martinez repeated the question. She snapped to,
and said, "Oh . . . oh, yes. Several," she admitted. "He . . .
he hunts."

Settler felt that little sizzle again. This was it. "Does
he have the guns here?"

Vera shook her head. "He always has them with him."

"Dad's a dead-eye with a rifle," Jensen put in. "Got
the shooting trophies to prove it. Sometimes he even
refers to himself as 'the Marksman.' "

"Go to bed." Half sprawled over Remmi's couch, Noah
had his computer on the coffee table. Once they'd gone
upstairs, they'd turned on the spy camera and checked its
memory, but watching it had proved futile because, after
swinging the baby off his feet and dancing, Vera had
cleaned off the dining room table, which meant she'd
placed the sunglasses in a drawer. All that showed on the
screen was darkness.

Already connected to the Internet on his laptop, Noah
was also linked wirelessly on Remmi's iPad to Emma, his
assistant, who, it seemed, never slept.

Remmi was next to Noah, her legs over his. "I'm not
going to bed yet. Too keyed up." They were too close to

finding out the answers to questions that had haunted her all her life. As tired and emotionally wrung out as she was, she couldn't just fall into bed and shut it all down, not with her mind spinning as it was.

Noah was FaceTime-ing with Emma, who was pretty and intense. In her early twenties, with brown hair that fell in loose, unkempt layers to her shoulders, Emma Yardley was chewing on her lower lip as she concentrated. Hazel-eyed and sharp-featured, with a smattering of freckles that she didn't cover with any kind of makeup, she stared into the screen when she wasn't checking other computers. According to Noah, she surrounded herself with electronics.

From the corner of her eye, Remmi saw Romeo saunter into the room, stretch, then hop onto the arm of the couch. She motioned for the cat to come closer, patting the vacant cushion next to her. Instead, he pounced onto the back of the couch just out of reach.

"So here's the interesting thing," Emma said as Remmi leaned in for a better view of the screen. "Oliver Hedges Senior, the old guy? He had a bad skiing accident that really messed him up. Lost part of his spleen, broke ribs and his legs, had a punctured lung, and a bruised spinal cord. From what I can see, he kind of gave up for a while, ended up in a facility called Fair Haven Retirement Center, one of those communities that has a graduated living scale, depending upon a person's needs. Everything from independent living to full-time nursing care, you know what I mean?"

Noah nodded. "Yep."

"Well, Hedges, he was in the upper limits of care requirement. Couldn't walk and barely talked. He wasn't that old, either. Sixty-one. So he goes to the hospital and then to the care center, and everything heals but his spine. The long-term diagnosis was that he would probably never walk again. So, his young, second wife—trophy wife—puts him into the home, as, apparently, she's now having second thoughts about being married to an invalid. Within six months, she divorces the old man and then . . . ends up marrying his son, Hedges the second."

"OH2," Noah said.

"Okay, whatever. But it goes a little deeper than that. I guess Marilee and OH2 had been college sweethearts, which is how she met his father in the first place. OH1 was single at the time, having already divorced his kids' mother. So Marilee and OH1 click and she dumps the son for his rich daddy. But after the accident and the awful diagnosis, wifey bails right into the arms of her former boyfriend. So much for 'until death do us part.'" Emma held up a finger. "But wait, there's more. The story isn't over because the old man in the care center, the original Oliver Hedges, OH1? He finds love again."

"What?" Noah said.

"At the nursing facility? In his condition? What were the chances, huh? But it's true. He recovered enough to take back the reins of the company and marry again."

Remmi just stared at the screen "Who?"

"Well, this is where your Shawna Whitman comes in," Emma drawled.

"Seneca?" Remmi whispered, feeling her pulse jump. "How?"

"Shawna Whitman, aka Seneca Williams, was one of the nurses at the care facility, and she worked directly with Hedges Senior. I guess you could say she gave him back the will to live again, and he started to improve."

Remmi couldn't believe it. After all this time? "Why an alias?"

"Turns out Shawna didn't have a license to be a midwife. Never registered with the state; she just did it on the side. She was really just a nurse's aide."

While Emma was talking, Noah was typing on his laptop and, from the looks of it, checking out information on OH Industries. He'd clicked on the board of directors and pictures of the officers of the company, and front and center was Oliver Hedges.

Emma went on, "Remember I told you there were two sons? OH2, who died at thirty-seven, and his younger brother, Brett. Well, OH1 also has a twenty-year-old daughter. A girl named Kayla."

"Ariel," Remmi said and turned her attention from the screen to Noah. "It's Ariel. Not his daughter. Though he might claim she is. Ariel's his granddaughter!"

He typed quickly, Googling Kayla Hedges. Pictures appeared, shots of her growing up, from a toddler with her father to a gangly adolescent and eventually to a young woman who was a thinner, younger version of Didi, right down to her secret smile.

Remmi let out a little cry, and tears filled her eyes. "She's alive," she whispered. On the very night she'd found out for certain that her mother had been murdered, she'd learned that her sister had survived! "Is there mention of a son the same age?" she asked, dashing away the tears.

"Let's see." Noah's fingers flew over the keyboard, as Emma said, "Yep. Kyle. Google him."

Noah did, and several pictures appeared on his screen.

Staring at the lanky teenager with straw-blond hair and a surly expression, Remmi gasped, "He . . . he looks like Jensen when he was about that age."

"They would be cousins," Noah said.

"Looks like both Kayla and Kyle are in school at UNLV," Emma said. "The Hedges family home is still in Las Vegas, too."

"How did you get this information?" Remmi asked.

Neither Noah nor Emma responded, but the answer was self-evident: hacking.

"I want to meet them," Remmi said, remembering the last time she'd seen her siblings. They'd been tiny infants, driven into the desert, unaware of the strange fate that would follow.

"We will," Noah promised.

Remmi shook her head. "I mean I want to meet them ASAP. Like tonight. They're either at UNLV or maybe at their home. Las Vegas isn't that far away."

"Tomorrow," he said, glancing at the window, where rain drizzled down the glass. "We'll get an early start."

She wasn't satisfied, felt an urgency from twenty years of not knowing. Now, she was close to not only finding the answers that had eluded her, but to meeting her siblings again.

"They may not want to see you," he warned. "Or believe you. You're going to upset their entire lives, change everything they know. The truth about Didi isn't all that pretty."

"I know, but I have to meet them," she said. "They're the key to what happened to my mother, to their mother."

He thought about it a second, then inclined his head in agreement and turned to the computer screen. "Okay, we've got to go, Ems. Thanks for doing all the leg work."

"Finger work," she corrected, wiggling her fingertips in front of the screen. "You're welcome and good night, er, morning." After she clicked off, Noah reached over to the lamp on the side table, snapping it off. The living room settled into a semi-darkness, the glow of computer screens the only illumination.

"You need to go to bed," he said, pushing her hair out of her eyes. "Long day." He pulled her closer to him so that they were stretched out on the couch together, wedged on the narrow cushions.

"Don't want to," she argued, but she yawned, her head against his chest.

"It's late." His arms tightened around her. His body was warm; she heard his heart beating in his chest, and it felt so right, so safe to lie here.

"I will," she said, closing her eyes, feeling her mind begin to wind down. "In a sec—"

"Take all the time you want," he said and kissed the crown of her head.

"Okay," she said, but she was already drifting off.

CHAPTER 33

The house was dark.
  Quiet.

Even the glow of television or computer screens was no longer visible in any of the windows. Just Christmas lights winking in the early-morning hours, bulbs casting off a blurry gleam in the rain that continued to fall.

The Marksman, as Milo Gibbs thought of himself, watched the big house for another five minutes, but nothing stirred within.

Go time.

Silently cursing himself for leaving the night-vision glasses in the truck, he snapped on a fresh pair of surgical gloves, making certain they were tight enough that he could easily feel a trigger.

Satisfied, he crept inside, through a basement window in the garage he'd left open earlier while the handyman was working with the electrical panel located on the back wall. Through the connecting door, he stepped inside the cellar, passing by a washer and dryer on his way to the bottom of the stairs, where he paused and again listened for any signs of life in the three stories overhead.

Nothing.

The house was quiet aside from the soft rumble of the furnace and, as he passed by the first floor, the hum of a refrigerator, the ticking of a clock, and rhythmic snoring of the old lady, whom he'd seen occupied the first-floor bedroom. And the Asian caretaker was still in the parlor, where, it seemed, she camped out overnight in case the woman in the bedroom needed her.

That was a bit of a problem, but not one he couldn't handle.

The bigger issue was the man. Noah Scott.

Last night, Scott had spent the night here, and tonight, as well, he'd stayed over, which was a piece of bad luck. Still, he was running out of time. The two of them had been at his house, poking around, trying to guilt Vera into talking.

He crept up the back stairs, passing what appeared to be an empty second floor. He'd been watching the house, and no one ever seemed to stay on the guest level, which he thought was a good sign—more space and insulation between the first floor and the third.

His plan was simple: with a silencer on his pistol, he would sneak into Remmi Storm's bedroom and shoot the man first, as he might be stronger, could more easily overpower him; then he would level the gun at Remmi and shoot. He felt the tiniest bit of hesitation at killing her, but it quickly withered. He'd do what he had to do. She was a problem.

Bang, bang—and out. No muss, no fuss. He'd take the exterior stairs and drive off in the Kris Kringle van, then ditch it down by the waterfront somewhere and hike to the nearest train station. Take the first morning train to an area where he'd parked his SUV.

The only real hitch was Noah Scott. He was the wild card, and, of course, he had to contend with his own damned leg, which hurt like a son of a bitch. He hoped the wound was going to be all right. As careful as he'd been, he still risked infection, especially while camping out in a dive like the Baysider, which he thought should be torched rather than cleaned.

That little fantasy warmed him.

He'd love to pour the gasoline and light the fire that would send that fleabag of a motel into a conflagration, with flames reaching to the sky.

But not now.

Tonight, he had a job to do.

He needed to concentrate and ignore the throbbing in his thigh muscles as he silently climbed.

In a short while, he would be home free.

Unless Vera talked.

He worried about that. Her Christian values were always at odds with her practicality. But she'd see the light.

She had to.

If they both were going to survive.

If not, he'd have to take care of her, too.

Yes, she was his wife, the mother of his sons. Yes, at one point he'd thought he loved her, but that had been years ago, before all the nagging and finger pointing and reminders of his past mistakes. There was no way he could ever atone for his sins. Not even with what he was planning now. Even that wouldn't vanquish Vera's recriminations and her continual reminders of how he'd never really lived up to her impossible standards.

Despite everything else, it was his seduction of her sister, Edie, that had been his biggest and most unforgivable

sin. Who would have thought that a few weeks of passion
would have changed the course of all their lives forever?

But he couldn't think of that now.

He needed intense concentration, razor-sharp preci-
sion.

On the landing between the second and third floors, he
paused, listening. Did he hear something on one of the
floors below? Some movement? A disturbance in the qui-
etude? Or was that his imagination?

He waited.

Aside from his own breathing and the rush of blood in
his ears, his pulse elevating with the adrenaline pumping
through his veins, he heard nothing. No signs of anyone
stirring.

Noiselessly, he slid the pistol from one pocket of the
jumpsuit, then eased out the silencer from the other
pocket and snapped it into place. It gave off a soft click,
but the sound was barely audible. Making certain the clip
was in the magazine, he started mounting the final half
flight to the nearly dark upper floor.

He crouched, not wanting his head to appear over the
top rail, but as expected, no one surprised him.

Good.

Confident, he stepped onto the upper level, guided by
night-lights and the map he had in his head.

After killing the handyman, he'd climbed up several
ladders and peeked into windows, orienting himself to
the house and, most intently, the uppermost floor. Earlier
in the day, he'd happened to catch a conversation between the owner of the house and the handyman, in
which she berated him for not doing a good job, demand-
ing he stay until he got it right: "Don't forget the sleigh or
Rudolph's nose. Red. Remember? And it has to be visible
from the street. I don't care how long you have to work,
how late it is, even if it's midnight!"

"Fussy old biddy," the handyman had said under his breath. The Marksman had heard it all from his hiding spot, a trellis covered with evergreen vines on the fence line.

Now, muscles tense, gun held out in front of him, the song from his youth rolling through his brain, he moved on the balls of his feet, easing around the corner, heading straight to Remmi's bedroom.

The door to the room was ajar. Lucky. He'd be able to shoot from the doorway rather than have to twist the knob. He would empty the clip at the bed rapid-fire, then hurry back down the stairway and into the kitchen, where he'd flee out the rear door. By the time the old lady or her aide woke up and either called the police or came up to investigate, it would be all over, and he would be in the wind.

Edging ever closer, he eased along the rail and then stopped. Did he hear a strange noise? Something that hadn't been there a minute earlier? A . . . whirring? Probably the motor of the furnace kicking in. But the basement was three stories below him. Could the sound be coming from the old vents?

Don't think about it. It's nothing. You're just keyed up.

The whirring continued as he stepped toward the bedroom.

This little light . . .

His heart was beating like a drum, and he was beginning to sweat, excitement at the prospect of the kill running through his blood.

Could he do it?

Murder his own blood?

Of course.

Three more feet.

Two.

One.

The door was ajar, not completely open, and he noise-lessly pushed on it with the business end of the silencer.

No lights. He kicked himself again for not bringing the night-vision goggles with him.

Finger on the trigger, he made out the outline of the bed in the darkness, leveled his gun and fired.

Pop! Pop, pop!

Backing up, he ran into something with his foot.

EEEEEOOOWWW!

The squeal of some ungodly beast echoed through the old house.

For a half-second, he thought it was one of his in-tended victims, but no, the sound was at his feet, and about the time he realized it, an immense furry beast sprang from the darkness, landing, and clawing at his leg.

"Aaagh!" he cried in surprise and pain. The cat—that's what it was!—had landed on his bad leg. He kicked, but the animal skidded around, clawing and howling. And then it bit into him like a savage tiger.

He cried out.

Shit. This wasn't supposed to happen!

Grrrrrwww. He shook his leg and batted at the animal, afraid to shoot it as he'd put a bullet through his foot.

Shit! Shit! Shit!

He had to finish shooting now! Backing up, cat on his leg, he fired into the bedroom, emptying his pistol.

Pop, pop, pop!

He fled down the stairs toward the kitchen, emptying the gun, kicking at the cat.

Pop, pop, pop!

"Hey!" a voice yelled from the living room. A man's voice. "What the hell's going on?"

Oh, for the love of St. Jude! Noah Scott isn't in the bed

*with Remmi! He's in the fucking living room, and he
probably has a gun!*

"Noah?" Remmi Storm's worried voice.

They were alive?

"Down!" Noah yelled. "Get down!" And he was coming. In the darkness, Milo saw a dark shape vault from
where the living room couch was backed against a window.

And he was out of ammo.

Fuck! Spinning, Milo headed for the kitchen and the
back door; he threw himself forward, dragging the stupid
cat, his leg on fire.

He should have shot the damned beast.

Crrracck! The sound of wood splintering roared in his
ears.

The kitchen wall seemed to explode.

He stumbled, nearly fell.

From what he'd thought was a cupboard, something—
no, someone—rolled out!

What the fuck?

He whirled quickly, the cat flying off his leg, his thigh
burning like a son of a bitch. Before he could react, the
tiny person jumped up and, in one motion, spun like a top
and, with a weird shriek, kicked his gun from his hand.

Jesus Christ!

In that second, the interior lights snapped on.

Blinking against the sudden illumination, he saw the
Asian caretaker, who had kicked her way into the room
from some kind of dumbwaiter. She was winding up
again just as he heard, "Stop!"

From the corner of his eye, he spied Noah Scott, standing behind the coffee table, legs spread, expression grim,
pistol aimed straight at Milo's head. "Don't move," he ordered.

For a split second, Milo thought about taking his chances

and bolting, but he noticed the Asian woman in a half-crouch, muscles coiled to strike again. The cat who had attacked was glaring at him from the top of the couch, its black lips pulled into a snarl of fury.

Remmi, her hair mussed, was off the couch and staring at him in shock. "Milo? You? You were going to . . . *kill me?*"

The back door was only fifteen feet away. If he could just—

"Don't," Noah Scott ordered again, as if he could read Milo's mind.

The female karate fiend's face was a hard mask, eyes glittering. She looked like she would enjoy nothing more than kicking him to kingdom come and back again.

Damn his bad leg. That was Ned Crenshaw's fault.

"Call the police," Noah told Remmi, but she was already picking up her phone.

This couldn't be happening. He couldn't be trapped by a couple of non-pros, a female martial arts student, and a damned cat. It was surreal; that's what it was, surreal, but he couldn't kid himself about what was happening.

He thought about being nailed for the Crenshaw murders.

He thought about the handyman dead in the back of the van.

He thought about the years of prison that were in store for him.

No way.

No fucking way.

"Don't move," Noah told him coldly. "I mean it: one step, and I'll shoot you, right here. Right now."

"You can't," he said, desperate to get away, trying to think of anything.

Scott held him in his sights, his face hard, recognition dawning. "You shot me. Out there in that desert. I saw your face, Gibbs, and I didn't realize who you were. But I do now. And I'm damned sure you tried to blow me away, just like you did Ned Crenshaw. Just like you did Trudie." His eyes narrowed. "You came back to the hospital to finish me off, but I ran, so don't tell me I can't pull the trigger. Because I can. And I will."

The bastard would enjoy killing him.

For the first time in a long while, Milo Gibbs felt fear burn through his blood. He knew if he didn't do something quickly, right now, he was doomed. Time to play his trump card and try like hell to ignore the pain pounding through his leg.

"I'm your father," he said, looking straight at Remmi.

Her mouth dropped open, and she stared at him, blinking and shaking her head. Her knees looked as if they might buckle, and if they did, and Scott had to steady her—if he was distracted for one half a moment—Milo knew he could grab the gun, could salvage this clusterfuck of an operation, could reverse this untenable situation.

"You're lying," Remmi said.

"Wish I was, but me and Edie—er, Didi—got together before she ran off to California and . . . and I went back to Vera. Didn't know about you for years."

"Oh, God. No, no, no."

He saw the truth sinking in, but, damn it, Scott was still holding the gun rock steady.

"It's true, Remmi," he said, in his best cajoling tone. "If I'd known—"

"You're saying that I'm your daughter and you came into this house to murder me?"

"It's not what—"

"After you killed how many others?" She was obviously stunned, disbelieving. Then the anger came. Instead of hanging her head, trying to sort fact from fiction, she raised her chin and glared at him through eyes that were hard and glassy with unshed tears. "You're not my father. You're no father. I don't care what you did or didn't do with my mother. I don't give a damn what blood type you have or DNA test or any of what the rest of it says."

He tried again. God, the door was so damned close. "But, honey—"

"Go to hell, Milo. Go straight to hell."

Shit!

He had to get out of here!

He thought he could hear the sound of approaching sirens. The cops were on their way. But there was still time. He could still escape, regardless of the gun pointed straight at his chest.

The stairs were mere steps away.

He glanced again at the post at the top of the stairs. Only three steps—

Then he saw her. The Asian woman. She was coiled tighter. As if she had anticipated his move. Before he could react, she spun around; foot outstretched, face twisted into a demonic grimace, she screamed and flew at him, all of her weight thrust upon his already throbbing knee.

Thud, thud, thud! Tiny, hard feet hit in rapid succession.

Pain screamed through his body.

He fell to the floor, knocked senseless, hardly able to stay awake.

"Stop!" Noah ordered.

Through his pain, he saw the muzzle of Noah's pistol aimed straight at his face. Remmi stood next to him.

"Don't," Milo croaked out.

"Jade?" A worried female voice called from a far, far distance. "Jade? Are you up there? Remmi? Is everyone all right?"

The old lady, he thought, his blurred gaze focusing on the tiny Asian woman.

And then she aimed at his thigh again and let loose with a wild cry. He slanted a look at her, and their eyes met.

He saw the pure hatred in her gaze.

"Jade, no!" he heard Remmi cry as the compact woman landed all of her weight on him. Pain screeched up his leg, and he shrieked, writhing, hearing his own bones crack.

"Stop!" Remmi yelled once more, but it was too late.

The viperous woman struck hard. Again.

This time he passed out.

CHAPTER 34

Settler wasn't satisfied.

She sat at her desk in the homicide department, her eyes gritty from lack of sleep, and she didn't yet feel that special little glow of gratification she always experienced when a case was closed, even though she'd found a new piece of evidence.

Maybe it was because everyone else in the department seemed to be in a better mood than she was, the hum of conversation and jangle of phones louder today, it seemed, than usual. Or it might be because the phone calls from the press had been non-ending. Or perhaps it was because Ted Vance had given her the once-over and hadn't bothered to hide his disapproval at her disheveled appearance, even though she'd been up most of the wee hours of the morning bringing a killer to justice.

Pain in the ass.

Knowing she was being petty just because she was tired, she pushed Vance out of her mind and sipped the double espresso she'd picked up on her way to work. The night had ended somewhere around 4:30, and she'd gotten less than four hours' sleep before she'd walked Earl, left him with the neighbors, and made her way like a zombie through her shower. Then she'd scraped her hair away from her face, snapped it into a ponytail, and dressed in black slacks, black top, and a jacket. Good enough.

She should feel a little more satisfied than she did, though.

Yes, they had Milo Gibbs in the hospital, a guard at his door, and statements taken from his wife, kid, and everyone at the Emerson house. Gibbs had already had surgery on his leg and should be rousing soon. She and Martinez intended to interview him once the anesthesia wore off.

It appeared as if Gibbs was, indeed, the assassin who had killed Karen Upgarde by giving her a little push, either psychologically, physically, or by lacing whatever she was drinking with psychotropic drugs. The autopsy and tox screen would clarify what was in her bloodstream. And, of course, he'd shot Trudie and Ned Crenshaw. She suspected the DNA from the blood found on the trail leading away from the crime scene would no doubt be matched to that taken from his body. Not to mention his killing of the handyman they'd discovered rolled in a tarp in the back of the man's Kris Kringle van. Then there was the attempted murder of Noah Scott and/or Remmi Storm, and all of the eyewitnesses to that thankfully botched crime and who knew how many more?

But there were still big pieces of the puzzle missing.

From a pile on the corner of her desk, she picked up her copy of *I'm Not Me* and stared at the distorted picture of Didi Storm on the cover, wondering if Milo Gibbs had killed her. He'd certainly tried . . . or been a part of it somehow. Noah Scott had IDed him as the assassin who had put a bullet through his throat in the desert that night twenty years earlier. And someone had died in that burned-out Mustang. That, too, looked like Gibbs's work, and the bullets confirmed it, though the male victim was still unidentified. She took another swig from her cup. Somehow, Didi had escaped in her white Cadillac that night, only to disappear the next day. It seemed as if Milo was the killer. But why?

Personal grudge?

Paid assassin?

Martinez showed up at her desk, all smiles in a pressed shirt, slacks, and jacket.

She eyed him and said, "I think I need a wife."

"Everyone needs a wife," he agreed. "Wives need wives."

She thought of some of the projects that she needed done around her house. "Maybe I need a husband, too. And don't say husbands need husbands."

Martinez leaned a hip against her desk. "I just got off the phone with Milo Gibbs's attorney."

"He's already lawyered-up?"

"I think Vera found the guy. In her church, no less. Anyway, it's been hinted that Gibbs is probably going to talk. Work with us. Try to come up with a deal to avoid a long sentence."

"Maybe we don't need a deal. There's a good chance we can figure this out ourselves."

"Of course, we can, but I'm talking about saving time."

"Take a look at this." She pulled up a picture on her computer screen. "It's the fake driver's license for Brandon Hall."

Martinez looked over her shoulder. "Uh-huh."

"And here"—she clicked the mouse, and another image came up—"this is Oliver Hedges's second son, the one who survived. He's got a beard now, but . . ." She hit a few more keys, and the screen changed. "I did some digging, and here's a shot of him twenty years ago, with no facial hair."

"Brandon Hall in the flesh."

"I think so, and the same initials? Both BH? Not very clever. But then he wasn't the smart one. OH2, the older brother, went to Stanford, but this guy"—she tapped a finger at the image on the monitor—"bombed out at a junior college."

"But he survived."

"Trouble was, from what I understand, OH2, the oldest son, thought he was smarter than everyone else, but . . ."

"He's the one who died."

"Apparent heart attack, and the family didn't ask for an autopsy. Nor was anyone in the P.D. interested at that time, so the body was released and he was cremated."

"You're thinking he was killed?"

She lifted a shoulder as she heard a cell phone ringing in a nearby office. "An awful lot of people associated with Oliver Hedges have been murdered, so it's a big question mark. I've got a call into OH2's wife, you know, Marilee? The woman who married both father and son? Waiting to hear back from her."

"That should be interesting."

"Very." She smiled thinly, then drained her cup. "Conveniently, she lives in Las Vegas. As does the rest of the clan. OH Industries is located, for the most part, in Southern California, but they have on-site managers and run the company from Vegas, only show up at the offices a couple of times a month."

"Okay."

"I think we can interview them. Get to the bottom of this without Gibbs's confession."

"It might make things easier."

"Do we really need to give this scumbag a break? He murdered two people for sure, attempted two more, possibly three, if you lump Jade Kim in with Remmi Storm and Noah Scott. How does he think he's got any wiggle room?"

"A deal would avoid the cost of a trial."

She knew that, of course, but it bugged her. She didn't want to think of Gibbs getting anything less than the worst sentence possible. It killed her to be practical, but she grudgingly asked, "Does he have any other bargaining chips?"

"He thinks so. Claims he was an assassin for hire, and he'll give up names if he gets a deal. We pushed, and he did admit this much: way back, twenty years ago, he was working two ends against the middle."

"Meaning what?"

"He was hired *by Didi* first. Apparently, once she swapped the first baby, the girl, for the bucks, Gibbs was supposed to get the kid back from Hedges. The baby was dressed in blue to look like a boy, but Didi knew he wanted a son even more, so she was going to make another play. But the old man got wind that something was up—maybe from Shawna Whitman is my guess—so he overbid Didi and hired Gibbs to make it look like Brett died. How? By killing a guy about the same size as Brett Hedges, in this case a homeless man Gibbs found at random."

"So, that was all for Didi's benefit? Because Brett Hedges is alive and well and living in Las Vegas."

"That's what Gibbs says. They wanted her to believe Brett was dead. But everything went haywire when Noah Scott showed up in the desert, and Didi double-crossed Hedges."

"So, she goes back for a second try the next day, and what? Gibbs somehow kills her and buries her and her Cadillac in the desert?"

"He's not saying yet. Wants a deal, but yeah, that's my

guess. Unless Brett himself killed her. That's always possible."

"But why?"

"For the kids. The entire Hedges clan is all about those twins."

Settler thought about it. She'd spent a lot of time reading up on the Hedges clan. "OH2 died without an heir."

"Right. And the old man might not have been able to father more kids after the accident, even if he did have a younger wife in Shawna Whitman."

Dani slowly shook her head, thinking about the Hedgeses. "I'm beginning to wonder if the old man's skiing accident was an accident."

"Who knows. No one has ever questioned it. OH1 never said anything."

"But then his son marries the wife who divorced him when he became an invalid. Maybe that started him wondering about his firstborn; maybe he questioned his motives, saw him for the louse he was."

She leaned back in her chair, the wheels turning in her mind. "Do you think the eldest son who stole the wife also tried to kill his old man? Maybe he wanted the whole enchilada."

"Could be. With this clan, I wouldn't say any bet was off."

"And then, tit for tat, the old man somehow has him killed. Has someone do it. Like Gibbs?" She asked, "Would a father kill his own kid?"

"Gibbs tried with Remmi Storm," he pointed out.

"Touché."

"Like I said, this whole family is one major piece of work. If we can believe Gibbs—"

"We can't. Seriously, Martinez, we can't believe a word he says."

"I know, but if we did . . . Just stay with me here. Gibbs

says, and I quote, at least from his attorney, that he's 'too old for this shit,' that he 'wants to turn over a new leaf.' He wants to talk."

She would have laughed out loud if she'd found anything funny this morning. "With the trail of bodies he's left behind? Come on. This hired assassin who tried to murder his own kid just last night suddenly finds Jesus and develops a conscience?"

"The Lord works in mysterious ways."

"Right. And I'm not stopping the investigation just because Milo Gibbs wants to talk. Forget it."

Martinez's smile grew, and he seemed amused at her bad mood. "So let me guess. You want to go back to Vegas to talk with the Hedgeses?"

"Yep. And let's not forget the wives. I want to hear what Marilee Hedges and Seneca Williams—aka Shawna Whitman and now Shawna Hedges—have to say. So yeah, I want to interview them all, more than I want sleep right now, so that's pretty bad."

"I'll drive. You sleep."

"First, I want to talk to Milo Gibbs myself."

Martinez was already straightening up from the desk.

Settler got to her feet as well. "Let's drop by the hospital and see if Milo is serious about confessing; then, once we iron the details out with his attorney and him, we'll fly to Vegas. I'll try to tee up Stinson, see if he'll take us there again." She was already reaching for her shoulder holster and sidearm.

"I'll call Davis in Vegas. We should give her a heads-up."

"Okay," Settler agreed, already heading for the stairs.

"Hey. Wake up. We're almost there," Noah said.

Remmi blinked and couldn't believe that she'd dozed. They were in her Subaru. Noah was driving, and she was in the passenger seat, her head resting against the window.

Yawning, she blinked and saw by the clock on the dash that it was nearly 5:00 in the afternoon. Twilight had descended on the desert, the stars glittering in a lavender sky. Far in the distance, rising like a spangled phoenix from the desert floor, the lights of Las Vegas loomed.

They'd been on the road for nearly nine hours. Once the police had allowed them to leave, they'd each grabbed a bag, Remmi with a quick change in a shoulder bag, Noah snagging his backpack from his truck.

Remmi had insisted she wanted to see her siblings, and rather than argue, Noah had agreed. They'd loaded into her Subaru and, avoiding the crowd of gawking neighbors and reporters with microphones and rapid-fire questions, had driven past the police barriers in the waning storm, where light bars had strobed the morning gloom, reflecting on the wet streets.

Noah had gassed up at the first open station they'd found, then hit the freeway.

During the first hundred miles, they'd talked about the arrest, how Settler and Martinez had shown up with backup and EMTs. Milo had been driven to the hospital in one ambulance, while the dead man found in the back of the Kris Kringle's Christmas Lights van, another of Milo's victims, had been whisked away in another.

Remmi tried not to think about Milo Gibbs. She was still numb inside at the thought that he—Uncle Milo—was her father. That horrid fact explained so much—why Didi had fled Missouri, why she would never reveal his name, why there was a deep rift between Didi and her family, why Remmi had felt so much resentment from Aunt Vera while she lived with them, and why Milo had been so distant. But her stomach turned sour that a killer, and most likely an assassin for hire, had been the man who had sired her. Even more devastating was the sorry fact that Milo, knowing full well that she was his daughter, would have murdered her without thinking twice.

A stone-cold killer.

Now he would spend the rest of his life in prison.

The police had evidence. His rifle. Vera's and Jensen's statements. Both of which would become testimony at a trial.

Vera, too, was probably going to spend some time behind bars. She had to have known what Milo was doing—and if not known, then at least suspected. And yet she'd stayed married to the prick. It was hard to imagine.

Didi had been right: Remmi had been better off not knowing the identity of her father.

However, now that she did, she wasn't going to let the fact that he'd sired her taint her life any more than it had. She wanted to meet her siblings and then finally, finally, once the chains of the past had been broken, get on with her life.

That which does not kill us only makes us stronger. She hoped to God that Nietzsche was onto something.

As they closed in on Las Vegas, she put in a call to Settler, at Noah's insistence, but the detective's voice mail picked up, so Remmi left a message. She and Noah had already decided they would stay out of the heart of the city, find as quiet a place as Las Vegas could offer.

"Is this good?" he asked, motioning to a two-story motel on a side street at least two miles out of town. The area was undergoing a renovation, it seemed; most of the surrounding buildings were empty or being reconstructed. "According to the motel's reader board, it comes with a pool and a twenty-four-hour restaurant."

"What more could we want?"

He pulled into the dusty lot of the Western Oasis with its illuminated sign of a cowboy in a Stetson riding a camel.

Within twenty minutes, they'd checked in, left their bags locked in the room, and were being seated in a faux-leather booth near the windows of the restaurant. The view was of the access road, but it didn't matter. Not much did. After the waitress, an impossibly tiny woman with hair teased high enough to give her another three inches, took their orders, Remmi's phone buzzed.

Dani Settler was on the other end of the connection. "Don't try to meet with Hedges," she ordered. "Not with any of them. We're still figuring this out, and until we do, it's just not safe."

"That's why I called you. I want to see my sister and brother."

"Just wait. Please. Martinez and I are already in the air. We'll be landing in about an hour. I'm serious about this, okay? I understand why you want to see the kids, but just hang tight. One more day is all it will take, maybe less, for us to wrap this up."

Her heart dropped.

As if she expected Remmi to argue, Settler went on, "Remember what happened last night. So, go into town. Gamble. See a show. Whatever. But do not confront the Hedgeses."

Remmi hesitated.

"You hear me, Ms. Storm? We don't want you in harm's way, and we don't want our investigation compromised."

"I get it. We'll wait." Remmi was frustrated as hell.

"Good. Where are you staying?"

"The Western Oasis," she said, sinking back into the booth before disconnecting.

"We wait?" Noah asked.

"Yeah." She felt deflated. "Story of my life." Taking a sip from her water glass, she said, "Settler suggested we take in a show." She let out a half laugh. "Do you know how many shows I watched from the wings while I was growing up? No thanks. I think I'll pass."

The waitress returned with huge platters of food. While Noah dug into a thick steak and French fries, washing it down with beer, Remmi picked at her pot pie and sipped her Chardonnay slowly, her appetite practically nonexistent.

She thought about her siblings. What if Adam and Ariel, now Kyle and Kayla, didn't believe her? What if they didn't want to know her? What if they thought she was a liar, someone trying to get close to them because of their rich family? What if the thought of Didi Storm being their mother was repulsive? She had no idea what they'd been told or how they would react.

She finished the wine and took another sip of water.

One step at a time.

First, you have to meet them.

If they choose not to be in your life, if they think you're a liar or some kind of scam artist, you have to be patient.

She found herself dunking her straw in her water glass, up and down, the ice cubes dancing, the water swishing, her thoughts a million miles away.

Noah grabbed up the check. "Let's go," he said, and she saw that he'd nearly finished his entire meal. "You're exhausted."

"What about you?"

"Feel like a million bucks." He slanted her a crooked smile that touched the corners of her heart. *Careful,* she told herself, *you could fall in love with this guy all over again . . .*

The thought surprised her, and she cleared her head. *You are tired. You barely know him.* But she let him pay

the check and watched him as he talked to the waitress—
how comfortable he seemed to be in his own skin, a boy
who had grown up in a difficult, if not impossible, family,
who had nearly been killed that night in the desert, and who
had hitchhiked to safety before reinventing himself.

You could do worse, she told herself, and then, as
Noah was distracted with his credit card, she felt it again,
that eerie sensation of being watched. She glanced over
her shoulder to the night beyond and saw only a few scattered cars in the parking lot, no one around, no one peering at her from the darkness.

Your nerves. Noah's right. You're overly tired. Still she
searched the parking lot and saw only the pale image of
her reflection staring into the night.

"Come on, let's get you into bed," Noah said, once
he'd finished paying.

"I'm okay," she said, wondering about the night ahead.
There were two beds in the room, and they'd each placed
a bag at the end of the one they had claimed. But . . .

She was distracted, considering the next few hours
alone with Noah.

As they reached their door, Noah began to slide his
key from his pocket, and Remmi felt a movement behind
her, a disturbance in the night. The hairs on the back of
her neck raised and she started to turn.

Too late!

Steely fingers surrounded the back of her arm as the
cold barrel of a gun jammed against the base of her skull.

"What?" she cried.

Noah reacted, reaching for the gun in his pocket.

"Don't," a strong male voice whispered just over her
ear. "Or I'll blow her brains all over you . . . and you," he
added tightly, his fingers clamping harder, "shut up." To
Noah, he snarled, "Put your hands in the air or I'll blow
off her head. Don't think I won't."

Remmi was frozen, her breath caught in her throat.

Noah's hands rose slowly to the sides of his head. The gunman reached over and grabbed Noah's pistol from his pocket, transferring it to his own. Then he retrieved Noah's phone and did the same.

Terrified, not daring to move with the cold metal jammed against the back of her head, Remmi stared at Noah. She couldn't see her attacker, but she felt him pressed hard against her, could smell some cologne. For a split second, she thought about trying to pull away, but she heard the click of the gun's hammer and froze. Noah's head gave the barest of shakes.

"Hedges," Noah said, "what the hell are you doing?"

Hedges? Brett Hedges? Why would he be here? What would he want with them?

"Shut up," Hedges ordered. "Just shut up, or I'll kill her. I will."

Noah's mouth clamped shut.

"Put these cuffs on," Hedges ordered and tossed a pair of handcuffs to Noah, who caught them on the fly.

Please use them to hit him! Don't do as he says.

But Noah complied. The handcuffs clicked. No one showed up.

The few people in the restaurant couldn't see them.

The occasional car on the road passed by.

No one pulled in.

No one came out of the damned motel.

"Test 'em," Hedges ordered in a low voice, the gun's muzzle never moving. "Snap your wrists apart, Scott. Do it!"

Noah did. The handcuffs held, the chain taut.

"Get into the car," Hedges said. "Now. Back seat."

"What car?"

"Her car, damn it," he said, and Remmi realized they were only a few feet from her Outback.

Oh God. No. This couldn't be happening.

"Don't do it," Remmi said.

Noah kept his gaze on Hedges as he opened the back door of the Subaru.

"Get in! Now," the gunman ordered fiercely.

Please, someone come.

No one did.

Heart pounding, panic setting in, Remmi watched Noah slip into the interior. Before he sat down, Hedges moved swiftly, slamming the butt of his gun into the back of Noah's skull. Noah crumpled with a low groan.

In that split second, Remmi tried to run. She screamed.

"Shut the fuck up! You want me to shoot him?" Hedges said, turning the gun on Noah's inert form. "You do as I say, or I'll gut-shoot him and you can watch him bleed out. Is that what you want?"

"Why are you—"

"Shut up, and get in the car and drive."

"I can't. He's . . . he's got the keys."

"This is your car."

"But he was driving," she said in a panic. "They're in his pocket." She started to reach for Noah, but she tripped over the curb, stumbled against Hedges, and fell to her knees.

"Jesus, what's wrong with you?" He yanked her to her feet, then to her horror, slid her phone from her back pocket. "Now. Get behind the wheel." He reached into Noah's pocket and extracted the keys, then handed them to her. "No funny business. Believe me, I'll shoot him. Now. Drive."

Telling herself she was being a fool, she did as she was told. In the time that it took him to open the door, she tried to start the car and knock him down, maybe run over him and lay on the horn, but he was onto her and kept his pistol aimed at Noah, so she merely waited as he climbed in.

"Take the road south," he ordered.

"I don't know why you're doing this."

In the flash of the interior light, she'd caught a glimpse of him, a beard starting to gray, hair thinning a bit, but a normal-looking man, not a psycho. "It doesn't matter. Just head south."

She pulled out of the parking lot. Her brain was engaging again, and she was thinking faster, trying to come up with a way to escape. He'd surprised her and scared her out of her mind, but now, she had to think, had to find a way to stop whatever madness he had planned.

She turned onto the access road.

"No! Shit. Not north. I said south. The other way, damn it!"

"Sorry," she said. She wheeled a quick one-eighty and watched the city grow smaller in the rearview. "I–I'm not used to driving with a gun pointed at me."

"I'm not moving the barrel."

"If you killed Noah—"

"He's not dead. Yet."

"But you intend to kill him? To kill me?" she asked. "Is that what this is all about?" If so, she should drive like a maniac and wreck the car, take him with them. But even as the thought came into her head, it fled. As long as they were alive, there was hope, a chance that they would find a way to escape.

For now, she'd do as he wanted.

CHAPTER 35

"Man, that was some weird shit," Martinez said as they climbed into the rental car at the Las Vegas airport. Stinson had flown them in his Cessna once more, and now Settler owed him not one, but two dinners. He was also hinting that she throw in a Vegas show.

As if.

"You mean the song?" Settler said. They'd interviewed Milo Gibbs after his surgery, and either he'd lost part of his mind or the anesthesia hadn't worn off because he kept singing some little song she'd heard long before.

"Yeah, the light shining song. Over and over again."

"Yeah. I heard it. And if anyone hasn't given him the word yet, he's not gonna make it on *The Voice*."

"Unkind, Settler."

They'd gotten more from Gibbs than the song. With his attorney present in his hospital room, Gibbs had confessed to the murders of the Crenshaws, Bob Rice, the handyman for Kris Kringle, and even to giving Karen Upgarde the drugs that literally pushed her over the edge.

He also admitted to killing the still-unidentified man in the car in the desert twenty years earlier and attempting to kill Remmi Storm and Noah Scott the night before. But he'd sworn he hadn't killed Didi, which meant, if he was telling the truth—a big leap, given the man's perfidy— that a killer was still at large. Settler wasn't sure what to believe. Gibbs was a consummate liar, but it was entirely possible that Didi's murderer was someone else, as she had collected enemies like dogs collected fleas.

So, it wasn't out of the question that the same killer who had helped OH2 to an early grave had taken Didi's life.

"She's on the move," Martinez said, staring at the cell phone that Milo Gibbs had given them. The man had admitted planting a tracker on Remmi Storm's car, and though it was evidence, they'd chosen to use it to keep tabs on Didi's daughter.

"Remmi is?"

"Yep. Heading south."

"Damn it! I told her to stay put."

"Apparently she doesn't take orders all that well."

"Apparently," Settler repeated grimly, as the entrance to the freeway heading south came up. "Let's see where she's going."

The city was far behind them, barely visible in the mirror as Remmi drove onward, angling into the mountains. They'd left the freeway for a county road and from there to a smaller, private byway that cut upward through the cacti, Joshua trees, and rocks. No streetlights. No cars. No people. Total isolation.

This is not good.

Heart pounding, her nerves strung to the breaking

point, she tried to come up with some way to beat Hedges at his own game, but the farther they got from the city, the more unlikely that was becoming.

She glimpsed reflective eyes caught in the beams of her headlights. "What the—" She slammed on the brakes as a coyote streaked in front of her headlights, a flash of silver gray and brown fur.

"What the hell!" Hedges yelled, then he, too, saw the furtive animal scurrying into the shadows. "Just drive!"

"Where are we going?"

"We're almost there."

She had to find a way out. There had to be some way to save them. He had the phones and the guns, and if she hit the car's panic button out here, no one would hear them and he'd shoot her or, worse yet, Noah.

The nose of her Subaru crested the ridge, and then the gravel road sloped sharply downward, ruts causing the car to bounce, tires spinning, gravel spraying as they slid downward. The steering wheel slipped through her fingers until finally the headlights found the valley floor. Here, the ground was more stable, though it still sloped and was surrounded on two sides by mountains of sand.

"What is this place?" she asked and felt a chill as cold as the desert night.

"Where OH Industries gets its sand. And where you're going to find out what it felt like for your mother in that Cadillac, all those years ago . . ."

At that moment, her headlights washed upon several oversized pieces of machinery. A dump truck, and a backhoe with a huge bucket. Parked next to the dusty construction equipment was a black pickup, its paint job so shiny as to nearly appear liquid.

Hedges's vehicle.

"Park it."

"Here?" she asked.

"Yeah, fine."

"I don't understand." The car was still angled about fifty yards from the truck and equipment, situated in the middle of the pit.

"This is payback," he said calmly. "For your mother. That bitch tried to ruin me. She sold me my own kid. For a quarter of a million dollars. Told me I had a son, and I paid her, only to find out that night that she'd had twins, and she switched out the daughter for my son. She planned on trying to sell me each of them, one at a time."

"But you cheated her." Remmi had yet to slip the car into park. She kept her foot on the brake, to keep the Outback from rolling down the slight incline.

"She was *selling* me my babies. Of course I cheated her. What mother would do that?" He stared at Remmi as if she were crazy. "And it was complicated on my end, because I wasn't the only one who wanted my kids. My older brother? Oliver, or OH2, as he liked to think of himself? He wanted them, too. Considered them *his* heirs when they were *mine*. He couldn't have kids of his own, so he thought, he really thought he could swindle mine. I was the one who dealt with Didi, and he thought he was going to take them from me. And how was he going to do that? Kill me, of course." His agitation grew, and with it, he began waving the gun.

Remmi kept her eyes on the gun's muzzle. She couldn't believe what she was hearing, but she wanted to keep him talking, not for his story as much as to buy time. If there was some way to get him out of the car, she could drive away . . . or if she could get the gun or the phones or something. She heard another groan from the back seat, and her heart soared. At least Noah was alive.

For now.

"But he didn't . . . your brother didn't get Adam and Ariel. He died," she said.

"Kyle and Kayla." Hedges barked out a laugh. The gun was pointed at her again. "Good old OH2. All his brains. All his education. All his plotting. For what? He ended up dead." Another harsh chuckle. "It seems we're all a murderous lot."

"What do you mean?"

Keep him talking. She was looking at Hedges, but in her peripheral vision she was trying to see any means of escape. That's when she saw the movement in the back seat. Noah was rousing.

Keep him talking. He can't know that Noah is coming around.

"My brother was poisoned," Hedges said.

"You killed him?"

"No. Oh, no." He gave his head a shake. "My father took care of that. He blamed my brother for his skiing accident, something about the bindings being tampered with, and it crippled him, didn't quite kill him, but almost did. Dad was sure his namesake planned not only to win his woman back, that bitch Marilee, but also to take over the company *and* my kids. Before he could, though, Dad got his revenge."

"I thought your father was in a retirement home. In a wheelchair . . ." If she could just get the gun!

Behind her, through the seat, she felt movement.

"Well, he had a little help," Hedges admitted, caught up in his story, seemingly unaware that Noah was rousing. Oh, dear God, if there was a way out of this . . .

"From you?" she asked, her eyes never moving from Hedges and the gun.

He snorted. "And I thought you were supposed to be smart."

She waited, ears straining for any signs that Noah was awake, while her mind was trying to piece together what Hedges was talking about. "Your father had help from . . ."

She felt some pressure on the back of her seat. Was Noah signaling her? She couldn't tell.

Hedges was waiting for her to finish her sentence, baiting her, she realized.

And then it dawned on her.

"Seneca," she whispered, her heart freezing.

"There ya go!" He waved the gun. "Give the lady a prize!"

"She stole Adam from me and brought him to . . . you?" Remmi said, disbelieving and silently praying for a miracle.

For a second, she thought she heard the whine of a car's engine . . . She pressed her foot on the brake a little harder, the Subaru still idling.

"Not to me," Hedges said. "She took Kyle to my brother, actually, but only temporarily, until she killed him."

"She what?" No! Remmi must have heard wrong. "Seneca killed OH2?"

He snorted his disgust. "Shawna," he said. "Shawna killed him. Can you not get the names straight?"

"I don't believe she would—"

"She's a woman of many talents, as it turns out. Excellent nursemaid. She helped raise the kids and gave my father a chance at life again. He's still in a wheelchair, but he gets around okay. You know what they say about the love of a good woman. And a damned good murderess, if she needs to be."

"I can't believe that—"

"Oh, believe." He was so much calmer now that he was in control, that he had Noah and Remmi unable to thwart him. He almost seemed to revel in telling his story.

She sensed that he liked drawing this part out, of having the power, of terrorizing and informing, almost bragging, while she was literally a captive audience.

"But Shawna won't like the fact that I had to get rid of

you. She was really fond of you, so this will have to be my little secret."

"Why are you doing this?" she asked and, from the corner of her eye, saw something shift in the back seat.

Hedges was into his story. "If it all hadn't fallen apart, if that damned book hadn't been published, if you hadn't started nosing around . . . But you wouldn't give up. You just had to keep poking and prodding, trying to find my kids . . . and that just can't happen."

"The police know," she said. "You can kill me, but the police will find them and tell them. The reporters? They'll be coming, too."

"But none of them know all the secrets, do they? Only you."

She saw now, through the slight crack between the two front seats, that Noah had positioned himself behind Hedges. There was just enough light from the dash to catch a glimpse of Noah angling his head back and raising his cuffed hands.

"You killed Didi," she said flatly.

"Of course I did." He sounded pleased with himself. "And I'd do it again, the way that bitch fucked me over, I would gladly—"

From the corner of her eye, she saw Noah gather himself. "Now!" he yelled "Now!"

She took her foot off the brake and hit the gas as she flung open her door. The car bucked forward. She rolled out, bouncing and scraping in the gravel, avoiding the rear tires. Scrambling to her feet, she watched in the incandescence of the dash lights.

Noah was pressed against the back of the passenger seat. He'd risen over the headrest and had thrown his arms forward and over the head of the unsuspecting Hedges.

But the car kept rolling, picking up speed on the incline . . . toward the pit . . .

"No," she whispered and took off after it.

It sped, rocking and turning as if someone were grappling for the steering wheel. Gravel, sand, and dust sprayed from the wheels.

"God, no!"

Choking, the clouds of dust thick, she raced.

No! No! No!

Vaguely, she was aware of another light, something bright piercing the canyon floor. Another vehicle, hurtling over the rise.

Was Hedges meeting someone here? Another killer?

She stumbled, just as the speeding Subaru bounced off course and smashed into the side of the truck. Metal screeched and groaned as it twisted and crumpled. She felt a split second of relief that the vehicle hadn't nosedived into the pit when she heard a horrid, blood-chilling scream.

Noah! Oh, God, Noah!

Blam!

A gun blasted!

The windshield shattered, glass spraying. That son of a bitch had shot Noah!

"Stop! Just stop!" she cried, coughing, racing, stumbling forward as the vehicle that had followed them into the canyon shuddered to a stop.

The doors of that car flew open.

"Police. Freeze!" Danielle Settler's voice rang through the sand pit.

"Help! Please!" Remmi cried, yanking open the driver's door of the Subaru to see the horror within.

Brett Hedges was pinned to the passenger seat, twisted metal and glass surrounding him; the chain on the pair of handcuffs had cut deep into his neck. His head was lopped over, and his eyes were glassy.

Dead. He had to be dead.

And Noah's hands were on either side of the headrest. "Noah," she whispered. "Oh, God, Noah." She reached into her pocket, found the key she'd stolen from Hedges when she'd pretended to trip in the parking lot, and unlocked the handcuffs. They opened, Noah fell back, and a horrid sucking sound escaped from Brett Hedges before he slid to one side.

"You had that?" Noah asked. "Why the hell didn't you use it sooner?" And then he fell back, and she noticed the red stain growing on his shoulder.

"Out of the way!" Settler ordered. "God, I could have shot you!" she yelled at Remmi as Martinez took charge. Remmi heard sirens. Far away, across the desert, but drawing nearer. "Backup and an ambulance are on the way," Settler added.

"Too late for Hedges," Martinez said. "He's gone."

"What about Scott?"

"Don't know. Doesn't look good."

"He has to be all right," Remmi said, shell-shocked. She couldn't lose him. Not now. Not after finding him after all these years. "He has to be all right."

"We'll do our best," Settler said as the next set of lights appeared over the rise, and Remmi thought she distinguished the bleat of an ambulance far away. Too far away.

"I love him," she whispered as the clouds of dust began to settle.

"Then you just keep loving him. And if he makes it," Settler said, "tell him."

"I will," she vowed—and only hoped she would get the chance.

Hours later, after he'd had surgery to repair the torn muscles of his shoulder and some stitches for the cuts he'd sustained when the window had shattered, Noah was taken to a private room.

Remmi had given her formal statement to the police and was waiting for him to wake up. Then she made good on her promise.

"Happy Thanksgiving," she said as he woke up.

"What?" He still looked bad, his face bruised, a cut over one eye. And he didn't seem the least bit surprised by what she'd told him.

"It's twenty minutes after midnight. Thanksgiving."

"Oh . . . yeah . . . I hadn't given it a thought."

"Me neither. Guess we had a lot on our minds." She grabbed his hand and twined her fingers with his. "I have something to say." Gathering her courage, she said, "I love you, Noah Scott."

He squinted at her a long moment, and her courage nosedived. Too soon . . . she shouldn't have said it!

But then he drawled, "Is that so?"

She nearly gasped with relief. "Yes."

One side of his mouth curved beneath the stubble that covered his jaw.

In for a penny, in for a pound . . . "You know, usually when someone says 'I love you,' there's an equal response, and it's a lot better than 'Is that so?'"

"I guess you're right." For a person who was lying in a hospital bed, he showed incredible strength in tightening his fingers and pulling her close, so that her face was mere inches away. "Let's do this."

"What? How?"

"By climbing into this bed with me and showing me just how much you love me."

At that moment, outside his door, a nurse wheeled a cart.

"You're crazy," Remmi told him.

"Maybe. Come on . . ."

Still close enough to feel his breath upon her face, she narrowed her eyes and said, "I thought you were different from the boy I met all those years ago, but I was wrong. You're still as incorrigible as ever."

"Incorrigible. Love that word."

She laughed.

He gave another tug on her hand, dragging her even closer, so he could brush his lips over hers. "By the way," he said, "I love you, too. And as soon as I get out of here, I'm going to prove it to you."

"Promises, promises."

"You bet." He got serious then. "Enough for a lifetime."

"A lifetime? That must be the anesthesia talking." But she saw in his eyes that he meant what he'd said.

"We'll see." His eyes sparkled, and he inclined his chin toward the window. "We're in Vegas. It's pretty easy to get hitched here."

"Now I know you're still under the influence."

"Think about it. We're not getting any younger, and we've waited a long time."

Was he serious? He couldn't be. Could he . . . ? "Okay . . . I will . . . think on it," she said cautiously.

"Think hard," he suggested as she pulled away and started for the door. "Think real hard."

She did, for the next three days, while she waited for him to be released. She thought about it a lot. It was a crazy idea, but she asked herself what was she waiting for? And what about her life wasn't a little off the rails?

She rented a car as what was left of the totaled Subaru was with the police. Though she tried repeatedly, her brother and sister refused to see her. As it turned out, they blamed her for the death of their biological father, Brett. Someday, when enough time had passed, maybe, they would sort everything out and want to reconnect. She hoped. She had left word with their attorney. They knew she existed; they could come to her. She wasn't holding out hope.

Shawna, aka Seneca, too, refused to speak to her.

Not a surprise, since in Remmi's statement to the police she repeated what Brett Hedges had told her, so Shawna might end up in jail, along with her husband, for killing OH2.

Or maybe not.

They could afford expensive criminal lawyers, and OH2's body couldn't be exhumed, as he'd been cremated. The only other person who had known the truth, Brett Hedges, too, was dead. She thought about that and how he'd saved Ariel from dying in the desert when the Mustang had gone up in flames. Somehow he'd helped his daughter survive. What had seemed certain death, which had been part of his plan, even though he'd expected to be saving his son. It had been a dangerous, near-fatal plan and a miracle that Ariel had lived. Maybe Brett hadn't been completely evil.

Then again . . .

She'd thought about that night a lot and was putting it behind her. She'd also considered Noah's proposal for three days, and when he'd recovered and was finally released from the hospital and ensconced in the passenger seat of the rented Ford Escape, she said, "Okay, I've thought."

He didn't pretend to misunderstand. "And?"

"And there's a little drive-through chapel in Las Vegas that would be perfect."

He grinned. "You're taking me there now? Right out of the hospital?"

"No way." Sliding her sunglasses onto her nose, she said, "Greta would kill me if she wasn't invited. Tell ya what. If you move your business to San Francisco, and we rent the upper *two* floors from Greta, and you work with Emma via FaceTime, or she moves up to the city, too, and things work out, then we'll come back to that chapel. Maybe on Valentine's Day."

She started the car, and as the wintry Nevada sun bore down on them, she slid a glance his way. "What do you say?"

"I'm in." He grabbed her knee. "But let's not wait that long. How about Christmas instead? I mean even though it's over a month away, people are already celebrating, have been for a couple of weeks. It feels right, don't you think?"

Catching the freeway that would eventually take them home, she decided she had nothing to lose and everything to gain.

Grinning, she said, "Looks like you and I are destined for a happy holiday."

"Is that a yes?"

"Yes!"

And they both broke into laughter as she hit the gas.

Dear Reader,

I hope you enjoyed *Liar, Liar*.

My next thriller, *Willing to Die*, will be coming out in August 2019. My editor was instrumental in coming up with the title and idea for *Willing to Die*. It was his idea to have *Expecting to Die* closely linked to its sequel, *Willing to Die*, because the heroine of the books, Detective Regan Pescoli, is pregnant in *Expecting to Die* and the mother of a newborn in *Willing to Die*. As such, *Willing to Die* will be the latest book in the Montana "To Die" series featuring Detectives Regan Pescoli and Selena Alvarez of the Pinewood Sheriff's Department in Grizzly Falls, Montana. *Willing to Die* takes up where *Expecting to Die* and *Deserves To Be Dead*, a novella I wrote with John Sandford for *Match Up*, an anthology that came out in 2017, left off.

Pescoli is struggling (again) this time with work and her new baby. She's torn; she doesn't want to give up her career as she's a dedicated detective, but leaving her infant is difficult. And then there's her teenaged daughter, Bianca, who is having her own life challenges after a near-death experience in *Expecting to Die*. Things only get worse when Regan gets a frantic call from one of her estranged sisters telling her that another sibling is dead, found murdered in her grand home in San Francisco. That does it, Pescoli is off to solve the murder and bring the killer to justice. What she doesn't realize is that in so doing she's falling into the carefully laid trap of an old enemy, one out for revenge, one you've met before. Things become increasingly dire as Pescoli discovers she's put her entire family, including her newborn at risk. Can she outwit a clever killer? Will she be able to act quickly enough? Or will those she holds most dear pay the ultimate price?

To find out, pick up a copy of *Willing to Die* in August 2019! Meanwhile I'll keep everyone posted on my website lisajackson.com and on Facebook and Twitter. For now, if you'd like to learn more about the book, just turn the page to read an excerpt!

Keep Reading!
Lisa Jackson

In this gripping new novel from #1 New York Times *bestselling author Lisa Jackson, a killer on the loose in Grizzly Falls, Montana, makes the business of murder deeply personal for Detectives Regan Pescoli and Selena Alvarez.*

Though Detective Regan Pescoli loves her new baby with all her heart, maternity leave has her itching to get back to her job. But the frantic call she receives from one of her sisters brings work home to her in the most violent way possible.

Pescoli's oldest sister, Brindel, has been murdered, and the crime scene is as puzzling as it is brutal. Brindel and her husband, Doctor Paul Latham, were found in separate beds in their beautiful San Francisco home, each the victim of a gunshot wound to the head. There are no signs of forced entry, and despite the emptied safe it's clear this isn't a random burglary gone wrong.

For Pescoli, the shocking news brings grief mixed with guilt. She and Brindel weren't close, and Pescoli barely knows her teenage niece, Ivy, a secretive girl who lands on her doorstep. Pescoli is soon mired deep in the investigation headed by her partner, Selena Alvarez, who's grappling with three more deaths that could be connected. The list of suspects is growing in tandem with the body count, but so is Pescoli's unease.

Maybe it's exhaustion or hormones, or the pressures of dealing with a new sheriff. Or maybe the chill running through her veins is justified. Because as the case takes a new, terrifying turn, Pescoli's loved ones and her life are at the mercy of a killer who'll go to any lengths to see her suffer . . .

Please turn the page for an exciting sneak peek of Lisa Jackson's WILLING TO DIE, coming soon wherever print and eBooks are sold!

Near San Francisco, California
July Fourth

Dead.
Her son was dead!

Cold to the bone despite the summer's heat, she couldn't breathe, had to gasp for air.

Her throat clogged with grief, pain, and a deep, intense fury.

Standing alone in this cemetery where gravestones stood in sentry-like rows, she clenched her fists and wanted to rail to the heavens where, across the night sky, fireworks burst in thunderous booms and great sprays of light.

The demons that had tormented her mind hadn't lied.

As bitter as the harshest Montana winter, desperation cut through her heart. Blinking against tears, she dragged her gaze from the inscription on the small marble stone at her feet.

A low-lying fog was rolling in, swallowing the lights of the city situated on the far shore of the bay. The iconic Golden Gate was partially obscured, only the bridge's tall towers knifing through the fog to a black sky glittering with stars, a backdrop to the fireworks. She watched another shooting star rise high, streaks of fiery glitter bursting, then fizzling before her eyes. For a few awe-inspiring seconds, the pyrotechnics bedazzled, then faded, their short life spans over in quick, brilliant bursts. Over almost before they'd begun.

Like her son's brief life.

Her heart tugged so painfully she fell to her knees. She'd known this was possible, perhaps even probable, that he'd died, but throughout these past lonely years, she'd held out a glimmer of hope that he'd survived, that they would be reunited, that she would feel the warmth of his arms around her neck as she held him close. "Oh, baby," she whispered.

Once again she turned her attention to the small gravestone, a tiny marker in a sea of larger, more elaborate tombstones. In various shapes and sizes, some tall, some ornately carved, others more plain, the headstones stood unmoving, hulking along the slope that curved downward to the city and the dark, black waters of the bay.

Why?

Oh, God, why?

Closing her eyes, she drew in several deep breaths.

Don't question. It is what it is.

More importantly: What are you going to do about it?

Jaw clenched, she thought of those who had wronged her.

Those who had used her.

Those who had abused her.

Those who had taken out their animosity against her on the innocence of her child.

Still on her knees, she reached forward and traced the dates inscribed on the frigid stone with the tips of her fingers. Barely four years from date of birth to date of death.

Her heart cracked with the pain. "Oh, honey," she murmured, her throat catching as thoughts of that unlikely birth swirled in her brain. The agony of labor, the fear of the unknown, the rush in her blood at hearing the newborn's cry, and then the emptiness as her son was stolen from her, taken from that isolated delivery room. She'd heard the whispers in the hospital.

". . . deeply disturbed."

". . . mentally unstable."

". . . severe psychosis."

All spoken in hushed tones. As if she couldn't hear.

And now this.

She squeezed her eyes shut and brought to mind the manipulators who had made the decisions, those who had determined that she was "unable," or "unwilling," or "incapable." More words she wasn't supposed to hear. And then there was the harshest of all: "unfit." Her teeth gnashed as she remembered the callousness with which that word was tossed about. How would they know? Yes, she'd been unstable—she knew that—though the word "insanity," which she'd heard throughout her life, surely was extreme. She wasn't "insane," and never had been.

Especially not tonight.

No, as the rockets screamed into the sky, blooming in wild explosions of color and light, she'd never felt more sane. She'd spent so much time searching for her son only to find him buried here—that bit of hope she'd felt at the thought of reconnecting with him, of seeing him, of explaining to him and holding him . . . that tiny flame of expectation was now dead. Extinguished. And in its place rose a new emotion, raw and acrid.

Vengeance.

Swallowing the lump in her throat, she gazed at the small grave marker again and now, dry-eyed, thought of what lay ahead. "They'll pay," she promised her child, hoping that he would somehow know. Her fingers twisted in the drying grass of the hillside, the long blades and dandelions that were tucked close to the marker and had escaped the gardener's mower clutched in her fingers. "Every last one of them. I will hunt them down and, I promise you, they will pay." In her mind's eye she saw them all. As she pushed herself upright, a series of smaller fireworks exploded over the bay, flashes of kaleidoscopic colors disappearing in fading fingers until the darkness was unbroken again.

She knew who they were, those who had betrayed her.

She knew where they lived.

She also knew she had the element of surprise on her side.

And she would destroy them all.

Tossing the dried weeds from her fingers, she dusted her hands.

She had a mission.

As she headed down the hill, stepping carefully between the marble and granite sentinels of the dead, she plotted just how to wreak her vengeance against them.

A sense of cold satisfaction displaced her desperation.

She turned at the locked gate, then climbed atop the wrought-iron fence and looked back over her shoulder. Spying the tiny gravestone, she whispered, "I love you," and waited for an answer that didn't come.

Armed with her new purpose, she hopped lithely to the ground, shoved her hands into the pockets of her jacket, and felt the cold reassurance of the Beretta Pico, a small .380. Jaw set, she strode through the darkness, avoiding streetlights as the explosions burst overhead.

No one would stop her now.

No one would dare.

Romantic Suspense from
Lisa Jackson

Available Wherever Books Are Sold!
Visit our website at **www.kensingtonbooks.com**